LAMORIAN CHRONICLES

BOOK ONE

AIRDLE'S REALM

DOROTHY GABLE

IRON
STREAM
FICTION

Birmingham, Alabama

Airdle's Realm

Iron Stream Fiction
An imprint of Iron Stream Media
100 Missionary Ridge
Birmingham, AL 35242
IronStreamMedia.com

Library of Congress Control Number: 2024936497

Scripture quotations marked TRB are taken from The Readable Bible®. Copyright © 2022 by Rodney S. Laughlin, Leawood, Kansas. Used by permission of Iron Stream Media.

Cover design by www.BookCoverDesign.us

ISBN: 978-1-56309-713-3 (paperback)
ISBN: 978-1-56309-714-0 (ebook)

1 2 3 4 5—29 28 27 26 25

The beginning of a sprawling world-building journey! Gable fastens the Christian reader's mind and heart to timeless biblical truths through this fantastical and speculative venture. Pen to paper, heart to mind. "Ask any of the pages. They'll take you there if you've forgotten the way."

—G. Wesley Cone, pastor, author of *The Empyrean Call: Isaac's Story*, tabletop game designer

In this compelling story, Dorothy Gable introduces us to a kingdom both familiar and refreshingly different. As she draws us in to become deeply invested in the characters, she artfully reminds us about the love of God and the truth of the gospel. The flawed and highly relatable characters treat the inner prompting of the Holy Spirit simply as an expected part of their daily lives. With simple easy dependence on God they exemplify for us what it means to walk by faith and not by sight.

—Larry Eiss

The CHRONICLES of LAMORIA

Parchments discovered written by an ancient mariner chronicle their encounter with the kingdom of Lamoria, a realm dwelling in a distant land, lost in time.

Four Tribes: Airdle, Dornan, Ayisin, Sanderfield

Six Councils: Airdle, Tholen, Dornan, Worstein, Stoddard, Sanderfield

Map illustration by Kelly Allen.

Prologue

The Prophecy of the Peacemaker

Hard raps sounded on the door to the prophet's chamber near Airdle Chapel. Lawreader Daliel, the seer of Whistler's Brook steeped in the Law of God, startled from a deep sleep and called out, "Who is it?"

"You must come quickly. Our High King calls for you. The healer fears our liege's days are few."

The man of God slipped on his cloak. He had been summoned to give the blessing at the birth of Crown Prince Eldridge's infant. The day before, no one had mentioned the king's sickness had worsened.

"Coming." Settling the hood, he stepped through the door.

The page tried to hurry the prophet along, but he kept to his usual pace. "The call is urgent."

"Fear not, young one. See, the steps to Airdle Castle are near at hand." He followed the page into the main hall. Two large chandeliers lit the foyer. At the base of the stairs, they heard calls from the second floor for water and staff scurrying about.

The healer's assistant stood at the top of the stairs. "Lawreader Daliel, the king awaits."

The seer paused by the top step and glanced to his left, the princes' wing. Crown Prince Eldridge paced outside the door to his suites. "And the crown prince's lady?"

"Giving birth. The healer and midwife are here." The young man smiled for the first time. "This one might live."

"As many have prayed." He followed the assistant to the king's bedside.

The seer sat on a stool by the bed and held the king's wrinkled hand, made thin and fragile from months of sickness. Despite his weakness, his liege fixed a determined gaze upon him.

"My lord, how may I serve you?" Daliel asked.

The king's chest rose and fell with every breath. Deep coughs shook his frame.

Daliel lifted a cup of water and helped the king take some sips.

The king smiled weakly and looked toward an upper corner of the ceiling. Joy and peace flowed across his face. "My time is soon." His brows furrowed as he met the seer's gaze. "We are the last of the ones who saw the birthing of Lamoria when God sent Daniel bearing God's words in the Leaves of God." He clenched Daliel's hand as he loosed a shuddering cough. "They must not forget Jesus or turn from His ways. You, the lawreaders, the preachers, must remind them." The king's chest shook.

Daliel slid aside for the healer's assistant to help him clear his lungs.

The assistant said quietly, "Keep it short. His strength is failing."

Bringing the stool back into place, Daliel patted the king's hand.

"You must pray Lamoria does not return to the old ways." The king's eyes widened when the cry of one drawing first breath could be heard from the prince's suite. "You may go. Give the blessing. The Lord of Glory sets our future." The king closed his eyes.

As Lawreader Daliel rose to leave, a gurgling sounded in the king's chest. He stepped aside for the waiting healer to aid him. Seeing his liege well attended, the man of God walked down the hall to Crown Prince Eldridge's chambers. Feeling the Spirit come upon him, the seer stumbled and reached for the paneled walls. For the king had spoken truthfully, doom would come upon the land when the people fell away. "Oh Lord," he prayed, "leave us not."

"My lord?" A nearby page noted the man's unseeing gaze, fixed on a distant point. He waited, ready to help, but the praying man of Whistler's Brook seemed to have been transported into a different world.

Moments later Daliel felt the wall and sensed the page hovering nearby. Why doom on a day of new birth? He forced himself to continue down the hall. At the door he watched the father bend over his wife, who cuddled the bundled newborn in her arms. Stepping in, he asked, "Prince Eldridge, is your child well?"

The prince turned to him with a broad smile. "I have a son, an heir, Prince Wallace."

Before he could reach the newborn to give the blessing, the bells sounded and cries of "Long live King Eldridge" echoed through the chambers.

The prince would soon receive the signet ring.

Once the holding lords and leaders had assembled, he would be crowned king.

Lawreader Daliel acknowledged the scribe in the corner waiting to record the royal birth with the blessing. He stepped closer to the infant. As he reached out his hand to utter the prayer, he saw a world not of this world. "A peacemaker of the four will arise in troublesome times; the wicked will be thrown down, but those who turn again will see the rising of a kingdom out of ashes." The seer sighed. The doom he had foreseen earlier would be lifted and peace restored.

"Ahh, Prince Wallace, a peacemaker," the midwife murmured.

The seer came to himself. "Nay, this one will remain

faithful to God and the realm, but in a day of trouble, God will send another to make peace again."

Lawreader Daliel reached for the newborn with full cheeks and dark eyes. He gave the blessing. In the midst of his unease, he knew God would one day restore the land after much strife.

Chapter 1

Prince Trillion

Prince Trillion, youngest son of King Wallace and King Eldridge's grandson, stared at the five horsemen lined up against his squad. Today he fought not only for the honor of the Second Royal Contingent, but for his place beside the other princes. Kewatin, his large buckskin charger, shifted beneath him and pawed the ground. They faced Marshal Galant, head of the Tholen City Marshal Squad, and four of his horsemen on the broad field behind Airdle Castle's tournament grounds. Trillion glanced to his right, lifting a brow at his second's nod. They held blunted swords in their right hands for this sparring contest. Their legs tightened in the saddles, holding firm the reins with their left. The five marshals were tightly coiled and ready to spring.

Trillion sounded the charging whistle. As one, five steeds burst toward the other line. Moments later, Galant's team leapt to the battle. Trillion's men moved to flank their opponents while Trillion sparred with Galant.

Trillion and Kewatin charged Galant.

A Tholen marshal drove his horse to block Trillion's path. Before the marshal could assault his left side, Trillion pulled on the left rein and dug into his seat. The buckskin planted his left foot, pivoted, meeting the other horse, shoulder to shoulder. With a quick arc, Trillion unseated the marshal with the side of his sword.

Galant's charger surged toward them.

Trillion dropped the reins and pulled out his dagger with his left hand. As he flung his sword hand up, he puckered his lips for a sharp whistle. Kewatin leapt into the air, kicking out with his back legs.

Galant crouched down in the saddle to avoid Kewatin's sharp hooves. His charger reared and turned to face Kewatin. Thrown by the sudden movement, Galant fell under his horse.

Trillion's charger shifted in the air to avoid colliding with Galant's horse. As they fell to the grassy field, horse and rider overturned. Curling to the right failed to bring Trillion clear of his own horse falling toward him. As if in slow motion, helpless to save himself, he watched Kewatin plunge toward him.

Images arose of the evening before. At the inn, Galant had boasted of his squad's achievements. His taunts that not only had Trillion recently been given the lead of the Second Royal, but that his squad had not accomplished any noteworthy feats, unleashed Trillion's fury. They nearly came to blows that night. Trillion's squad had been quartered at Airdle, near the castle with parade and escort duties, while Galant's squad distinguished themselves by vanquishing marauding bandits along Tierney Ridge.

His sins rose up before him, one after the other. God's heavy hand of righteous judgment bore down upon him.

The weight of his horse drove the dagger still clutched in his left hand into his thigh. Jolts of pain shot up his leg and along his spine. A heavy blow to his chest forced the air out of his lungs. A great sorrow engulfed him. Struggling to breathe, he cried out in his soul, "Jesus, save me!" Acknowledging his blame, he confessed, "Forgive me."

Before Trillion's world went dark, pure light and love enveloped him.

Kewatin and Galant's steeds writhed on the ground in a jumble of reins, stirrups, and thrashing legs. The marshals rushed toward the pile. One slashed a rein tangled around the buckskin's leg. Another helped him roll the steed away from the fallen prince.

Kewatin found his footing and stood. He shook his hide to clear the dust and reseat the saddle. The whites of his eyes showing, he skittered away. A marshal jumped onto his horse to chase down Prince Trillion's stallion.

Two pulled Galant clear so his horse had room to stand. Another grasped the bridle and tied the horse to a nearby fence.

Trillion lay crumpled on his side. Blood pooled from the gash in his left thigh.

His second knelt beside him to feel for a pulse. "He lives. Call for help! Bring a healer and a board to carry him." Looking about, he lifted his voice. "Does anyone have a band to stop the bleeding?" He gently rolled Trillion onto his back.

One of Trillion's marshals removed his belt and affixed it above the gash.

Word spread quickly. Many came from the stables and marshal headquarters. They stepped aside for Healer Anselm.

The healer of Airdle Castle wrapped the wound with clean linen cloths. Feeling along the ribs, he lowered his head to listen to the prince's breathing. "We can move him."

Four from Trillion's squad arrived with a carrying board. Two helped the healer position him on the litter. Each holding a corner, they walked toward marshal headquarters.

Head Marshal Vaughn emerged from his office in the main building. "Prince Trillion!"

"He's not awakened, Head Marshal," Trillion's second said.

"Will he live?"

Healer Anselm said, "It's uncertain. I must tend to him in the healer's suites."

Vaughn watched them head through the courtyard to the lower castle entrance. He approached Marshal Galant. "Do you have an explanation for this? Who drew the sharp sword?"

Still shaken from the fall, the marshal blinked, trying to recall.

"Prince Trillion, my lord," Galant's second said.

Reports of last night's argument at the inn had reached his ears. "Duels are forbidden in Lamoria. Do we not have enough to keep us busy without attacking each other? Have you not heard of the incursions in our eastern plains?"

"This was a practice sparring match, five against five." Galant avoided the head marshal's glare.

"Oh, I think it was more than that. But see to your injuries. We'll talk later about this." He stalked off to his office to open an investigation.

Healer Anselm leaned over the wounded prince. The gash on the leg had been thoroughly cleansed and bound with an herbal poultice to prevent infection. He had not completed his examination when King Wallace stepped into the main room of the healer's suites. "They found you, my lord. You came quickly." The healer turned on the stool to face the king.

"The only child of my lovely Queen Lillian." King Wallace's shoulders sagged, unable to turn away from his son who bore the face of his beloved departed wife.

"She died too soon." The healer rose to see about the preparation of the rest of the medicinals. "He is young too. We can pray for a full recovery. Is it true that a horse fell upon him?"

"That's what I heard. But the gash to his leg. Will it heal?" The king stood fixed, unable to reach out to a son who had fallen to depravity.

"I believe so. While deep, no major vessels were cut. If no infection follows, he should recover. Too soon to know if he will regain his former strength. The blow to his chest worries me more." Anselm knelt again to listen to Trillion's chest. The prince struggled with short, rapid breaths and writhed on the bed. Peering carefully at his throat, he noticed the trachea curved slightly to the side. He called to his nearest assistant. "Keirsin, bring a short blade with a tube! We must clear the chest that he may draw in breath."

Trillion stirred. His eyes darted about, scarcely able to see. A wall of pain from his leg to his chest threatened to crush him. Unable to draw breath, he felt death drawing near.

"Hold him steady," Anselm called. Three assistants gathered to hold the prince in place.

"Prince Trillion, lie still while we help you breathe." Anselm relieved the pressure on Trillion's left side.

Anselm rose and glanced at the king. "Please try to calm him, my liege." But when he saw his father, the young man's eyes widened, and he drew in quick breaths, pain etched on his face.

King Wallace found a place along the other side of the bed, between two healers.

"My son, be at peace. You live." He glanced down at the wide bandage on his son's leg, at the blood-spattered, torn breeches and tunic. There was so much to say, yet no words formed. Eighteen years had passed since the Lord had taken Queen Lillian home. Trillion had been only twelve. "You're all I have left of your mother."

Trillion shuddered. "Father . . ." Too many were about for him to share his heart. "Forgive me."

"I do, and God does too." He caressed his son's hand until the healers finished their treatments. He pulled over a nearby stool. "Now we can talk."

Head Marshal Vaughn tapped on the door jamb. "My liege, if I may see you for a moment?"

Vaugh asked Healer Anselm, "His condition?"

"Fair, but there is hope." The prince's breathing had settled, and his color had improved.

"May I speak with Prince Trillion?"

Healer Anselm tilted his head toward his king. "If the king grants you leave. He has regained consciousness." He shooed the rest of the healers and assistants into the apothecary storeroom. "Let's give them some privacy."

King Wallace rose to face the marshal.

"My lord, it was reported that Prince Trillion pulled a sharp dagger during a sparring match. Everyone had dulled swords for the practice bout."

"You may ask your questions, Vaughn."

The head marshal turned to the prince. "Why did you draw a blade?"

"To scare him." Trillion worked to draw breath. Would they believe him? "I wasn't going to use it. But the horses collided and we fell."

Vaughn said, "This was a duel between Galant and you, disguised as a practice bout." He leaned forward and said with clipped tones, "Duels are forbidden."

"Blame them not. Galant boasted any of his squad could take mine. Said we were good only for performing at tournaments and parades." Trillion pushed past the pain to draw in breath. "Our requests to patrol and protect Esther's Spring had been denied." His own father had gained renown for defending the kingdom by leading the Second Royal Contingent, a marshal squad of eight, along with troops to repel an Amhavran invasion. Yet he had not been accorded the same opportunities.

"Be not eager for combat, my son. The sorrow of spilling another's blood lingers throughout one's days." King Wallace stepped to the side. "Vaughn, you may continue."

The king listened as Vaughn stepped through the questions, but he heard none of his son's usual evasive answers.

Trillion did not excuse or try to justify his actions. He

avoided looking at his father. Instead, drawing courage, he met Vaughn's gaze. "Will I be released from the marshal service?"

To lead a squad of marshals had become his life. If not in the service, what would be left for him?

Vaughn knelt by his side. "Prince Trillion, it is too early to say. Much depends upon you making a full recovery." Vaughn rose. "We will prepare a full report."

Left alone, Wallace sat on the stool. He brought a cup of water to his son's lips and extended a tentative hand to stroke his son's arm.

"Thank you." Beyond the searing pain, Trillion's sins still crushed him. Hope fled. Life, a future, dissolved away. "Father, I have sinned against God and you. I've done a terrible thing."

Wallace lifted his brow. "Only one thing?"

Trillion looked aside. Were his sins too many even for God to release? "I know I've cheated at table and deceived many." His striving to be the best, to win every race, had been futile attempts to save himself and regain his father's approval. He would never have his love.

"But these pale beside my greatest sin." Trillion forced himself to meet his father's eyes. "I have a son by Lady Lisze, daughter of Lady Elwin of Dornan and Marshal Rothsum of the Sanderfield, one of your Mighty Three."

The king sat up, withdrawing his hand. "I remember my dear friend. He has a land grant in Dornan that I gave him years ago. Is she there with her child?"

Trillion's face fell and his breath labored. The enormity of his crime overcame all else. Taking courage, he shook his head.

"How did this happen?"

"She's the keeper of Clefisch Way Station. Her son is probably twelve or so." Something had changed within when he had pled for Christ's forgiveness lying under the horse. He prayed for the right words and found himself able to speak. "Lord Nordrum's holding shared a border with their land grant. After her parents died . . ."

"Marshal Rothsum and Lady Elwin are dead? Why hadn't I heard of this?"

"Nordrum, as well as others in Dornan, conspired to drive them out, even though Lady Elwin was Lord Nordrum's older sister. They couldn't bear a Sanderfield having an estate in Dornan Council. Rothsum had been attacked along the ridge south of Clefisch Pass." Trillion remembered the lords boasting that they had overcome a great marshal. "The Dornan lords squashed any investigation. They said he fell down a cliff during a storm, as if it had been an accident. They made certain you never heard. A few years later, Lady Elwin succumbed to an illness."

His voice quavered. "Their only daughter, Lisze, was not yet of age. Lord Nordrum filed a motion with the courts to add the land to his holding. She put up a good defense but couldn't find the papers with your seal of a perpetual land grant. The judge gave her two months to find the documents. She came here but her uncle used me to thwart her plans. She worked as a baker in this castle. Do you remember the maiden who made the sweet bannocks?"

"Unsurpassed."

"Nordrum paid me to dissuade her. We thought it would be easy to stop her, but she was determined."

"A true daughter of Rothsum."

"You were touring Worstein and wouldn't be back in time for her to plead her case here. She needed to find the original decree in the archives and had obtained permission from the librarian to search. Running out of time, I hatched a plan." His inner pain rose and he struggled to breathe, but something within gave him strength. "I told her if she married me, I would use my influence as a prince to have another land grant issued. I staged a sham wedding with a few friends."

He looked aside. "After one night, I sent her away, ridiculing her for even trying to run a Sanderfield estate in Dornan. The mayor of Whistler's Ridge, the leading lords of Dornan City, besides Lord Nordrum, all conspired against this daughter of the Sanderfield." He paused, seeing the shock on his father's face. "There's more. When she told me she carried a son, I tried to force her to have an abortion. Rothsum's friends helped her escape. Later, I heard about a woman with a young boy who tamed horses, managed a king's way station as its keeper, and baked the best sweet bannocks. I lacked the courage to face her." Trillion met his father's gaze. "I have asked God to forgive me. Now I ask for your forgiveness."

"You've found your faith again."

"I never had it." Trillion looked away. The day his ama, his mother, died was also the day his father was no longer his aba. He had been pushed out of the king's suite to live in a room next to the other princes. Love died that day. His older half-brothers tempted him to lie, steal, and cheat. Sometimes they encouraged him to join in their mischief, then laid the blame on him. The king grew cold toward him. The bond between father and son became irrevocably severed.

"What? Your prayers as a boy? All the verses you learned for us?"

"Works to please you. Nothing more." How surprised he had been to feel pure love for the first time, even surpassing his ama's, when he surrendered to God.

Trillion's father's approval had always rested upon deeds. Cascading pain grew as he recalled the sorrows he had brought upon himself and Lisze. "Lord Nordrum paid me with a bay stallion that died of a twisted bowel a year later. Again, the hand of God. The Lord struck me down today. At least I made my peace with the Lord before the end."

"End? Son, the healer believes you are young and healthy enough to heal. I do love you." He sat up and looked aside. "There will always be a place for you here, but what of your son and his mother? I will have them brought here." King Wallace reached for his son's hand, cradling it in his. "Do you have any feelings for her?"

"I do. She far surpasses the ladies of the land—the only one who ever caught my eye. If I had only known how what I had done would rend my soul! How do I know that I love her? But I do. Shame kept me from going to them." Despair rose up, for how could she forgive him?

The king leaned forward and with steady voice said, "I will dispatch Marshal Thielen to fetch them."

He rose, tapped on the door to the apothecary, and called the healers to care for the prince. "I have a matter to attend. Call me if there are any changes."

Trillion shifted to try to find a more comfortable position. One moment he felt joy, then fear for the coming days overshadowed all else. He had expected to feel better confessing to his father, but recalling what he had done to Lisze had rekindled overwhelming guilt. At the same time, his heart lifted recalling her tall stature, trim figure, and long, slightly wavy hair. He had watched her train her horse to perform marshal maneuvers. Well read, she knew and understood the Leaves of God. Kind and generous, she was one of the best bakers of the land. In time he had realized that he had traded away a family for a horse.

He found himself praying again. "Oh Lord, if there are to be future days, may I do good and not evil; build up, not tear down; and may You restore Lamoria to the unity we had once enjoyed." He recalled the days when he had traveled the land with the king and queen. All had welcomed them, taking no thought of their clan, tribe, wealth, or standing.

But forces had risen, pulling them apart. The people of Dornan despised the Sanderfield. The townsmen despised the plainsmen. He had helped Lisze's uncle steal her land.

Was forgiveness possible? Had his father hinted they would have to marry? Yes! They would to protect his son.

Even though he had never laid eyes on him, he knew his son would need the shield that only being registered as a grandson of the king could afford.

What of his future? "Oh Lord. Give my days purpose, whatever that might be. I surrender all, even my marshal squad to You. If You so will, use me to raise my son." Tears flowed, for the future needed to be secured for him. Unspoken were his last two requests—that he could have a part in preserving Lamoria and see the king as his aba once again.

Chapter 2

Of Wilm

At the firepit along the far ridge behind Clefisch Pass Way Station, Wilm sat beside Marshal Esrilin on the end of a worn, twisted oak log. He watched tongues of fire encircle the next piece of wood. Embers carried by the fire's wind glowed red against dark outlines of leaves, eventually evaporating in the inky black of night.

"Tell me again," he asked, his voice high and reedy.

"Of what?" the marshal replied, wrapping his bronzed arm around the lad. "You did water the horses as your mother requested?"

"Oh, give the lad a story," Cesim, the older blacksmith muttered, stirring the fire and then adding more logs to the pile.

Wilm smiled in anticipation of the fire's surging again. He raised his hands and felt heat wrap around his fingers. "When the ring of fire encircled our land, stopping boats from coming. When the streams of fire grew to mountains of black rock."

Marshal Esrilin held the boy close to him. "Don't get too close to the fire, little man. You asked of the beginning stories."

Wilm's shoulders sagged, thinking the marshal would retell the story from the Leaves of God—*In the beginning God created the heavens and the earth.*

He knew that story well as his mother drilled him daily on God's writings. The stories he longed to hear told were of the rising of Lamoria, how they came to know God's writings, and painted them on leather leaves. They were the horse lords of the plains. He remembered his mother telling him that the Lamorian were no better or worse than the Amhavran in the mountains or the Regnard who lived north of the mountains, but he knew. The Lamorians were not simply the horse people of the plains; they ruled the land with might and right.

Esrilin shifted and gazed into the glowing fire. "In the beginning, when the earth was young, our ancestors came to these shores by the sea."

"But they loved the broad, grassy plains and horses running free," Wilm said.

"Do you want a story?"

"Yes, Marshal Esrilin, I will hear your story." Wilm settled himself on the log to listen.

Esrilin stroked Wilm's dark brown hair, glancing fondly into the lad's rapturous gaze. Settling into the singsong of a storyteller, he continued, "Strong of bone and sinew, brown with flowing black hair, the four founding tribes—men, women, and children—piloted their small boats to the next large island. They found this land and made it theirs." He pressed his finger gently against the boy's mouth as he felt him gather breath for more questions.

"We do not know why they fled their homeland or what they were seeking, but this land became their home. Spreading out across the hills and plains, they forgot their ocean journey until one day the ground shook." He looked up at the stars and continued, "Fire grew up from rocks beneath the waves. Those who still ventured to the sea for fish fled the shores as ash, fire, and terror rained down for days. When all grew quiet, they returned to the shore. Small islands now ringed their land. Tremors continued. Ash and flame heated the lagoons, and dark islands reached up to the sky." He paused to take a quick drink of boiled tea.

"Grew to the black pearls of the sun," Wilm added. "Someday I will swim from island to island."

"When you are older and can battle the many-toothed

shark, eight-armed octopus, and swim from channel to channel, then and only then shall you take the young man's journey."

"Yes, marshal." Wilm sighed. He felt as if he would be forever young.

"Little changed, life went on, generation after generation, father to son to son's son, until our coming became a distant memory. We nearly tore ourselves apart, seeking but never getting, grasping but never keeping. One family hunting another family, brother killing brother, we were close to reaping the full judgment of God. Few reached our lands from the ocean. Few ventured beyond the coral reefs and sharp rocks until one day a battered boat washed ashore. They found a pale man with red hair."

"Like the Regnard who live north of the mountains?"

"Back then we didn't know of the people who lived in the far north. We knew of the Amhavran in the mountains, and we kept them from our plains with our bows and swift horses."

"They don't dare step on our lands now," Wilm said.

Cesim pulled the fire together to keep it going. "Best if we keep to ourselves, that I say, lad, but all peoples need God. Inside, we're all the same, even if we live differently."

Esrilin continued, "The pale man, Daniel, brought us the gift of God's writings. In time, we perceived our only hope for a future lay with Christ." He traced the scrolled edging on his blade's handle poking out from his belt scabbard.

Wilm held his breath.

"Daniel began with the villages by the ocean bays. One by one, more came to hear God's words. Some mocked and scoffed, but when Tholen came, he heard and led his tribe to make peace with the Stoddard. In time, we were a nation at peace, not war, working to settle and build a nation, not simply survive."

"And the House of Airdle led the great fire council that

created the kingdom of Lamoria and set the boundaries of the councils."

Esrilin looked at Wilm in the glow of the fire. "You're interrupting again. I hear your mother's footfalls. Time for your prayers."

"And recite my verses," Wilm muttered.

"Your mother hands down to you the sacred writings from the Leaves of God and the law of Lamoria founded upon God's ways—not the old ways of sin and savagery." Esrilin patted Wilm's shoulder. "Never despise your learning. It will guide you along paths none can see the end of. The future is a blank slate to us all. Those who follow God will find their ways to the Halls of Christ and the Throne of God. Say your prayers well, little one."

Wilm turned, hearing his mother walking toward them in her short leather boots. Story time was over.

Lisze stepped near in her work skirt that covered soft breeches. Her long hair swept down as she reached for her son of twelve years. She winked at the marshal and encircled Wilm with her arms. "Is he telling stories again?"

With Wilm's nod, she said, "Time to recite your verses, my son."

With a wave, the two walked past two paddocks and through the stable to the reception hall. Their quarters consisted of a spare room beyond the dining hall, beside the kitchen.

"Now then, Master Wilm." Lisze stepped back as he peeled off his tunic. "Dusty from riding the horses?"

"Yes, Ama." He turned to the basin to wash before slipping his night robe over his head.

"Psalm 23."

"'The LORD is my shepherd; I shall not want.'" He paused. "Is King Jesus my shepherd?"

"Yes, since you took Him as your Lord two years ago." She peered into his piercing dark eyes. She had looked for signs of the Holy Spirit working in her son. Separating the true moving of the Spirit from his desire to please her was hard. "As you say you did."

"Yes, Ama, I did." He looked away, recalling those days when he could no longer ignore his guilt and his end if he rejected the one true God.

Lisze moved him toward his bed beside the back wall under the window. She felt along the ledge, making sure the latch was up. "Never forget." She lifted the window and closed it again softly.

Wilm settled on the rush mat. "I know, flee to Esther's Spring, avoiding the Dornan, find the Imbus cache, follow the ridge through the Imbus Wastelands, and seek the Sanderfield on the eastern shores." Last moon they had found the Imbus cache. "When will we travel to Sanderfield?"

Lisze pushed a few strands of hair from his eyes. "When you are older. Now, say Psalm 23 for me." She tucked him into the bedsheets and rested her hand on his silky hair as he recited the familiar verses.

Lisze looked through the window to the moon before it fell below the dark horizon. Even as a keeper of a king's way station, a place designed for quartering squads and providing respite for weary marshals, her days revolved around her son. "The King's first song of ascent, Psalm 120, 'In my distress I cried to the LORD; He answered me . . .'" Lisze turned from her fears and completed the citation along with the next, Psalm 121. "'I will lift up my eyes to the hills. Where does my help come from?'" Her mind's eye saw the waving, open plains, dotted with distant grouping of trees.

Wilm watched her gaze out the window as if she longed for other places, yet he never dared ask. "Did your mother teach you these lessons?"

"Yes, she did." Lisze turned her attention to Wilm. "My father and mother taught me as I teach you. These lessons will give us life if we choose to follow the Lord of life, who is . . .?"

"Jesus, I will follow Jesus!"

"Good boy. Now, your turn, the third ascent."

She listened to her son repeat the week's lesson.

"The third ascent of the king. 'I was glad when they said to me, "Let us go into the house of the LORD."' Is it true there are fifteen steps to Airdle Castle, matching the number of Psalms of Ascent?"

"The first king designed the fifteen front steps of Airdle Castle after the Psalms of Ascent." Lisze's gaze turned inward. "That we would never forget Lamoria's birth rested upon God's Holy Word." She remembered mornings at the castle— soft ocean breezes, flags waving from the turrets, gulls calling, and stained-glassed windows twinkling with the sun's last rays. Fond memories could not overshadow the deep hurt and lingering bitterness of Prince Trillion's betrayal. Yet she did not want to poison her son against King Wallace and Airdle.

"Why is our House of the Lord a tent?"

With a start, she returned to the present. "Because we live at a remote king's way station, my son, not in town." She bent to kiss his forehead, leaning down until her son's sweet breath caressed her cheeks. Lisze grasped his soft hand. "Now, to sleep." She circled his face with her hands and bent for a last goodnight kiss. "I love you."

"I love you, Ama. Don't ever leave me."

Lisze bent forward to hug him closely, as if she could shield him from all harm. Sitting up, she turned to go and said under her breath, "Not yet, Lord. I need more time with him."

She blew out the candle and stepped out to take in the stars filling the sky with their brilliance now that the moon had set.

"Airdle's lights blocked out God's stars," Esrilin said, walking quietly to her side.

Lisze nodded. "His lights are not easily seen at the castle."

"You must tell him."

Lisze glanced toward the marshal's strong profile, mostly straight nose, and firm chin. Esrilin was one of the best of the king's marshals in her estimation—smart, loyal, and true. Her shoulders sagged. "I can't. He's too young to understand."

"Lisze, he knows, perceives, more than you realize. Do you want him to hear it from someone else? Only you know the true story of his father and his birth."

"And if I don't? If he never knows?"

"You can't hide him here forever. It's becoming more evident every day with his looks."

"Wilm and I both bear the shame of his illegitimate birth. If I had an assurance that one would come forward to sponsor him, I would not hide him away." She faced the tall marshal. "I would sacrifice myself to ensure his safety, but I have no such pledge." She looked away, fearing the pain this subject must bring to Esrilin, her true love. She knew the marshal's loyalty to God and Lamoria kept him from adopting Wilm as his own.

Esrilin drew breath. "Lisze, a courier bearing dispatches brought word that Prince Trillion was gravely wounded during a sparring match."

"Will he live?" Her voice tight, she couldn't even utter his name.

"The prince is Wilm's father. In the future, might he not be bitter that you had kept this from him? Many have died from such accidents. During a flying maneuver, his horse fell upon him, and a dagger wounded his leg."

Perhaps the hand of God had finally moved to exact judgment upon the wayward prince. Lisze forced down a rising anger but refused the temptation to pray for his quick demise. "And then what? I tell him of his mother's great sin? I bear part of the blame!" She wiped away hot tears with a hard hand. "I vowed never to return to that place."

Her hopes and dreams of raising horses with Esrilin had wilted away as Wilm grew. The visage of the Airdle kings had been stamped upon his face. Any who saw him would know he was a grandson of the king.

Esrilin reached for her arm and drew her into an embrace. "We rest in God's forgiveness. He makes no mistakes. Fear not the reproach of man, my love, or what the future holds, for God has already set it in motion." He released her.

Lisze nodded. "God's will, though I can't see it." Lisze watched him head to his quarters. She turned to the back door. "Good night, Esrilin."

She paused at the doorway to their back room, knowing the position of her bunk in the darkness. "Lord, make a place for us, a home, a community that will welcome us."

Lisze shuddered at what the prince's wounding might mean for them. Yet he had kept their secret, as they were both to blame. She narrowed her eyes. If exposed, they would flee to the Sanderfield. Straightening, she recalled how the Lord had provided during the months she carried a child.

Cesim, dear friend of her father, Rothsum of the Sanderfield, and Esrilin, who had grown up with her, had sheltered her over the years and secured this position for her, upon her qualifying certification. "May the prince take our shame to his grave."

The Holy Spirit struck her conscience. "Forgive me, Lord. I pray You heal him, bless him. But don't let him tell anyone." She found her bunk and drew the blanket to her chest. For if the lords of Dornan would not countenance a Sanderfield home on their plains, the leading lords of Lamoria would never welcome such an illegitimate spawn at Airdle Castle. "Even if they take my life, Lord, preserve Wilm's."

Chapter 3

The Fourth Contingent

A few turns past dawn, Lisze carried plates from the dining hall to set them by the washing table beside the main building. Stepping through to their sleeping quarters, she glanced over Wilm's copying of the next ascent. He had finished his numbers, figuring, and script lessons. She reviewed her plans for the month. This afternoon they would have another lesson on the ways of the fish, if they were to be left alone. So far, she had taught him the way of the horse and the whistles of command, the ways of the snare and how to catch rabbits, the ways of the forest, its plants and berries that were good to eat, and the various woods good for cooking fires and warming fires.

"Keep him safe," she prayed as she set about cleaning up after morning mess.

As keeper of a king's way station, she ensured adequate food and supplies for travelers and quartered horsemen. They would soon need to lay up sufficient feed for the horses overwintering at the station. She reminded herself to inventory the stores and make a list. Esrilin could buy supplies at Whistler's Brook, the nearest trading post situated by a small village.

After cleaning up, she went outside to watch two horses trot in the paddock. They had been left behind by a squad due to badly torn hooves.

Feeling a slight vibration beneath her feet, she walked around the building to view the southwestern trail. Dust clouds rose from the distant highway. An unscheduled troop riding hard crested the ridge. She held her breath.

Esrilin and his squad had not yet left to survey the plains east of the city of Whistler's Ridge. As the quartered marshal, he could greet a squad in her stead. Lisze stepped close to the edge of the building where she could listen out of sight. She tilted her head to discern their mission. If they had come for respite or a meal, she could emerge to extend a keeper's greeting. If not . . . the blood chilled in her veins as she remembered Esrilin's news the night before.

Lisze heard a worker cry out that a squad approached. She was thankful he called for Marshal Esrilin.

She peeked around the corner as Esrilin emerged from the stable. Lisze slid out of sight, holding her breath. She heard him give the greeting. "Marshal Esrilin of the Clefisch Pass Squad bids you welcome and aid."

"Marshal Thielen of the Fourth Contingent. We bear a summons."

She heard them dismount and rustling of a parchment being handed off to Esrilin.

Breaths caught in her throat.

Esrilin read aloud, "Keeper Lisze is summoned to Airdle Castle along with her child, if one is with her."

Lisze ran along the side of the building and entered by the back door. She pulled their knapsacks from the rafters and headed to the nearest barn. In the dimness of the stable, she nearly toppled into Cesim standing in the center hallway.

"Tack Tesla and Whinny?" he asked, his brow furrowed.

"Yes, I'll find Wilm."

She returned quickly with Wilm.

Cesim hugged them both. "Off with ye now. I won't tell."

They were quickly astride their mounts. Cesim secured fresh water skins to the saddles.

"Many thanks, Cesim. You don't have to lie for us."

"But I don't have to talk. Go with God's speed, milady and Wilm. May you find your home."

Lisze urged Tesla forward at a fast walk through the tall grass behind the station.

Wilm gave a wave to one who had been like a grandfather to him. He urged Whinny, his mare, to follow close behind Tesla.

Reaching the nearest patch of bushes, Lisze led them through a gap and down into the eastward valley. They didn't transition to a fast gallop until they were far enough from the station not to be heard or their dust trail seen.

They would seek the safety of the Sanderfield, her father's people. Her heart beat with fear as well as beseeching prayers. The Leaves of God promised that the Holy Spirit would give the words to say in times of need.

"Dear Lord, shelter us." She buried deep within the urge to pray for God's will.

Esrilin felt Cesim come through the door to the dining room and stand to the side. He glanced over, recognizing the chin tilted toward the back stables. With a slight answering nod, he turned toward Marshal Thielen.

"Well, where are they, this keeper? I hear she is tall of stature. Daughter of Rothsum, one of King Wallace's Mighty Three from the Amhavran Wars?"

"She is. I will have our blacksmith fetch her." Esrilin nodded to Cesim. "Please find our keeper. Perhaps she is in the garden or schooling a horse?"

Esrilin smiled innocently at the renowned marshal of a royal squad. "This might take a few moments. Have you need to slake your thirst?"

"Much obliged." Thielen gestured for his men to hitch their steeds at the rail.

Esrilin heard Cesim call two stable boys to serve the

squad. The marshals appeared tired with pinched eyes and drawn faces. "Have you traveled far?"

"Directly from Airdle Way Station. The moon afforded enough light for a good part of the evening. The northern road is well known and easy to follow. We rested for a few turns." Thielen looked about, slapping his gloves on his thigh. "The keeper, Lady Lisze, does she have a child?"

"A son."

"And his age?"

"Turned twelve this past month of the eagle, the third moon after the winter solstice."

"And where would he be?"

"Cesim will fetch them both. Shall we sit at table while we wait?" Esrilin paused, watching the marshal look about and purse his lips. He needed to give Lisze as much time as possible to flee. He understood why she ran, but perhaps with the possible news of Prince Trillion's passing, this was not the right choice. Praying for guidance, Esrilin followed Thielen through the door.

Esrilin knew the bond of love between him and Lisze transcended time and place. His call to the marshal service had never dimmed over the years. That they had been together had been a blessing he knew would someday come to an end. The ache would linger until he crossed over. In the Lord's heaven they could be together again.

Thielen sat, watching most of his men come in, and accepted a short mug. He took barely a sip before he rose to pace. The squad leader stepped toward the kitchen, disappeared into the back rooms, and returned. He glared at Esrilin. "Outside!"

Esrilin followed Thielen through the front door to the corner of the building. The dust trail from Lisze and Wilm's horses had dissipated. He snapped back to attention when he realized the marshal's sharp eyes stared fixedly at him.

"You knew Marshal Rothsum? Wasn't he a close friend

of your father's?" Thielen paused only briefly. "So she has a child. We don't need to know how or why the king needs to see them, but the summons is urgent." The marshal drew in his breath. "Where are they?"

Esrilin looked to the side, saying nothing.

Thielen glowered at the younger marshal and called his squad to form with a sharp report whistle.

Esrilin ordered the few of Clefisch Pass who had appeared with Thielen's whistle to assemble the quartered squad and staff.

"That you helped them escape will be reported to Head Marshal Vaughn, Marshal Esrilin."

The younger marshal made no excuses. "She has her reasons."

"We will pursue and find them."

"Do you know to where she flees?"

"We have a tracker."

"Do you think she will leave much sign?" Esrilin watched Marshal Thielen shift his eyes to look at him. "Our squad can aid you in your search."

"You will?"

"Yes." Esrilin leaned closer. "To see they receive a proper hearing and are escorted to the castle with all dignity. We must fly, as they seek the safety of Sanderfield Council. Do you have leave to search to their eastern shores?"

Not waiting for a response, Esrilin turned to his squad. "We are tasked with helping the Fourth Contingent escort Lady Lisze and Wilm to Airdle Castle. I ask for three volunteers. One marshal will oversee the way station. The other four will proceed with the scheduled patrol of Whistler's Brook and through the upper Weaver's Plain. Any questions?"

Esrilin maintained a stern face though he was pleased that Marshal Lance, his valued second, along with two others, volunteered immediately. He gave further orders to the remaining five.

Quartered marshals at a king's way station always ensured their gear and steeds were ready at a moment's notice. In a short time, the four joined Thielen's squad.

Once mounted, Marshal Thielen whistled for two abreast, with the tracker beside him. "You may lead, Marshal Esrilin, as you seem to know the paths she might have taken."

The road dropped quickly with steep declines. Esrilin held his horse to a canter, mindful that the squad's horses had traveled most of the night. They took the northern trail to cross the Imbus River.

"Lord," he said under his breath, "help Lisze to see this might be Your will for them." Putting aside his swirling emotions, ever the dedicated marshal of Lamoria, he took the lead, knowing exactly the path they had taken.

Lisze paused by a stream not far from the Imbus River. She needed to think, to plan.

Wilm let the horses drink. He glanced at his mother staring off toward the horizon as if she had no idea what to do next. "Ama, did you know the prince who has been injured? They told me about it this morning while I fed the horses."

"What? Oh, yes." But she would not tell him that the prince was his father. They would shelter with the Sanderfield. In a few more years, when he was older, she could tell him.

"Ama, is he my father?"

Lisze stared in shock, her jaw slack. At first, she wanted to deny the truth, hide from it. There her son stood, young, innocent, unspoiled by the troubles of the larger world. She would shield him. Almost stamping her foot, she strove within herself for the right words.

"I heard them talking about me one day."

Tears formed in her eyes.

"That a prince was my father. That's why you hide me away. For a while I thought you were ashamed of me, but I think the Lord let me hear so I would understand."

She felt his arms around her. Holding back her sobs, she melted into his embrace. "You are a treasure, a gift from God. Never forget that. I will never be ashamed of you. After my father served as a marshal with King Wallace during the war, the king gifted him with a land grant. It lay north of my Uncle Nordrum's holding in Dornan. My ama and my aba preserved the land, drove out the bandits and vagabonds. Their herds were glorious. But my uncle hated that a Sanderfield had a small holding in Dornan Council. When Ama and Aba died, I was still young, seventeen. My uncle conspired to steal the land, convincing the judge it needed his care. I pleaded with the judge, but I could not find the papers of a perpetual land grant with the king's seal. I went to Airdle to see the king or find the land grant."

She stopped, feeling the blood pounding through her veins. Would her son still love her once he knew? "Uncle Nordrum hired Prince Trillion to stop my search, but I was determined." She gazed into the distance, remembering Trillion's charms. "The dashing prince, skilled on a steed, made my heart beat faster. I thought he would be a friend."

The betrayal rose up. She shoved down all feeling. Her voice quavered. "Trillion told me that he knew of my plight. I worked as a baker in the castle while I searched for our land grant. He loved my sweet bannocks. He promised that if I married him, I could keep my family's land. I not only betrayed God, but Esrilin." She saw the understanding in her son's eyes. "Such an honorable man, our Marshal Esrilin." Lisze turned away, unable to face him as she confessed.

"Deep down, I knew it was a sham, but I was desperate to keep our land. He held a mock wedding with two of his friends. I should have known when the one posing as lawreader couldn't find the passages to recite from the Leaves of God. We were together one night, and then he cast me out. I prayed that he would keep the secret of our one night together. I stayed in Airdle until I discovered that I carried you." She turned, staring into his face. He took her outstretched hand. "You are God's blessing from that dreadful time. Cesim and Esrilin helped us, and I became the keeper of Clefisch Pass."

Wilm's answering smile warmed her soul.

"I vowed never to return. Never to see him or Airdle or that castle again." Her bitterness ran deep.

"But, Ama, what if he's repenting? What if he's sorry? He will need our forgiveness before he passes."

Lisze drew back. A shock ran down her spine. She shook her head, turned, and paced. How could she tell him that those of Airdle and Dornan would never accept one of the Sanderfield or the Ayisin? Prince Trillion's own troubles had made that clear. But the Spirit whispered that her son spoke truth.

Truly, as Christ had forgiven her, she must forgive Trillion. She stopped and faced her son.

"Ama." Wilm reached for her hand. "I would like to see my father and tell him that Jesus loves him."

She did not pull away. Glancing about, her mind surveyed the quickest way to the castle. "Then we must go now. They will not be far behind us."

"Wouldn't they help us?"

"As freeborn, I will go. Not dragged to the castle like a criminal." Her lip quivered, reliving how Trillion had ruined her. The shame would never go away. Doing good, raising a son, seeking to make up for her sin was all that she had left. Perhaps this would be another good deed to add to the rest.

Wilm brought the horses, and they mounted. They turned back to reach the southern trail through the Weaver's Plain to bypass Whistler's Ridge.

"Why do some hate the Sanderfield?" Wilm asked. "I heard a stable boy say the Ayisin are lazy and the Sanderfield are rude. Marshal Esrilin scolded him severely."

"Son, our people are dividing once again, as we had before Daniel brought the Leaves of God. There were four tribes—the Airdle, of the sea; the Dornan, of the plains; the Ayisin, the nomadic people; and the Sanderfield, who dwelt along the rocky northeastern shore. When our people found the Lord, they were able to live in peace."

Lisze recalled their days with the Imbus Ayisin midwives. They had asked no questions, made no judgments. Had showered their love upon a young woman in her time of delivery. "The Imbus Ayisin sheltered us in our earliest days. We owe them our gratitude. Ayisin live in every council, but travel often, depending upon the season, and to visit their cousins." Her eyes misted. "The townspeople and herdsmen traded and sheltered the Ayisin as they traded and sheltered them."

"What changed?"

Lisze smiled. "Hard to make peace with others when we are warring with God in our hearts. When we ask Jesus to save us, for the first time in our lives we can have peace with God through Jesus."

"I remember when I accepted Christ a few years ago, it was easier to accept differences in others. If someone is of Airdle or Dornan, does that make them better people?"

"No, of course not."

"So you are of Dornan and Sanderfield. Why did one tell me that I was also of Airdle and Ayisin? Why would it matter?"

"Some people look too closely at things that don't matter. I believe how one acts, their faith, love, and purpose count more than their tribe or clan. But yes, many of Airdle or Dornan look down on an Ayisin or Sanderfield." She was glad he hadn't asked about the prophecy.

Before Wilm could ask another question, Lisze lifted a fist to call a halt. "Shh, listen." Had she heard galloping horses drawing near?

Looking about, her heart fluttered. They were in the open with no place to hide.

Lisze held Tesla at a stand and set her face to hide her fear, but her heart pounded. Thoughts swirled in her head. The only prayer she could form was a desperate plea for help. Remembering that the Spirit fixes the prayers of the faithful, she felt a small relief until more than a squad rounded the bend and bore down upon them.

Wilm backed Whinny off the trail. "Ama! Move off the trail."

Lisze faced them with her back ramrod straight, for she knew who they were and their charge from the king. Her heart skipped a beat when she recognized Esrilin in the lead.

Marshal Esrilin to her now.

She flinched not when they continued at a canter, pulling their horses to a stop in front of her at the last moment. Some slid to the side. The group surrounded them.

"Well, marshals, have you found your quarry?" She avoided Marshal Esrilin's gaze, focusing instead on Marshal Thielen. What would he do with them?

Chapter 4

To Airdle

Northwest of Dornan City, Marshal Esrilin called a halt at a marshal camp with a good well, lean-to, and firewood. While Thielen was the lead, he was not as familiar with the best place to overnight. "We can stop here and arrive at Airdle tomorrow."

Too tired to argue, Marshal Thielen began to assign camp chores. By the time he retrieved his own bedroll and saddle bag, Lady Lisze had assembled a camp kitchen by her side. The boy called Wilm had a fire going and kept an eye on the warming pan. Flour, some lard and rising powder, with the right amount of water, had been formed into two bannocks. Marshal Esrilin had already begun to heat their trail meats.

She held her hand over the large pan and declared it hot enough.

"Ama, do I set snares?" Wilm asked.

"No, we will break camp quickly on the morrow. One bannock for tonight and one for the morning." She noticed he watched the squad. "You can see if any would like some help."

Wilm ran to help the marshal ordered to fetch more firewood.

Esrilin sat next to Lisze.

"Lisze, does he know?" Seeing her nod, he glanced about to make sure none were near. "I'm sorry."

"Don't be. You were right. Wilm does want to see his father. He thinks he might be repenting." She would have stated that would never happen, but she saw Esrilin's agreeing nod.

"My love, God can save any, even the worst of us."

Lisze trembled as she blew out breath through her lips. She blinked back hot tears. "He saved us, didn't He? Really, who's good enough? Not me!" She lightly tilted the hot pan from side to side to spread the grease and then dropped the bannocks in the pan.

"Lisze, you are forgiven. Do you believe it?"

"Doesn't feel like it." She blinked tears away. "How can I face him? If I didn't fear for Wilm, I'd send him in without me." She hid a shaking hand under the slit skirt covering her riding breeches.

Esrilin moved closer to embrace her in a hug. She was more important than fearing any would see. "I will never abandon you, even with the coming changes."

"The fault is mine. We wouldn't be in this mess if I hadn't been so set on our family's land grant. So what? We could have built a home anywhere." No longer able to hold back her tears, she buried her face in his shoulder.

He wrapped his arms around her and stilled her shaking arm. "God is ever with us. Give not into fears that might never come to pass. Can we be happy for Wilm to meet his father?"

"And his grandfather. Trillion hates me. I'll never forget how he sent me away with a look of disgust and contempt. But we share a son. One that must live in the castle. Where would I go?"

"The light of God sometimes shines only the path before our feet. God will never abandon you."

Lisze leaned back to wipe away the tears. She heard a crackle from the pan and saw they had turned a light brown. "The bannocks!" She checked the bottom and sighed. "At least I still can make a decent trail bannock."

"That you can." Esrilin slid aside and rose. He checked the placement of his squad's bedrolls and gear.

Tired, hungry, and thirsty, the men accepted the water

bags provided by Wilm and the meal provided by Esrilin and Lady Lisze. The sun set before they found their places for the night, with each assigned their share of guard duty.

The next morning came too soon.

A fresh squad with trail-conditioned steeds could reach the castle in one day from that camp.

They were on the road as dawn broke. By late afternoon, the castle and stables' roofs came into view. The sun hung low over the horizon when they slowed to a walk on the paths leading to the courtyard. Lisze assumed they would stop at marshal headquarters, but the troop continued on to the front steps of the castle.

They must have been seen as King Wallace, Head Steward Kiel, Supreme Judge Prince Joshua, several pages, and castle guards waited at the landing before the carved, wooden front doors.

Lisze noticed her son gaze in wonder at the group adorned in royal attire standing before the doors of the castle. "Wilm, the slender man standing to the side with the tunic bearing Airdle arms is your uncle. He is Prince Joshua, the Supreme Judge of Lamoria. He ensures the courts make good and fair decisions." She didn't have the time to list the rest of the staff that hovered by the king.

Lisze noted that Esrilin kept his horse close to hers. They dismounted at the stairs.

Marshal Thielen looked at Esrilin for a moment. "Our work is done here."

Lisze pointed to her best friend. "I request he accompany me, please!"

"Is that your wish, Marshal Esrilin?" Thielen gestured to his squad to take the horses to the stables.

"Yes, I'll report to Head Marshal Vaughn as soon as I've seen this through. Can you arrange billets for myself and my men?"

"Very well."

Lisze and Wilm stood before the first step and looked up. The waiting crowd parted for King Wallace, an older, slightly stout man wearing a richly embroidered tunic. His round face was framed by plaited jet-black hair that reached his shoulders.

As if they had already met, when King Wallace put out his arms, hands palm up in greeting, Wilm ran up the stairs before Lisze could stop him.

"Grandfather!" Pausing at the top, he began to blush. Trying not to stammer, he said with a bow, "I am Wilm, son of Lady Lisze."

Hearing cheers and clapping, he glanced back at his mother still standing on the flagstones.

King Wallace bent slightly to greet him. "I am glad you are here, Master Wilm." He stood and looked at the two standing below. "Well, you may approach."

Esrilin came to Lisze's side. She slipped her arm in his, happy for the escort as her heart fluttered within her. She dared not glance at the king but fixed her gaze on her son. Wilm stood confidently by his grandfather, as if he had always lived at the castle. Swallowing a groan, she tried to remember Esrilin's words. She would trust in Christ. She would be joyful.

Reaching the top, Lisze curtsied before the king, thankful that Esrilin stayed by her side.

"So this is our bannock-maker. Pleased to see you again, Lady Lisze." He turned and the group made way for the king, Prince Joshua, Wilm, and Lisze. Esrilin followed close behind.

Steward Kiel and his staff returned to their stations.

King Wallace approached Healer Anselm who waited in front of his suites in the eastern hall. "Is he still awake?"

"Yes, Your Majesty."

King Wallace continued forward. Entering his son's sick room, he was pleased to see Trillion sitting, propped up by pillows. "They're here."

The group gathered along the side wall and the door leading to the apothecary. The healer stood to the side of the bed. He had dismissed everyone else, as the king had requested a more private audience.

Wilm came through, pausing only a moment before going to the man on the short bed not far from the door. "I am Wilm. Are you my father?"

"I am. Many call me Prince Trillion, but only you can call me father." His eyes drank in the boy, tall for his age with the visage of the Airdle kings stamped upon his face. His mostly straight black hair had been tied back for the trail. "Please come."

Wilm stepped closer and knelt to see his father's face better. "Father, I, we, prayed for you." Breathing in, he said, "God told us to come. Do you know Jesus?"

"I do now." Trillion looked at Lisze, momentarily transfixed by the beauty of one who had weathered many storms. Yet he had no idea of her heart. He tried not to move for the pain it would bring. He returned his gaze to the youth before him. "I hope and pray we have a chance to get to know each other. But first, I have to talk with your mother."

Wilm nodded and went to stand by Esrilin.

Trillion, with flushed cheeks, pale face, and shallow breath, held out a hand. "Please come."

Lisze's heart missed a beat. She felt Esrilin push her gently forward. Moving as if in a dream, she sat on the short stool near Trillion. She looked fixedly at him, ignoring his extended hand. She should harden her heart, walk away.

Striving within, she watched his hand droop, pain wash over his face, and his eyes teared.

With shaking voice he said, "Lisze, please forgive me. In the name of Christ, forgive the terrible things I have done to you."

No! Never! Yet Wilm's words returned. Had this one truly repented? Even so, the Lord demanded she yield. "I do." Forcing herself, she reached for his hand. "For if Christ can forgive me, I must forgive you." A pulse of love and grace flowed through her arm. Her weight of guilt and shame fell away. "I am glad to hear you found Christ. I have to ask you to forgive me. So stubborn, so set on my goal, I allowed you to use me as I used you." There, she had said it, what she hadn't realized all these years. "Well, now you've seen your son."

Trillion glanced at his father for a nod of confirmation. He returned his gaze to Lisze. "He is your son as well as mine. I would guess that you love him greatly."

"More than anything in the world."

"Would you be willing to do a hard thing to keep him safe, protect him?" Trillion looked aside. How unimaginable his proposal must seem to her, but his pain was rising and he would soon have to lie down. Praying for strength and courage, he reached again for her hand. "If you marry me, Wilm's future will be assured. He will be registered as my son and the king's grandson."

The king leaned forward. "This will secure your son's future. All sons and grandsons of the king are fully trained and receive a holding or land grant." The king looked at her. "What say you?"

Lisze stood quickly. The stool fell to the side. She looked away from the eyes watching her. Unable to breathe, or draw in air in the crowded room, she moved to the door.

Wilm rushed to her side and held her hand. With lowered voice, he said, "Ama, our prayers have been answered. My father has repented."

Tempted to be rid of all of them, be done with this place and the House of Airdle, she could not avoid her son's open, honest face. That Wilm bore the face of the Airdle kings had closed the door to Esrilin taking him legally as his son. This they had come to know as the boy grew. Had they not sacrificed already that he might have a future? Even if her life had been undone, could she not take this step for Wilm's sake?

Lisze glanced back at the prince. His sunken eyes were now red-rimmed. Sorrow cast a shadow over his face. Had her forgiveness been mere pretense, a show of civility? *Lord, do You require this of me?* Betwixt the door and the hand of Trillion, her battle raged.

"Ama, this is of the Lord," Wilm said. He cradled her hand in his and walked her back to his father's bed. Righting the stool, he helped her sit.

Lisze stared at Trillion. "Do you wish this? If things were different, would you still . . ." Before she could finish, he reached for her hand.

The movement sent pain rippling along his side and around his chest. His hand shook, but he did not loosen his hold on her. "What a fool I had been to not have courted you properly. Yes, I must admit. Yes, I confess that I not only pray to be a good father to Wilm but a good husband to you."

Lisze nodded and said softly, "Yes, I agree." She looked at the prince, once so full of pride, now barely able to sit. For the first time, she felt love and tenderness, kindness. Perhaps it would be, could be, real. With or without his love, she would still do this for Wilm. He needed a father, a heritage, a place. "When?"

"Now."

"Now?"

King Wallace stepped toward them. "Lady Lisze, his wounds are severe. An infection has started in his leg. To ensure Wilm's registry in the list of princes, you must wed while he lives."

Prince Joshua opened the door. "Clerk Glenn, we're ready."

A middle-aged lawreader in jerkin bearing the Airdle seal of justice carried a slim book of order of services and a registry.

Lisze sat unmoving beside the fallen prince. Prince Joshua read aloud the passages that she had heard years before. One part of her screamed this was another deception, but the Lord's Spirit whispered, "Peace, child," to her soul. Stealing a glance at Trillion, she recognized again that the arrogant, vain prince had been transformed. Perhaps it was true, yet her mind spun with hearing the words they were to repeat for their vows.

Trillion's voice quivered occasionally, but he never broke his gaze upon her face.

Lisze repeated the words. "May we not break the circle of life between us whether good or ill, with many herds or empty barns . . . till the Mighty God calls us home."

The king drew two rings from a pocket.

Trillion slipped one over her finger.

Lisze slid the other over Trillion's finger. Their eyes met and a pulse ran down her spine. The past was done, forgiven, as far as the east was from the west. "May you have many days to get to know your son."

She felt the heat emanating from his body. "Trillion, you have a fever."

"Oh, I know."

"What have they given you?"

Healer Anselm stepped toward the bed. "We have everything well in hand, Lady Lisze. I am the royal healer. As you so rightly observed, the prince needs some treatments and rest. So be gone, all of you." He disappeared into the apothecary room to prepare the medicinals.

She rested her hand on Trillion's arm. Closing her eyes, she prayed, "Oh Lord, heal this man." Her heart yearned that he would have a future.

With a low voice, as if it were his last breath, Trillion said, "After you, no one else caught my gaze or stole my heart. My pride and arrogance kept me away all these years. But each day given to us will be a heavenly gift."

Tears fell. Lisze wiped them away. As she rose, Esrilin quickly left the room.

"A moment." She curtsied briefly and followed after him.

"Esrilin, wait!" Lisze quickened her steps. He turned, rigid and straight. His face was a hard mask.

"I am done here. My call to the marshal service remains. I will request postings along the eastern shore."

She should nod, agree, but her heart ripped within. "At least say goodbye to Wilm," she said with trembling lip. As if he had been summoned, she glanced back and saw her son coming their way.

"Marshal Esrilin." Wilm ran to hug the one who had been like an aba to him. "We will never forget you. Will you return to Clefisch Pass?"

"Prince Wilm, quite the title now. I would go back, or to wherever they send me. I was not much older than you when the Lord confirmed that I would be a marshal. Even as a prince, you can still train and serve with us."

"I would like that." Wilm furrowed his brow. "But we will miss you."

"As I you, both of you. Sorrow to part, but happy in that you have taken the path God lays before you." He gave Wilm a final hug. "Spend as much time with your father as the Lord provides. Only God knows the future and how many days you will have. Never waste them."

They watched Wilm head back to the healer's suites. Esrilin allowed himself to feel Lisze near him. "We didn't know how God would work this out, but He has. Remember, few will be these days, even if given to sorrows, in the light of the love we will share for all eternity."

She had never seen the stoic marshal driven to tears until this day. "Our prayers go with you."

"For his sake and yours, I will not return unless the service calls. I've a few incursions to report to the head marshal. Whatever he decides to do with me, that I will do."

"I understand. They are blessed by your service. Lamoria needs marshals like you." She watched him walk down the hall and turn toward the stairs. His steps down were whisper quiet. A finely trained marshal indeed.

Lisze gathered her wits about her and returned to the suite. Trillion, still propped up, stared intently at Wilm as her son told him stories about life at Clefisch Pass. She stood beside Prince Joshua. King Wallace sat in a chair past the end of the bed and the clerk had gone.

Prince Joshua said, "Lady Lisze, you have done a remarkable job raising the prince."

She tilted her head. "I had help from Marshal Esrilin and Master Cesim."

King Wallace turned toward her. "Cesim yet lives? He's a marshal?"

"Serves as the blacksmith and grounds manager."

When Wilm began to yawn and Lisze perceived her hunger, she stepped toward the bed. Despite Trillion's directed attention on his son, she noted the dark circles around his eyes had deepened. He shifted occasionally as if to lessen his pain or to draw breath. Coughs came from deep within his chest. She tapped Wilm's shoulder. "Son, the prince needs his rest and the treatments Healer Anselm mentioned. And you need a good meal and a dry bed."

Lisze glanced at the king sitting on a nearby stool. She rose and headed to the apothecary room where the healer instructed his assistants at a long preparation table. "Healer

Anselm, we must help the prince lay down. Are the treatments ready?"

Anselm sent two helpers out to settle the prince.

King Wallace rose. "Prince Wilm, we will find the steward to assign a room and have a meal brought." He held out his hand and the youth accepted it with a smile. They headed to the door. "I need to retire as well. Lady Lisze, it is good to have you back with us. Are you coming?"

"Your Highness, may I stay to oversee his welfare?"

"Very well, when you're ready, find any guard or page and they will show you your rooms."

Prince Joshua rose from his chair and joined them. "Let me introduce you to your new home."

"May I call you uncle, Prince Joshua?"

"When we are in private or with family, you may. But I am Prince Joshua when we are about or at the school. While chief judge of the land, I also supervise Airdle Day School and teach sometimes."

"You're a lawreader? You teach God's Word?"

"Prince Wilm, from whence came the laws of Lamoria?"

"From the Leaves of God. The codes of the moral law and the civil law. But the sacrificial law has been overturned with the Lord's sacrifice on the cross."

"Well taught, young prince. Lawreader can refer to one knowledgeable about our laws or to one apt to teach from the Leaves of God."

"The stories of our Savior, the history of the kings." Wilm scrunched his brow. "The prophets' words. They're sometimes hard to understand."

"I see we will have much to talk about. Shall we?" Joshua ushered Wilm out the door after the king.

Lisze smiled, hearing her son ask more questions as they walked down the hall. She went back into the room, sat on the stool, and reached for Trillion's hand. "Wilm asks many questions."

"That is good." Trillion coughed again.

Lisze's fingers touched his chest, feeling the rumbles through his lungs. "Are you better lying down?" She watched him nod, followed by a grimace. "I must make room for the healers."

She stepped aside to watch the healer direct the assistants. Sitting on the chair a short distance away, she prayed. They worked for another turn. Once his breathing had settled and his wound cleansed and bandaged, Anselm gestured for her to follow him into the preparation room.

"How may I assist?" She was his wife now. Not one marshal, stable boy, or worker had been lost under her care at Clefisch Pass. She was not about to leave his healing treatments to others without her supervision.

"Please sit with him until the sleeping draught takes effect. Time will tell. He must rest." The tired healer patted her arm. "Loving care is its own balm. Good lady, I will be honest with you. We have done what we can, but with an infection his—"

"Healer Anselm, spare me not the truth, for I have nursed wounded at Clefisch Pass."

The healer nodded. "Many his age are able to overcome infection, but I am also concerned about his left side. There are no assurances that he will fully recover."

"I understand. If he has any needs in the night, your assistant may call me. And, if this is not too bold, could you provide the recipes for the herbal teas and instructions for the exercises to keep his chest clear?"

Anselm nodded. "Most definitely. That would make it possible to let him return sooner to his suites. I believe you would know when to call for us?"

"Most assuredly." She curtsied and sat near Trillion. She held his hand and whispered prayers. He stared at her for a long time, but his eyelids grew heavy.

"Sleep well . . ." She tried again. "I'll pray for you . . ."

When his hand clenched hers, she said, "Then I will stay."

His hand in hers, she willed him to breathe with each rising of his chest. Suspended beyond time itself, he lay. She sat beside him. When his hand loosened and he had fallen asleep, she pulled away gently and left the room to stand in the hallway.

A light on a table by the stairs directed her gaze. From what she had heard, but never seen, the princes' suites were in the west wing on the second floor. Walking along, she saw a royal guard and stopped for directions.

In moments, she was in Trillion's suite with her packs beside the door. She lit some candles and felt the deep, down bed. Somehow she had to stay awake until the promised sup could arrive.

Lisze grabbed a candlestick and peeked into Wilm's room across the hall. Hearing the rhythmic breathing of one deep in sleep, she returned, satisfied. A page arrived and placed her meal on a small round table. She ate what she could and then succumbed to exhaustion on the bed.

Chapter 5

A Guardian for Prince Wilm

Light streamed through a lead-trimmed window, warming Lisze's cheek. Consciousness returned, and she opened her eyes. Beige-colored walls bordered with delicately sculpted dark mahogany trim rose to a white vaulted ceiling supported by thick beams. Rich burgundy curtains, embossed with the royal filigree, were drawn back by gold-threaded cords. She vaguely remembered hearing someone pull aside the curtains, but the siren call of sleep pulled her down once again.

Feeling strength return, Lisze pushed back the covers. She stood, wondering how late it was. Had she slept the day away? Her eyes scanned the delicate furniture, rich curtains, and golden recliner draped with a vibrant blue gown.

At first glance, it hardly seemed like this was Prince Trillion's room, until she spied the large, battered trunk beside two sets of boots. But the blue gown?

A head peeked in. "I thought I heard you stir, milady. No time to lose." A middle-aged chambermaid stepped through the door, shut it firmly, and approached the recliner. "Ah, just the one." She turned holding up the dress. "It should fit."

"For me?" Lisze noticed her dusty clothes were gone. "My riding breeches, boots?"

"To the cleaners, Lady Lisze." The maid approached with the undergarments. "Remember me?" Seeing Lisze's bewildered look, she said, "Maid Alice, but I remember you." Alice chatted while she handed clothes and undergarments to Lisze. "You do know how to dress?"

"Of course." Lisze reddened and looked about.

"Oh, still modest." The maid nodded toward a three-leaved privacy screen painted with a dashing figure astride a rearing stallion. "You could dress behind the divider." She quickly gathered all the articles and draped them over the panels. "Used to be Prince David's rooms, but he has his own estate near Roanin."

"Now they are Prince Trillion's. I would have thought he had more gear, as a marshal. Thank you." Lisze washed briefly at the chamber basin before heading behind the screen. "Where is Wilm?"

"Prince Trillion keeps his marshal gear in his locker. Head Steward Kiel doesn't like mess in the royal suites. Prince Wilm is with the prince in the healer's chambers." Alice removed the nightgown Lisze had slung over the screen. "Need any help?"

"I can manage." She put on fresh, white undergarments, a blue bodice, and slipped into the gown.

"No one made a sweet bannock like you did, lass. The prince will be asking for one soon, no doubt."

"When he recovers enough to enjoy it. Have you heard any reports?"

"He yet lives."

Lisze reached back to draw the gown tight. "Could you fasten it?" She stepped out from behind the screens, turned, and sucked in her breath.

"I'll have to see this adjusted. Made for a maid with a smaller waist."

"Just secure it with a pin. I can fix it later."

"My dear, you'll have more to think about than altering clothes. That's my job, and what I can't handle, the tailor will see to." She directed Lisze to the standing mirror. "Now for your hair. Sit." Alice pulled a padded chair to the side and began to arrange Lisze's long locks. "Castle's been without a proper lady for many years now. Since Prince David is the heir, his wife was the lady of the castle until they moved to their own estate. Prince Joshua, next in line, moved before they did. His wife never took to the busyness. She's a more private person." Alice paused, holding the brush in midair. "You might like Lady Jessica." She smiled. "Prince Joshua and Lady Jessica. Has a certain ring to it. He's next in line after his brother."

"Wouldn't Prince David's sons succeed to the throne after him?"

"The Crown Prince has only six daughters. Nearly tried to find a different wife, but then he grew attached to Clinton. That's Joshua's oldest son. Taken him under his wing, he has. Uncle and nephew are tighter than father and son. Rumor has it, if trouble comes, Prince Joshua will transfer the crown to his son." Maid Alice shook her head. "Well, time's a-wastin', so no more palace doings. You'll have your fill of it soon enough, I reckon."

"May I grab first sup from the kitchen?" The lower levels had a long dining hall for staff. Years ago, if anyone, even a member of the royal family, had missed a meal, they could eat in the common hall.

"Of course."

"Thank you, Maid Alice. You've been so kind." Lisze stood in front of the mirror and rotated, barely recognizing herself. Her hair, tastefully pulled back, flowed past her shoulders. The blue skirt twirled with her movements.

"Oh, the shoes." Alice brought over some slippers and walking shoes. "See if you can find any that fit. The cobbler will be by later."

A pair of soft brown leather walking shoes fit well. "These will do, but I'll want my riding boots back."

Grabbing a light shawl, she opened the door.

"Off with you now. Can you find your way?"

"Yes, down the hall to Healer Anselm's suites."

Quickly finding a few items from her pack, Lisze placed

them in her pockets and nodded. "Maid Alice, under the head chamberlain? Your room's in the east wing?"

"Yes, you do remember. Lower level, naturally."

"Naturally." Lisze smiled and walked with Maid Alice to the lower level. The halls were quiet and still.

Lisze ate quickly and took a back staircase to the end of the eastern wing. A royal guard nodded as she made her way to the healer's suites. Knocking softly on the door, she turned the knob and entered.

Her heart dropped, and she brought her hand to her chest. The low bed was empty, cleaned, and tidied as if waiting for the next patient. She must have cried out, for Wilm emerged from behind a tan curtain.

"Ama! You look beautiful! Come see. They made a room for Father."

Lisze followed Wilm around the curtain to a large room. The back section seemed dedicated to storage. Folded cots and shelves with blankets and supplies lined the left wall. A bed had been pushed closer to the other side, by the window. When Trillion turned toward her with a broad smile, her heart melted.

"What manners! I nearly slept the day away." She sat on a chair Wilm brought. Light streamed through the window. Lisze turned to Wilm. "Did you rest well?"

"Yes, Ama. You should see the room I have all to myself."

"I will." She turned her attention to Trillion. "This is better by the window." She hesitated to ask how he was doing with Wilm beside them. Trillion's face was pale, and the gray, pinched look ringing his eyes remained.

Trillion looked at Lisze. "Could you check on my charger, Kewatin? He's a buckskin stallion with the most beautiful golden coat. He's probably in the royal stables. You can ask the trainer or stable manager for a horseman to escort Wilm, if he wants to ride."

"May I go today?" Wilm asked.

Lisze gave her son a knowing look. "Wilm, for today exercise Tesla and Whinny in a paddock. We will have time to explore the grounds later. Had you not heard your father's request?"

"Son," Trillion felt the strangeness of having a twelve-year-old for a son. "No one has told me how Kewatin is doing. He fell with me. Can you do this for me?"

Wilm nodded.

Lisze turned to Trillion and patted his hand. "We'll be back with a report." It felt too warm for her liking, but she had confidence in Healer Anselm. She hesitated to add her concerns over what the healer had shared the night before. All was in doubt, strange and bewildering, but, if Lamoria were to be set back on course, perhaps this prince could rise and help. "Has your lawreader been by? Would you like him to pray with you?"

"Definitely. Lawreader Garth stills preaches at Airdle Chapel. Remember it?"

"Of course, I do. I'll be back."

Lisze flagged the first page to send for the lawreader. She led Wilm down the main stairs to the first level near the guest rooms and dining halls. At the end of the hall, they followed a narrow staircase to the lower level.

"This is the easiest way to reach the stables." She had another reason for going this way.

Hoping and praying, Lisze stepped into the kitchen, and her emotions tumbled. Good times had been had working with the kitchen crew to prepare meals, clean up, and keep the pantries in order. She hadn't seen an old friend when she stopped by for a meal that morning.

Perhaps now? She looked about the island in the center of the kitchen.

A slender woman with long, shiny hair emerged from the pantry down the short kitchen hall. Her eyes widened and she gestured for Lisze to follow.

"Wait here," Lisze said to Wilm. She stepped down the hall to the pantry she remembered well. Before she could speak, Patrice wrapped her arms around her.

"So it's true? You're really here." Patrice moved out a little to view their latest prince. "Why did you come?" She looked back at Lisze and reached for her hands. "But it is good to have you back. Don't leave him there."

Lisze nodded for Wilm to join them. She noticed the look of recognition on Patrice's face.

The slender woman pulled out a coin of Lamoria stamped with the face of King Aaron.

Lisze accepted the coin and handed it to Wilm. "I'm sorry, I tried to shield you, but this is why—"

Wilm felt its heft in his hand. "Was this the first king? I do look like him."

"Wilm, meet Lady Patrice, my best friend while I was here." Lisze tilted her head. "Did you learn the knack of kneading bread?"

Patrice's melodious laughter filled the pantry. "I'm the head cook now. I find maids and pages who are so gifted." She glanced at Lisze and Wilm. "You must be careful. How old are you, young prince?"

"Twelve."

"Is it true Prince Trillion now believes?" Before they could give voice to their assents, she said, "Can't believe all the rumors, but some are true. That bout was no mistake. Marshal Galant had been told to call him out. They know what will set him off." Patrice leaned closer to them. "Request a guardian be appointed to watch over him."

Lisze furrowed her brow.

"I am sure you've trained your son well." Patrice curtsied slightly to Wilm. "Beware those who mean to trick you into doing mischief, fair prince." They turned, hearing the clattering of pans and pots from the kitchen. "Must go."

"And we have an errand to run." Lisze noticed the band

on her friend's finger. "Is that a wedding band on your hand?"

"Recently wed to Arlen, a lorimer. One of the finest saddle makers and leather carvers in Airdle Council. He had been a marshal until an accident."

Lisze hugged Patrice. "I'm so happy for you. May we go out the back way?"

"Of course, and don't be shy to stop by."

"I won't." Lisze led Wilm back down the hall.

They stepped out into bright sunlight. Lisze blinked to get her bearings. The royal stables should be to their right, past the first of the marshal's buildings.

They found the royal stable close to a grassy paddock beside a riding ring. Heading into the stable, Lisze found the horse trainer checking a large buckskin tethered in the center hall. "Good morning, good master, I am Lady Lisze. Prince Trillion has asked me to check on Kewatin. Is this his steed?"

The horseman stepped under a tie across the hall and bowed. "Welcome, Lady Lisze. Your reputation precedes you. Master Tonson at your service." Pausing for a moment, he stepped back to view the horse. "Skittish, as expected, but then the prince is not around to calm him. A back leg is sore. We've wrapped the right front, and the swelling has already begun to go down."

"Is he spurning oats and hay?"

"Nay, he eats enough for two horses. I believe that is the secret for his strength and endurance."

Lisze began to coo, approaching the stallion with an open palm. She came beside him to stroke his head, neck, and shoulders. "Have you a brush, Master Tonson?" Moving slowly, she began to groom the horse with rhythmic strokes. Kewatin leaned into the brush. His ears relaxed, and his head lowered with the grooming.

"You are a beauty."

If she wasn't in what she would have considered a ballroom gown, she would have completed the job. Without proper boots and her riding breeches, that would have to be left for another day.

She handed the brush back, forcing herself not to laugh at Tonson's astonished gaze.

"Mother trains the marshals' horses," Wilm said proudly.

Mother and son exchanged smiles.

"I'll let Prince Trillion know how Kewatin is doing. As soon as I have my riding gear, I'll be by to school him. Wouldn't do to have him soften during the prince's convalescence."

"So he will return?"

"One day, we hope and pray." Lisze remembered her other errand. "Prince Wilm needs to school Whinny and Tesla. Where have they been stabled?"

She followed Tonson to the last stalls by the back barn door. "Looks good. And where should we store our tack?"

Once they had the tour, Lisze said to Tonson, "Wilm may exercise the horses in the paddock. Soon we'll ask for a guide to show us the trails and best places for training."

"So the young prince aspires to be a marshal one day?" Tonson lifted his brow.

Wilm bowed slightly. "If God so leads, to serve and protect our land. May I exercise our horses? They're probably restless."

"Remember, son, ride in the paddock and do not venture forth today."

Tonson bowed. "The prince will be well looked after."

Lisze returned to the castle and to her husband, Patrice's warning ringing in her mind.

Prince Trillion shifted in the bed with the head partially raised. His brow furrowed. "That took a while. Wilm?"

"He's exercising Tesla and Whinny. I met an old friend in the kitchen and took the time to become acquainted with Kewatin. He's a beautiful steed." She reported Tonson's findings. "I was thinking of schooling your charger until your recovery."

Trillion smiled. "Still the horse master, or should I say lady of the horse?"

Lisze narrowed her eyes, but seeing his teasing smirk, she smiled with him.

"Well, my turn to check on you. Feeling better? Be honest." She reached to hold his hand, and it felt a little cooler. Some of the light had returned to his eyes. "You do look better today."

"Having you here is . . ." He looked aside.

Lisze brought a chair over and told him about Patrice's warnings. "Is she right?"

Trillion nodded. "Yes, we need a guardian for Wilm, and I let Galant goad me. They know me too well."

"Knew you. Remember, we are made new in Christ."

"The accident was God's final warning. I was doomed unless I repented." He turned his head to gather breath. "As we flew into air . . ."

"You did a flying maneuver during a match? Had you trained for that? It's not too hard during an exhibition or performance, but to land properly during a skirmish requires mastery of the skill."

"We'd only practiced alone in a ring. None offered to train us for its use in battle. As we fell, I heard God's voice and felt His love. A brilliant, overpowering, unconditional love. For the first time in my life, I realized everything Father had tried to tell me—all those lessons, all those verses, the songs, the services, the sermons were true. Lying there, before my world went dark, I remembered you and acknowledged my sin."

Trillion forced himself to meet her gaze. "I came to faith that day. Of all the things I had done, hurting you bothered me more than anything else. Very little brought joy anymore. I finally understood that without God, my doom was certain. For love, I surrendered and for love I had to confess. God showed me that I had a son, and I have to make him ready."

Trillion paused to catch his breath. "I prayed to see you one last time. Even back then, I knew you were too good for me. Bent on sin, anger, bitter resentment, and there you were, facing impossible odds—so loyal, so faithful. God also told me Wilm has been set apart for a special purpose. I have no idea what this would be, but we must shelter him, guide him, prepare him." He looked at Lisze. "God told you too. Before you even showed, you knew you would bear a son. Do you remember?"

"I spoke without thinking." She looked to the side. "I only knew I had to keep him safe." She furrowed her brow. "The princes, your half-brothers, persecute you because you are of the Ayisin. Do you think they will also try to hurt Wilm?"

Trillion met her eyes. "I fear they will. Crown Prince David has no son. Prince Joshua, next in line, has three boys. Prince Ricard's only child is a son, but he's younger than Wilm. That he is my son, many will see that as a threat because my mother was of the Ayisin."

"As well as of the Sanderfield, through me." She lifted her eyes to look out the window. "I never understand such hate. We've had many dealings with the Imbus Ayisin, and they are a gentle, kind, patient people."

"When one's heart grows cold to God, it becomes easy to despise and belittle others. That I know very well." Trillion shifted to dull the pain. His heart beat with the exertion. "Do you know anyone you would trust to keep our son safe?"

"Master Cesim, the blacksmith. He was my father's armor bearer for a time, but he's more than a faithful friend. He's been watching out for us."

"I remember Cesim. Would he do it for you and Wilm?"

"I have no doubt." She turned her head and gave him a sideways glance. "He is a believer and will forgive you, if you ask."

"I'll ask, anything . . ." Coughs interrupted his attempts to lighten their mood. "I feel better already. Go to Steward

Kiel's office. It's down the hall. He can send the message to the king."

"I'll make the request." Lisze held his hand. She desired to know more about him. "Tell me of your faith."

"How had I missed that surrendering to Jesus would be my liberation and not my bondage? That faith was a gift, not earned by vain deeds?"

"Oh, many miss the reality of a life lived with God until He does come in." Lisze remembered her confession to God when she was eight. "In the cities and countryside where many frequently hear the Word of God, some do not understand it's so much more than following a set of rules." She remembered something her mother had told her. "Even if born to Christian parents, even if we go to church and can recite many verses by heart, even if our lips speak of faith, our heart is dead in sins until we invite the Savior in."

Trillion held her hand, and they talked of their lives in Christ.

Cesim's commission was transferred from the marshal service to the royal guard. He arrived, having received no explanation. With a new marshal leading the Clefisch Pass Squad and Esrilin off running special errands for Head Marshal Vaughn, he was glad to leave the memories of their time together at the station. Yet fears rose up for Lisze and Wilm. The aging warrior stabled his steed at the second royal stable and went to find Steward Kiel. With measured steps he walked to the prince's suite on the other side of the castle and knocked on the door. He smiled from ear to ear when Wilm nearly toppled him over with a hug. "You've grown more! Careful of this old man!"

"Old man! If only some of middle-age were as fit as you!"

Lisze rose to meet him. "Come in." She exchanged glances with Trillion, now settled in his former rooms. The healer's treatments had kept bouts of fever at bay. "Wilm, I remember your room needs straightening. Don't dawdle." She hesitated to promise a surprise upon his return.

Once he had left, Lisze gave Cesim a hug. "Do you need some time with Prince Trillion?"

"Nay, this won't take long." Cesim met Trillion's gaze, and his jaw went slack. The vain, arrogant, lost prince had been transformed. Patting the arm of his best friend's daughter, he strode to the young man sitting on a long seat. "Greetings, Prince Trillion." He bowed. "I have come to the summons, yet none have described my duties."

Lisze pushed a chair closer. "Cesim, please sit." She sat by them.

Trillion wet his lips. "Cesim, I must apologize for my behavior—"

"Nonsense. You never offended me personally, although your former ways brought shame to the House of Airdle. Not that Prince Ricard and the crown prince don't also sully the people's trust. As a redeemed one, you are cleansed in Christ."

"But, who told you?"

"Aye, I heard many tales, Prince, but the Spirit within confirms what the Lord had tried to tell me—you are new in Christ. I apologize for never having believed this could happen. How may I be of service?"

"To guard Prince Wilm."

Cesim stood in front of the prince and Lady Lisze. He placed a closed fist upon his heart and bowed. "I most gladly accept the commission to protect and serve Prince Wilm from all threats and harm, so may the living God who raised up Lamoria ever be my watch."

Trillion said, "Thank you. Our hearts will rest easier now."

"Shall I fetch the lad?"

Lisze rose as well. "It was to be a surprise."

"Aye, I will surprise him. His room is the last across the hall? And mine is the small one next to it?"

"Yes, with a narrow window. We could find you a larger room."

"No need. I'm a man of action, not the chambers. The lad will experience a proper inspection." He left to seek his charge.

"I see we made the right choice." Trillion glanced at Lisze. "With the stories of his marshal exploits, I had no idea he was such a tease."

"Life was never dull at our way station."

They settled well into the prince's suites, but Lisze feared the busyness of the second floor impeded his rest. Within a fortnight, Trillion requested they be allowed to move to the Garden Suites at the back of the castle.

That afternoon, while Wilm was still in classes for the summer session, Lisze pondered aloud. "Maid Alice said both Princes David and Joshua's households reside at their own estates. We could request a land grant some place out of the way."

"But Wilm's schooling?"

"We can school him with the help of tutors. We could raise the best horses, see the land well tilled." She smiled. "That would be enough for me. Would it be enough for you?"

Trillion's eyes lit up. "It would. With our own estate we could shelter him until he's ready to face the challenges of his heritage."

"He longs to join the marshal service."

"As each prince has." He glanced at Lisze. "God will help us, lead us in training him not only how to take the field, but to navigate the deceptions of men."

"My daily prayer." She leaned close to him. "I'm learning I must trust God with everything, especially our son."

Chapter 6

The Garden Suites

Acooling late-summer afternoon breeze drove Trillion and Lisze back into the sitting room of the suites on the northeastern side of the castle. Through large picture windows they watched the wind bend the flowers in the garden. Lisze adjusted Trillion's lap robe. "Are you warming up?"

"Merely a chill." He squinted at the trees surrounding the garden. "Seems early for leaves to turn."

Lisze glanced around their temporary quarters—a small suite of rooms off the rear flower garden, bursting with day lilies, morning glories, and other flowers. Quiet and out of the way, it had sheltered the small family for almost a month.

"Sit with me." Trillion extended his hand. "Joshua and Jessica will be here soon."

Lisze glanced about for chairs to draw up around the small table in front of the windows. Before rising, she recognized a worried look on his face—set mouth, pinched nose, and two furrows between his brows. "Trillion, how did your meeting with Prince Joshua go?"

"Better than I feared, but it was hard. I confessed, told him everything." Trillion narrowed his eye. "And he apologized for his former treatment of me. He said that God had told him he had to be nice to me, but by then I mistook his gestures of kindness as another subterfuge. I hope and pray that we can now be friends. He's coming here to discuss our land grant."

Lisze breathed in, conflicted. Was it wise to leave the palace? Would it harm Wilm's chance to get to know his grandfather? "I assume it wouldn't be in Tholen, Airdle, or Dornan."

"That leaves Worstein or Stoddard, closer to the Imbus Ayisin. Princes David and Joshua's mother was of the Airdle from Tholen. Some years after she died, the king married a Dornan woman from Wasson."

"Prince Ricard's mother, the second queen?"

"Father waited a long time before he married my mother, Queen Lillian. She was young and beautiful, a daughter of the chief of the Keyayisin in Worstein. She transcended the divisions between us."

"All speak of her grace and loving-kindness."

Trillion sighed. "And now I know we will see each other again in heaven. I must forgive my brothers for what they have done. I am thankful that Prince Joshua came to me. Reconciling brings peace." He leaned back, his chest rising, phlegm catching in his throat.

After his coughing fit passed, Lisze laid a gentle hand on his chest. Slight vibrations danced up her fingertips. "Your throat is clear?"

"Yes." Trillion repositioned and coughed again.

"You had your troubles growing up as well, daughter of Sanderfield."

"How I hated to hear that! Some said it with a smile on their face and daggers in their eyes. What of the family we came from? Matters not our character and way of living? Yes, during the short time at a day school they teased me for my dark-brown hair. Muskwa, they called me, brown bear!" She took a breath and shook her head. "I must forgive their ignorance; that's what the Lord told me. My companions were the horsemen of the plains, my testing grounds, the open ranges. My parents taught me all they knew of book, field, husbandry, and holding."

"Like you've taught Wilm, preparing him well for the days ahead."

"Begun, anyway, though I had no idea of the depths of Lamoria's growing divisions, or the forces levied upon a youth who lost his ama too soon." She looked deep into his eyes. The sound of distant voices filtered past stone walls. "I think they're here."

"Prince Joshua and Lady Jessica are punctual as always." Trillion reached for his cane.

Lisze rose, helped him stand, and they walked to the glass doors.

The tall, slender prince, in a jerkin emblazoned with the shield of justice, stood by a lithe woman almost as tall as he with wavy black hair secured in a bun. Her light lavender gown with lace and delicate bone buttons flowed with her movements.

Lisze opened wide the doors and curtsied.

Trillion bowed. "Welcome, Prince Joshua and Lady Jessica, to our humble rooms."

Joshua looked about. "Nonsense, Brother. You may call us by our given names. This garden has the prettiest late summer flowers."

Lady Jessica extended a hand in greeting to Lisze. "And this guest suite looks very cozy."

Lisze directed them to their chairs.

Joshua settled on the one near Trillion. "Good idea to rest here through the summer but not for the fall or winter. Tends toward damp with cold drafts."

"We'll soon be going back to my suites. This was quiet, out of the way." Trillion looked about for his wife, but she was busy with the afternoon tea.

Lisze set cups and plates of pastries on the round glass table. Lady Jessica smiled sweetly as she sat in the next chair. Seeing Joshua drinking his strong coffee and Jessica her brew of mint and lavender, Lisze pushed a plate toward Trillion.

"It's good to see you are finally on the road to recovery," Prince Joshua said.

"We take it one day a time."

Lady Jessica shared a knowing smile with Joshua. "Wise decision. We've all been praying for you."

"We can't tell you how happy the king is to have his son and grandson by his side." Joshua pulled out three rolls of parchment. "I've been talking with the king about the best place for your land grant. Here are some possibilities. It's also time to select the holding where Wilm could squire."

"Squire? He's just twelve." Lisze looked about. "Sorry for interrupting."

"Not at all. Yes, they squire when they are older, but the holding is selected in advance. This is not too soon." He nodded toward Lisze. "You had mentioned something closer to the eastern shore, but there is another area that might work." He pulled out a fourth scroll. "Worstein, just south of the Amhavran hills."

"West of Havransen Pass and the Invien Cliffs, in the shadow of the mountains?" Lisze leaned forward to study the holding nestled in the northwest corner of Lamoria.

"You are correct, Lady Lisze. I considered your history, both of yours." Joshua cleared his throat. "The people there accept a person for who they choose to be, not the family they come from. They'll test you and give you a chance to prove yourself."

Trillion looked aside. "I made myself a pariah in some parts of Worstein Council."

"You'll have opportunities to make amends, Brother." Joshua laid out the scrolls.

Lady Jessica rose and looked at Lisze. "Let's walk the garden. I'm usually at our estate at Seagull Bay and have looked forward to meeting you and Prince Wilm."

Trillion and Joshua watched their wives chatting gaily as they walked the inner path. Jessica bent to admire the flowers, and Lisze picked some for her.

"How great is our God who gives us lovely wives." Joshua sighed and sipped his coffee. "She makes good coffee too."

"Blessed beyond my imagination. If only I had found faith in time to do things right with them."

"And raise your son at Airdle Castle?" Joshua lifted a knowing brow. "His sheltered upbringing shielded him from the controversies of the castle. Even so, God can work good out of our misdeeds."

"I have to ask, since Wilm graduated to the fifth level in the second quarter trials last month in July, is he still doing well at fourth level in school?"

Joshua set his cup down. "Fear not, he's a better fit in size and strength at the fifth. I've approved his graduation to the fifth in his studies as well. Lisze schooled him well." The prince sat forward. "But he will need to give more attention to his studies. I'm certain, as the novelty of living here wears off, he will be more diligent."

Trillion nodded. "Ever the leader of students. I hear you still teach from time to time."

"Occasionally, as I can fit it in."

Trillion shifted to find a more comfortable position. "Will his time as squire be for only a year?"

"Yes, as customary, with a possibility of living with the Ayisin for a month. Why do you ask?"

"Clinton, your oldest, has been squire with Prince David for years now."

"He now assists the crown prince as he oversees several marshal squads and Airdle's courier service to the southern councils." Joshua shrugged his shoulders. "The Lord gifted me with an understanding of the law and the courts."

"As well as in the classroom." Trillion remembered the rumors that if something happened to Prince David, with no sons, Joshua would transfer the crown to Clinton, his eldest.

They turned to drink their coffee, gazing out the picture window to the stately oaks rimming the garden with vine-covered arches leading to beds of roses. Sounds filtered in of running feet, trailed by deliberate steps of heavy boots.

Wilm burst through with Cesim working to keep up

with him. The youth stopped and bowed with a grin on his face. "Prince Joshua, is not Lady Jessica with you? I have wanted to meet her." Prince Joshua lived at Seagull Bay, and Wilm had not yet met his aunt.

Trillion spread his arms for the after-school hug. "Do not run ahead of your guardian. Pull up two chairs and bring him a drink. We have tea." They laughed with the teasing for he knew Cesim drank only coffee or fresh spring water. "And what of that scroll you hold, son?"

Once two slim chairs were in place and Cesim situated with his coffee, Wilm stood at attention before his father holding the scroll close to his chest. With a flourish, he presented it to his aba.

Trillion caught Joshua's smile and nod toward his son. "Conspiracies afloat, I see." He unrolled it. "So you are now officially registered in the fifth level in your classes."

They all turned when they saw the ladies heading their way. Wilm rose to open the door, bowing ceremoniously, as they drew near.

Holding back her laughter, Lisze said, "Prince Wilm, this is Lady Jessica."

"Very pleased to meet you, Prince Wilm." Lady Jessica held out her hand.

Frozen, Wilm said, "You're beautiful."

"Thank you, Prince Wilm."

Joshua said, "Prince Wilm has an announcement."

"I am now in the fifth level at field and in class."

"Prince Wilm, are you doing well in that level for horsemanship?" Trillion realized he had failed to ask, distracted by his own concerns.

"Yes, Father. I gentled Candy, the mare we culled from the plains this summer, my gift from grandfather. She runs the courses most quickly, and the other princes could not make me fall off. Best of all," he leaned closer and said with a conspiratorial whisper, "she's a buckskin like your horse."

"My charger?" Trillion glanced between Lisze and Wilm. "Maybe soon we could all go for a ride."

"Next warm day you should visit Seagull Bay. We're not far." Joshua noted the life returning to his brother's eyes. "The leg has healed enough for you to ride?"

"I hope to be taking my first ride soon."

"Well, our time to depart." The three stood. Joshua stepped forward and wrapped his brother in a close embrace. "We are so happy for you. Let's not lose hope and fail to pray for David or Ricard."

"We do pray for them."

Trillion felt Lisze come by his side and her hand squeeze his. They walked out to the garden and waved goodbye as Joshua and Jessica left. He leaned close to his wife. "You by my side makes me a better man."

Lisze squeezed his hand. To hide her blush, she asked Cesim and Wilm, "Have you plans for us this turn?"

"Aba, can we walk the market? There's someone I'd like you to meet."

"You up for that walk?" Lisze asked. Trillion appeared pale, but then he'd been inside most of the summer.

He held out his hand to Wilm. "Yes, but first my after-lesson time with my son?"

Lisze and Cesim watched them walk hand in hand to the chairs.

"Need a nap, Cesim?" She laughed with his grunt, but he headed to his room near the back entrance to the lower levels. She puttered about straightening as she listened to Trillion pry every detail and happening out of his eager son. Once they were done, she reached for her shawl and then brought Trillion his cane. "Wilm, tap on Cesim's door and ask if he'd like to join us."

Trillion, setting his left leg aside, used his good leg to stand in one smooth motion. He winked at Wilm, who returned and grasped his hand. "Lead the way, young prince."

He led them past the stables and followed a side street, crossing Main Street filled with fine shops to Second Street. Small houses and craftsmen's showrooms faced the road.

Some sat outside on stools, their day's efforts strewn around them. "Father, I want you to meet my new friend. He makes the prettiest bridles and saddles."

"Good day, Prince Wilm," called out a man perched on a stool, surrounded by baskets of leathers, some plain, some carved, others painted.

Wilm ran up, gesturing to his parents to step across the busy street. "Please greet Master . . ."

"Marshal Arlen," Trillion stated, extending his hand.

"You know him?"

Trillion laid his hand on his son's shoulder, staring at Arlen's upraised face. "It's good to see you." He glanced at the small house behind the young man.

Arlen extended his hand. "You'll pardon the offense, my lord, but I cannot rise."

"Of course. I see you've met my son."

"Yes, I have. A fine young gentleman he is. This must be the beautiful Lady Lisze."

Lisze curtsied. "So you are Lady Patrice's husband. She's a dear friend of mine."

Arlen noticed Trillion's pale face and grimaced expression. He called back toward the house. "Father, can you bring a chair?"

A grizzled, older man lugged a rough chair out to the doorway. Lisze positioned it by Arlen for Trillion to sit.

"Prince Trillion, tales are told of your newfound faith. This is wonderful news and answers to our prayers."

Trillion laughed. "I can imagine your disbelief, considering how I used to be."

"We were so far from God." Arlen shook his head, exchanging smiles with his former squad leader. "Quite the team, giving no quarter at trials or at table." He straightened. "My pardon, my lady, but we digress. Have you heard of the Airdle Seaside Fellowship?"

"I've not." She glanced at Trillion.

"Pray tell, my friend." Trillion gestured for Arlen to elaborate.

"We meet at the northern part of the seaside around the large rocks for prayer and fellowship late afternoon most Saturdays through the summer. Our song leader and lawreader are very good. You are welcome to join us."

"You believe?" Trillion asked.

"I do." Arlen slapped his leg. "Losing the use of one leg forced me to let God into my life. I had a decision to make—spend the rest of my life in bitterness or thank God for His love. Thankfully, my father took me in and helped me acquire an internship with a lorimer, one of the best saddle makers in the district. This I can do sitting down. My praying grandmother never gave up on me. And the Lord has provided a wonderful wife. Soon we will open a saddlery shop."

"Father, look at this one." Wilm brought over a leather etching of a stallion poised to stomp a snake readying to strike.

"It's beautiful." Lisze studied the rich colors of the plains, the snake's mottled hues, and the stallion's sleek black sheen.

"It looks like Master Cesim's old horse."

"Probably looked like that a long time ago, son. He's been dead a few years now."

"How did he see him?"

"Many beautiful stallions roam the plains, Wilm."

Arlen smiled and pointed toward his head. "I made it up. This is one of my most popular leathers. Many like it because the horse is brave." His voice trailed away when he glanced at Trillion. "Well, they like bravery, Prince Wilm."

"Time to go." Trillion settled his walking cane against the worn stones.

"Perhaps we can catch up again." Arlen added, "See you at the meeting?"

"We'll try to be there." Lisze returned his smile.

As they walked back, Wilm asked, "Can the king accompany us on our afternoon ride Saturday?"

Lisze began to nod, but Trillion stated, "Oh, it's the last Saturday before the new moon when the king holds Public Judgment."

"What's Public Judgment?" Wilm asked.

"The people of Lamoria bring cases to the king the magistrates can't settle. He listens to their complaints and renders judgment. If a matter is too complicated, Prince Joshua assigns a special judge or council circle to settle the matter."

They turned toward the castle grounds rising to the east. Trillian said, "I had forgotten this will be a quarter banquet, and all of the royal family must attend. Also, leaders of the various councils come for the feast."

"Father, why is this called Airdle Castle if the king rules Lamoria?"

"Lamoria is the name of our country, but as the kings came from Airdle . . ."

"And the castle is in Airdle . . ." Wilm said.

"The mysteries of history." Trillion glanced at Lisze. "Do you remember the details? It had to do with more than King Aaron's tribe."

Lisze pondered the question. "I think that they had several terrible incursions from the Amhavran north of Worstein. Many were lost and villages burned. They decided to make Weirstone the capital of Worstein Council and gave the holding to a prominent leader. Airdle City seemed a safer place."

"How soon after did a series of earthquakes close the northern route to the mountains?" Trillion asked.

"Shortly after Airdle Castle had been completed, but perhaps our young scholar can research to see if I remembered correctly." They both laughed at Wilm's frown.

Wilm stopped in his tracks. "If Jesus came, why are there still wars?"

"The time of great peace will only come with the Messiah's second coming. Until then, we must remain ever vigilant. Why I joined the marshal service." Trillion saw his son's nod.

Chapter 7

The Banquet and Public Judgment

Lisze lifted her napkin to her lips to hide a wide smile. While they had practiced formal table manners with Wilm, this event rivaled any she had attended in her lifetime. A small band of musicians softly trilled through traditional plains melodies on harp, lyre, and flute. Several long tables forming a "u" shape were draped with pale beige linens and a full set of silverware for each place.

The king, his stewards, Prince David and his family sat at the head table. Prince Joshua on down to Prince Trillion sat in order along the king's right side. Being a new moon gathering before the fall harvest, the children sat with their families. The leaders from many prominent cities occupied the table to the king's left. Representatives from Worstein, Sanderfield, and Stoddard in the north were absent. In time, the king rose to conclude the meal with a toast and prayer for the harvest and coming winter. Head Steward Kiel rose as well.

"Do we have to leave now?" Wilm asked. He had not quite finished his meal and looked longingly at the tempting dessert at the center of each table.

Trillion leaned over and said in his ear, "No, the king leaves, so we can do what we want." He smiled and lifted his eyebrows.

Wilm looked at the dessert and back at his grandfather striding along the far wall near an ornate doorway. Setting his brow, he leaned toward his father. "May I watch the judgment? Prince Joshua came in to talk about it in class last week."

"Not only can you watch, you can accompany him to the king's chair, but you must be on your best behavior. You'd miss out on dessert."

Wilm glanced one more time at the frosted pastry and the king nearing the door. "I wish to see and hear what judgment is like."

"Well, then, Prince Wilm, Steward Kiel will make your introduction. Tell him you wish to accompany the king."

Trillion leaned back as he and Lisze watched the eager boy disappear through the door. "He'll be back shortly for his dessert."

"I wouldn't count on it." She watched the door to the hall close, her throat constricting.

"Relax, Lisze. A contingent of palace guards, a host of pages, along with a squad of marshals are at the ready. Public Judgment is the best-guarded affair, I believe, in the land." He looked about as many had sat back, more relaxed, and their voices a little louder than before. "Shall we retire to our chambers?"

Lisze glanced at the circles around his eyes. "Yes, of course. Nap time?" She stood to help him, but he used the table for leverage.

Standing close together, her face inches from his, her enchanted gaze sank into the bottomless depths of his eyes. His straight dark hair framed his high cheekbones. She recalled the attraction she had felt years ago.

Trillion wrapped his arm around her waist and stepped forward to guide her toward his side, but his foot caught on a table leg.

Lisze grasped his upper arm. "Careful," she whispered, noting his pinched eyes and shortened breath. "Yes, we need to be along."

Prince Ricard pushed back his chair, holding a goblet

in his hand. "Need any help?" His eyes lingered over Lisze's trim figure.

She felt Trillion tense. "No, kind prince. All is well in hand, but thanks for your offer of assistance."

"Any time." He winked at Lisze and smiled broadly.

"Godspeed."

Many raised their glasses and smiled back. Joshua rose to escort them out.

"Prince Wilm will be in good hands, Lady Lisze," he said. "See you soon."

"Of course," Lisze replied.

Trillion accepted his cane from the page once they were in the corridor. "Ricard." He glanced at Lisze. "If only I had not been like my brother."

"You were never that boorish. Worse, you were charming and captivating. Let's not waste time looking back. All is forgiven. We have a path to follow and a son to raise." Lisze rotated to face him, mesmerized again with his eyes.

Trillion pulled her toward him, pleased she hadn't pulled away or stiffened. He longed to kiss her full lips, but the time was not yet. The Spirit whispered a day would come they would be friends, companions, lifemates.

Lisze smiled and held his hand.

Trillion leaned back on his cane.

He set his face with the pain of each step, trying not to think how far it was to their quarters.

How easily he drew short of breath. Lisze noted the circles under his eyes. Filing her questions about his slow recovery away for later, she matched his pace.

Wilm watched as the king listened intently to the landlord's explanation, restating his complaints about his tenants.

King Wallace asked the tenants, "Did you withhold the rent?"

"Aye, and for good cause." The plainsman spouted his litany of complaints and list of items stolen or damaged. His wife stood silently by his side with a young daughter clutching her skirt. "Our family has rented from the Third Imbus Holding for generations. Always have our water rights been respected and our grazing lands not overrun by vagabonds. But now fences are flattened, a campfire set a grove of trees to blaze, cattle run off, some left to butchery, and livestock missing."

"Your grandfather understood his part. He patrolled the open ranges," the holding lord interjected.

"That we do, as the rangers will attest. But the lord kept the land in peace. Yes, we have done our part, but you have failed in yours. I haven't seen a fit patrol in over a year." He raised his gloved hand and began to pull it off, one finger at a time to raise his ungloved hand above his head. "I challenge."

The bailiff stated, "No challenges in the Judgment Hall."

Seeing the bailiff's sharp look and hardened stance, the tenant tucked his gloves under his belt. He lowered his hand and bowed. "My apologies, my liege."

King Wallace rose and lifted his hand, his eyes scanning the throng standing before him. "Has the pact between lords and tenants been altered?" He eyed the landholder directly.

"No, my lord. The pact stands."

"What do you have to say about the mischief to your tenant's lands?"

"My horsemen patrol. Our magistrates levy judgments." He turned and scanned the crowded court. "I see four other landholders with the same problems. Our herds are pillaged, our brands overwritten, our homes attacked." He looked at the king. "And the marshal squads are not to be found. These assaults are not done by local gangs, many tracking from common lands. Are not the marshal squads to aid when attacks come from outside our borders?"

"Bailiff!" The king lifted his hand again for silence when loud murmurings rose up. "This is an open court for all complaints, and yours will be heard today." He turned to the bailiff. "Summon Prince David."

The court sergeant approached the chair. "He might have left for his holding."

"Then bring him back." King Wallace turned to the restless crowd. "All who have holding concerns see the assistant bailiff at the sideboard. The rest, form a line."

Consulting with the court lawreader, they settled three cases, and decisions were registered with the magistrate clerks.

Wilm stood beside the king's high chair. Questions swirled in his head. In class the law seemed so fixed for the duties of each—landowner, landlord, and marshals. Why would their own countrymen desert them? Some complaints were about theft of livestock, yet others seemed to lack any purpose.

As the last case was referred to a waiting lawreader, the groups surged forward. Disgruntled plainsmen congregated on the right-hand side of the room as Prince David, flanked by the lords of Roanin, Dornan, and Airdle, approached on the left. Other holding lords gravitated closer to Prince David.

The crown prince snapped his gloves on his thigh as he said, "High time we put a stop to these raids by the Ayisin."

"The Ayisin who are our kinsmen and fellow travelers?" The king rose, nodding to the round leather shield, painted and etched with Ayisin markings that hung over the hall. "Tread carefully with your accusations, Prince David. Long our plainsmen rode in peace with the law of God in our hands."

King Wallace's piercing eyes scanned the plainsmen,

their families, the holding lords, their scripted men, and the few Ayisin with their hooded cloaks. He raised his clenched fist. "Our families drew each other's blood until we made peace with Christ." His finger followed the shields and standards of the holdings that ringed the upper ledges of the great hall. "We made peace with our Ayisin brethren as they chose to follow the nomadic life with their herds, and we agreed to trade with them, shelter them, as they us." He nodded at the plainsmen and holding lords. The corner of his mouth bent up slightly with the nods and assents that flowed through the gathering. "Accusations of robbery and pillage are serious charges, Prince David."

The king rested his hand on the hilt of the ceremonial short sword by his side, settled his robe, and sat on the judgment throne. King Wallace leaned forward. "Where is your proof these incursions are of the Ayisin? Why now would they threaten the peace of generations?"

Wilm grew puzzled. He had not heard of Ayisin clans who broke fences or stole cattle, apart from unexpected brigands who could come from any tribe.

"Your Majesty," Prince David stated as he lowered his head and softened his voice. "In our father's and grandfather's days, we dwelt as one. We also traded openly with the Amhavran." He cast his eyes about the room. "But the Amhavran are as apt to burn down a hall as to trade with it, and the plains have become more lawless by the day."

Wilm furrowed his brow. Not one marshal had spoken of the Amhavran invading. King Wallace sat tall on his raised chair. "Your duty, Prince David, is to keep the open plains safe and secure. We will talk of this later." He swung his eyes back to the plainsmen. "Pay your rents, but report every instance to your landholder." He leaned forward, narrowing his gaze. "They are to make right whatever has been lost to unprovoked attacks that should have been prevented. Bring proof of incursions from aliens for the marshals to investigate."

The king stood to his full height, swinging the ceremonial sword on his belt around to grasp the hilt in his hand and began to draw it out. Beams of sunlight streaming through the west windows glinted off the top edge of the polished metal, momentarily blinding the king. Visions of his father came to his mind, and he heard his words. *A king can rule by might, but a true leader will win their hearts.*

Blinking, he pushed the sword back into the scabbard and gestured toward the raised, hand-carved, fire circle ten strides beyond the dais. Field stones, polished and etched with the tribes' emblems, formed a large circle. Decorative flagstones ringed the raised stones in concentric arcs. "Let us gather round the fire circle."

As a ceremonial gathering had not been planned, the roof's windows and vents had not been opened. Fresh wood and kindling had not been laid. The blackened foundation stones were visible, swept for the next gathering and lighting of a council fire.

"Come, gather round."

Prince Wilm walked beside his grandfather down the four steps as the crowd shifted and flowed. He watched each one find his place. Prince David stood at the western jeweled stone. The king approached the northern point, studded with diamonds.

The king nodded and pointed toward the Ayisin's herald stone in the northeast quadrant. The Ayisin walked to the circle and lowered their hoods.

"Let us never forget that Lamoria is one."

Beginning at the king's right, the Ayisin stated, "Lamoria is one." The first pledge flowed around the circle. Landholder, plainsman, and Prince David repeated the pledge.

The king said, "Our God is one."

The second pledge flowed around the circle, followed by the third, "Our law is one."

"Our unity is easy to forget when conflicts arise. Let us

seek the Lord of heaven that we might live in peace with one another." The king raised his arms. "Let there be one rule of law for all. For the Ayisin." His gaze swept to the landholders and their company. "For those who live off the plains." Glancing at the townsmen, he said. "For those who live in the towns." Lastly, he locked eyes with his eldest son. "And the same law for the lords of Airdle. May the one true God ever chart our course and guide our way." The king smiled at the group. "Together, we can heal our land; together we can work for the peace of this land as we follow God. Go with God."

"Go with God," the people replied, some smiling, others with grim expressions.

Wilm heard some muttering, but also light laughter. He smiled and slid close to his grandfather's side when an Ayisin's gaze lingered on him.

"May we have a word, Your Majesty?" the elder in a simple hooded cloak asked.

"Of course." The king gestured toward the far corner of the hall as he nodded to a nearby sentry. "Prepare the seats for a meeting."

The sentry ducked through a doorway, reappearing moments later laden with cushions and a stout page behind him carrying more.

Cesim approached the group. When the elder Ayisin noticed him, he reached past the outstretched hand to wrap him in a hug. "Is this Cesim? One of the Mighty Three?"

Cesim smiled. "That was a long time ago, Eriason. Now I guard the prince and, from time to time, shoe a horse."

"Is this the one we heard of?" Eriason asked, staring fixedly at Wilm.

"Prince Wilm, son of Prince Trillion," King Wallace said. He gestured toward the circle of cushions.

The page brought in a low table where he prepared the traditional golden tea in short, round cups.

They sat, asking of the health of family, the strength of

their herds, and sharing news of recent storms and harvest yields.

Wilm listened to the talk of daily life, yet their faces looked worried. Why did it take so long for them to talk about what really mattered? He held his cup and sipped the unsweetened tea with little flavor. Keeping a neutral face, he smiled when his grandfather asked him if the tea was good. He furtively glanced over at the Ayisin staring at him.

Judging that the appropriate pleasantries and latest items had been covered, the king pointed his chin and upper lip toward Eriason to hear their complaint.

The elder Ayisin began, "The plainsmen are not the only ones experiencing mysterious attacks. A small number of our own encampments have been overcome by small, quick-strike forces. Their arrows and blades, like the ones you saw from some of the Imbus men, were not forged in our winter villages nor by Stoddard or Amhavran blacksmiths. Our men have searched the trade routes and council fires, but no such weapons are ever found." Eriason drew one out for all to see. "These blades come from a far place. The Regnard perhaps? Inquiries to Prince David have fallen on deaf ears. We had hoped since Prince Trillion has returned that he could help." He leaned forward. "News reached our ears of the prince's grievous wound and of his recovery. My king, as he once negotiated a truce between the Imbus Ayisin and the plainsmen, could he help once again?"

"I will consider the part he could play. We are overjoyed at Prince Trillion's recovery. Let us all number our days, as the future is unknown to all."

"Journey's end lies hidden with the turning of the trail," Eriason said.

King Wallace smiled at the Ayisin elder. "Are you planning on staying overnight?"

"We hadn't planned to linger here."

The king looked at Cesim. "Fetch Prince Trillion."

Once Cesim left, Eriason said, "We had heard the rumor and wondered if it were true that he has married and has a son."

"This is true."

"But this boy was not born in Airdle or Dornan." Eriason paused, looking between the king and Wilm. "Yet he bears your face, my king." Seeming to hesitate, he said after a long pause. "Many winters ago, Cesim brought a maid to us of the sons of Sanderfield and of the daughters of Dornan, the Eastern tribes. She bore a son. Is this the child?"

The king reached for Wilm's hand. "Through the providence of God, his life was preserved."

Eriason sat back, nodding at his companions. "Then he is the one. The one foretold in the prophecy of the four who would bring our peoples together." Eriason nodded toward the king. "You have done well all these years. You showed no one favor above another—not even for your own sons or near kin—but the people have begun to grow apart."

"They have left God," Eriason's companion said. "The plainsmen are correct. Not only are there attacks upon travelers and missing herds, but a coldness grows between the peoples of plains and towns. Some say Airdle no longer stands for the people or the plainsmen. We are growing apart when we should be coming together to discover the identity of these infiltrators." He wet his lips and drew out a worn leather skin with ancient markings. "Perhaps the time spoken of in the words of our forefathers is now upon us. Is he the one who is of the blood of all four branches, the one who will bring us together during a time of trouble?" The Ayisin set their gazes on Wilm.

Wilm shifted uncomfortably as all looked at him. What was this prophecy of the four they spoke of and how did it concern him?

"My heart is heavy with what I see," King Wallace said. "We were one because of God's grace. As many drift away from the one true Lord, our hard-won peace also withers." He shifted, looking down at his grandson. "Prince Wilm is the son of Trillion of the House of Airdle whose mother, Queen Lillian was the daughter of Ichwan, leader of the Keyayisin. Wilm's mother, Lady Lisze, is the daughter of Marshal Rothsum of the Sanderfield and Lady Elwin of the Dornan."

"So the boy is of the four branches of the Lamorian peoples." Eriason lifted his chin with upturned lips.

"Many prophets have come forth, some recently. God's Word and its prophecies are complete, set, and will come to pass. Words that seem to be from God concerning our tribes are not the same. Time will tell if they also speak of God's work in Lamoria. Talk of one to unite us once again might be true, or it might not be. One thing we do know." He patted Wilm's knee and searched their faces. "God holds each one of us accountable for our own deeds. We walk righteously; we seek the true way; we help the stranger and the pilgrim."

He nodded his head toward the Ayisin. "And I thank you for sheltering a young woman in her time of trouble. What comes of this? Our duty is to walk each day the path God sets before us." He raised his palms, and all stood as one.

The king raised his hands to give the royal blessing from Numbers 6:24–26. "'The LORD bless you and keep you; the LORD make his face shine upon you and be gracious to you; the LORD lift up his face toward you and give you peace.'"

One by one the men stepped forward, grasped the king's forearm, and embraced him.

Wilm watched them leave. "Grandfather, I've never been taught this prophecy. Is it found in the Leaves of God?"

"No, Wilm. The words of the seer were spoken the day I was born. Yet they are not like the prophecies of God's Word that span the ages. We wait and see what God will do."

"And my part, Grandfather? Is there a place here for me?"

"Always, and God will lead as He directs all who are known by Him."

A sound at the end of the hall drew their attention. Trillion approached with Lisze and Cesim beside him. Wilm went to his parents, wondering why his ama had never mentioned the prophecy.

Lisze gestured to Cesim and Wilm. "Son, you've had a long day. Time for bed."

Cesim laughed lightly, hearing Wilm groan. "Your eyes betray you, my boy. Off we go."

"Many thanks, Cesim. Sweet dreams." Lisze turned to stand beside Trillion.

King Wallace and Eriason exchanged glances. "There is always hope. We can pray." The Ayisin elder embraced his friend.

"Prince Trillion, please entertain the company in the south hall." The king pointed to a far door. He stepped closer and, with lowered voice, said, "And, Trillion, time for my sons to take up the shepherding of this land. You will have a place and tasks to do as you have skills some of your brothers lack in languages and negotiation."

"My desire, Father. Why I train and am rebuilding my strength." He stood straighter and forced himself to walk without a limp. Trillion had told no one what Healer Anselm had said about his fewer days. Again, he begged the Lord for full recovery that he might fulfill God's purpose for him.

Chapter 8

The Council Meeting
with Eriason of the Ayisin

Trillion watched the group of Imbus Ayisin sit beside him. His heart warmed when Lisze sat to the side. Truly they would be life partners, working together side by side. He let the men settle. The way of the Ayisin was to feel the other, not rush into speech. He lifted his eyes and met Eriason's.

"Chief Eriason, please begin with a prayer to the God of heaven." He ignored the look of surprise on the elder's face that he had requested prayer.

"We beseech thee, Oh Lord, for only from You can we chart our way. May we seek Your face, may we be united in You. Guide us, Oh Lord, for apart from You, we can accomplish nothing."

"Thank you, Chief Eriason." Trillion surveyed the room. "I have heard rumors but not the facts from those who have knowledge of these attacks. Who would like to begin?"

As one, all faced Eriason.

He listed the details of the incursions, the targets, the trails, and the recovered weapons made of strange metal.

"And none of our marshals or your men have been able to capture these intruders?" Trillion asked in frustration, for he knew the Ayisin were superb trackers. If these interlopers evaded even the Imbus, they were more than bandits but skilled warriors.

"We find only traces. They leave little sign. But they have become bolder, encroaching farther south and west. Some landholders, enraged at their atrocities, captured three warriors, executed them, and burned their bodies. We had no chance to examine who they were, who sent them and why. As you know, many Ayisin have lost faith in fair dealings with the landholders as some have expanded their holdings onto our tribal areas. Others believe they are agents of Prince David or Ricard." He smiled. "None list you or Prince Joshua."

"Which marshal squad took the reports?" Trillion's eyes widened when all shook their heads.

Eriason said, "None. We serve now the marshal squads. They rarely come to our aid. For a long time the plains were at peace and most only needed aid if lost or lacking food or water. But not today." He lifted his hands.

"Let us begin, one by one." He glanced at Eriason on his right. "State the facts of each attack—time, place, what destruction had been done, how many slain."

Trillion glanced at Lisze. "Find the supply of parchment and quill pens to take notes."

Trillion listened to the descriptions. "And not one squad answered the call to investigate and help catch the intruders?"

They listed the few who had come to their aid, but most attacks had been in remote areas with few clues to follow.

"At the next marshal meeting with the king, I will request that I am permitted to lead the investigation." Trillion knew they needed assurance that they had been heard and action would be taken. Here was a task he could do.

"Prince Trillion, you were not at today's session to hear that plainsmen also have experienced attacks—slaughtered cattle, damaged fences, and fires left unattended. We've seen burned holdings on the open plains, stopped to help bury the dead. We are not alone in our troubles. At first, many did not believe the tales or the failures of the marshal service." He peered into Trillion's eyes.

Trillion sat back, pushed down his exhaustion, and

extended his hand, palm up. "The bond between our peoples is not yet broken. I will take your concerns and suggestions to the next marshal meeting with the king. I will make every effort to discover who is behind these attacks and raise up defenses against them. I will follow up with the court reporter. We must all work together. Please spread the word. If any are captured, they must be kept alive until the marshals can question them. One must know the enemy to have victory."

"You speak truth. Yet God is not unaware of our troubles. It is on Him we must rely. Prince Trillion, may God guide you in this search for truth, justice, and peace," Eriason said.

"Amen and amen." Prince Trillion lifted his hands and they rose. "I am honored to take up this task and appreciate your prayers." He would also look for proof that holding lords or greedy plainsmen were seeking to seize their neighbors' lands.

The Ayisin contingent declined the offer of rooms but welcomed a trip to the armory. They picked out finely crafted arrows and bows. They would stay with their Ayisin cousins a little north of Airdle.

"Godspeed," Trillion stated as the groups parted. He felt Lisze come to stand beside him, and they headed toward the Garden Suites.

"Will I have a part in this investigation?" she asked.

Trillion reached for her hand. "Most assuredly. There's a room above our suites where we can map each incident. Puzzling that none of Prince David's squads have taken up this matter."

He heard Lisze draw in her breath before saying, "Are you strong enough for this task?"

"My love, I want my days to count for something."

"Oh, Trillion, we missed the Seaside Fellowship. May I tell Patrice we will try to make it next Saturday?"

"If something else doesn't come up." Trillion walked close to her side.

The next week, Trillion rapped on the frame of the door to King Wallace's office in the Hall of Justice. "My liege, I have a request."

His father glanced at him for a moment before waving him in.

Trillion stood in front of the wide desk, suddenly tongue-tied and awkward. Having failed at even leading a marshal squad, dare he ask now?

The king lifted his brow. "Yes? What is it? Prince Trillion, begin with your request."

Taking courage from the Lord, Trillion blurted out what he had heard at Saturday's meeting. "I wish to head the investigation of the attacks on our lands. The Ayisin as well as the plainsmen have similar reports. I need copies of yesterday's cases, as well as any Head Marshal Vaughn has collected. Assembling the facts, we can assign appropriate squads to investigate." Trillion continued with his list.

"I concur and will have an order written up giving you authority to investigate." The king's lips rose slightly at the corners.

Trillion almost felt as if he had his father's approval and respect. At last. "Thank you. Also, I must attend the marshal meetings." They were usually held shortly after a Public Judgment. He watched the king's brows draw down. "That will be the best way to hear what has been done and help me discover which squads' reports to search."

"You may attend. I will let you know when you may speak."

Trillion nodded. The Lord reminded him that this task was first for God and justice, not to merely earn favor in his father's eyes, though that temptation ever lingered. Reminding himself to please the Holy One above men, he left the room. The Garden Suites were quiet and still when he arrived.

Wilm was at the Airdle Day School, and Lisze was helping someone with a need somewhere in the castle. Not willing to seek after her, Trillion set the reports that Lisze had recorded on their dining table. The area was too small though, and his papers would leave no room for sup.

He surveyed the large, open room cluttered with a menagerie of chairs, small tables, and trunks. How many did they need?

He headed through the back door to the lower store-rooms, praying to find a few pages to help transform their living room into an office.

In a short time, two long tables ran most of the length of the back wall. Two small tables with chairs remained nearby, along with a few carefully selected items. Trillion laid the reports on a table and began to sort through them, creating piles. He stopped as if frozen, remembering how David had foiled his earlier attempts to fulfill promises by tricking him with lies or distracting him. *Lord, empower me. Let this not be in vain.*

The Spirit whispered that all service was ultimately to the Lord of Glory. With that, he continued.

Two days later, Lisze adjusted Trillion's collar and settled the embroidered prince's jerkin upon his shoulders. "I've heard about these marshal meetings. Hadn't you attended before your accident?"

Trillion held back a bitter laugh. "This is the first time I've even asked. If we can't stop marauders from traversing our lands, we have become weak indeed. And Lisze, even worse." Their eyes met. "What if some of these attacks are from our own people?" He was pleased they could work together.

"Biting and tearing one another. My own uncle had his men break our fences, start fires and leave them unattended. I would imagine some of these attacks are orchestrated by greedy landholders or brigands not brought to justice. Why do some grasp for more than they need or can hold?" Lisze stepped back to survey his courtly attire.

"Like your family's land. Pray I receive the permission to request the records to prove it." Trillion stood, encouraged and strengthened by her support. She hadn't complained about the changes to their suite or him heading the investigation. "And I will be looking for your help. There is something I want to show both of you when Wilm comes home."

"So I have to wait!" Lisze's eyes crinkled with a laughing smile.

"Have you always been so impatient?" Trillion teased back. "Where are you off to today?" She kept herself useful most days helping someone in the castle.

"With the banquet after the meeting, Patrice could use help in the kitchen. The king asked me to ensure the banquet hall is properly set."

"Save a sweet bannock for your men. Don't forget us." Trillion watched her leave. Pushing down the flutters in his belly about the marshal meeting, he reached for parchment and quill. He remembered that a leader had a scribe take notes. There should be a clerk to record the session. He adjusted his vest and wound his way through the passageways to the upper floors.

The wide Hallway of Justice led to the Judgment Hall on the first floor. Portraits of the royal family graced the wall closest to the door leading to the main hall, which housed the king's throne. Trillion paused to stare at his mother's portrait. *Oh Lord, help!*

The hall was quiet, and he had forgotten to ask where the meeting would be held. He relaxed a little when head marshals began to congregate in front of the pair of doors leading to the northern conference room. A few glanced his way, but he did not feel comfortable joining them. When the king announced that Trillion would lead the investigation and would be attending their meetings, then he could mingle with them.

Two royal guards opened the doors and found their posts on either side. Prince David arrived, followed by Prince Clinton, Prince Joshua's son. David's usual retinue accompanied them.

Trillion stepped forward when King Wallace and his clerk entered the hallway.

Although his father did not acknowledge him when he approached, the guards gave leave for him to enter. At least he was in.

One lone chair remained toward the end of the table. No one protested when he stood behind the chair. He watched the clerk take his place at a side table with parchment, quill pens, and two ink wells. His father walked to the head of the table, and a waiting page pulled out his chair. His brother David stood behind the armed chair at the king's right-hand side. Head Marshal Vaughn sat catty-corner to the king. When the page pulled out the chair for David, the rest pulled out theirs in unison.

His father gestured palms down. As the men sat, the rustle of chairs shuffling forward filled the quiet room.

The king rang a silver bell. "The meeting of the marshal heads has commenced. Prince David, you may call for reports."

Trillion listened to the reading of various reports, beginning with Head Marshal Vaughn. They reported herd strengths, feed inventories, structures maintained, number of caches resupplied, and on and on. He glanced at grains of sand slipping through a large hourglass sitting on a tall side table. When would they bring up what had been reported at Saturday's Public Judgment?

Prince David rose and called for new matters to be heard but avoided looking in Trillion's direction. One by one, each marshal stood and spoke once the crown prince gave him leave.

Trillion tried to catch his father's eye to gain any hint that he would be given leave to speak. But the king allowed the crown prince to lead.

Knowing he had to take action, Trillion stood as the last speaker sat. Prince David did not turn to look at him even when the king cleared his throat.

King Wallace said, "Prince Trillion has been tasked with heading the investigation into the mysterious attacks reported this past year."

Trillion's eyes flicked toward his half-brother, whose face reddened as his jaw tightened.

"To fulfill his mission, he needs to have your aid and support. I grant Prince Trillion admission to these meetings. I want to hear that you will fulfill any requests from him." The king looked directly at each one. His voice rose. "The strife and tension between our peoples grow, along with attacks that threaten the safety of our people and our unity. We must seek the cause and craft the solution to regain peace and stability for our lands. After all, that is our call and duty."

After the king's nod and permission to speak, Trillion briefly described his meeting with the Ayisin and the list of reports he needed to see.

"With all due respect, my liege," Prince David interjected. "Is this not also what my squads have been doing? What qualifies you, Prince Trillion, to pursue this matter?"

Emboldened by God, Trillion kept and held his brother's eye. "I endeavor to come alongside the noble efforts of the marshals. You are busy, and may know only of attacks in your assigned regions. But the assailants likely transcend those borders. One investigation, looking only into these matters, will more quickly expose the forces behind these events." Trillion held his gaze, waiting for a challenge or rebuttal, but his brother looked away.

King Wallace rose. "The time is done for this meeting. I concur with Prince Trillion. This matter is too important to be left unattended. Dispatch to him all reports of mischief in our lands. The prince will sort them out and keep us abreast of his findings. You are dismissed."

"My liege, is there a record of his appointment?" Prince David asked.

The king turned to his oldest son with a stern, fixed gaze. "The copies are with the clerk and will be dispatched." He headed out of the room.

At the far end, Trillion waited for the room to empty. A few marshals congratulated him on his appointment and wished him well. He followed Head Marshal Vaughn's path, but many squad leaders surrounded him as the crowd headed toward the banquet hall.

Trillion turned away, nearly bumping into Marshal Thielen in the crowded hall. "Marshal, it is good to see you."

"Is there somewhere we can talk?" Thielen shifted, looking about.

"I will return to my office in the Garden Suites after noon sup. Perhaps you care to view the latest flowers to bloom when you are done with the banquet?"

Trillion felt satisfaction at having managed to squeeze in his request during the marshal meeting. He had felt the Lord come alongside, giving him assurance. The usual tiredness began to creep in now that the meeting had ended. He pondered how to ensure cooperation, but that would be a problem to solve another day. Now, he needed his reserves replenished. He headed to the kitchen.

Trillion padded softly down the steps leading to the

kitchen. Workers scurried about on the lower levels. He had no desire to attend the banquet following the meeting. He timed his steps to the coffeepot hanging by the nearest hearth and poured a cup.

"Prince Trillion!"

He turned. "Lady Patrice, sorry to interrupt, but I'm in need of a slice of . . ."

"Bannock?"

"Yes." Years before he would have chased her around the island, although he never did any harm. He had been demanding and impatient. Today he felt the difference in his reception now from years ago. With new eyes of faith, he understood why so many had avoided him in the past.

Lisze approached from the pantry carrying a box of peaches. She set it down and took him aside, studying him carefully. "You look tired."

Trillion accepted a small plate of pastries from a cook. "Thank you. This will help."

"How was it?" Lisze asked.

"Rough. I'll tell you about it later."

"You could sit at sup with them in the hall."

He made a face and shook his head. "That would not be wise."

"Join us?" Patrice asked as she passed them going from the oven to the pots burbling over the fires.

"I will. Very gladly."

As he had hoped, the conversation around the worker's table in the lower levels was light, friendly, and welcoming. He leaned toward Lisze. "Is this what it was like for you when you worked here?" He returned her saucy smile.

Despite the good sup and the chance to relax, Trillion could no longer deny his exhaustion. He lay down on their bed with the door open, hoping he could rest before Thielen arrived. Despite himself, he fell asleep.

A knock sounded, and Trillion rolled off the bed. Trying

to wake up, he smoothed his hair and vest, embarrassed to be caught napping midday.

"Coming," he said, walking as swiftly as he could to the outer door.

Marshal Thielen entered and looked at him. "Prince Trillion, are you able to do this task? Have you recovered enough?" He scanned the parchments piled on the back table.

"This is my duty, and I will be ready. As you can see, this is an office, not a field assignment." Unsaid was the truth that his days riding with a squad were over.

They walked to the table, and he tapped a pile of paper. "The beginning of the search. Reports from my evening meeting with the Ayisin."

"And? Are the attacks of strangers or of us?"

"That is the question, Marshal. Too soon to tell. The ones reporting the sharp daggers made of metal never before seen are most likely of foreigners." He paused, thinking through the possibilities.

Thielen stood quietly for a moment. "But our people can be cunning. Knowing of these attacks, some could pretend to be of the strangers, all the while seeking to run a family off their land. It pleased me to hear you will look into this, for Prince David has not ordered such an inquiry."

"That is well known. The Ayisin complained about the lack of marshal squads willing to hunt down the offenders."

"Echoing what was reported at Public Judgment."

"I have requested the documents for the cases from the king."

"You will be more quickly served seeking such papers from Prince Joshua's office. They are recorded as official court decisions."

Trillion's face brightened. So there was more than one way to ferret out the information they needed. "An excellent suggestion. I will write up an order."

"Prince Trillion, not all requests require formal writs.

I have found the Supreme Judge most kind in helping with many matters. He will not take offense if you ask. If an official order is necessary, he will not only tell you but also assign a clerk to draft it."

"Good to know."

"Also, while you are with him, request to see court decisions from the plains and nearby areas reporting similar attacks."

"Shall we sit?" Trillion led him to a pair of chairs facing large windows overlooking the flower garden. "What is your opinion of the matter? What do you make of these attacks from ones we have hardly seen?" When the marshal hesitated, Trillion leaned forward and said with measured gaze, "Our people need answers. The uncertainty leads to attacks between our tribes." He smiled with the marshal's nod. "Sifting out attacks perpetrated by our own people, we should be able to discover if these are isolated events from marauders lurking on our borders or warriors surveying our land for invasion."

Thielen nodded. "I agree. My heart fears that we have made ourselves appear weak and ripe for the taking. With our people dividing, they are not joining together to aid or halt the attacks."

"Let us not imagine fears and demons that do not exist. I will make every effort to stay to the task until it's done. But the speed of finding answers also rests with receiving full reports. Do you need a formal request?"

Thielen laughed. "For many of us, your declaration today, along with the king's charter for your investigation, will be enough permission for us to send our reports to you. Here are the names of the squads where you will be bound to dispatch formal requests." The marshal pulled out a folded parchment. "I drew it up this morning upon hearing of your appointment. Well done, Prince Trillion."

They sat and talked of what they had seen and the days

ahead. Trillion relaxed, feeling camaraderie with the head marshal overseeing two squads beside his own.

After Thielen left, Trillion trudged up the stairs to Prince Joshua's office. Seeing his brother at his desk, he tapped lightly on the door and entered. "Supreme Judge, I have a request to make. Do you need a formal petition?"

"Trillion, sit. You may call me Joshua when in private or alone. We have enough parchment here to fill several suites. Let me hear your request."

He gave a brief description and then asked, "Have you received the document from the king's office? He said he ordered copies made."

"When?"

"Day after Public Judgment."

"Hmm, they usually come more quickly." Joshua glanced at his brother. "You attended the marshal's meeting? How was the banquet?"

"Didn't go."

"Not surprising, as Prince David's associates and marshals mostly attend. I'll check with the king if it doesn't arrive soon. But that doesn't hinder me from assigning the search to my clerks. I'd like the parchment in hand before I send the report." Joshua sat back. "I've also a similar charge—to expose court decisions seeking to steal and defraud. This is a pile of suspicious court cases. I'm glad you're taking this on. Was disturbing to read the cases from Public Judgment. Letting incidents like this linger unpunished will tempt the wicked to commit more offenses."

Trillion nodded, pleased to have another who applauded and supported his efforts.

"Looks like you've had a full day. Want some brotherly advice?"

"Of course."

Joshua tilted his head. "Leadership is hard, as you have no doubt discovered. Sin ever taints our efforts. Yet to stand against the darkness is never in vain."

"For the one true God in the end will make things right. Until that day, that He includes us in His work is an encouragement. Do you find being the supreme judge a burden?"

"Only when I take my eyes off the Savior."

To talk with his brother of faith giving strength for the day's work warmed his heart.

Chapter 9

The Investigation

Prince Trillion awoke from a sound sleep. He sat up, swung his legs over the edge of the bed, rose, and was halfway to a water pitcher before he realized the pain was mild and he had not stumbled or limped. A glance at the hourglass he had set before his afternoon nap told him he had slept for half the usual time. The suite was quiet in its emptiness. His family had not yet arrived.

He felt in his pocket for the key he had acquired from Steward Kiel. It unlocked the back door of the passageway that led to the map room. Trillion turned to the book of Isaiah as he waited.

He heard Cesim and Wilm enter through the garden doors at the same time Lisze arrived through the lower levels.

Trillion rose to greet them. "Ready?" He pulled out a long black key.

Lisze's eye grew wide. "Is that the key to the library archives?"

Trillion glanced at Cesim. "Ever see the map room?" It shouldn't have surprised him when the old warrior nodded.

"I did fight in the Amhavran war. Rothsum and I viewed the room many times with Prince Wallace."

Wilm glanced quickly at his guardian. "I've never heard that story."

"Perhaps you will, son, but today we all may see it." Trillion had seen it once. Peace had reduced the need, though the king liked to keep the map up to date.

"No one is to enter without me, Lisze, or Cesim. I have the key." Trillion stepped to the right corner of the back wall and pushed aside a bookcase, revealing a narrow door. "Oh, bring two lanterns."

Cesim lifted his arm. "I'll grab a torch from the passages. Will make it easier to see."

Trillion unlocked the door to a dark, narrow passage-way that led to a winding staircase. At the landing for the first level, he pushed the unlocked door open to a square room with short windows close to the ceiling. The staircase continued to the king's suites on the second floor.

Trillion heard both Lisze and Wilm suck in their breaths as they saw the Kingdom of Lamoria laid out in miniature on a large, square island. He watched them study the model, following the ridges and rivers coursing through the councils. Their faces displayed the wonder he had felt when he first saw it as a boy. He stepped beside Wilm, who hovered by the miniature castle. "It's okay. You can touch it carefully. Crafted from the substances of this world: resins, sculpted wood, stone, and leather."

Cesim rocked back on his heels. "Came in handy during the war. What do you have in mind, Trillion?"

"Tracing the eastern attacks. The king announced my investigation at today's marshal meeting." Noting Wilm's questioning glance, he briefly described his day.

"About time. Prince David not too happy?" Cesim smiled.

"Not at all." Trillion turned to the three. "And I would welcome your help. I've reports to gather, study, analyze, and note. We'll look for patterns to sift out attacks by outsiders from those by our own people."

"Meaning we're staying in the Garden Suites for a while longer?" Lisze looked at her husband.

"I believe so. We'll be too busy to move with the project. And it has to be completed quickly, for Lamoria needs answers."

Late Saturday afternoon Trillion, Lisze, Wilm, and Cesim headed for the Seaside Fellowship.

"Can we find a place to sit?" Wilm asked.

Lisze glanced his way. "Patrice promised to save seats for us by the first terrace, but let's not be late."

Trillion and Cesim followed.

"What do you think of the group?" Trillion asked.

"Meeting Sundays in the Airdle Chapel is enough for me." Cesim looked at Trillion carrying the Leaves of God. "Your first time?"

"Of course. First time for many things lately."

"Prince Trillion, Lady Lisze," Patrice called, waving her hand. "This way." Walking quickly to meet them, she gestured toward the front. "We've saved you a spot."

They followed close behind Patrice, her long locks swinging with her steps.

Trillion smiled when they drew near to Arlen. He reached past Arlen's outstretched hand to wrap him in an embrace. He directed Lisze and Wilm to the empty seats at the end of the row.

Trillion scanned the crowd. Plainsmen with town dwellers, farriers, merchants, cooks, and landholders sat side by side. No padded area had been reserved for the wealthy or landholder but terrace by terrace all blended into one—one people—because of one faith. Trillion sat down next to Arlen, worn Bibles lying on their laps.

A small group performed an ancient melody on harp and lute; a young man recited a poem filled with praise to the goodness of God in the midst of hardships. After several stood to recount a lesson or grace from God, a young, slim man stepped forward.

His voice carried on the winds of sound as a salty breeze infused the air. He talked of new beginnings and forgotten ways. Not looking back but pressing forward, whether the past was littered with pain or resplendent with victories, all needed to start each day anew for the glory of God.

Hope that had been slowly rising burst forth within Trillian. *Confirm my calling, give me strength to complete my mission*, he prayed. His mind traced the path of seeking the intruders, finding a way not only to stop the attacks but to heal a fractured people. *May I have a part in restoring peace.*

He had heard God again. He had a purpose. His life had meaning. Trillion glanced at the rapt attention on Lisze's face. He wondered how God had touched her heart today.

Trillion spent the days following the seaside service in diligent research. Apart from sleep, building up his strength, and receiving the last of his treatments, Trillion spent every spare moment on the investigation. Healer Anselm had agreed to him riding Kewatin. Lisze had been true to her word, and his steed had not forgotten any of the marshal maneuvers.

Wilm helped sort reports coming in, noting areas that had sent nothing. The squads under Prince David sent sparse records. Trillion suspected many were incomplete. With no squads stationed in Sanderfield Council, Trillion and Prince Joshua sent a traveling merchant to see if he could uncover any strange events.

Lisze read each one, making a list of the important facts, noting their locations. Once laid out, they added colored flags to the map. In time, they were able to isolate the number of incursions by strangers.

Finally, Trillion figured they had enough information to submit a report to the king.

That night, Trillion and Cesim entered the map room to put in the last of the flags. Red meant a strange blade had been found. The rest had blue flags.

"Does it look to you like they made a circuit?" Cesim studied the dates written onto the flags.

Starting with the first one between the Imbus Ayisin and Esther's Spring, they traced a path across the river to a spot east of Whistler's Ridge.

Cesim leaned over the map. "They avoided Whistler's Ridge. Next one is north of Dornan City."

"Near the ridge. Probably too many patrols and heavy traffic."

Cesim nodded. "Prince David's friends traveling to Dornan City or the holding."

Trillion traced a northward path closer to the sea. "Had to skirt the canyon?"

"Went through it." Cesim pointed to the burnt horse farm not far from the canyon's end. "The rest is a puzzle."

"Stymied by our stations along the ridges, along with the cities, they tried to cross at Tholen Ridge." Trillion held back a laugh. "That's steeper than the rest. But what about this flag?"

They both stared at the blue flag north of Esther's Spring. "Maybe they hadn't left a blade or dagger?"

Tracing the path again, Trillion included the blue flags in line with the red. "So a survey trip? Check out the defenses?"

Cesim nodded. "What are you going to write about the rest?"

"The truth."

"Good man."

"It's mostly ready. I'll finish it up tomorrow and give it to the king."

Chapter 10

Attack on Wolf's Bane

A large, seafaring ship with six sails open and waiting for the wind began to move toward a distant shore.

The captain squinted to see their target. "Head for the northernmost black island. Our man says the water is deep enough to pull around its northern tip."

"That's close to shore." The navigator turned the wheel. The ship cut through the waves as the wind grew stronger. "How're we going to keep from running aground onto a sandbar?"

"Trim the sails and use the rowboats to pull her in."

The navigator shook his head.

Orders were to arrive at night, and the timing of the wind couldn't have been better. The Lancer Teams were ready. The rowboats were in place for lowering to the sea. The captain shouted the order to trim the sails and drop the anchor.

The ship creaked and groaned. A few boards scraped a tall coral reef, but their progress was not impeded.

Midnight had come and gone by the time the rowboats dragged the ship into position near the northern tip of the small island. The captain's officer called for the rest of the boats to drop, and the Lancers climbed down hemp ladders to their vessels. Sailors lowered their gear in bundles. Wordlessly, they rowed to the shore of a small fishing village.

House by house, they took every person they found, unless too young, old, or weak. When one managed to cry out, the village awoke. A group of men ran toward them, but they were short of stature and lightly armed. The invaders subdued most of them. They only had to thrust through a few with their lances. Some managed to escape into a nearby dense, dark forest. A few jumped into the sea.

Bound and taken to the boats, the ship received its latest cargo. The row boats led the ship out to the open sea. They sailed north, out of sight of any village. Not one Lancer had been wounded—a successful mission.

The fishing village called Wolf's Bane in the northwest corner of Worstein Council had been emptied. The people of Lamoria, unaware of the tragedy, slept peacefully in their beds.

Fillan, one of the few to escape, swam south until he could scramble onto the rocky shore. Still tense with fear and horror, he ran to the nearest town, Invien Springs. They listened to his story and brought him to the orphanage.

The sheriff waited until the market stalls opened to investigate the claim. They gave little credence to what the people of Wolf's Bane had to say, and the messenger had been but a youth. He patrolled the fishers' market. No one had seen anyone from Wolf's Bane. Perhaps the lad's report was true. The sheriff assembled some deputies, and they rode to the village.

A dread stillness lay upon Wolf's Bane. The houses appeared unharmed, but some doors swung in the breeze. No voices cried out. No one came to greet them.

The sheriff returned to his office to report the slain and missing of Wolf's Bane, not mentioning the survivor. He handed the dispatch to a waiting courier. "Take this to the nearest ranger station."

With the report done, leaving their suppositions and follow-up questions for a marshal team to uncover, Trillion and Lisze packed to move back into his suites in the royal wing.

"What did the king say about the report?" asked Lisze.

"He hasn't had a chance to read it." Trillion pulled out another sack for his books. "He liked what we did to the map. That was a relief."

"When will Prince David see it?"

"Didn't ask. My part is done." Trillion tied the bag closed and packed another one. "What more does the Lord have for me to help our country come together?"

"Husband!" Lisze stood beside him. "You are on the mend. Your strength increases daily. Your lungs are mostly clear."

"The fevers are gone." He glanced out the windows to see late summer butterflies flit from flower to flower. "Did I tell you Prince Joshua wants to train me to be a judge? Well, a magistrate first. He thinks I might one day be the Supreme Judge."

She stepped closer. "Is that what you want?"

"I think so. Someone will need to take his place someday."

"Say increase, decrease prayers." Lisze laughed. "Something my mother taught me. If you are in doubt about something, ask the Lord to either increase or decrease your desire to see it happen. We'll see what God will do."

Trillion pulled her toward him. "Lisze, you working with me on that report made the work a joy." He blinked away a mist and put an arm around her waist. She did not pull away. "I love you."

Lisze's eyes grew full, and she laid her head against his shoulder. "I love you too." This was right. It was good. Wilm had grown close to his father, and Cesim had wholeheartedly accepted him. Their little family was doing well, with friends in the castle and Airdle City.

They pulled away when a knock sounded on the main door.

Trillion opened it to see a page. "Yes?"

"The king summons both of you."

They followed him to the king's office. Trillion paused when he saw Marshal Rysen and his second, Marshal Nolan, plus other members of their squad, sitting in front of the king's desk.

Lisze followed him into the room.

"No time for pleasantries, Lady. This is a planning meeting." Marshal Rysen's lip curled at seeing a Sanderfield in their midst.

The king rose. All worked to stand with him. He looked at Rysen. "There was no mistake. Lady Lisze will be the cook."

The marshals made room for them to sit.

The king shifted and looked at the hourglass. "We are waiting for Prince David to arrive. He should be here shortly." He glanced at the report on his desk. "But I will say that yesterday, we received a disturbing dispatch from Marshal Karith of Stolein Way Station. The village of Wolf's Bane in the northwestern corner of Worstein Council has been emptied. All the people are missing or killed."

Trillion soon heard the quick steps of booted feet, and Prince David entered, followed by his clerk and Prince Clinton. He glanced at Lisze, but she seemed as puzzled as he was about the news of Wolf's Bane.

When all were seated, the king leaned his elbows upon the desk. "These are dark days. Along with the report Prince Trillion completed days ago, the news of the stealing of our people points to grave threats to our land. Neither the Worstein Council leaders nor Lord Bierl have requested our aid. I am thankful for Marshal Karith's dispatch that alerted us to this attack. Until proven otherwise, we will assume this is connected to the eastern incursions."

The king turned his gaze to the heavy-set marshal sitting in front of him. "Marshal Rysen will lead the squad. You will leave at first light. Head directly to Weirstone and offer your assistance. If Lord Bierl, the lord of Worstein Holding, rebuffs your offer and forbids you entrance to Weirstone, continue on to Wolf's Bane. That village does not lie under Bierl's authority. Copies of Prince Trillion's report concerning the eastern attacks will be made available to you."

The king paused to draw breath. "Not knowing who the culprits are, many on the plains are accusing and attacking each other. I am sending you to keep open warfare from happening between our tribes. Karith has learned the people were taken away by sea, not by land."

"A village taken in a boat?" Prince David asked.

"Another riddle to solve." The king continued with his instructions. "You are released to complete your plans in a nearby conference room. Bring them to me when they're done. Lady Lisze, you may find Prince Wilm and Cesim. Prepare for your journey."

"Sire, I will have to requisition supplies, oversee their packing."

"Lady Lisze, you may do so once the initial plans are drawn up." The king turned to Trillion. "Prince Trillion, stay for a moment."

After the room cleared and the door shut, the king said, "Worstein has essentially withdrawn from the realm. I noticed no mention of reports from that council."

Trillion met his gaze. "Marshal Karith hadn't heard of any in Worstein Council. Most were in Dornan or Stoddard."

The king nodded. "I task you with searching out the reason for their withdrawal and possible solutions. I pray the offer to help with Wolf's Bane will encourage Lord Bierl and the other Worstein leaders to reestablish relations. Also, here is the request that Wilm squire for Lord Bierl, as Prince Joshua told you. In the past ties were strengthened when our youth learned the ways of another council. Prince Wilm will be our ambassador, as will you."

"I will do my best and report my findings."

"You may help your family pack." His father walked around the desk. He placed a gentle hand on Trillion's shoulder. "My son, you've done well, and it pleases me that you are willing to serve Lamoria." Wallace looked closely at his son. "Are you fit for this journey?"

Trillion straightened his back, squared his shoulders, and said, "I am. I welcome the chance with each breath. No more wasted days." He found himself wrapped in a hug. Joy filled his soul. Along with trepidation at having to ride with Marshal Rysen. The marshal's dislike for him and his family was evident for all to see.

"Son, it's good to have you with us. Prince Joshua has shared of your growing faith. Let us not fail to pray for Princes David and Ricard." He stepped back. "You may prepare your family for the trip."

Before Trillion turned to leave, he remembered his sins. "Father, there is one problem. I cheated some people at Worstein. Should you send Prince Joshua? My sins follow me."

King Wallace leaned against the desk, tapping his finger. "Perhaps this is your opportunity to make restitution."

"I will bring payment with me."

Trillion met Cesim on his way down to the Garden Suites. "Packed already?"

"Lots of practice."

"Cesim, I'll need you to watch out for both Lisze and Wilm."

"Wouldn't think of doing anything else."

They heard voices through the back door. Trillion headed straight to Wilm's small room. "What's the problem?" He noticed his son's frustrated face.

"Ama's redoing my pack."

"Of course she is." Trillion stepped forward. "He has

everything he needs in there?" Seeing her nod, he reached for the pack. "He's old enough to do it himself."

Cesim stepped in. "Lad, we've got this. You two need to pack."

Trillion and Lisze entered their room. He glanced at her usual dress of riding breeches and vest with short boots. "While we'll have to pack light, could you bring a nice dress?"

"I can pack many useful provisions in the space a dress takes up."

"Roll it up in your bedroll." Trillion stepped closer. "The king has good reasons for you and Wilm coming."

"Of course, I count my blessings I can keep an eye on you."

"Just stay clear of Rysen."

"I will. I have to attend the planning meeting to draw up our requisition. Pray that all goes well."

Trillion watched her leave, walking quickly.

Lisze rushed to the conference room where the marshals' planning meeting would be held. Hearing voices, she paused to catch her breath and smooth her skirt. Lisze knocked twice on the door and stepped in, assuming the stature of a way station keeper—confident strides, straight back, and steady gaze. She had cooked and aided many a marshal expedition.

"This is most irregular. A lady does not cook for a squad." Rysen nodded curtly toward Lisze. "The party leaves at first light with no supply train or cart."

"Well then, having served as cook for marshal squads"— her voice hung in the air, and she stood to full height, slightly taller than Rysen—"each member of the squad will carry his own provision bag, as is customary. What is the number of the party?"

"Twenty."

"We'll need resupply."

"We resupply at Worstein."

"Very well, Marshal Rysen. Is the supply requisition ready?"

Marshal Nolan handed her a parchment. "Already done, Lady Lisze."

"Excellent." Lisze nodded to Sean, the young marshal assigned to help. "Let's find the quartermaster."

At the supply barn, Lisze set down the first sack. "We will also need some flint fire kits, wire snare rolls, and arrow tips."

He started to protest, then noted her determined look. "I will do what I can." Turning to the supply room, he paused at the door. "Some of these items have been disposed of by order of Prince David. He considered them no longer necessary."

"Let's see what we can find." Surging past, she rifled through the stores. She grabbed a torch to peer into the far corners of the supply barn.

Sean looked under the lowest shelves. He smiled when he pulled out an old provision sack with the missing items. "Not enough."

"But a start." Lisze counted out the sacks. "Sean, I will keep a fire kit and snare wire. Here are four more. One for the lead marshal, his second, and you pick the other two."

"Of course, my lady. Jason and I usually make the fires and see to the horses."

Lisze approached the quartermaster perched on the edge of a stool beside the open door. "My thanks." She helped Sean load the last of the provisions on a small cart.

"Where to, my lady?"

"The third stable barn to put this with the tack."

Chapter 11

Journey to Worstein Council

The squad assembled in the far field. Uncertain of their position in the company, Trillion, Lisze, Wilm, and Cesim hung off to the side.

Marshal Rysen cantered up to Trillion. "Quaint." His eyes flicked over the family. "This is no lady's afternoon ride. Take squad leader position. The cook and her retinue follow in the rear." He nudged his horse past Cesim's. "And you, take rear guard—if you're able."

Wordlessly, Cesim wheeled his steed to the back of the column. Lisze motioned for Wilm to stay beside her as they positioned themselves a half-length ahead of him.

Rysen whistled. The squad advanced at a walk until clear of the outlying buildings. They settled into a ground-covering canter along the King's Highway.

Lisze drank in the stillness of an early dawn. As the trail crested a hill, she leaned toward the warmth of the rays of the rising sun. Glancing over she caught Wilm's gaze. His smile spread from ear to ear.

They traveled through the day with brief stops. Halting for fresh water as the sun set, Lisze drew out her fire starter kit. She stood when Marshal Rysen approached.

"No fires. This is not a maiden's pleasure trip."

"As you wish, Lord Marshal. I will ensure everyone is well supplied before bedding down, and Cesim can check the horses."

"We rest only for half a turn. Moonlight affords enough light."

Curtsying slightly, she said, "Then I will be quick about it." No one admitted any needs, not even Trillion.

Early on the second day, they cleared the gap through Tierney Ridge. Worstein uplands rose so gently Lisze hadn't realized their rise in elevation until she looked back to see a village perched midway up the ridge, overlooking Tierney Fair. On their left spanned tracts of forests with hawks flying almost below them. Well-watered and tilled, she had heard much of this prosperous northern holding. The road led to a way station. Worstein and holding flags, without a Lamorian banner streaming above it in the stiff breeze, contained emblems of sheep and wheat.

"Ama, the mountains!" Wilm pointed his chin to the tall, white peaks of the Amhavran Mountains in the distance dominating the sky above forested foothills.

Cesim reined his horse beside Wilm's. "Behold the hills of Worstein." He nodded to the west with forests and plains. "And the plains of the Keyayisin, where your grandmother was born."

Before Wilm could ask for more details, Rysen whistled for their final approach to the group of buildings and corrals ringing the road into the holding.

Trillion urged his horse to the front of the squad behind Marshal Nolan, arranging his outer robe to cover the royal insignia. The squad unfurled the royal flag and banner. He remembered that Lord Bierl, the holding lord, was a trim, barrel-chested man slightly past middle age with grandchildren of his own. Hopefully, they would be allowed passage to the grand keep at Weirstone. The main building sat close to the Invien River that flowed from Invien Ridge to Wolf's Bane. After Airdle Council had been chosen to lead Lamoria, they built Airdle Castle on the southern coastal extremity, patterned after Weirstone Keep.

They recognized Lord Bierl, the holding lord of Worstein, leading an armed troop carrying Worstein's colors of forest green upon fields of yellow. The man with the round face, wide hands, and broad shoulders brought his black charger to a stop, blocking their path. Their rangers held spears and bows, with fighting leathers in place on forearm and shin.

"Marshal Rysen, state your business."

Rysen smiled and nudged his horse forward. He didn't bother to ask if the message had been received, as the couriers would have reported such a refusal before their leave-taking from Airdle. "As stated in the dispatch from King Wallace, we have been sent to render any aid we can provide for Wolf's Bane."

"Council affairs rest with our rangers. We take care of our own." Bierl studied Rysen with a hard face. "Aid is not required—not the kind Airdle sends."

Trillion's jaw tightened, but they had one last appeal to make.

The marshal bowed his head. "As you wish. We will search beyond your holding borders. May we resupply?"

"No." The holding lord positioned his steed to the left of Rysen's.

Prince Trillion swung his robe away, handing it to the nearest horseman, and advanced to Lord Bierl's other side. "My father, King Wallace, requests any information of the matter you can provide."

Bierl leveled his gaze at the prince, disgust evident on his face.

Trillion urged his horse forward. "My lord, I understand your disapproval of me, but I have repented of my sins and bring restitution."

Lord Bierl studied the prince's open face and the tired

squad. "Very well." He gestured to a distant grouping of buildings in the lower left field. "There, and step not one foot farther into the holding."

"Our resupply?"

"Take what you need from the outbuildings. The river's close behind—where the squad waters their mounts. Anything you lack, you can find at the nearest town." Bierl wheeled his mount. His rangers followed him through the gate. He paused to give instructions to the pair at a small guardhouse before galloping down the highway.

"Not unexpected," Rysen stated.

"Disappointing," Trillion said. A useless endeavor, as he had feared it would be. He fingered the royal request to squire for Wilm.

The lean-tos and pasture areas close to the river afforded ample food and water for the mounts but not for the riders. Lisze pulled out her pot and pan. With instructions to Wilm and Sean, she set about providing for the troop.

By first turn after nightfall, the squad feasted on fresh bannock, rabbits snared by Wilm, and pheasants taken by Sean and his companions. She brewed tea and boiled coffee. Later, she prepared Trillion's herbal tonic and waited for him to join her. She had almost drifted to sleep when he approached.

"Your tea's cold." Lisze handed him the mug.

"Do I have to drink it?" he asked.

"Definitely. I sense this trip will test your endurance. Pace yourself, you'll need all your strength." Once he emptied the cup, she lifted the wrap. "Now, can you tell me what's going on? I thought Wilm would squire here."

"Not likely." He ran his fingers over the back of her hand. "There were rumors, but we had to confirm it with a surprise visit." He stilled his voice, beating down the anger. "This reception confirms our fears. Worstein has essentially separated from Lamoria."

The next morning, as Lisze set about to break camp, she greeted the heavy-set Marshal Rysen, close confidante of Prince David.

Rysen smiled with set lips. "You stay. We have no need for another cook."

Lisze sent Trillion a pleading look, but he shook his head imperceptibly before taking his place in the formation. Once in the field the lead marshal had say over the expedition.

"That's that, then." Cesim hovered over the last still glowing fire. "And I had doused the best of the firepits."

"We didn't know," Lisze said.

"What about us? Do we have to stay here?" Wilm asked.

Lisze eyed the tall, towering trees ringing the open area of sagging buildings. The small shed had not seemed to have held provisions for quite some time, but would provide good shelter in a storm.

"Ama, could we go see the mountains?"

Cesim said, "As long as we avoid Worstein Holding. Days long past I knew a way up the southern cliffs. Years have not erased my memory of the secret passage to the Amhavran Mountains in Worstein's backyard. We head east to Invien Ridge, south of Havransen Pass into the foothills. Invien Ridge is broad and wide with a northern trail with views of the Amhavran Mountains."

"Do we have the time?"

Cesim leaned back on his heels, thumbing his finger on his lips. "It's almost two days' ride to Wolf's Bane. That's four days traveling. Then they have to follow the tracks."

"Six days, half a fortnight?" Lisze watched Wilm's face light up. "We won't have any sweetmeats or soft rush beds."

"Ama, I wasn't raised in a castle. I want to see the mountains."

"Very well." She added, "We've not been welcomed by the people in this area, so we stay out of sight." Lisze smiled at the thought of a chance for adventure with Wilm and Cesim, two of her favorite people, but she prayed often for Trillion's safety.

Cesim stopped, trying to recall the landmarks for the mountain passage. "Now, my lad, never forget—there's the broad paths or the back ways the horsemen know." He nudged his mount forward down a narrow valley. "Perhaps around this bend . . . or not." More hills rose up, blocking the way. A distant waterfall coursed down a rocky hillside.

"So that's what I've been hearing," Wilm said.

Lisze hid a giggle. "It seems not all landmarks survive the ravages of time."

"Not all." Cesim turned his steed about, and they retraced their steps. "Ah, here we go," he said, stopping at a barren, silvery stump reaching twice a man's height. He shook his head. "This was once a magnificent oak."

"I will call it bone tree," Wilm said.

"Bone tree, I like that. Now, let's see if this is the trail."

When the land sloped down and twisted back to the uplands, Cesim shook his head. "I thought I knew how to go."

Wilm pushed his horse past his mother's as he gazed at the plains below.

"It's beautiful, isn't it?" Lisze said.

Cesim described the vista laid out below them. "I can see the ocean past the Keyayisin Forest, and Tierney Ridge on our left."

Lisze looked about. Although only midafternoon, it was not too early to find a good place to rest for a day or so. "Let's find a place to camp and rest."

Wilm dropped his head back to stare upward. "The trees here are so tall it's hard to see the mountains."

"We can push on to higher ground in a day or so," Lisze said to encourage Wilm.

Cesim laughed. "But I bet there are some good caves nearby." He winked at Wilm when he said, "Cook's assistant, you are charged with finding a cave suitable for shelter and a fire circle."

"Yes, Master Cesim, sir." Wilm nudged his horse ahead and headed back to the nearest deer trail. Winding along the ridge, dipping every so often into short valleys, only to reach another rise as the plains opened before them. Pausing momentarily, he gestured for all to be still. After the horses settled their breathing, he heard again a low moan.

Lisze noted Wilm's questioning gaze, and she nodded. Wordlessly, she dismounted. Cesim and Wilm followed her lead.

Wilm held the reins of the three horses while Lisze and Cesim searched for a sign. Light moaning, carried by the slight western breeze, directed them to a low clump of bushes. Cesim pulled on a bush. It came away in his hands. Lisze pulled off the rest. They stared at a barely conscious, older Ayisin man.

Cesim gave the usual greeting, but terror did not leave the man's eyes.

Lisze gestured the friendship greeting. "We won't harm you. What happened to your leg?"

"Broken." He set his jaw and spoke no further. Using his arm to try to sit, a look of pain washed over his face.

Lisze knelt to support him. He grasped her arm and tried to rise but fell back.

"Good sir, we can find shelter, see to your wounds. We'll linger here until you're ready to travel," she said.

He nodded and worked to catch his breath.

Lisze walked to Cesim and said quietly, "He might be hunted." She turned to Wilm. "Find a cave with space for a fire, but defensible, and report back. I'll ready him for transport."

Wilm nodded, and Cesim followed the lad around the bend.

111

Looking for a good splint, she set to straightening and securing the man's leg.

When they returned, Cesim asked, "Is he ready?"

"Yes." She pointed to the splint on his leg. "Hope it's close by. I suspect he has other injuries. Is it far?"

"A little, but it's hidden well."

"We must obscure our trail."

Cesim approached the Ayisin man, who pulled back in alarm.

Lisze asked, "What do you intend to do?"

"Move close enough to carry him, unless you have a better idea."

"No." She knelt again by the man's side. "I'm Lisze, and this is Cesim. He will take you to a cave where we can make camp."

He looked at the young woman and older warrior, nodded, and let the burly man lift him.

"Lady Lisze, obscure our tracks." Cesim paused, waiting for her to find the right switches.

Lisze handed the reins of the other horses to Wilm, who was sitting astride his mare, Candy. "Wilm, lead the way." Taking a switch and boughs, she removed what evidence she could of their steps, making sure to leave no items behind. Although it seemed as if Wilm had led them to a blind canyon, an opening appeared past several large rocks.

Down two more canyons and into a sheltered area, Wilm continued to the next ridge and seemed to disappear into another canyon. They followed. He tied the mounts to a low-hanging branch and pulled back piles of brush to reveal a large cave opening. Wilm said, "It's empty except for a small cache in the back."

"Leave it be, for now." Lisze stepped past and set up an area for the injured man.

Their camp was completed before dusk. Lisze made a small, smokeless fire for tea and to roast the rabbits Wilm snared. Cesim brought an herbal broth to the Ayisin man.

Drinking deeply, he held out his cup for more tea. "I am Aiden. I welcome your aid." He accepted the plate of trail meats.

Before daylight disappeared, Lisze had tried to encourage the man to move to a rush bed in the cave, but he insisted on sleeping outside. Wilm found him a place protected by a rock overhang, and they helped him settle in for the night.

Lisze followed Wilm out to the small valley. The light of the moon shone a path to the darkness of steep hills, mere foothills before distant, towering mountains.

Wilm glanced back at the short ridge hiding their camp. "We can't leave Aiden, can we?"

She moved aside a few strands of wayward hair. "Time will come when you'll be able to see the mountains, even visit them, but the Lord has provided a far greater opportunity for now."

"I know. People are more important than our plans. Who will go for help?"

"Let's see if he can recover enough to ride." Trying not to shiver with the chill of the setting sun, she wrapped her arm around her son.

He leaned back and gasped at the myriad stars, twinkling, some joining into bright orbs. "There are so many! More than at Clefisch Pass."

"Beyond count, but the Lord knows their number and gives to each a name."

"Where mountain and plains meet," Cesim said, coming up beside them. "The best of both worlds."

"I never knew you loved the mountains," Lisze stated.

"While I prefer more even ground, mountains have their own charms and dangers."

Wilm lay on his back and drank in the sight of the twinkling stars. As he studied the patterns of each grouping, his eyes rested on the jagged line where the distant mountains swallowed the lights.

When Wilm began to sigh and yawn, she tapped his shoulder. "Time for your own bedroll." The three walked back, and she settled him onto the rush bed in the cave.

Lisze sat by the fire and spoke to Cesim in a low voice. "We must stay until Aiden can be moved."

"If there's no progress, I'll have to return to Worstein. They will never know to look for us here."

"Agreed, but we can wait a few days. Let us pray. He's so quiet."

Cesim began to spread the logs apart. "An Ayisin for certain. You can tell an Airdle gathering by the persistent conversations filling a hall until one can hardly hear himself think. The plains people, Dornan and those of the north, are quieter but seem averse to dealing with any matter until they've told the story of the day, their firstborn's ride, and their grandmother's pies." He rose to add to the fire and glanced at the Ayisin. Aiden seemed to have drifted off to sleep. "Not certain of the Sanderfield, but the few gatherings I've seen, they've been loud and crude. The Ayisin, when they first meet, even ones they've known for years, sit and feel their presence, speaking only when necessary. He shared his name and thanked us. That is much talk for an Ayisin."

Lisze nodded. "We are all different."

She thought back to the marks on Aiden's shoulders, and down his arms. His color seemed pale, almost blood-less, with darkened rings around dull eyes. She had seen such before on her father's body. A shudder ran through her. "My father's death was not an accident?"

Cesim glanced her way. "You don't miss much, Lady. Bad rains and riding the wrong trail didn't send those boulders tumbling down upon your father. He bore signs of having fought off attackers. We weren't able to catch them. Lady Elwin didn't want to worry you." He poked at the coals. "Let's pray Aiden's pursuers don't find this little cave."

"I don't understand such hate." She separated the logs,

banked the coals, and emptied her canteen. "My father taught me many things—how to ride, gentle a horse, make a saddle, live off the land—but little of himself."

"And your mother's lessons. You were well taught. Your father was a private man, never sharing personal feelings with even those closest to him. Whatever happened when he tried to go home, he never spoke of." Cesim rose. "He courted your mother with an intensity I had seen only on the most dangerous march. They dreamed of taming the land, making it fit for herds of horse and cattle. Even planned a small way station."

"What's done is done, Master Cesim, and judgment will be rendered by the one true God. That out of my parents' deaths came a son." She turned and blinked away the tears. "To see how God can work even when evil seems to have the upper hand."

"Ready?"

Lisze bowed her head, entered the cave, and felt her way to the rush bed by Wilm. With a goodnight kiss, she found a comfortable position. She could make out Cesim in his bed-roll at the mouth, guarding them. She recalled a well-known passage in the Gospel of John. "Lord Jesus, You are my gate. You protect us well. You said, 'I have come that they may have life and have it abundantly.' Thank You for Your many blessings."

Camping brought back memories of Esrilin, and she thanked the Lord for having had time with him at Clefisch Pass. Yet, she could not deny her growing feelings for Trillion and hopes for their years together. That the Lord would use the prince in a mighty way, she had no doubt. Had she not been called to help him? *Lord, Your will be done and keep them both safe.*

Chapter 12

Back to Worstein Holding

The day was dry and not too hot. Clouds partially obscured the sun, now cooler than at the height of summer. A fair breeze rustled the leaves of the trees. Hummingbirds flitted about, fighting and pirouetting around the last of the summer's flowers. Wilm and Cesim returned midmorning with a brace of rabbits. Wilm skinned and cleaned the meat. Cesim, observing, set up the supports to roast the rabbits on a slim pole.

Lisze retrieved her bow from her pack and examined the wood for new breaks. Pressing resin into a crack before it could split, she reached for rawhide bindings.

Cesim glanced her way. "Can't keep it together much longer, milady. You could have your choice of any fine bow in the armory."

"I know, but this is the last one Father made for me." She sat back. "Did he explain why he settled in Dornan and didn't return to Sanderfield?" Lisze noticed Aiden fast asleep on the mat. The man seemed to be on the mend and had taken a few steps, with Cesim's help.

"Something happened back home but he never spoke of it. When your father returned from the Sanderfield, he found the Lord and vowed never to return. I remember him remarking that a few wicked leaders could turn a region to violence. He said without God we would all rip ourselves apart. Your father almost spoke of his people as if they were a lost cause, unredeemable."

Aiden stirred, having listened as he dozed. He sat up. "Did you trap the rabbits, young man?"

"Yes, Master Aiden." Wilm looked aside, trying to avoid the Ayisin's sharp gaze. He heard him laugh lightly.

"You may call me Aiden, as I may call you Wilm? Are of Airdle?"

"I guess so." Seeing his ama's nod, he said, "Prince Trillion is my father."

"So you are the one Eriason talked about. You are of the four founding tribes."

Lisze met Aiden's gaze. "He comes from the four branches of Lamoria. Time will tell of God's call and what it will mean."

"Lady Lisze, I remember your father well. And Cesim, I didn't recognize you in your old age."

"Old age!" Cesim laughed, rocking back and winking at Aiden. "You've shown the years, although I don't think we knew each other. It was a long time ago."

"It was, and we were warriors of the land." Aiden looked at Wilm, brow furrowed. "So, young one, someday will you spend a summer with the people?"

"We came to ask Lord Bierl if Wilm could squire, but he's not receptive to those from Airdle," Lisze said.

"Not surprising, with having to expel the Airdle judges and install their own magistrates."

"Prince Joshua could help," Wilm said.

Lisze cautioned, "We will see where the trail goes before we make such an offer. But you must talk to Prince Trillion for he has never spoken of this. Do you know who attacked you, Aiden?"

"A mob of men, I thought from Tierney. I had come for supplies at the fair. They ambushed me at the gorge. Only by God's grace did I manage to slip away. But now I am in doubt as their speech was different, more clipped, harder to understand."

"Marshal Rysen is here with a squad to investigate what happened at Wolf's Bane. The town was emptied. There were some dead, but many missing. We'll have to report your attack."

Aiden said, "Strange times. We blame each other, yet it seems as if ghosts run through our land unchecked, only these ghosts carry blades and arrowheads." Aiden drew one out from a pouch. "Like this."

Lisze reached for the blade, feeling its heft. "We've seen them as well. Prince Trillion prepared the report for the initial investigation. The king's marshals are trying to discover where they're from."

"The attackers could not enter by the coast, so they must come from land. The Amhavran traders have not seen them. I doubt they could have come by the mountains," Cesim said.

"The Sanderfield Gap, that runs between the foothills of the Amhavran in the east?" Lisze asked.

Cesim rose to fetch more wood for the firepit. "In years past, that was so well guarded we never worried about strangers from the northeast. Now, everything is in doubt, including ghost ships." Wilm opened his mouth as if to speak, but Cesim shook his head. "Many questions, few answers. That is why we have come, to let Worstein know the attack on Wolf's Bane was probably not done by any of our people."

Lisze rose to start the sup. "We should head back to Worstein tomorrow. Can you handle a ride at a walk? We'll have to find a doctor who can help you recover." She felt relief at his nod, for he needed more healing than she could give.

They headed out after breakfast the following day. Wilm gladly offered Candy. Lisze helped settle Aiden into the saddle as comfortably as possible, and Wilm walked beside his mare. They were not quite clear of the canyon when Lisze heard the dull rumbles of many hooves with high-pitched ticks.

"Ama, shod horses!"

"I heard." She brought Tesla to a stop, and Cesim rode ahead to find a place to hide. "This way," she said when she saw Cesim's wave. Wilm led Candy behind a fissure, with Aiden fighting to stay conscious. Lisze settled the horses.

Cesim whispered, "Lad, climb up and take a peek. Be careful."

Wilm eagerly made his way up the steep rise to work his way over and out of sight.

Cesim shook his head when Lisze asked if Aiden should dismount. He guarded the entrance, sitting tall on his mount, sword drawn.

She tried not to jump when she heard Wilm's familiar whistle and Trillion's answering call. Cesim urged his horse forward. Lisze mounted Tesla and grasped Candy's lead. She followed when Cesim said, "All clear."

The narrow path led to a wide trail. Lisze couldn't hold back her smile when she saw Trillion astride his mount next to Marshal Nolan.

Wilm returned from having told the group about the injured Ayisin. "Ama! They had been looking for Aiden!" Wilm ran to Candy and led her to Chief Pagiel, Aiden's son, and three Imbus Ayisin next to the marshals and some rangers. The Ayisin called out with joy, seeing him alive and rode up to him. Aiden tried to smile despite his pain.

Rysen said, "We'll head for the closest Worstein way station. Pray they are more welcoming this time." Rysen gave the signal for the unit to form up and reined his horse to the side. He gestured for Cesim to approach. "What were the extent of his injuries?"

"I couldn't say. Lady Lisze rendered aid. She is a fine healer."

The marshal glanced at Lisze. "Do you have a tongue, Lady?"

Refusing to show her irritation, Lisze spoke without emotion. "I set his leg and gave him what herbs I had with me. He needs a doctor's care, as he has internal injuries."

Rysen wheeled his charger and headed to the front of the column. With a lifted arm and shout, they moved forward. Lisze followed at the rear.

Trillion brought his stallion around to her side. Wilm, Cesim, and two marshals took the rear guard.

Lisze noticed the strung bows and short swords in their free hands.

"Don't fret, my love."

She leveled her gaze at him. "I learned long ago that a good deed unnoticed will yield treasure in heaven. Too many are like Rysen." Lisze glanced at her husband. "Is your time done with this squad?"

"You three have likely gifted Rysen's squad with an open door to Worstein, even though he might not be aware of it. Many in Worstein are friendly with or related to the Ayisin."

Lisze told him what Aiden had said about having to expel Airdle judges.

Trillion almost smiled. "Perhaps we can discover the rift and heal it."

Wilm couldn't hold back. "But Wolf's Bane? What did you find?"

"Son, in time we will travel to the village, but Aiden's injuries must be seen. I would prefer to investigate Wolf's Bane with Bierl and his rangers and not behind their backs."

Chapter 13

Worstein Holding

Worstein lay before them after they passed through the foothills close to the holding's southern border. The station on the main road consisted of houses and corrals. A guard sitting on the porch called out when he saw the horsemen. Three more rangers emerged from the building. Chief Pagiel and another Ayisin urged their mounts to the station at a fast trot.

When the lead ranger recognized Chief Pagiel, he called out a greeting and called for the wagon to be brought.

In moments, four Ayisin dismounted and gently lifted Aiden onto a clean wagon.

Rysen waved Trillion to come beside him. The head marshal raised his fist, and the column halted a stone's throw from the gatehouse.

The land of Worstein holding spread out on an upland plain. Lisze glanced back. This station had a clear view of all roads leading to it, as Clefisch Pass had.

Hearing pounding hooves, she saw several horsemen approach from the ranger's station.

Lisze prayed as the rangers stopped to talk with Marshal Rysen. She relaxed when he waved the company forward.

All followed the column through the gate and onto the plains of Worstein holding—neat farms, long fields of hay and grains, with small vegetable gardens, lumber mills near quaint villages, and expansive pastures for horses, cattle, and sheep.

The broad road led to a tall, dark castle.

"Weirstone Keep!" Wilm said.

Cesim smiled. "Dark mountain rock might make it appear foreboding, but it's cozy enough inside."

Wilm noticed the holding lord standing beside a short, plump lady and a tall maiden with frizzy hair. They stood at the top of the stone steps and waved. "Cesim, who are they?"

"Lord Bierl's family. The short one is Lady Katrina, and the tall girl is his youngest daughter, Giselle."

"I've heard of Lady Katrina. She's very active in charity work with Marshal Karith's wife, Lady Dara." Lisze tried not to stare at the lady of Weirstone in a velvet dress and her daughter. Squaring her shoulders, lifting her head, she set her lips, concerned as to what their reception might be.

Lisze, Wilm, and Cesim found their place alongside the squad following the wagon. Rysen and Pagiel dismounted and walked up the steps to greet Lord Bierl.

Lisze noticed a throng at the wagon. Was something wrong? Lisze wheeled her horse, rode around the group, and approached the doctor, dismounting quickly. "Healer, if I may."

He looked over, almost in irritation.

"He has suffered a broken leg, internal injuries, and endured a day's journey on horseback. He has much pain, but also needs water, food, and more medicine than I could give on the trail," she said.

"You dosed him with capsaicin?"

Was this a rebuke or his way of asking for more information? Lisze stepped back.

The healer rose and took a step toward her. "You are?"

"Lady Lisze, at your service, good healer. Wife of Prince Trillion." She smiled when Trillion stood by her side.

"Mother of my son, Prince Wilm. Well, Healer Trent, I see you are still patching up the wounded. Lisze, meet the fine healer who kept me alive years ago when I had an unfortunate encounter with a sword."

"Prince Trillion, I heard of your grave injuries. You've recovered once again?"

Trillion laughed at the healer's look of disbelief.

The healer turned to Lisze. "Well then, Lady Lisze, do I have to ask for a report?"

Trying not to blush, she relayed the events of the past days and Aiden's progress.

"Very helpful. Sounds like you did everything that could have been done."

Lisze watched the healer follow the litter carrying Aiden to a side door. "Then he is in good hands." She turned, happy to feel Trillion beside her. "And have I said how thankful I am that we have a master healer at Airdle who saved your life?"

He felt her arm slip into his. "No, the Lord did, when He brought you."

His smile sank into her soul, and she knew she would endure whatever was necessary.

"From what we've learned, we're going to need this holding's help." Trillion took her arm, and they walked arm-in-arm, a stable boy having gathered the mounts to lead them away.

"Father, you must meet Lady Katrina and their daughter, Maiden Giselle." Wilm paused seeing their glances. "They have many questions."

"I suspect they do," Trillion said and turned to face the steps. He tried to look relaxed and positive. Perhaps this time they would be warmly received. They would be the last to mount the steps.

Lisze began to sort their saddle bags once they arrived in their small suite. The rooms were spacious and tastefully decorated. The staff had filled a tub in an adjoining room with warm water. Trillion went to wash the dirt away while she tried to find suitable clothes for evening sup in Weirstone's main hall—a place she had heard grand tales of since her earliest years. Wilm had left for a quick visit to the stables with Cesim.

On their way to the guest wing, Lisze stared in awe at the castle's grandeur. The walls were trimmed with gold, the floors were of crafted marble, and the crystal chandeliers held scores of candles rumored to emit specific scents for each hall.

She heard a quick knock, and then the lady of the castle flowed in, followed by a maid with garments over her arm.

Lisze left the packs on the floor with her crumpled dinner gown draped on a chair and went to greet her. "Lady Katrina!"

"Nonsense, you may call me Katrina. What is your name, dear?"

"Lisze, wife of Prince Trillion, with my son Wilm."

Katrina glanced at the sad state of Lisze's dress. She turned to the maid standing beside her. "Will a skirt and blouse with a shawl do?"

Lisze accepted the soft brown skirt and elegant cream blouse with burgundy shawl. "Perfect. Thank you."

Katrina handed Lisze's gown to the maid. "Take this to the launderer. Have it cleaned right away."

Once Katrina left, Lisze made Trillion's tea and set the bed. After his bath, he could not hide his exhaustion from her.

"More tea? Haven't I proven I can handle excursions?"

"You put on a good show. Fear not, I'll keep your secret. Healer Anselm gave me instructions before we left. Is the bath still warm?"

"You could call for more hot water."

Lisze grabbed her small bag and borrowed clothes. She didn't have time for a leisurely bath. Ducking inside, she cleaned up as quickly as possible and donned the skirt and blouse, loosely wrapping the shawl around her shoulders.

Lisze entered the room and gazed at Trillion's still figure on the bed. A jolt ran through her. Had he passed, overcome by the rigors of the trail? *Lord, give us more time together*, she prayed silently. They'd barely come to know one another.

Lisze walked softly to the bed and sat on a nearby chair. She leaned forward tentatively, drinking in the sight of his peaceful face. The corners of his lips curving up slightly. This was her husband. Bending over, she listened to his light breath. She raised slightly and rested her hand on his upper arm. Prayers burst forth for him—not for the son of the king, but for the one becoming her beloved.

Trillion's eyes opened, and he brightened at the sight of her. He tenderly touched her hand. "You clean up remarkably well, my lady."

Lisze wiped a tear away, with his kind and gentle words. She stroked his hand over her other hand. "I need to hear your breathing." She placed her ear against his chest and sat up to look at him.

"Will I live, fair maiden?"

She watched a smile form. As if coming to herself, she cocked her head. "The gurgling rails are diminished but not gone." She gazed at his face once again and placed a gentle hand on his arm. "I should let you sleep. Were you dreaming? You looked happy."

"I've had enough." Trillion watched her sit back on the chair.

He sat up and swung his feet over the side of the bed. "As I dozed I remembered the joy of us working together on the report. And we found a few answers. A beginning."

Her hand slid down to rest upon his hand. "Really? High praise, good sir, that we now enjoy clerical tasks." Feeling his hand tighten, she slid on the bed to sit beside him and leaned against his shoulder. "I didn't mean to belittle your efforts.

Lamoria needs answers." She slid her fingers over his wedding ring. "Perhaps we can embrace our new life at the castle."

"I fear failing father and the kingdom—again. What does the Bible say about fear?"

"Fear not!" Lisze stroked his arm. "Easy to say. Hard to do. We must trust by faith that we will perceive God's path each moment of every day." She thought a moment. "How did that verse go? 'Do not be anxious about anything, but in everything, by prayer and petition, with thanksgiving, let your requests be made known to God.'" Her voice softened. "'And the peace of God, which transcends all understanding, will guard your hearts and your minds in Christ Jesus.' Philippians 4, verses 6 and 7. Favorite memory verses my mother urged me to never forget. If we can keep our eyes on the Savior, clouds of fear and doubt lessen."

He nodded. "Like you said, easy to say, hard to do. The Leaves of God contain truth for our lives today. I had not known or understood the source of my parents' faith and the help God provides."

When a knock sounded on the door, Lisze pulled aside and stood. "Coming." She hurried to the door. "Just a moment."

They heard a faint, "Steward Ashin," through the door.

Lisze glanced back at Trillion before quickly opening it.

"I am Steward Ashin. Is Prince Trillion here?"

She swung it wider for the steward to see Prince Trillion standing by the bed.

"My pardon, but Lord Bierl has seen the value of your help with the Ayisin. He wishes to speak with you, Prince Trillion, in his library."

Trillion stepped to Lisze's side.

"I am honored." He gently squeezed Lisze's arm. "I'll be back. You're not rid of me yet," he said, trying to ease the worry on her face. "No fears, remember?"

Trillion walked beside the steward with full, even strides

along the corridors. They entered the library on the left. He glanced at the shelves filled with books. So the rumors were true that Lord Bierl was a learned man. He sat in a chair in front of the roaring fire, thankful for warmth as he waited for the holding lord to arrive. Could it be that they might have a chance to find favor with this man?

Trillion rose when the door opened, and Lord Bierl stepped through.

"Good to light a fire when summer's heat wanes." Bierl sat in the chair opposite Trillion and sighed, glancing past the young prince, deep in thought.

The holding lord seemed conflicted, as if he didn't know how to begin. Taking a guess, Trillion said, "I regret past actions and am ready to make amends."

Bierl raised his hand. "I will not stand against your attempts to reconcile. Today I see in you your mother's faith." He rubbed his brow. Meeting Trillion's gaze, he shook his head. "That our people attacked Aiden is deeply disturbing. How could they have believed that he had been involved in the emptying of Wolf's Bane?"

Trillion waited, hoping this was the time they could work together, mend the break with Worstein.

"I heard disturbing news from Aiden as well as Rysen. Other attacks have occurred?" Bierl looked at the prince, waiting for an answer.

Trillion nodded. "On the eastern plains and the forests of the Imbus Ayisin. Some formed bands to hunt down the assailants. The plainsmen would have warred with the Ayisin if not for the marshals."

"Who are these people that can steal a village in a night?"

Trillion shrugged his shoulders. "They left weapons crafted of metal not seen before."

"How could this be happening? What are Prince David's marshals doing? Polishing their boots for parades?"

"King Wallace and Head Marshal Vaughn will order all

marshals to pursue any and all intruders. The king commissioned me to open the investigation by collecting all reports of attacks. My findings will help focus our efforts. That is the reason I was sent to Worstein, to see if these attacks are related." Trillion breathed, gathered his courage, and asked, "If I may, Lord Bierl, be so bold? Why were you reluctant to accept our aid?"

The holding lord sighed, rose, and walked to the window. Lifting his head, he closed his eyes as if in thought. Bierl faced the prince. "Judges and magistrates, trained and certified by Airdle, have fallen to corruption. They take bribes, allow witnesses to be intimidated, drop cases at the request of the rich, and allow the disinheritance of poor widows and landholders. Even ones we thought had not been tainted failed to expose the wrongdoing of their peers. The auditors sent from Prince Joshua dismissed the charges and helped conceal the crimes."

"My lord, Prince Joshua sent no auditors."

"Who sent them?" The holding lord sat. "Is this Prince David's doing?"

Trillion pondered his answer. "Maybe through associates. Prince David leads many of the marshal squads while Prince Joshua deals with judicial matters." Perhaps Prince David did have informants posted in various positions in the departments, as he had suspected. "Prince Joshua has not mentioned any of this to me. Have you sent a dispatch to him about these appalling decisions?"

"Through the auditors." Bierl sighed. "We are still considering how to deal with this mess. Prince Joshua has not visited in many years. The king no longer tours the holdings."

Trillion shifted in his seat. "Have you found magistrates and judges fit to serve? Are they trained?"

"Most were exceptional clerks or worked for magistrates in Tierney or Stolein. Others returned home to see justice served." Almost slumping in his chair, Bierl stared at the fire.

"Lord Bierl, I assure you." Trillion leaned forward. "Prince Joshua's faith would never allow him to support or aid any who break God's laws. His desire to see justice cover the land has not waivered. May he come and help in this matter? His breadth of knowledge and experience . . ."

Bierl lifted his brow. "The wisdom of the Supreme Judge is not in question. Our faith in the House of Airdle is."

Trillion nodded. "This helps us better understand your situation. Prince Joshua can aid you while we investigate the slaying and kidnapping of our people. The king desires to set things right with Worstein." Feeling the time was right, he asked, "Can you tell me what you know about Wolf's Bane?"

Bierl relayed the bare facts of the attack on the village.

"Not only for our safety, but for the peace of our land, we must work together to uncover who is behind these events. If they are able to steal away a village in one night, that is indeed a foe to fear. Were you able to catch any of the intruders? Is it true they came by sea? Have we relied too long on the Black Pearl Islands and the reefs that line our shores?" Trillion drew in his breath.

"The sheriff believes they anchored beside the northern tip of the last island where the deep draws near to shore." The holding lord met his gaze.

Trillion nodded. "I will confer with Marshal Rysen. We should alert stations along our coasts to watch the seas. Perhaps they've seen alien vessels, but were unaware of their importance."

The room fell silent.

"I should let you return to your family. A page will stop by to escort you to the banquet hall. We don't often have guests from Airdle."

Trillion rose with Bierl. The well-respected holding lord extended his hand, and Trillion grasped it for a firm handshake. "Thank you for meeting with me, Lord Bierl."

He took his leave, walking with the page to their suites.

Sharp voices could be heard through the door. Stepping in, he saw Lisze standing by Wilm with set mouth and clenched jaw.

"Young prince, do not give your mother a hard time. What is the matter?"

When Wilm shook the formal princely jerkin in his hand, Trillion said, "This banquet will be a formal affair. We are required to dress accordingly. See, your mother is already properly attired."

"Is this adequate?" Lisze swung her arm along the light brown skirt that flowed as she moved. Trillion's eyes were only for his wife. "You look ravishingly beautiful." He wrapped her in an embrace. "A beauty like you has no need of fancy gowns. Had you brought this?"

"Lady Katrina lent it."

"I saw you pack a brown bodice." Trillion brought it to Lisze after Wilm unfurled it from her saddlebag. "Not bad. Let's see how that completes the look."

Lisze set aside the shawl and gathered the corseted bindings, pulling in the billowy blouse. She combed her long hair and pinned back her front locks with small, jeweled combs. Trillion changed into his semiformal short brown jacket. Embroidered panels on the chest displayed the Airdle cross on an amber field.

The three stood side by side in front of a long mirror.

"We make a fine family," Trillion said.

"Perhaps Maiden Giselle will be there," Lisze said, watching her son's cheeks redden.

Wilm rolled his eyes.

Seated toward the front near the lord's family, Wilm noticed Giselle's frizzy hair had been secured with barrettes. Her dark curls flowed down her back. She scratched at her laced cuff and smiled shyly when she saw Wilm watching. He returned the smile and adjusted his cuffs as well.

Lisze glanced at her son. "She's younger?"

"My age. Their youngest. Her brother is ten years older."

Lisze accepted a platter of meats from a waiter and turned back to Katrina, who had asked about fashions in Airdle. "I've been so busy settling in and helping when I can, along with caring for Wilm." The mothers exchanged smiles. "I remember horse lines, saddles, and the latest bridles more readily than the latest cut of dresses."

"I imagine you're busy with the balls and banquets at the castle. Have you heard about Prince David's banquets at his estate?" Katrina resettled her long, forest green jacket over a soft cream dress.

"No." Lisze looked into the distance of the long hall. "King Wallace takes his duties seriously and wishes for all to be well throughout Lamoria. Perhaps we can come together to discover who is behind these troubles."

"Our prayers as well. Many here had friends or relatives in that small village. It didn't help they kept to themselves and rarely invited visitors."

"So this happened a while ago?"

"Less than a fortnight."

"How did they send word?"

"A young boy escaped and made his way to Invien Springs. They say he swam to the cliffs close to Invien River's outlet."

"What is his name? Is he safe? Have they questioned him?" Lisze would have turned to ask Trillion, but he was listening intently to the head Worstein ranger and Chief Pagiel.

"I wouldn't know. Busy with holding affairs. It would be noticed if the larder were bare, riding breeches not mended, or the wool crop not prepared for market." She knit her brow. "My pages had to spend weeks cleaning the spring's shearing."

Lisze smiled. "I understand. I recall a time when we ran

out of dried berries. They're an expected relish on our sweet bannocks." She sat back and listened to the lady of the holding share her management secrets.

The meal progressed to a traditional, fine-layered confection slathered with butter, honey, and tree nuts. Before the ladies escorted the young ones to the drawing room, Lisze quickly said to Trillion, "Lady Katrina mentioned a young lad from Wolf's Bane who escaped to Invien Springs. Have you heard of this?"

"No, but I'll ask around. With no trail inland, we must look to the sea."

"Will pray you make headway."

Trillion reached for her arm but stopped short of a quick kiss. "Enjoy your time with the ladies. We are ambassadors to this fair council."

Chapter 14

Meeting in Weirstone's Judgment Hall

L ord Bierl led the group to Weirstone's Judgment Hall. He gestured for Trillion to sit by the fire in a tall wingback chair. Even though the hall did not have a fire council pit, the chairs encircled a large fireplace.

Momentarily surprised when they asked him to lead the meeting, Trillion stalled for time to decide when and how to begin. He asked the lawreader to open with Scriptures and prayer.

The lawreader quoted from Psalm 19 and 119 without notes. His concise prayer pointedly reminded them of the common bond and purpose God laid upon the governments of men.

Strengthened in the Lord, remembering to fear not, Trillion rose and called for rounds of introductions. Most kept their comments brief until the men from Invien Springs accused the Keyayisin of murder and theft.

A tall Keyayisin in a richly embroidered tunic refuted the charges. "And where are the people? Did you find their fishing nets and spears in our homes? We lost our people who lived at Wolf's Bane too."

Lord Bierl tried to calm the throng of raised voices. Some even rose, gesticulating with clenched fists.

Trillion stood and whistled a piercing note. "Be seated! This is a time to state the facts, what you know—not to lay accusations. Lord Mayor of Invien Springs, you may begin."

The meeting progressed with each reporting in turn what they knew, along with their concerns.

Pagiel's statement hinted that the blame rested with the people of Invien Springs but uttered no direct accusations.

The wide doors to the hall swung open, and three figures entered. Aiden walked slowly beside Healer Trent and a young man. Trillion approached the elder leader, lowering his head in respect as he laid his hand over his heart with a greeting of honor. "You are most welcome, Aiden of the Imbus Ayisin. Do you wish to speak?"

The former chief nodded and walked with Trillion to stand between two high chairs. "Aiden of the people of Lamoria asks to stand before the council," announced Trillion.

Lord Bierl spread his arms in greeting. "Your presence is most welcome, and we long to hear your words, Chief Aiden."

Aiden waved his hand and stood in front of the fire. "As you know, my son Pagiel is now our chief, but that does not remove my duty to speak." His eyes roved the group. "The Law of the Lord is perfect, reviving the soul. When the Lord of Glory walked this earth, He spoke of divisions, divided houses. A kingdom divided against itself will not stand. Long ago we formed a people united under one God and His law, each allowing the other to live as their customs dictated from the plains to the towns to the fishing piers to the Ayisin tribes. We lived in harmony, our peoples moving and trading freely at fairs, towns, and markets. A visit to Tierney Fair and my Keyayisin friends have been marred by violence in which I had no part."

Lord Bierl would have stood to make a quick report, but the elder lifted his palm to the Worstein leader. "Quick action taken by the Worstein rangers by order of Lord Bierl has found the culprits, and they will have their day in court to be held accountable for their crimes against me. My favorite mare, along with my pack mule, have been returned, but the spirit behind the attack lives on." Aiden lifted his eyes to the vaulted ceiling, as if hearing a distant voice.

He continued, "We have grown apart, and whether we have lost faith in God or have become complacent with our years of peace under King Wallace, I know not." His measured gaze looked at each one. "I have come to tell you that strange incursions have been happening in our forests and the plains south of Imbus. A mob went out when an Ayisin encampment had been pillaged and burned. They met an angry group from a nearby village, having discovered a home had been destroyed with all slain. Only the actions of the marshals were able to keep open war from breaking out. Items left behind in those places are made of metal we have never seen before. Prince Trillion, did you bring their blades?" Chief Aiden turned to the prince.

Trillion reached for a large leather bag, splayed it open, and laid out before the assembled group knives, hatchets, and short swords. "Made of iron not forged in Lamoria and not seen by traders." He passed them around for examination. "The king has allowed me to lead the investigation into the incursions. It seems most happened over the past year. The attackers' route, beginning in Stoddard, through the eastern section of the Weaver's Plain, and back toward the Sanderfield gap, seemed to be a survey trip—warriors spying out our land."

One toward the back called out, "What of the Sanderfield? Is this their doing?"

Aiden glanced over the men. "Traders state these blades were not forged by the Sanderfield. Time to work together and not apart. Age allows me the excuse of retiring, but I pray that you see clearly." He turned and left, his Ayisin companion by his side. The healer paused by the door, studying Trillion carefully before he closed the door.

The prince ignored Trent's pointed look and called for the Invien Springs sheriff to describe the state of the village of

Wolf's Bane. A memory returned of the time he helped Nordrum take Lisze's homestead. Judge Severn of Worstein had written the request for the land transfer, and Prince David had discussed it with them.

None reported finding evidence that a group had marched overland to Wolf's Bane. He waited to hear of the boy Lisze had mentioned, but no one spoke of any survivors. Representatives were selected to go with Rysen's marshals to investigate along the sea. Lord Bierl seemed satisfied and closed the session.

As the groups rose to depart, Trillion sought out the Invien sheriff. "Sheriff, how fortunate to have heard so quickly. I understand the people of Wolf's Bane keep to themselves."

"We trade frequently with them for their catch from the seas. We investigated when they failed to come to the market."

Trillion asked, "Did any escape who could tell us how this was done? Anything at all about the attackers?"

"Can't believe every tale, especially of young lads. Usually running away from home. We have a place to put them until they're claimed." The man avoided his gaze.

Trillion thanked him. It seemed the sheriff had something to hide. He approached three Worstein rangers. "Lady Lisze heard a boy escaped to Invien, but the sheriff refused to acknowledge that a survivor had alerted them to the attack. We must go to Invien Springs to find this lad."

The ranger drew his brows together. "First I've heard. Who told Lady Lisze?"

"Lady Katrina."

Lord Bierl joined them. "My lady volunteers and brings donations to the children's homes. I might know a teacher in the area who could help locate him." Lord Bierl glanced at the lines on the prince's face and his sunken eyes. "You and your men will need at least a day of rest."

"We would welcome that, unless the need is urgent to

leave tomorrow. Lord Bierl, I would like to accompany you to Invien Springs when you have word of the boy's where-abouts." Trillion held Bierl's gaze.

"Very well, you may travel with us. I suspect they've already handed him over to their orphanage." He straightened his back. "We try to ensure none of the children there are mistreated."

Trillion nodded. "I am at your service, Lord Bierl. Have you thought about having Prince Joshua come? I could make the request through Marshal Karith of Stolein."

"I will let you know." Lord Bierl lowered his head slightly and spied a tall man on his way out the door. "Enjoy our suites, Prince Trillion."

"We do. Good night." He headed back to his family's rooms. It had been a long day, joining up with the rangers to find Aiden and heading for Weirstone. Lisze would want to hear everything. Thankfully, Lord Bierl would grant leave for a day of rest.

The next day Trillion tried to gather the energy to join Wilm and Lisze for a trail ride with Maiden Giselle, but his wall of exhaustion could not be hidden from his perceptive wife.

Lisze sent Wilm on ahead. She walked him to the bed. "Don't be embarrassed. Rest. I wish you didn't have to go with them to Wolf's Bane."

"The king requested I see the situation firsthand. Enjoy your time. Glad to hear Lady Katrina has been friendly."

Lisze, dressed in her riding leathers, left with a wave and smile.

Before he could lay down, a rap sounded on the door, and Healer Trent walked in with a mug.

Trillion rose quickly. "Yes?"

"Remarkable recovery, young man. You took the lead last night?" Trent surveyed the room and returned his gaze to the prince.

"At Lord Bierl's request."

"Sit, let me examine you."

"I'm fine."

The healer headed for the small round table near the fireplace. He set down the mug and plopped his heavy body on the chair.

Trillion marveled that it didn't collapse under the load. Deciding whether to order the man out or humor him for a few moments, he recalled the healer's careful tending years before of near-fatal wounds. He pulled out a chair, keeping distance from the table. The odor of the herbal brew constricted his throat.

"The House of Airdle will ever take the lead, I fear." The man leaned forward, studying him closely. "Quite the remarkable stories about your new family. How many other Wilms are there running around, waiting to be registered? The good King Wallace has such a kind heart."

The blood pulsed in Trillion's neck. "There are no others."

"So, you're as impotent as Prince Ricard?"

Trillion reminded himself to stay in control. His half-brother was known for his infidelity. Ricard's wedding had been quickly consummated when a maiden of Tholen had been found with child. His son, Lars, had been a surprise. Rumors surmised the child was the son of a wealthy judge from Stoddard. Tempted to kick the healer out, Trillion tried to explain his actions. "I know I gave the impression—"

"Prince," he interrupted, "your indiscretions are well known."

"Yes, I drank, gambled, raced, and engaged in sparring matches."

"Cheated at cards and games, laid waste the ladies of the land. You admitted yourself that you raped your wife."

Trillion felt the heat rise in his cheeks. He leaned forward with a threatening timbre in his voice. "Lisze consented." The Spirit warned that was only partly true. "I deeply regret deceiving her." He rose, clenching his fist. Tempted to take out the arrogant man with one blow, he yielded to the Holy Spirit's urging to take no action. Instead, he faced his accuser. "The pretty maidens of the land with their lace, fancy gowns, and layered hair were vain and shallow. Only Lisze captured my heart. She was smart, determined, with a drive I'd not seen in other women. How I treated her haunted my days until I surrendered to the Savior. I rest in God's forgiveness."

The healer's eyes squinted, and a corner of his mouth lifted. Blowing through his lips, he leaned forward. "I know you, Trillion—your smooth grace and charming ways. No one really changes. You said it yourself. You used your cunning wiles to destroy a fine daughter of Dornan. I have no idea what game you're playing. Lord Bierl should have sent you packing, but it seems you've swayed him to your side."

"What game do you speak of? What malevolence am I crafting?"

"Aren't you really here to spy out the sins of Lord Bierl?" Before Trillion could protest the accusations, the man continued. "And to have an illegitimate son registered as a grandson of the king and in the line of succession! You have beguiled King Wallace with your craftiness." He paused to take a breath.

Trillion leaned forward. "The sins of the father do not adhere to the children. Each will account for his own actions. I married Lady Lisze to protect him. As the youngest son with others before me, there is little likelihood that Wilm will someday be king. We seek a place for the family the Lord has granted to me. I admit I don't deserve it, but that shows the stature of God's grace and love."

The healer stood. "So here I am, sent to bring a sleeping draught as the master wants you fit for tomorrow's journey."

"What is it?"

"A simple sleeping draught."

"Very well."

"Need to see you drink it."

"I'll sip it as I read the Leaves of God, which is how I usually settle down. It will be gone within the hour." He would have shared his faith, the reason behind the change, but the man left quickly before he could frame the words. A warning rose in his soul, and he bent to sniff the tea—a slight acrid odor with almost a hint of almonds. Not daring to taste it, he poured the liquid into a bottle, hid it in a cupboard, and drank deeply of fresh spring water. He reached for God's Word but then fell to his knees before the dying fire.

Praying, he cried out to the Lord. "How I must look to them! Will they never forget; never forgive? Lord! Do I not deserve their condemnation?" Although made alive in Christ, his sins rose up, crushing him.

"What can I do to overcome my past? How do I make things right?" His sins, along with Prince David's, owned the blame for the fracture with Worstein. Would Tierney Ridge one day be their northern border?

He sat back on his heels and stared fixedly into the fire's glowing coals. When his mother, the queen, had died, his father had descended into mourning, refusing to be comforted. She had been his traveling companion, uniting the realm with her warm, easy grace. Yet, even then, signs of division had begun to appear with some regions' cold acceptance of an Ayisin queen.

He strove to withstand the inner onslaught—the reason why his strength had not returned. Despite his profession, it was already too late for him. Damaged beyond repair, his regeneration opened heaven's gates but not any missions here on this plane. "Lord, what can I do to serve You? Will You even accept me?"

Believe. Trust. You are accepted in the beloved. You are a child of God with a hope and a plan and a purpose.

Trillion bowed in prayer. He only needed to do what lay before him each day. "And those who will not forgive?"

Leave them to Me. You follow Me.

God had things for him to do. His days, although numbered, were not done. He would ensure the House of Airdle rendered aid to Worstein. He would teach his son all he knew, including the speech of the Amhavran and Regnard.

After a sound nap Trillion rose from the bed, splashed water on his face, put on his vest, and bent to renew the fire. He heard the voices of Lisze and Wilm grow stronger.

His wife and son entered with glowing faces and broad smiles.

"I see I missed out on a grand adventure." Glancing at the mug from Healer Trent, he tried to forget the man's accusations.

"Ama rode a wild stallion named Thor. She helped Giselle school her mare, and we explored the holding." Wilm brought a few logs to restore the fire.

Lisze reached for Trillion's hand. "You hadn't told the half of Worstein's beauty." She studied his face, his slumped shoulders and drooping lips. "Wilm, wash for sup. I see your father is already dressed for the dining hall."

Once they were alone, Lisze asked, "Trillion, what happened?"

Not wanting to let their son hear, Trillion sat. "We'll discuss it later. Time for noon sup." He glanced at Lisze. "Don't you need to wash?"

A short time later, Wilm emerged from the bathing room, washed and dressed in his Airdle jerkin. Lisze passed him with her laundered dress.

Trillion's heart lifted seeing a son of Airdle, who walked with the Lord as the kings of old, step toward him. He spread wide his arms to hear stories of their morning adventures until Lisze was ready.

They slipped into the smaller dining hall closest to the kitchen as the bell tolled for sup.

"Wilm, shall we?" Lisze lowered her head in his direction. He stopped talking about their ride and let his father escort them to their side of the table.

Giselle smiled broadly at them.

After the prayer and the bowls had been passed, Katrina said, "Giselle reports you are quite the horsewoman. Said you were able to ride Thor in the back pastures. I had wondered if we would have to sell him if we couldn't make good use of him."

"Do you manage the herds?" Lisze asked.

"We both do. I manage the breeding lines; Lord Bierl is the trainer. Usually seems to know how a horse thinks, and that stallion's been a disappointment."

"Put him to work. He's bored. Give him to a stern rider who would make him work every day. I spent all morning riding him, and he hardly tired. It would be a shame to have him gelded."

Trillion watched the ladies talk about herd management. He once again realized how well they fit together. He had not the energy to open conversations with the others sitting around them. Rysen and his squad sat at the other end of the table.

As the meal ended, Trillion excused himself. He would have fled back to their room but paused when Lisze stood as well.

"Thank you, Katrina. You set a lovely table. And Lord

Bierl, for the use of your horses. Giselle was an excellent guide to your beautiful holding." Lisze bowed to the young woman. "We will retire for a short while." She slipped her arm into Trillion's, and Wilm followed with Cesim beside him. The youth winked at Giselle, his new friend.

"We need to talk alone," Trillion said when they reached the hall.

Lisze smiled and paused for Wilm and Cesim to catch up. "You have time to explore the stables and paddocks." She lifted her brow to Cesim, and he gestured to the door leading to the courtyard.

"Off we go, lad. I will show you how to trim our steeds' hooves."

Once alone in their room, Trillion described Healer Trent's accusations and his suspicions about the potion. Lisze took one sniff and opened the window to dump the brew on the ground. She scoured the cup and bottle.

"I was right to not drink it." Relieved, yet mystified, Trillion shook his head. "What were his intentions? Poison?"

"Hard to know. Perhaps to make you sick, sending you home early?" Lisze sat at the other side of the table. "Trillion, your new life in Christ grows more evident every day. You care for others, give of yourself, and avoid the drinking halls to worship the Lord with us."

"While I played the part my brothers set for me, something held me back from completely giving myself to evil. Why did it take so long to find my sanity?" Trillion rose to pace. "I am forgiven. I have to remind myself that I am new in Christ. The old has passed away."

"With Trent's accusations, I think we should all leave after investigating Wolf's Bane."

Trillion turned to face her. "Lisze, my father asked me to find a way to reestablish relations with Worstein. They've had problems with some of the powerful leaders in their council using corrupt judges for their own gain. I will be going with

Lord Bierl to Invien Springs to find the survivor you told me about. Pray they will let Prince Joshua come to help them appoint fair judges."

Now that he had a family, he had to think about their needs too. "When I travel with Lord Bierl, would you want to stay here or go with the squad to Wolf's Bane?"

Lisze furrowed her brow. "Wilm and I would like to see the village. When I return to Airdle, I was thinking of working with Lady Jessica to raise aid and donations. And I am the squad's cook."

Trillion's face opened and he reached across the round table for his wife's hand. "The Ayisin have another word for husband or wife. The coming alongside of a man and woman, pledging themselves to one another, that God's will might go forth." His voice grew tender. "You have become such a life-mate to me."

"You are mine as I am yours. How have I never heard this word before?"

"The Ayisin remember well the earlier words many in Airdle and Dornan have forgotten."

"I see. Maybe that's why the best of the preachers hail from the Ayisin of Imbus and the woodsmen of Stoddard."

"My parents were truly lifemates."

"I saw her, Queen Lillian. I must have been eight or so. Her long black hair flowed down her back like a waterfall."

Trillion pulled aside, his breath catching.

Lisze cradled her hand in his. "I'm sorry, I didn't mean to bring up the past."

"Lisze, you can speak freely. You never have to worry if you'll hurt me. I hadn't realized how devastated my father had been with her death, hadn't perceived that no one came alongside to help him. We both grieved alone."

They gazed into each other's eyes until they heard a quick knock on the door.

Trillion said, "Come in."

The holding lord stepped in. Rising awkwardly, Trillion spouted a greeting.

Bierl looked about the large room. "I love these suites. Slip in here to get away once in a while. Have to remember not to barge in when we have guests. Sit?" He stoked the fire and drew a third chair around. "So how do you like Worstein, Lady Lisze?"

"It's beautiful."

"Prince Trillion, I know you've ridden it before. Lady Lisze, I've heard you've tamed our wild stallion."

"Merely challenged him to a good workout. He should carry one of your rangers who rides daily and would have need of his quick wits and fearless nature."

He nodded. "Glad my lovely wife heard this from someone other than me. She had secured him as my mount and for breeding, but he's gone wild without vigorous, daily exercise. I prefer a more settled mount, but she wants me to look the part. Lady Katrina will be going to Dunilian Market in a few days and welcomes your company. Will Wilm stay here with you?"

"We'll be going with the marshals to Wolf's Bane. I am their cook."

"You're the cook?"

"Yes, I've been on many excursions. My father taught me well."

"Yes, I remember Marshal Rothsum, a most impressive man." He furrowed his brow and looked at the couple. "Healer Trent was of the understanding you were not well. He mentioned you might require a wagon for your journey home. Remarkable recovery."

"God is good." Trillion squared his shoulders. "I'm fit to travel with you tomorrow."

"Well then, do you have a letter for me from the king?"

"A letter?" Trillion looked at Lisze. She widened her eyes in encouragement with a slight smile. "If this is a good time." He drew out the folded parchment from his pocket. "If it would please you, my lord. Would my son, Prince Wilm, be accepted as squire under your care? He's twelve now. That would be at the time of your choosing." Trillion held his breath as Bierl read the letter.

"It would be an honor. Did Aiden talk with you before they left?"

"No, I hadn't imagined he would be able to travel so soon. Sorry I missed him."

"He longed to be home. Best place to recuperate is in one's own bed. Felt ready to travel in a wagon we provided. Your healing touch has great benefit, Lady Lisze. Aiden was of the impression Wilm would be squiring here and extended an invitation for the young prince to spend time with the Imbus Ayisin on the plains during his time as squire. In years past, the people of Worstein and the Ayisin beyond Invien Ridge had been close. We would like to see those bonds of friendship renewed. If our peoples had not become strangers, they might not have mistaken Aiden for an enemy."

"It seems the further our people are from God, the further we are from each other," Trillion said.

"Quite right. It's as much a spiritual as a community issue. But how do you change a man's heart, even if you can force him to change his ways?"

"Faith is a gift. The transformation of God who works from the inside—one I wish I had discovered sooner." Trillion met Lisze's warm eyes.

"I spoke with Trent a little earlier. He had some warnings. Are you aware of his views?"

"He made them quite forcibly this morning and left a sleeping draught that he said had been at your request."

"Was it helpful?"

Trillion sat silently, rendered speechless for a moment. His days of speaking ill of others, sowing discord, had passed. "I hadn't the need. Rested well."

"I requested no such tonic and do not question your actions. Not all share our faith or understanding that when a man allows God to enter his soul, an incredible transformation can occur." Bierl relaxed in the chair, looking at the fire's glow.

"To be taken from darkness to light, from death to life, I couldn't imagine returning to my old ways."

"Our fine healer lacks faith. I know of your history, Prince Trillion. I can see the wonderful change in you. Don't lose faith or hope." He leaned closer. "You might have more to do in Worstein than you think."

"The gift of getting to know my son and my lovely wife." He reached for Lisze's hand. "I pray we have more time together."

"The Lord's gifts are without measure and more than we deserve. Let us never take them for granted."

Trillion felt the Spirit's urging. "Lord Bierl, Prince Joshua is most experienced in identifying corrupt judgments. Do I have leave to send for him?"

"Would your Marshal Rysen be involved?"

Trillion held back a knowing smile. So Rysen was an issue. "My lord, I would recommend that Marshal Karith provide the escort. His squad would be an asset to the effort. Could a ranger carry the dispatch to Stolein?"

He stared at the fire, shifted in his chair, and turned to Trillion. "You may send the dispatch. Give the package to Steward Ashin. He'll send a courier with instructions. They will be granted safe passage through Worstein."

They rose as one. "Thank you. I can't guarantee how soon he could arrive."

"Prince Trillion, I've found over the years that the Lord's timing, mysterious though it might seem to us, is never wrong." He bowed slightly to the couple. "Our home is your home. Take your rest. Walk the gardens."

"May Lisze peruse your library?"

"Of course. Ask any of the pages. They'll take you there if you've forgotten the way."

After he left, Trillion walked to the small table.

Lisze fetched his supply of parchment, quill, and ink. Setting them beside him, she sat on the opposite chair and noted the dark circles around his eyes and hollowed cheeks. "You have beautiful handwriting. Much better than mine."

"Is that so?" He wrote quickly and then rose to deliver the letter.

Lisze stood and reached for the folded, sealed letter. "I can take that. Not quite fully recovered, are you?"

He rubbed his forehead. "I've been delaying telling you. Few know of the damage the infections wrought. I'm pretty good with the leg." He met her gaze. "The fevers weakened my heart. I have to pace myself."

"You told Marshal Rysen?"

"I did." He stroked her hand. "I wanted to give it a little more time. See if perhaps the doctor was mistaken. After all, God could heal me."

She met his gaze. "I needed to know."

He squeezed her hands. "I have fewer days than most my age. I intend to put them to good use."

That evening, after last sup, Lord Bierl took Trillion aside. "My rangers and I will ride with you tomorrow to the village. We need to see what we're facing. You and I, with a few rangers, can travel to Invien Springs to find the boy. It's a short ride from Wolf's Bane."

The Spirit whispered assurances that he could make the journey. Trillion smiled. "How early do you want to leave?"

Bierl laughed. "When we're ready on the morrow."

Chapter 15

Wolf's Bane

Logan of Wolf's Bane crouched behind bushes at the edge of the forest a short distance from the narrow footpath not far from his home. Stillness hung in the empty village—no women hung their wash on the lines, no children raced through the yards, no older ones cleaned and mended the nets, no men prepared the day's catch for market. He had left his slingshot behind in the rush of that terrible night. It would be nice to have the slingshot so he could catch something to eat besides porridge and root stew.

He rose from his hiding place, confident all was still and that the Invien sheriff had left. Tentatively, he stepped from behind the shrubs. A click of metal on rock sounded in the distance. The road to Wolf's Bane, a small collection of houses nestled between a rocky shore and dense forest, had been worn down to bedrock in spots. He slunk back to his hiding place.

He looked down, unable to forget what had happened. The seer had kept them safe. Had told them not to trust the men from Invien. The fish merchants of Wolf's Bane never went alone to Invien Springs Market. They knew the ones they could trust, and even then, there was no friendship.

The sounds of many horses grew louder, with no calls or coarse jesting. Logan lifted his head and peered through a hole in the bushes, waiting for the column to come into view. The banner on the pole of the marshal next to an older man who rode with stiff back, sharp eyes, and insignia on his chest, hung limp in the still air. The horses held to a slow walk. The boy could not make out the herald or perceive the colors in the folded silk.

A guard, a squad, a troop of some sort. Had the men that night been dressed like this? That night, a visit to their small outhouse close to the woods had rendered him a hapless witness and one of the few survivors. Should he fetch the seer? He would have to watch to judge their intentions.

He noted the strung bows, unhooked swords, and fine steeds with dark eyes, champing at the bit. He squinted to make out another older rider with some gray peppering his hair whose warhorse trotted sideways, impatient with their cadence. Could that be the holding lord of Worstein?

Fear rose up, and he stilled his breath. The number of horses and armed riders convinced him not to run out. Some from Worstein, and a few Ayisin who didn't appear to look like the Keyayisin, rode with them. His town hadn't expected help from any of Worstein. The people of Wolf's Bane preferred to be left alone. The last four riders came into view, and Logan nearly fell into the bushes. He stepped out with a leg to stop his momentum but not in time to prevent rustling leaves. He slipped behind dense brush and stilled his movements when a figure looked in his direction. The face of a boy, not far from his age, wearing fancy riding clothes sat confidently astride a war horse.

"Mother," he heard the boy say in the voice of one who had not yet begun the change to manhood. "May I ride Thor to tire him out? He still wants to run!"

"Wilm, don't forget your chores. You are Master Cesim's helper. Find a good corral with lean-to, hay, and watering trough."

Logan leaned forward despite himself to see the kind face of a woman sitting tall in the saddle with two braids down her back. Her large war horse was alert and under her control. Logan remembered his mother and his heart nearly broke.

How had the seer known to come and rescue them? Perhaps the One had told him. Some whispered the mysterious man who lived in the forest wandered in the night. Had he discovered the attack by happenstance or did the God he followed truly care for them? Where did they go—the neighbors, the uncles and aunts, the basket weaver, the net and hook maker, his parents? Many children and some adults had fled to the safety of the woods. They met the seer on the path, and he led them to a hidden cave. Leaving them, he went to the village. Upon his return to the cave, he told them that their village had been emptied but for a few dead.

As the riders rounded the first set of small homes, Logan began to work his way behind the bushes to draw closer to the water's edge. The sound of a wagon drawing up between two huts on his left stopped his motion. Barely breathing, he watched the woman appear with the wagon following.

"We'll set up the cooking fire here." The woman gestured for a young horseman to turn the wagon's bed to face the firepit and the trail into the woods. Thankfully, she hadn't heard his slow, cautious steps to the bushes opposite their neighbor's firepit. What if they went down the path in search of firewood? He breathed more easily when a young man arrived with an armload of short logs.

Coal was rare, and few wished to venture too deeply into the dense forests by the village. Many set out their stones in the sunlight, and by afternoon, they were hot enough to roast fish fillets from the day's catch. His stomach churned and burbled. He almost stopped breathing when the woman paused and glanced his way as she carried a pot nestled in a skillet to the tripod set up over the pit.

Logan missed their midafternoon meals where he mostly felt full. Milk, nuts, and berries had begun their days. The main meal of roasted roots and fish fed them, with jerky to munch on before bed. He remembered then that he had originally come to dig for clams and oysters—for something familiar to bring to their small band. Where were the cows, the ones to give milk and the ones for a feast?

The lady sat on a short stool and set a bowl on her lap. She poured in fine flour, along with clumps of lard. Kneading it carefully, she added another powder. Before she poured water from a pitcher, she held out her hand to feel the heat emanating from the large frying pan suspended over a kindled fire. With a contented sigh, she reached into a small bag by her feet and added some berries with just the right amount of water for a sweet bannock. He tried not to drool. A pot held an assortment of beans and meats. With a little water and spices, the aroma of a fine meal almost drove him to step forward. Would they give him some?

But memories of the men with raised blades, the warnings of the seer, along with the closed, mean face of the warrior who stepped past the wagon removed all thoughts of revealing himself.

Logan held his position on the slight rise and waited.

Wilm approached his mother as she stirred the pot. "Ama, will it be ready soon?"

She raised her brow. "Chores done? All the horses watered, rubbed down?" Noticing his look, she asked, "What's that smile for?" Lisze drew her brows together. "He let you ride Thor."

"Ama! Like you said, he needs a lot of exercise."

"In a paddock, I hope?"

"Yes, we found a large paddock. He wasn't doing well with a few of the other horses. Lord Bierl let me ride him."

"You asked?"

"Yeah, but I think he wanted me to ask. He smiled and watched for a little bit."

"Thor minded you?"

"Yes, Ama."

"Remember, that one's smart enough to know the difference between a paddock and the open trail. You'd have had a fight on your hands."

"I'd show him who's in charge, as you say, Ama!"

She hid her smile and checked the bannocks cooling on a nearby stone.

"May I have a piece?" He leaned forward so others couldn't hear. "I'm really hungry, and sup doesn't look ready."

Lisze glanced about to ensure they were alone. "A little bite, to see if they're good."

Wilm dropped his hand for a piece and slipped a portion into his mouth. A rustle and a movement out of the corner of his eye raised the hairs on his neck.

Someone watched.

Trying to look relaxed, he turned slightly sideways and chewed, all the while scanning the bushes for movement.

Hearing shouts coming from his right, he turned back to his mother's firepit.

Lisze looked his way. "Find out and report."

Wilm followed the sounds into town. No mules or donkeys were in the pens, no dogs barked, not even a cat slithered past. Had an invisible hand bent down and swallowed the village up whole? Wilm wondered if some had escaped to the woods and were watching even now. If he had the chance, he would ask Master Cesim to request a search of the forest. If only he were older, larger, he could have gone himself.

Wilm smelled the garbage pit before he could make his way past several rangers watching Rysen, his father, and Nisayin, one of the Ayisin, sift through the remains.

Rysen stated, "The village dogs. This is where they are." He bent down and examined a bloody hide, lower legs, and furry tail. "Two donkeys and a steer, looks like butchered for meat."

Nisayin carefully pulled a dog's carcass aside to reveal a hand. He glanced up and saw Wilm behind the three who had come with him. With a flick of his head, the other two looked at Wilm. "No place for children here!"

Before he could embarrass himself further with his burning cheeks, he turned to go. When several rangers arrived carrying more bodies, Wilm hovered beside a nearby house. He heard one say, "We found many slain in their beds."

Wilm headed back to Ama. This time he saw the bushes bend and sway, and not by any breeze. Acting as if he had seen nothing, he continued to the firepit. "Ama, they found bodies. Some were killed in their homes, but they sent me away. Plus two donkeys, a steer, and several dogs. I think the rangers are going house to house. The invaders seemed to have been in a hurry because the donkey hides had large clumps of meat. The legs had been hacked off."

Logan tried not to cry. Perhaps a whimper had sounded despite himself, and the boy had turned to look at the woods again. Had he been seen? Both of the donkeys slain! While Clam and Shrimp weren't beautiful, they had been his friends, braying when they saw him, looking for the roots he brought. He had to be patient. Once the cook called for sup, they would gather by the wagon. Plates and forks had already been piled on an opened tailgate.

He watched mother and son carefully. When they turned away from the forest, he inched his way along, for he had to travel to the next part—the section closest to the beach and far away from the men. The bushes thinned, crowded out by groups of white trunks with peeling bark.

Wiping his eyes, he paused. Too many still dug through the pile. They had laid out the dogs, and he held back more cries. He counted ten—more than half. Perhaps the wild ones had fled. He turned his head when the rangers brought more bodies and laid them apart from the others. They studied the cuts, discussing what weapons might have caused them. When they looked away, he slunk past the largest gap to a ridge with a tall tree and slipped behind a clump of bushes.

Logan eyed a tree, working through the best spots for climbing. Most of the men faced the pit. Every so often, one of their short swords in its scabbard would catch the last rays of the sun, reminding him of the death they could bring. He would wait, force himself to count the bodies, maybe even go closer to see. Tears fell, tracked down his cheek, and wet his hand.

They seemed intent on their task, even ignoring the call to sup. Half went, but the older ones stayed. One took notes on a thick leather board. Logan tried to be patient, but his leg wanted to twitch, and his back ached from hiding. As the light failed, he wondered if the seer noticed he had been gone.

Eventually, the area cleared. He carefully made his way and tilted his head to view the corpses lined up. Stilling his heart, he couldn't count for the number was too high—aged grandfathers, silver-haired women, the town's invalid, children, and infants. Aisling had escaped with her baby. He placed a hand on the ground to steady himself when he recognized her husband. She had said that he had called out the warning and tried to stop the invaders.

Logan could see well enough to make it through the white woods, but the back trail, obscured by tall trees, had an inky blackness with greedy fingers. Yet, he had to return that night to the cave to warn the others and tell the seer of the group camping in their village. He tried to walk carefully, hoping his eyes would adjust to the darkness. Stumbling over a root, he fell to his knees.

Say a prayer to that God, Logan argued with himself. The short, quiet people of Wolf's Bane kept to themselves, preferring the solitude of fishing or diving in the ocean over crowded markets and towns. Long had they bitterly complained of the church people who would often be the ones to cheat them. Yet the seer had told wondrous stories of a merciful God who loved them.

"Jesus, help me get back." A feeble prayer with little hope, yet the moon emerged from behind clouds and shone rays of light on the path. He set out and remembered to say, "Thank You, Lord, if You are there."

Eventually he recognized the area not far from the cave and drew close enough to hear voices. His heart warmed. Wherever they were, they were his people, his tribe. That made the cave home, for now.

All heads turned when he stepped into the cave. The seer stood quickly and then smiled, pointing with his chin to a place in the circle. They would talk later, he hoped. The old man continued with his story of the end of the ages and the Lord of Glory coming to rid the world of all wickedness. The images of the bodies lined up refused to leave his mind. That death had come to them, and the others had vanished, caused shivers to form.

After final prayers, the seer led him outside.

"You were gone a long time." He studied the quiet boy in the dim light of glowing embers in a fire pan. "You went back?"

"Yes."

"Did any see you? Follow you? We do not know if we can trust them."

Logan gathered his courage. "Horsemen came with swords and bows. They looked at the bodies." He described what he had seen, his voice empty of emotion. "I returned in the dark." He would have mentioned his prayer, but he felt frozen inside.

"The boy and his mother. Did they share their names?"

He searched his memory and said, "Mother . . . Wilm,

Master Cesim. The one called Mother rode a warhorse like a marshal. She had a bow and a short sword. Even Wilm, a boy my age, I think, had a blade on his belt. There were Ayisin with them, perhaps from Imbus, not Keyayisin. I think Lord Bierl of Worstein."

"I know the lord of that holding," the seer said. "Sorry, carry on. Not from Invien Springs. Maybe Airdle marshals, Worstein rangers, and Ayisin from Imbus? A puzzle." He looked aside for a moment. "Find your bedroll. Tomorrow will take care of itself. Seek peace in rest, Logan."

He followed the seer to the cave and found his place. How could he sleep? The images of the empty village threatened to overcome him. *Lord, if You're there, help me sleep.*

Chapter 16

Wilm Meets the Seer

L isze kept her seat on the log next to Trillion and Wilm. She held her peace when Marshal Rysen ordered two young marshals to dismantle the tripod and clean the pots and dishes.

"Do I have to set up again tomorrow morning?" She kept her voice low, asking when the head marshal had left.

"They found a suitable house for our headquarters while we're here," Trillion said.

"These are people's homes! How can we move in?"

"We'll only be here long enough for a thorough search. The people are not here right now, and it's easier to defend ourselves in a home than out in the open."

"I don't want to cook in a stranger's kitchen—especially when I've not been invited."

Trillion sighed. He recognized that tone. Time and prayer might settle her mood. "Shall we find our assigned room?"

They rose, headed for their packs, and walked the main road to the center of town and the only two-story, stone building.

"A poor village indeed," Lisze said.

The doorways were low, along with the ceilings, and they bent slightly not to hit the doorframe with their heads. A narrow kitchen gave way to formal dining and sitting rooms. Some bookcases along the back held some volumes. The narrow stairs creaked under their weight.

Trillion headed straight to the double bed on a tall frame. Lisze rolled out two mats for Wilm.

"Ama," he said after she heard his prayers. "I think . . . did you feel?"

"That someone was watching? I did for a moment."

"Two times I thought I heard sounds. One time I saw the bushes move."

"Yet, no one's come charging in."

"Will they search the woods? I think they should. Some might have hidden there, and they might not know they can trust us." Wilm searched his mother's face.

"We're definitely not in charge, but I will inform Lord Bierl."

She bent to kiss him goodnight after their prayers.

The next day, Trillion mounted Kewatin to ride beside Lord Bierl. Two rangers followed. They headed east on the road out of the village a little way before crossing Invien River on a worn bridge. The town was farther east down a wide road.

Lord Bierl glanced at Trillion. "We'll head straight for the orphanage."

The pretty town of Invien Springs came into view. Concentric rows of modest homes circled the main business area. Their chapel's cross rose above the rooftops. Bierl took a fork to the road that skirted the town. They turned left toward the eastern end. Trillion frowned when he saw large wood buildings not quite resembling barns. "What are those?"

"Workshops." Bierl's mouth set in a firm line. "They think they've found something new—creating spaces for people to work on their trades instead of in their homes." He tilted his head toward a tall, light-stoned, three-story building. "The orphanage."

Trillion took in the small, dingy windows, trampled dirt

in front of the building, with a scratched door missing half its paint in the center of the long building.

Bierl had one ranger keep the horses, and they entered a dark, musty hall. They walked to the first door with a large window. He tapped a few times and pushed it open.

"Master Besiel, Lord Bierl, head of Worstein Council, greets you."

A tall, slender man with sunken cheeks and shifty eyes rose. He walked around his desk and bent for a sweeping bow. "Lord Bierl, master of Weirstone. It is good to see you. Has Lady Katrina accompanied you, or has she sent you on an errand of mercy?" His eyes gleamed, as if in anticipation of gifts.

"I am here to see the lad of Wolf's Bane who arrived a few days ago. What is his name? Fetch him."

"My lord, many orphans come here regularly. I would have to consult my books." His gaze shifted away.

"Don't bandy words with me, Besiel. I know you've heard of Wolf's Bane emptying and the one who fled to your fair city for aid and comfort." Bierl leaned forward, his voice deepening. "Bring him to me at once!"

"He's not here."

"What?"

"Well, he's . . ." The man worked to catch his breath as his eyes darted about. "The boy, I recall he goes by Fillan, was old enough to be assigned to a tradesman."

"You put him to work already?"

"We can't accommodate all who need shelter. Those old enough to work are allowed to live near their masters."

"Where is Fillan?"

"He's up the road working for the tanner. But the tradesman has already paid for the boy to serve him for the next year."

"You sold him!"

"No. He'll be given food, clothes, whatever he needs, in

exchange for his service. Consider him an apprentice. The payment covers our expenses."

Trillion watched Bierl work to contain his anger.

"Provide directions." Bierl leaned in. "I'm curious, how many coins did he pay?"

Besiel swallowed. "Five, my lord." He stepped behind the safety of his desk. "I'll provide a map."

They quickly exited the building and mounted. "I see we'll have to investigate this orphanage, but we must first set Fillan free." Bierl turned Thor to the eastern road, and they set off at a fast trot. Past the town's limits, they transitioned to a hard gallop.

The tanner's workshop was a sprawling complex of low buildings by a tiny stone house. The smell of death and astringents filled the air. Several large vats and stretching racks occupied lean-tos jutting out from the barns. Trillion noted the stages of tanning and finishing a hide.

Bierl brought Thor to a halt and surveyed the young people in tattered clothes laboring at various stations. His eyes shifted to Trillion. "Shall we?"

They both dismounted, but he signaled the rangers to remain upon their steeds.

A broad man with rough hands and a stained leather apron walked up. His pockmarked face, with tangled hair pulled back, stared at them with beady eyes.

He asked sharply, "What do you want?"

"I am Lord Bierl."

"I know who you are. Have you brought a hide for tanning?"

"We are here for Fillan." Bierl leaned forward when the man spread his feet and put his hands on his hips.

"He's mine for the next year."

"We were told you paid five coins for him." Bierl reached for his money pouch.

"I'd need more than that, seeing I'm out a year's labor."

"How old is he? If he's underage, he cannot be signed as an apprentice without a proper guardian."

"I'd need ten coins." The large man shifted, the muscles in his arms bunching. His eyes flicked between the rangers and the two finely dressed lords glaring at him.

Trillion pulled out his wallet. "I can pay the rest."

Bierl exhaled sharply and brought out five coins from his bag.

The tanner closed his fingers over the payment.

"Call Fillan. We are leaving with him."

"Fillan, come!" the tanner yelled as if the boy were a dog.

A short, slender youth turned from stirring a large vat and headed their way. He glanced at the well-dressed visitors and stood before the tanner with downcast eye.

"These men will take you."

The youth stepped back with fear in his eyes. Bierl reached out a hand. "Fillan, we've come to take you home. Would you like that?"

Fillan smiled and looked at them for the first time. He scrambled up behind a ranger, clutching tightly to the saddle.

They took the road skirting the town. Bierl looked at Trillion. "Thank you. You kept me from giving in to the temptation of sending that man to his eternal reward."

"There will be a time and place for that, I fear." Trillion shifted Kewatin to a canter once they reached the open road. Lamoria's troubles reached beyond foreign invaders, to the very heart of her people. *Lord, save our land, revive us!*

They reached Wolf's Bane in a short time. Cesim walked up to them. Trillion glanced about for his wife. "Is Lisze in the house?"

"She's set up in the kitchen preparing sup. Wilm's wandering about somewhere. I'll get him. He wanted to meet the boy."

"His name is Fillan." Trillion watched Cesim walk down the road. He turned back when some of the rangers and marshals gathered around them.

Lord Bierl brought Fillan to his side. "Everyone, this is Fillan."

"Young man, we have come to help. Please tell us what happened." Lord Bierl tried to encourage him with a smile.

Everyone listened gravely to the story. "And you were the only one to survive?" Trillion asked.

"Many of the children ran into the woods, and some tried to swim away. But there's a terrible riptide near the village. I hope some made it. They didn't come back." Seeing their shaking heads, he looked down.

"Tell us about this ship and their boats."

"The ship was huge." Fillan tried to describe it.

One of the marshals drew an outline of a large sloop with ten oars.

"No." Fillan drew a tall, enclosed ship many times larger.

"Did you recognize their speech?" Trillion asked.

"No, their words were strange—harsh—more like the Amhavran but very fast." He described where the ship anchored and how the soldiers took the people in boats.

After Trillion, Bierl, and Fillan headed toward the largest home chosen for temporary quarters, Cesim and Wilm ran up to meet them.

Trillion hugged his son. "Wilm, you told us last night you thought someone had been watching." He directed his gaze toward Fillan. "Could some be hiding in the forest?"

Fillan tilted his head as if in thought. "Only the seer lives in the woods. Maybe they are with him."

Lisze arrived and announced noon sup was ready.

After the meal, the group continued asking Fillan questions.

When Lord Bierl said it was time to bring Fillan to the pit of the slain, Trillion told Wilm to go and play.

Wilm explored the forest's edge and found a narrow, well-worn trail. He entered the forest canopy and paused, waiting for his eyes to adjust. His nerves jumped, and he clamped down his surging imagination. The woods, still as stone and silent, felt heavy. He ventured a little way in and checked behind him for the way out, remembering Cesim's lessons.

The path held the footprints of many having passed through recently. In time he saw a boy even shorter than Fillan. He smiled.

"I'm Wilm. What's your name?"

"Logan." He stood for a moment, staring at the youth in fancy clothes.

"Are there others? Where are they? Were you watching us?"

He nodded. "We had to make sure you weren't from Invien Springs. When I saw the horsemen were kind to Fillan, I knew we could go home." He turned his head. "Look, they're close."

Wilm watched Logan's face light up when he talked about returning. Did he know what had happened? "Did you see the pit?"

Logan looked at him with determined eyes. "Yes, I told the seer. Everyone knows. But Wolf's Bane is our home."

Wilm glanced down the trail. A few women and a man, along with many children, followed an older man wearing an overcoat down to his feet. He carried a walking stick. Perhaps he was the seer. Wilm stepped aside to let them pass.

He had heard of seers. They often resisted being called prophets to avoid people thinking they spoke with the authority of the prophets of the Leaves of God. But they heard from God, sometimes in visions or dreams with God's message for the days at hand. And some for the days ahead. Wilm remembered the test for whether a seer was true or false—if his words aligned with the Leaves of God and the prophesied events came to pass.

The seer stopped beside him. "Go on to the village. It's safe now." He encouraged them to find their way home.

"We bring help," Wilm said, wanting them to feel safe.

The strange man peered at him and glanced up toward the leafy canopy. As if dreaming with eyes wide open, frozen in place, his mouth moved but no words could be heard. Then he looked at Wilm again with sorrow in his eyes and a slight smile.

"Remain here, young prince."

A shock ran through Wilm. This man felt strange, yet he felt the Spirit's assurance. This was a man of God. How had the seer known he was a prince?

Once they were alone, the seer drew a small flask from his belt. "Young man. What is your name and the names of your father and mother?"

Wilm bowed slightly. "I am Wilm of Airdle. My father is Prince Trillion, and my mother is Lady Lisze."

"What is her parentage? Is she also of Airdle?"

"No, her father was Marshal Rothsum of the Sanderfield, and her mother was Lady Elwin of Dornan."

The boy looked familiar, bearing the face of the kings of Airdle. *This is the one.* The seer faltered, and Wilm stepped forward to steady his arm.

"Kneel before me, Prince Wilm."

He knelt, forcing himself not to quiver.

"Do you know the Lord Jesus Christ? Do you seek to learn of the Leaves of God and follow in the footsteps of the Lord of Glory?" The man paused, flask in hand.

"I do." The strange older man pulled down his chin and lifted a vial over his head. Frozen, unable to move, he felt a glow of life rise in his chest as if a warm fire had been kindled.

"Prince Wilm, I anoint you king of Lamoria. May you rejoice in the Lord your God and adhere to His ways. May He deliver your enemies into your hand. May you bring peace and justice, rule with wisdom and righteousness. May none stand against you." The oil dripped down over his hair. Shock, joy, mixed with dread close behind. How could this be?

The man of God grasped the boy's shoulders to lift him up, feeling their heft and power. *This one will rule, and he will take vengeance on enemies but not yet.*

"The thing is certain, but it is not soon. Learn of man and beast, field and court. You will have many hard journeys, but the Lord will never forsake you." He bent closer and kissed both cheeks. "Tell no one of this until the time."

Wilm watched him disappear down the path. As if having returned from a far journey, he stumbled but did not fall.

"Tell no one," the man had said.

Wilm pondered the anointing. His father was the youngest prince with three brothers and their sons ahead in the line of accession. What disaster lay ahead in days to come that would remove all his Airdle uncles and cousins from this earth?

"Tell no one until the time," echoed in his mind.

When would that be? How would he know?

The Spirit moved within, and he recalled his parents talking about trusting God instead of fear. He would know when the time came. God would tell him.

Wilm turned, momentarily uncertain of the way back. He studied the ground, listening carefully to the distant voices of the people returning home, and he ran toward the sounds.

The figure of the seer in his robe came first into view.

Everything felt very strange now.

Wilm quickened his steps as the afternoon light increased with the lessening of the dense, leafy canopy. Cries of joy and laughter filtered through the air. He emerged to see the children and many of the rangers crowded round the seer and the children beside him. For an instant, it was as if he saw the Lord with His arms outstretched gathering His children before Him.

Running to join them, he saw Fillan rushing to Lord Bierl's side.

"Lord Bierl, we must keep them from going to their homes until they have been cleansed," he said.

The holding lord called to the nearest rangers with orders to check every house and clean them well.

His mother stepped toward them. "Hi Fillan. I'm Lady Lisze and am preparing sup. Where do you gather for community feasts?" After he told her, she leaned forward. "Maybe the older children can start a few games while I cook. I'll try to be quick. They must be famished."

Trillion walked up to Logan and Wilm. "Let the games begin!"

Fillan and Logan led everyone not cleaning or cooking to a level grove within sight of the sea with benches and short chairs around a stone-lined firepit.

Logan walked beyond the gathering place to a wide, mown field. "We can play games here."

Trillion let the older boys organize the children. They quickly divided into teams and were intent on a game. He tilted his head when Rysen came to stand beside him.

The marshal said, "Things seem well in hand. I assume Worstein Council will care for their own, as they have so vigorously attested. Our liege's charge for this mission was clear—to discover the matter and assess the risks to the realm. We've seen enough here." He pointed with his chin to the growing throng. "This type of news spreads quickly, and several have already returned. I think our time here is done." He stared at Trillion. "We leave today. Prepare your people."

Trillion straightened his jerkin. "I received a charge from our king to discover what aid we could render to these people. This is how we will remind Worstein Council that Lamoria is one. Also, Lord Bierl has invited us to linger. I'll send my report when it's complete."

Rysen didn't need to know about his letter to Prince Joshua.

In less than a turn, Rysen and his squad headed south for the King's Highway.

Chapter 17

Mayor Enoch

The seer emerged from the main house in an embroidered vest over a linen tunic and deerskin breeches. He directed the children and rangers to gather blankets. The children sat in small groups with a ranger beside them. Others brought the meal and handed out plates filled with food.

Yet they waited for the one who had exchanged a seer's garb for that of a mayor to give the blessing. He looked at everyone with misty eyes. "God provides." Wetting his lips, he said, "Today, I take up the name I had been given upon my father's knee. I am Enoch, Fillan's grandfather. I had been the mayor. Most of you are too young to remember me."

He bowed his head. "Oh Lord, let this be the beginning, not the end. We are thankful for the help and provision You sent. Bless us, let us walk with You and thank You for this food. May it nourish us. In the name of Jesus Christ, ever our Lord and Savior." Lifting his head, he spread his arms. "Eat, enjoy."

After Fillan finished his plate, he stepped toward the one called Enoch. "You are my grandfather?"

"I am." He bent to hug his grandson for the first time. "I watched you walk by the woods when you were young." He straightened and gazed at him. "Fillan, take me to the place where the House of God once stood."

They walked to the firepit near the grove. Wilm noticed their leave-taking and went to join them.

Wilm stood beside Fillan.

"I see two before me." Enoch looked at both of them.

"Grandson, have the offerings to the gods been removed from the grove?"

"No, Grandfather."

"Are you covered by the blood of Christ?"

Fillan drew his brows together.

Wilm said, "Have you asked Jesus to save you from your sin? It's easy. You only have to ask in your heart. Don't even have to speak it aloud. Pray. God will forgive and cleanse your soul."

"That is a decision each must make on his own." Enoch rested his hand on his grandson's shoulder. "Fillan, make fire." The seer prayed for their protection. "Covered by the blood of Christ, there is no condemnation, and the wicked spirits have no hold over us." He turned to Wilm. "Prince, assist me in removing the amulets and figures tied to the trees."

The seer went from tree to tree, carefully removing the baubles and amulets tied to the lowest branches. They were cast into a large basket Wilm found nearby. When they walked over to a tree with baskets of gifts or figurines placed beside its trunk, he had Wilm add them to the collection.

Fillan's large fire had drawn a crowd when they returned with the overflowing basket. The seer dumped the contents in front of himself and called for an assembly. When all had gathered round, he said, "Years I prayed and fasted in the forest. You know me as the seer, a name I at first rejected for I am a man, like any other man. The Lord's protection was ever with me. The fearsome beasts that hide there, remnants from the age before the flood, could not touch me."

There were so few remaining, mostly children and a few adults. Yet God could work even with few. "Welcome to those who have returned. All who are of Wolf's Bane, step forward." Enoch singled out the men of the village. "Come stand beside me."

When all were in place and the fire refreshed, he began. "I fled Wolf's Bane when the old ways returned. With the passing of our lawreader and the burning of the House of God, I despaired. Retreating to the forest, I fasted and prayed for God's judgment to fall. We who had been so highly blessed with the coming of the Leaves of God, who had known the ways of the Lord's grace and mercy, had turned back to Satan's lies. We sought the future through omens, skin-walkers, and those who talk to wicked spirits. Many set up images of this world and worshiped them." Enoch stepped back and swung his arm over the pile of offerings. "In time, God showed me that He is not only judge but also the loving Savior, waiting to forgive. God the Father desires that all men be saved. Judgment tarries to give time for people to choose to love Him in return, trust Him, follow Him.

"See the pile of amulets, gifts, and trinkets from the grove of white trees." Enoch lifted his hands and spread them wide. With a voice of power and authority, he said, "I am redeemed, a child of God, filled with His Spirit, covered by the blood of Christ. Mighty Lord, cast out the dark ones from this place. Set a hedge about Wolf's Bane. Drive out the dark spirits from the woods and cleanse our grove! Call us back to You!"

Enoch lowered his hands to hover over the people. "You have been created by God to walk with Him. Turn now to the Savior. Call on Jesus that you may be whole in Him. He has the power to place you into God's family. Be made His child, if you seek and ask. Never forget, dear ones, beloved of the Lord, if the Mighty God is for us, nothing and no one can steal us away from our Father God." The skin crinkled around his eyes with his broad smile. "Do you choose this day to follow God?"

"Yes, we do," many said.

Wilm held his breath. In his few years, he had not felt such darkness or light. He prayed for these people to find Christ.

"Then throw these vile objects into the fire. May we

remember this day that God tests all to see if their hearts are set upon Him. That God saves to the uttermost those who draw near to Him. There is not one sin we can do that would prevent our transformation when we ask."

He stepped aside, and the men threw everything into the fire. One began a song of praise to God. Many joined in harmonious worship. Enoch lifted up both hands. "'The LORD bless you and keep you; the LORD make his face shine upon you and be gracious to you; the LORD lift up his face toward you and give you peace.'"

Trillion looked at Enoch, surprised. He had uttered a blessing reserved for the king, beginning with King Aaron. Each generation had honored that tradition.

Yet, that is what it was—mere tradition of men. The Leaves of God stated believers were called priests. Could not one who had given his life to pray for his village extend that blessing to his own? He frowned. Perhaps that is where Lamoria had begun to turn, by choosing to rely on the king and lawreaders to guard their faith.

When he caught Enoch's eye, he smiled and nodded his head in agreement.

On the next Lord's Day, all gathered for the first assembly of worship to the Lord of Glory. Lord Bierl encouraged Enoch to lead.

Enoch's words at the fire by the grove echoed in Trillion's mind—saved to the uttermost. As he sang, he knew that he had been rescued by God and no force of darkness or evil intentions could keep him from his heavenly home. May the turning begin at Wolf's Bane and spread throughout Lamoria.

A few days later Lord Bierl and his company prepared to return to Weirstone. Four of the rangers volunteered to watch over the village and help them restore, rebuild, and renew. Word spread quickly throughout Worstein, and many returned to the remote village. Prayers for the community, donations, and willing workers began to arrive. The seer agreed to live in the mayor's house and oversee the restoration. For the first time in years, all assembled on the Lord's Day for prayer and worship.

As they headed toward Weirstone the next day, Wilm pondered the seer's words in the forest. Many had warned him not to put too much stock in prophecies. On their way back to the castle, to a boy under the watchful eye of Master Cesim, that future seemed dim and far away. Yet, he never forgot that empty village, the dark forest, or the oil running down his hair.

Wilm returned his father's smile and urged his horse to walk beside his. They shared their joy with Wolf's Bane turning to God again. Trillion said, "May this spark light fires of salvation throughout the land."

Keeping pain and fatigue at bay, Trillion prayed for the strength to do God's will.

Chapter 18

Return to Weirstone

Trillion, followed by Lisze, Wilm, and Cesim, entered the main stable last. He dismounted and held Kewatin's reins. Pain radiated up his left side, and his chest felt full. He barely noticed Lisze call Wilm to take care of Tesla. He watched listlessly as she unhooked his saddle bags.

"Trillion?" When he tried to bend to pick up his bedroll, she said, "I can get that."

Before they exited the barn, he saw Cesim secure Kewatin with ties to groom him. He forced himself to walk evenly to Weirstone's main entrance. Lisze slowed to match his steps. Trying to allay her fears, he said, "Merely spent. Need rest, that's all."

At least there were only a few steps up to the main door, carved with images he suspected were of the earlier times—scrolls of waves, outlines of a large bird with horned head, along with the seven-branched candlestick, palm trees, and cherubim described in the Leaves of God.

Steward Ashin greeted them at the door. "My lord and lady, a filling repast will be provided in the dining hall."

Lisze curtsied. "We will freshen and rest in our room. Send a page when sup is ready."

The steward bowed and stepped aside. "Will you need a warm bath?"

"The wash basin and pitcher will be sufficient, thank you."

Trillion slowed as even the slight jarring from ascending the steps had increased his discomfort. He welcomed Lisze's firm hand on his upper arm.

In the room, he shed his vest and stood staring at his dusty breeches.

"I saved a clean set of clothes before we left." She pulled out fresh breeches and a tunic. "Wash up quickly and you can lie down."

Trillion almost complained about her hovering but had to admit he was thankful for her care. "I will rest."

"Hungry?"

"Not really." At least she let him slip on the clean clothes by himself. He lay down, expecting her to attend to her needs, but she sat on the side of the bed.

"You are in pain." Lisze bent down and pressed an ear to his chest, listening for breath sounds.

"What is the prognosis, fair healer?" Trillion tried a light-hearted jest, but she smoothed aside some stray hairs and bent to smell his breath.

"Your breathing is hindered on your left side, and your breath is not as fresh as I'd like." She tilted her head. "Tell me truly, how do you feel?"

"Riding faster than a walk wrapped pain around my chest. My left lung feels full, yet otherwise seems clear. I am exhausted after a little more than a half-day's ride." His hand lingered on her. "But I am not feverish. It seems I must turn to clerical work over that of a marshal."

"No one knows the future. Healer Anselm taught me how to make your tonics and which teas to prepare. Having lounged around the castle for the summer, hiding away in the Garden Suites, you've done remarkably well. Rest, and I'll brew your teas."

Trillion held in his groan. Would he always be weak? When he heard metal grating on metal, his eyes opened to see his enterprising wife suspend a small camp pot over a revived fire. "Yum, more herbal concoctions. Did I tell you I enjoy them?"

"Never." Lisze rose and felt his hand. Indeed, it was not

hot, but cool and somewhat clammy. "Good we are free to speak truly to one another."

Trillion began to doze. Sounds of someone entering barely reached his consciousness until he recognized Lord Bierl's voice. He pushed to sit up and swing his feet over the bedside. "I'm fine, my lord. Need some rest."

Bierl narrowed his eyes and watched the prince have difficulty sitting up.

"I'll call Healer Trent."

Lisze said, "My lord, we told you of his visit to Prince Trillion but did not reveal that the sleeping broth had been tainted. I would not trust him to attend to the prince. Is there a noted healer in a nearby community we could call?"

Bierl furrowed his brow. "Why hadn't you spoken of this earlier?"

Trillion pushed himself to his feet and walked to the nearest chair. "That no harm had been done I did not wish to speak ill of another. If I may, Lord Bierl. There is something else you need to hear."

When Bierl sat, Trillion asked, "Does Judge Severn still serve Worstein Council?"

"He is the Supreme Judge of the council."

"Is he well known to Healer Trent?"

"He is. In fact, our esteemed judge recommended him to me."

Trillion paused to catch his breath. "The judge might have a part in the council's troubles. Severn instructed Lord Nordrum, Lady Lisze's uncle, in how to petition a Dornan judge to transfer Rothsum's land to his holding. Judge Severn was the one who carried Nordrum's proposal to have me stop Lisze from finding their land grant sealed by the king's signet ring. He arranged the payment when she fled Airdle. I fear your well-known judge is at the heart of your problems, and I don't trust Trent."

"Why would a Dornan holding lord seek to meddle in our affairs?"

"Not Nordrum, my lord, but Prince David. From his estate at Roanin, he has turned many of Airdle's and Tholen's judges to see his favor done. Judge Severn advises them where to file their cases to receive favorable decisions. He has instructed the judges on how to write up the matters of particular cases so they will pass Supreme Judge Joshua's scrutiny."

Trillion recalled his time helping distract Lisze at Airdle. "I know Prince David has used his influence and power to sway decisions for the benefit of his landed, wealthy friends in Dornan and Tholen. After all, as the crown prince, he has the king's ear."

Bierl sat forward, his jaw dropping. "Are you certain? These are serious charges."

"I observed this while helping Nordrum take Lisze's land, I am ashamed to say. Also, shortly before my accident, I heard a Tholen marshal boast that Prince David would soon control Worstein."

"That is hard to believe. Any such miscarriage of justice in my holding is swiftly investigated. We seek impartial judgments, not favoring either the rich or poor, as the Leaves of God direct."

"I'm sorry to be the one to bring this to you." Trillion rose. "Lord Bierl, does not Supreme Judge Severn review cases to assure justice is done? Judges can be turned, as well. Once a favor is done, they are reminded that their actions have been recorded and stored away." Trillion rested his hand on the table to steady himself. "When we go to the orphanage with Prince Joshua, we should be accompanied by a full ranger squad and marshals. Before I saw the orphanage and the indentured servitude of those young people, I had considered recommending that you act on your own, without the help of the House of Airdle. But, if Prince David has already begun to subvert your largest cities, there is no time to waste."

Bierl stood and extended his hand. "Then I pray you can regain your strength."

Trillion grasped the holding lord's forearm and laid a closed fist on his own chest. Tilting his head forward slightly, he said, "Since my heart change, I have set myself to restore Lamoria. May we see God's justice rule throughout our land."

"My prayers as well, fair prince. May the Lord's favor speed our way and bring their plans to confusion."

After he left, Trillion lay down. Lisze sat beside him.

"Talking with the holding lord was better than my teas? I see your visage brightened somewhat."

He held down a laugh. "I see you jest. I am relieved he believed me." His hand traveled down her arm. He felt her hand accept his grip. "The days I lived by lies and deception are gone."

"Sleep, rest. I will bring up soup and soft bread in a little while. But I am famished and want to check on our son." Lisze paused by the door. "Let us pray the Lord moves at Invien Springs as He has at Wolf's Bane."

Trillion watched her leave. "May it be so."

Prince Joshua arrived a few days later, escorted by Marshal Karith and five of his marshals, along with Worstein rangers. A courier had brought news of their arrival and Lord Bierl, Trillion, Lisze, and Wilm waited for a tired Prince Joshua to walk up the steps with Marshal Karith beside him. Lord Bierl bowed. "Greetings Prince Joshua, Marshal Karith. Did you make the trip from Stolein in one day?"

"Yes, never imagined traversing such a distance in a day. Naturally, I usually proceed at a civilized pace." Prince Joshua extended his hand. "Lord Bierl, I appreciate the chance to serve Worstein."

"Please come in." Bierl looked at the steward waiting

by the stairs. "Steward Ashin, please take Prince Joshua and Marshal Karith to their quarters."

The steward bowed and directed a page standing beside him to take their bags.

"Lord Bierl, won't I billet with my marshals?" Karith asked.

"Marshal Karith, your guest room awaits. Our rangers have prepared rooms for your men at our ranger station. When you are ready, join us for sup."

The family waited in the dining hall for their guests to arrive.

Wilm asked, "Aba, how can Marshal Karith also be a way station keeper?"

"Most of the larger way stations are run by marshals—important marshals. He had been my instructor and mentor."

"Were you friends?"

Trillion had to speak the truth. "Not really. Marshal Karith is a faithful Christian who tried to dissuade me from my sinful ways. He could have been a good friend if I had not wasted those years." He looked at his son. "But God works all things for good, Wilm. He gave us you."

Wilm's attention was drawn away when Prince Joshua and Karith entered.

Wilm stepped forward to greet the middle-aged marshal. "Hello, Marshal Karith. It is good to see you."

Karith gave a slight bow and asked, "Now that you are Prince Wilm, are you different?"

Several laughed, and Wilm looked at his mother. "No, I don't think so. I have to wear formal clothes, but I think I'm adjusting."

"Wilm, when did you meet the esteemed Keeper of Stolein Way Station?" Trillion asked.

"He stopped by Clefisch Pass several times, though not recently."

Prince Joshua mentioned they had brought coin to

aid Wolf's Bane. "I knew we would be traveling swiftly and wouldn't be able to accommodate wagons."

Lord Bierl accepted the prince's hand. "Many thanks. Our leading ladies are still gathering supplies from the list we had drawn up. I will direct you to the treasurer for its safe keeping."

Trillion added, "A few days ago I dispatched my report to the king with the items they needed. It was good to see many from outlying communities arrive to help repair the boats and fix their homes."

As the meal drew to a close and Marshal Karith left to check on his marshals, Lord Bierl said, "Prince Joshua, we can discuss the matter of the judges on the morrow."

"I need to hear the details immediately. I will hardly be able to sleep without having an idea of the nature of your concerns."

"Very well, we can talk privately in my library."

When Trillion stood to join them, Wilm rose too. He turned to his son. "Wilm, don't you want to play games with the others in the drawing room?"

Wilm directed his attention to his uncle. "Prince Joshua, may I go with you?"

"So you think you have something to share?" Prince Joshua asked with tilted head.

"I might."

"Prince Wilm, we will be discussing weighty matters, aspects of the law. You might become bored."

"Prince Joshua, I apologize for not having paid attention in class, especially yours when you would come to talk about God's law." He drew in his breath. "But the Lord told me I must learn all that I can from you." He glanced at the others when stillness hovered in the room.

"Very well, young prince, may this be the beginning of your learning of the matters of state."

In the library Wilm tended to the fire and sat beside his father.

Lord Bierl described what they had discovered at the orphanage.

Prince Joshua pondered the news. "Do you have a copy of Fillan's contract?"

"Yes. Fillan reported that some are charged for various items they need, putting them in debt. Their contracts are renewed until the debts are paid. He said some have been held by their masters for years."

Prince Joshua studied the parchment carefully and looked closely at the symbols on the bottom right of the page.

"What do you see, Joshua?" Trillion asked.

"A notation that this wording has been approved by the Supreme Judge of Worstein." Joshua looked at the holding lord. "Who is your Supreme Judge?"

"Judge Severn."

"Do you think he is aware of the abusive nature of these contracts? Hard to believe that he would agree to such oppression."

Lord Bierl turned to Prince Trillion. "Please share with Prince Joshua what you told me yesterday."

Trillion glanced down at Wilm. "Son, you might not have heard what I am about to say, but I, at one time, helped powerful men take advantage of others."

"Ama already told me."

"I don't think she knows about this. Remember, as Christ has forgiven us, we must forgive others, no matter what they have done." Trillion then described the inner workings of Prince David's network of associates.

"And you think corrupt decisions are also contracted in Airdle?" Joshua tightened his jaw. "Have I been asleep?"

"I believe this attests to Judge Severn's value to Prince David." Trillion leaned forward. "An investigation to uncover such fraud would involve sending marshals to search out the

truth, as some of the records of court decisions are themselves a fraud."

Prince Joshua examined the contract again. "How were
these workers treated?"

Lord Bierl and Trillion exchanged glances. "Son, did Fillan mention this to you?"

"Yes, Aba. Fillan said they slept on thin mats where
they worked. If a storm came in, they were crowded into a
shed. A few tried to run away. The people who lived nearby
returned them to the tanner who chained them to their stations." Wilm's mouth turned down, saddened that a Lamorian would be so cruel. "Fillan said that when you came for
him, he feared he had been sold to another master. They ate
gruel in the morning and thin soup at dusk. Some days they
even lacked sufficient water."

Lord Bierl lowered his brow. "This angers me beyond
words. We have provided much aid, along with gifts of beds,
food, and medicinal herbals. I wonder where those gifts
went." He sighed. "Do we have sufficient cause to act?"

Joshua nodded. "With this contract and Fillan's statement, we do. We will have to travel to Wolf's Bane for an official statement. But first, I have to ascertain if Supreme Judge
Severn is complicit or has himself been deceived."

"You must go with proper escort and see him with a
ranger by your side. Severn is cunning and resourceful. Be
wary." Lord Bierl waited for Prince Joshua's response.

"I agree. Marshal Karith can go with us."

"I understand your faith in the Stolein keeper; however,
for this interview with the judge, I recommend Ranger Zander also escort you. Have you heard of him?" Bierl waited for
the answer.

"I have." Trillion sat forward. "He was an excellent marshal who had been a second at some of the more notable
Tholen way stations."

"Why is he now a ranger?" Joshua asked Bierl.

"When Prince David began to appoint his wealthy friends as squad leaders, Zander grew tired of serving under ones not fit to wear the marshal shield." Bierl surveyed the princes. "Knowing the lowering of standards for marshal appointments added to our decision to withdraw from Airdle. Along with the auditors who certified the fraudulent judgments I showed them."

"Auditors?" Joshua asked. "I sent no auditors as I had no idea this was happening. Do you have copies of these cases?"

"I do. There are five." Bierl rose, walked to a back shelf, and brought a pile of carefully folded parchments.

"I see I have the night's reading." Joshua looked at Bierl and Trillion. "Anything else I should know?"

Lord Bierl studied the fire. "What are the remedies?"

"Fire the orphanage director, set up a board to oversee the running of the facility, have the council strengthen their statutes by outlawing abusive contracts. Restitution is usual for these types of cases. The rest will have to wait until I have a chance to see the exact nature of the crimes."

Trillion had to ask. "Could a decree from the king overturn any of these actions?"

Joshua sucked in his breath. "Our king is a faithful keeper of the realm. He knows the law, and as required in the law of the king, reads the Leaves of God each and every day."

"However, Prince David could sway his thinking, poison his mind, and blind him to the truth." Trillion paused, not wanting to bring up his past. "Prince Joshua, I would recommend that once we move to restore justice to Worstein, you return to Airdle and see the king before Prince David has a chance to deceive him."

The next day, at first sup, Trillion sought out Marshal Karith. He brought up the matter of the large ship that had been used to empty Wolf's Bane.

Karith knit his brow. "If large ships had been seen, you'd think we would have heard about it. Stolein City is built on a triangle-shaped peninsula that juts out past the reefs. Its harbor has the best access to the deep ocean, rivaling Airdle's. Perhaps that's why they chose Wolf's Bane. The large northern islands would have obscured its coming, even from Invien Springs on the bluff."

"Send a post if you hear of strange happenings."

They turned to greet a bleary-eyed Prince Joshua entering the dining hall.

Trillion rose and offered to find a cook to bring a meal. "You look like you'll need a nap to recover from your journey."

Prince Joshua accepted a mug of coffee. "My plans. But first I must find out when Severn will be at his seaside estate. Where is Lord Bierl?"

"Surveying the fields. Perhaps Steward Ashin might know who we could ask." Trillion knew he would be a good choice to ferret out this information.

"Oh, Marshal Karith, your squad has no assignments today. You may direct your men to refresh themselves, but you should tell the stable manager if they wish to take a ride."

"My thanks, Prince Joshua. We can tend to our steeds, have a short practice session, and let them rest." Karith rose and took his leave.

"Would I have caught this if I had followed through with marshal training?"

Trillion shook his head. "I respected you for realizing your skills in the court above the field. Remember well the tales of princes forced to the marshal service and performing terribly. I believe Judge Severn's skill with the law enabled him to devise ways to legally subvert justice."

"I can perceive the logic of the law and its application. But leading men, that was not a gift the Lord has bestowed upon me." Joshua studied his brother's face. "You look much refreshed from yesterday. Will you return to the marshals? Father has not yet instructed Head Marshal Vaughn to choose a new leader for the Second Royal."

"I'm in doubt as to the Lord's plans for me. I will recommend a replacement. My marshals are honorable and highly skilled. It's a shame my squad was reduced to the parade grounds. They deserved better." Trillion's shoulders slumped.

"Brother, Father directed the marshals to keep you from engagements that he might not lose you. Head Marshal Vaughn told me you were an admirable squad leader." He reached out to encourage his brother.

Trillion forced himself to nod. He had grieved the break between himself and his father long enough. Bowing his head, he silently prayed to forgive his father and for the Lord to bless him. He turned with a smile on his face, feeling cleansed somehow. "I'll fetch your meal."

Prince Joshua left for Wolf's Bane in the early hours of the next morning to take a statement from Fillan. Ranger Zander and a ranger of his choice, along with Marshal Karith and his best archer, provided the escort. The marshals would guard the horses while the rangers would ensure the prince's safety for the meeting.

The villagers of Wolf's Bane greeted them warmly.

After speaking with Fillan, they had enough time to sit at table near the shore where Enoch shared his desire to rebuild their House of God. Prince Joshua wished he could stay to get to know them better and explore their lagoon, but the time came to journey to Judge Severn's seaside estate, a little farther south along the coast. Their coastal road linked up with the King's Highway south of the Invien River. They would not have to travel through Invien Springs.

A road led past tall trees to a wide meadow beside a set of stone buildings with a view of the rocky shoreline. Ranger Zander led the way, having received exact instructions from a close associate of the judge. Before they drew near to the front gate, they took a narrow side path around to a long stable opposite the back of the last building.

Joshua sighed, reminded himself to breathe, said a silent prayer, and with a nod to the rangers, stepped to the back door with a crosshatched window. Tapping lightly, he walked in.

The mudroom off the kitchen held aromas from a sumptuous sup. "Is Supreme Judge Severn in? Tell him he has a visitor."

The cook's helper turned and disappeared down a long hall. Severn's guest retreat, also a place for private meetings, remained cloaked in secrecy with dire consequences for any who violated the master's confidence.

Joshua shifted, wondering how long the man would keep him waiting. If his information proved true, this visit would not be as friendly as their last one years ago. It had been too long, and he had held close to the lower coasts of Airdle and Dornan. The more isolated areas had been too long neglected by himself and the king. The loss of ties with the Sanderfield had not been unexpected, but to lose Worstein? He shook his head, praying for the Holy Spirit to give him the words and the vision to ferret out the truth in the midst of evasive answers. He had seen enough at Weirstone to believe that corruption had taken root. Either the esteemed judge would aid their efforts, or he would be one of the first to be judged.

"Prince Joshua! I've been expecting you." Severn stepped through to the vestibule and gestured to the main hall leading to a set of small rooms. "I hadn't heard before today that you were in the area. So tragic about Wolf's Bane. You're part of the relief effort from Airdle? Will be a comfort to know they are not forgotten."

Joshua worked to keep his face neutral. The man seemed to have hardly aged, looking only slightly older than when he had left for Invien Springs with a commission as justice to the northern district surrounding Worstein Holding. In time, Severn had risen to Supreme Judge of Worstein Council. All these years, Joshua had assumed his star pupil remained true, seeing the law fairly applied.

"I have come to hear your opinion on a matter. It's been a long time since we've had a chance to talk." Joshua stepped into an office with a lit fireplace. Two chairs faced the hearth. A large wooden desk looked toward the sea. Undercurrents of the rolling surf lightly vibrated in the study. Severn had not extended a hand for a shake or welcomed him with an embrace. He did not greet the rangers either who stood a short distance away from the padded wingback chairs.

They sat across from one another, a gulf between them. Severn's answers were short, almost monosyllabic. "My prince, where do you get your information?" the judge asked. He pretended no knowledge of the contracts forced upon the older orphans or their appalling working conditions.

Hopes dimmed that Severn would dispel Lord Bierl's and Trillion's assessment of his character. He deflected, excused, and belittled their concerns.

"You know the people of Wolf's Bane, are, may I say, from lowly stock. They're fishermen, and while we appreciate their work, they are poorly educated." He waved a dismissive hand. "I wouldn't consider them intelligent, enterprising, or resourceful. We've done what we could to help the children, but some aren't fit to live on their own once grown. Our workshops and apprentice programs help reimburse the orphanage."

"You call the hovels they live in, the wretched feed they're forced to eat, and keeping them toiling in the workshops charity? Explain why they were not allowed to return home upon their majority."

Severn's replies only fueled Joshua's anger. He turned to the matter of Bierl's five cases. A bribe had been accepted, and favoritism had been shown to the rich and powerful by taking land and fields from two widows and a wood hauler. Joshua also brought up the case that had been dropped at the request of powerful business owners.

When Severn began to excuse the decisions, he could not hold back. "That is not how you were trained. At one time you knew not only the letter, but the spirit of the law. Your judgments halted corruption. You were commissioned to see justice reign in the sea villages, towns, and cities of Worstein Council. Instead, you made Invien Springs and Tierney Fair your domain, subjecting it to your will. What happened?"

Severn smiled, hardly noticing the outburst. "Prince Joshua of Airdle Castle, in the settled lands along our southern shores that ideal, righteous judgment, as you call it, may be sought. But here in the wilds of the north, we can have no such luxuries. We are on our own, mostly, having to deal with storms, bandits, besides drought and disease. Far removed from the aid of your marshals, we do what we must to survive." He spoke quickly, his words clipped. "To render judgments that keep the peace, allow the towns to function, and commerce to continue requires compromise."

Joshua hesitated to rebut that Severn's corrupting influence had affected the whole region. He set his jaw and let the judge ramble on. When the man paused, he rose and stepped to the door.

Severn pushed back his chair and hurried forward. "Prince David is aware and in agreement. Why risk upsetting this hinterland's delicate balance? We've not the resources and must rely on our own devices." Severn met the prince's steely gaze. "You would have understood this if you had taken the time to consult Prince David. Surely, the king would agree."

"I believe no such thing of our king. What of your faith? Do you not tremble that the people's oppression cries out for justice to the living God? Joining land to land so the poor have nowhere to lay their heads. Master tradesmen allowed to misuse their workers." Joshua leaned toward Severn. "Did you not take an oath before the Lord of Glory to uphold the law derived from His Holy Book?"

"Faith! What does that have to do with settling disputes where no one is innocent and all bear some measure of guilt? Does not your vaunted Leaves of God consider all men sinners? Think, man! We make some allowances for those who can provide stability, progress, and a civil order. We all know our place in the scheme of things. Would your holy law do better?"

"Does God not exist?" When Severn failed to answer, Joshua leaned forward. "Does His Holy Spirit live in your heart?" Coming to full height, unable to mask his disappointment, he turned his back on the judge. Zander opened the door. "I can find my way out."

"What will you do?"

Joshua turned to answer for the last time. "These matters will be taken under consideration. Not the last you will hear of this." Something had to be done. Trillion's and Bierl's warnings had proven true. A chill ran through Joshua, realizing one of the judge's associates had warned him of their coming. What else did he know of their plans?

They would have to take action immediately. If they could halt corruption in Worstein, they might be able to reverse the damage already done in the other councils. Severn erred. Truth and justice were the bedrock of civil order. Without them, Lamoria would fall.

Chapter 19

Prince Trillion and Prince Joshua Help Worstein

Having arrived at Weirstone late that night, Prince Joshua awoke the next morning to see the sun climbing in the sky. They would need to prepare their strategy for freeing the orphans and begin packing for the trip.

He prayed there would be no bloodshed.

He headed down the hall to the banquet room. Maps covered the tables. Bierl, Trillion, and many others pored over the parchments, some making lists and checking distances.

"Ho, what is this?"

"Prince Joshua, you have returned to life." Lord Bierl waved him over. "We are making plans."

He brought forward a detailed map of Invien Springs and drawings of the orphanage and its grounds. "The orphanage first started as a charity work, but the town took it over when the last caretakers left. We will have no help from the sheriff or his deputies."

"Or from many of the townspeople, according to Fillan." Joshua feared what their efforts might yield, yet it was clear the children must be rescued.

Bierl handed a neatly penned parchment to Joshua. "Here is a copy of the proposed contract I asked Judge Halperin to write yesterday. The idea of giving the older children the opportunity to learn a trade sounded like a good idea. I hadn't realized how this plan could lead to abuse.

The Council of Worstein must do better. Now, Judge, if you would help write the warrant to arrest the Supreme Judge of Worstein, that would be most appreciated."

Joshua read the document. "Excellent. This Judge Halperin is near?"

"He oversees my holding, and I can attest his decisions are what Severn's should have been."

"The arrest warrant cannot be signed by any but . . ."

"I know; the Council of Worstein or the king. You could sign it yourself, but it would be better if we have the council's approval." Bierl paused. "Eat first, then you can write that warrant."

Seeing Joshua's meal had not yet arrived, Trillion sat by his brother. "It would be good if you came with us to advise or answer questions. But Bierl will present the motions."

His head spinning, Joshua asked, "When?"

"A turn or so after noon sup." Bierl turned to Trillion. "Do you have the orders for the squads?"

Bierl strode out the door to summon a page. "Bring sup for Prince Joshua, and make sure it's hearty. Coffee too." He entered the room. "Prince Trillion will direct the rangers and marshals at Invien Springs."

"Invien Springs is at least a day's ride away. Can you arrange a nearby staging area?" Trillion asked.

"Would be a good idea if we had the time. We'll leave right after the council meeting—hopefully with the leave to arrest Judge Severn," Bierl said.

"If not?" Joshua asked.

"We free the children and find them other places to live until we can secure a proper director, compassionate staff, and board oversight. I pray many will find homes with relatives. From what I've heard, once a child was enrolled, he was not allowed to leave, and the magistrate refused to grant guardianship to cousins or older siblings. Some will be old enough to apprentice with honest craftsmen." Bierl rose to speak to the men assembled in the hall. "I appoint Marshal Trillion to lead this mission. Save your comments and questions until the end and they will be addressed. I hold the right to challenge any action as chairman of the Council of Worstein." He bowed slightly to the prince. "Marshal, you may proceed with your plan."

Joshua moved to a clear spot at the end of the table when his food arrived. He listened with pride and joy as his youngest brother laid out the strategy for ridding the town of corruption, beginning with the orphanage.

Once Trillion finished, Joshua waved Bierl over.

"Lord Bierl, I will also draw up an order for the council to appoint a commission with authority to investigate all disputed court decisions."

Bierl stroked his chin. "Our council works by consensus, you understand. It takes only one to defeat a motion. We must free the orphans and obtain permission from the council to arrest Severn. You may write up the request for an investigation, but that project must be held for another time." He leaned closer. "Perchance there might be a few who have already aligned with Severn and Prince David. Have we any options from the crown?"

"The king could issue an arrest warrant for Judge Severn. Though I'd rather decisions be rendered by force of the council, not the crown."

"I agree. A matter of prayer." Bierl rose. "We all have much to do."

The turns passed quickly until Trillion, Joshua, and Bierl cantered down the main road to the Council of Worstein chambers halfway between the Keyayisin and Worstein holdings.

Prince Trillion spied wisps of smoke rising above the council chambers. The session had almost begun. They increased their pace to a gallop. A shingle-sided, oval building with a vented chimney reaching upward through the center opening in the roof came into view. A wide firepit, bordered by quartz stone, had curved vanes that directed the smoke upward. Evidently a modest fire had been built, judging by the size of the smoke cloud. Traditional councils produced a smoke trail visible for miles, signaling to the people the care and watch of their leaders.

A waiting stableman took their steeds. Trillion and Joshua followed Lord Bierl to a series of narrow tables that surrounded the firepit spaced for members to step into the center to speak.

"I see my second will chair, assuming I would be absent." Lord Bierl looked around. "Prince Joshua and Trillion, sit at the table closest to the recording clerk. I can't chair the meeting anyway as today I am a petitioner."

The princes sat at the end of the table and watched Lord Bierl approach the clerk. The man barely nodded at Bierl, but added their petitions to the business of the day.

Bierl sat beside the princes. "Our God is with us."

The meeting dragged on. Their petitions would not be recognized until the end. As they had not had time to make copies, a public reading would have to suffice.

The chair recognized Lord Bierl. He rose and walked to the center, acknowledging the members with a hand upon his heart. "Honored council, I bring before you a matter of great urgency. The attack on Wolf's Bane has also uncovered injustices that cry out for remedy." Lord Bierl eloquently summarized the situation beginning with the plight of the orphans.

Trillion perceived the sympathy of some and the cold indifference of others. He feared the warrant for the Supreme Judge's arrest would not be supported.

Bierl proceeded to read the petitions. "Prince Joshua, Supreme Judge of Lamoria, has graciously agreed to attend and answer your questions."

The council chair rose to look at each councilor. With a slight nod of his head he said, "Lord Bierl and our guests, Prince Joshua and Prince Trillion, as is customary with petitions of this magnitude, please retire to the waiting chamber for the members to discuss this matter."

Bierl's eyes widened, but he worked to hide his surprise. With a bow, he walked up the narrow aisle to the princes.

Joshua glanced at Trillion. "What does this mean?"

They rose to follow Lord Bierl. Trillion said quietly, "I believe that means they are ready to vote."

Lord Bierl walked around the outer corridor that rimmed the inner chamber to a long, narrow alcove. He directed the princes to padded benches and pulled closed curtains of sheer, translucent fabric for privacy.

Bierl's lids drew down and his brow furrowed. "Even if they decline our petitions, we must rescue the orphans."

Trillion nodded.

They sat in silence, pondering, praying, pleading.

Joshua considered what he'd say if even the petition to deal with the orphanage was denied. As Supreme Judge, he could demand action be taken.

They all rose when a clerk called to them and pulled back the curtains. "The council is ready."

As they entered the chamber, the chair rose. "In the matter of the petitions to arrest our esteemed judge, the council is not in favor. However, Lord Bierl may lead a force to overturn the crimes of the men running the orphanage near Invien Springs. So help us God, may His will be done on earth as it is in heaven."

Trillion noticed anger in his brother's eyes. Bierl tried to draw Joshua aside for the leave-taking. Trillion lowered his head. "Bierl, may I address the council, briefly?"

Bierl quickly stepped toward the center and flicked his hand for Trillion to follow. The holding lord rotated to face the council. "Prince Trillion requests a moment." When all sat, he lifted his hand toward the prince and stepped aside.

With prayers in his heart, Trillion lifted his head. "My lords of Worstein, we are thankful that you approved the petition to deal with the orphanage. Our faith is seen by our actions. The Lord Jesus commands us to love our neighbor as ourselves. Let me leave you with these questions—who is your neighbor, and are you being a neighbor to him? Also, the House of Airdle stands beside the council in seeing the Lord's justice and mercy ring across the land."

With a bow, Trillion walked up the center aisle. He saw Bierl come beside him and Joshua as well once clear of the table.

Lord Bierl nodded at Trillion. "Good job." He turned to Joshua. "Walk with us to receive our petitions and parting farewell to the councilors."

"We must hasten our leave-taking."

"I agree." Bierl walked to the council leaders lined up by the door. He shook their hands with his other hand placed on his heart. "For Lamoria," he said to each one.

Trillion and Joshua followed Bierl's lead.

They heard a few behind them say "For Worstein" instead.

Chapter 20

Rescuing the Orphans

Trillion and Joshua headed to their horses in a small paddock by the barn. Seeing their gear lying on the grass beside the barn, they quickly tacked their steeds. Trillion snagged Thor's lead. Bierl caught up and slid the saddle and bridle in place. Before the stableman could reach them, they opened the gate. As one, their horses pivoted to the east and lunged forward into a gallop toward Weirstone.

"Judge Severn's arm is strong here," Trillion said. "He will raise up henchmen to take the orphanage. We must arrive before they do."

Their steeds ran with the wind at their backs. Nearing Weirstone, Bierl led them to the main steps. "Page, see to the horses."

They ran up the steps and to the dining hall. Bierl lifted the petitions in the air. "The council approves our assault on the orphanage but not Judge Severn's arrest." He glanced at the princes standing beside him.

Trillion lifted his voice. "The Spirit warns me that we must not give our opponents time to assemble." He looked at the horsemen. Perhaps some standing around the table were in league with Severn. "Pack your gear and all necessary supplies. Be ready at a moment's notice, for we will leave soon for Invien Springs. Tarry not, sup well, but do not linger long at the table, for at an unexpected time I will call you to action. For Lamoria!" His charge echoed through the room when they raised their fists with him. "For Worstein!" Their voices, in unison, sounded in the hall and surrounded the keep. "For the glory of God."

Trillion lowered his fist. "We have forgotten what is most important—beseeching prayers. For if we build not with Him, we build in vain. If we lead apart from His paths, we will be led astray. If we go forth to set aright the land without yielding to the Savior, we will fail. Let us pray." They joined hands.

As if a force drove them to their knees, a sorrow from the Lord came upon them. One began, "Lord, You promised that if we humble ourselves before You, confessing our sins, and seek Your face, You would heal our land." One prayed after another.

Trillion felt the peace of Christ within his soul. Jesus would stand with them at that dread house. He prayed, "Lord, go before us, with us, and through us. We will see what You will do."

All rose and went to their assigned tasks. Trillion glimpsed Wilm hovering by the door. "Are the horses, gear, and supplies ready?"

His son bowed with a broad smile. "We—myself, Ama, and Master Cesim—with many others, have fulfilled our tasks."

All those chosen to go slept on straw in a nearby barn. At midnight, the Lord awakened Prince Trillion and Joshua. Rising, they called the troops to action. Hooves thundered in the night as they traveled the road south of the Invien River directly to the orphanage.

At a convenient field they stopped to unload supplies, set up canopies, and ready themselves to be in position before morning's light crested Havran's Peak.

Trillion reviewed the battle plan. A pulse ran through him, seeing rangers and marshals standing together. The Lord's promise for a united Lamoria stood before him.

The prince sounded the whistle to form up. "Make ready!"

Kewatin shifted and Trillion bent to soothe his charger

with a pat and soft words. Marshal Karith's marshals with six rangers lined up in pairs to his right. Lord Bierl sat confidently on Thor with his squad beside him. Ranger Zander's squad of twelve formed to the prince's left.

Trillion rotated Kewatin to his right for the final orders. "Marshal Karith and men of Lamoria, guard the children and escort the staff to Lord Bierl's keeping." Pivoting to his left, he withheld a smile for it felt good to lead again. "Ranger Zander, guard the outer perimeter and see to the safe keeping of Lord Bierl's squad."

Facing the center, the holding lord before him, Trillion bowed slightly and raised his hand, palm up toward Lord Bierl. But the man gave a slight shake and bow of his head. They were Trillion's to command.

Sitting tall in the saddle, he gave the last charge. "Lord Bierl, Prince Joshua, direct your men to detain and hold the staff and the director, delivering the council's order for his removal."

Trillion pivoted Kewatin and they trotted before the warriors. He should give the charge for the battle, but it was of the Lord. Completing his circuit, he called for Prince Joshua to give the prayer.

All were still, horse and rider, as the Judge of Lamoria called upon the God of heaven to guard and secure their way.

Trillion rode close to Bierl. "My lord, lead the way." He and his brother rode beside him, with Karith and, lastly, Zander following at a gallop.

Moon's light lit their path, but the men of Worstein knew it well. Slowing to a trot and then a walk, they drew near to the three-story clapboard building, sitting upon a barren field. Silently, Lord Bierl's squad with the princes dismounted. Rangers secured their horses. Eight dismounted to guard the home.

Karith's men followed the ranger assigned to lead them

to a side door where a teacher, a close friend of Lord Bierl's, would give them entrance.

Trillion held his breath, waiting to see a lit candle in an upper window signaling that the children were safe and the staff collected. A few horses shifted, pawing the earth with a hoof. Some coughs could be heard, but he detected no sign that they had roused the town.

A candle in an upper window cast its glow upon Marshal Karith. With his wave the three stepped forward with two pairs of rangers behind them. Trillion looked at Bierl. "Here is the warrant. Go forth for Worstein!"

Bierl walked to the door and pounded on it with his fist. "Open the door by order of the Council of Worstein."

A voice sounded from inside the door. "Who are you?"

"Lord Bierl who holds the warrant for you to come forth!"

They heard a cackle from within. A ranger stepped forward with a sledgehammer and shattered the door. Bierl rushed through to enter, but an invisible hand held him fast.

Trillion felt a chill. A malevolent presence stood in their way. He heard the Spirit laugh within—the Lord scoffs at them. "Cast out the darkness! In the name of Jesus Christ, the Lord of lords, expel these demons of the night. Fill this place with your light!"

Beisel, the measly director, lurked in the entryway. His sneer gave way to rage. "You have no means to enter. The way is shut to you, followers of a weak and crucified petty—" A shriek came from his mouth, and he cowered as if invisible angels had reined blows upon him.

Trillion felt the way open. "Go in!"

The holding lord stepped through the doorway and pushed the director against a wall. A ranger bound his arms behind his back.

Joshua heard a commotion behind him. He looked back

to see the sheriff and his deputies riding up. Ranger Zander with his men rode to stop them.

Trillion gave his brother a reassuring glance as they stepped inside.

Bierl faced the director. "You are charged with abuse of your duties and defiling children." The man growled deeply, and his eyes emitted a reddish hue.

Trillion felt the power of darkness exude from the tall, emaciated man. "Put him in the office." An eerie darkness dimmed the room. They stood transfixed at the sight of a carved wood plaque dedicated to the gods of old hanging on the wall behind the desk.

Joshua stepped around to a narrow door beside the plaque. Early morning sunlight poured through the east-facing window, lighting shelves filled with roughly bound parchment books. "The orphans' records," he called out.

Trillion ordered a ranger to guard the room. A door to his right caught his gaze. "What is that?" When the man refused to answer, his eyes widening in fear, Trillion opened the door. He worked to catch his breath. As if transported back to the day he fell, Trillion felt the fingers of Satan reaching for him. "You have no business with me. I am covered by the blood of Christ!"

"My quarters," the director said with slippery joy.

Bierl called to a ranger nearby. "Take him out and hold him fast. Set four guards around him." Joshua joined him, and they turned to the back room.

"Fear not. We have a mighty God!" Bierl entered the room with Joshua close behind.

Blackness hovered in the corners of the ceiling, and the stench of hell filled the air. In the power of the Spirit, Trillion knelt and spread his arms toward heaven. "We are covered by the Blood of Christ. Lord of Glory, send Your mighty angels and cast out the demons, for You are worthy. You have conquered. None can stand against You."

The rangers behind them began to sing, "Holy, Holy, Holy is the LORD of Armies; the whole earth is full of His glory."

Trillion felt the room brighten, but while the presence had moved toward the window, it still lingered. *Go outside and meet the sent one.* He stepped out of the room and said to a ranger in the office, "Sing praises to God. Pray and believe!"

He ran down the hall and out the doorway to see a tall man, broad of girth, dressed in the simple clothes of northern Stoddard.

"Sir, why have you come here? We are . . ." Trillion stopped when the man turned his way. *This is the one. He has been given the power to clear and restore.*

"What is your name?" he asked instead.

"I am Lawreader Shelton from Stoddard. The Lord told us to come that we might take care of the children. They won't tell me where they are."

Trillion's eyes glanced toward the upper levels. "They are safe, but you must come and implore the Lord to complete the cleansing of this house." He urged Shelton to follow him inside. "You were also sent to cleanse this place. This way."

They entered the room, and Shelton breathed deeply, uttering groans. "Great evils have been done here. To the one who touches the children, may a millstone be tied around his neck and he be thrown into the sea."

For an instant, darkness rose and the outline of death laughed. Trillion felt their raging hatred along with the Spirit's undercurrent of joy. For the battle had already been won.

"Be gone, in the name of Christ. Lord, send them to the depths. Lord, may this place be holy. By Your Blood, we pray in Your name." Shelton stood with raised arms, his head bowed slightly. The singing stopped. All stood.

God's light appeared, brilliant, with emanating love. Beginning in the room, the light filled the home, surrounded the building, and shot up to the sky.

The sheriff and his deputies lifted their arms to shield themselves from the light. Pulling back on the reins, their horses reared, pivoted, and galloped away. The people of the town and those on the roads paused to look. For a moment, angels' singing filled the air with sweet joy. Then it vanished, and the light of the sun seemed dim in comparison.

"Lawreader Shelton, come with me to see the director. This had been his room." Prince Trillion led the way to the staff assembled beside the slim man.

Shelton pointed with his chin to Beisel. "Is that the one?"

"He is. You may proceed, lawreader," Prince Trillion said.

As Shelton drew near, the director began to writhe, crying out, "Do not come closer! We cannot bear one who walks with God. The pain! The agony! His burning presence."

Shelton lifted his arm. "Oh Lord, deliver this one from the demons. Free him!"

The director uttered a terrible scream. Crying with a deep voice, he burst his bounds and ran faster than a horse to the cliffs by the sea. Two staff workers followed him. They leapt into the air, plunging over the side to the rocky shore below.

Several rangers followed. They looked down and saw their lifeless bodies broken on sharp boulders. Waves crashed upon their carcasses, and an undertow pulled them to the depths.

The rangers returned to the home, keeping an eye out for others seeking to stop them.

As if the weight of a heavy blanket had been pulled away, Trillion looked over at Joshua standing behind him. "Well? Is this your part?"

Joshua shook his head and bowed slightly to Lord Bierl opposite him. "Lord Bierl, these are your people. Examine them and deliver to the magistrate the ones you choose."

Trillion noticed many had come. The rangers surrounding the home kept them a short distance away. He saw Shelton, with Bierl beside him, talk to the staff, one by one.

He looked along the road to the east when the crowds parted; a narrow, long wagon with a tattered covering drawn by two mules approached. Before Trillion could take a step, Shelton walked past.

A broad woman almost as tall as Shelton and seven children clambered out of the wagon. They stood beside the lawreader. "Lord Bierl, fine princes, meet my family. We struggled on our travels here." Shelton shook. "Met many strange roadblocks. Are we late?"

Bierl walked up to greet them. "No, your coming was at the Lord's perfect time." He squinted in the sunlight. "Will you care for the orphans, restore them to their homes, see them educated, and help them find apprenticeships?"

"We will!" Shelton beamed.

All turned their heads when a ranger rode up at a gallop. "Prince Trillion, a mob is cutting down our rangers!"

Trillion glimpsed their horses tied not far away. He whistled for Kewatin and his steed reared and pulled back to surge toward him. "Bow and arrows!" he called out.

Karith ran to their gear and returned with the weapons.

Once astride, Trillion held the arrows with the bow and galloped after the ranger.

He saw a rabble with picks, axes, shovels, and clubs fighting hand to hand with the rangers. Not slowing, he called to a horseman beside him, "Go back for the rest to join the fight."

He leaned forward, letting Kewatin run at top speed. The large tanner at the head of the pack swung a massive, double-bladed battle axe. Three rangers surrounded him, but none could close in.

Directing Kewatin toward the tanner, he dropped the reins, notched an arrow, and let one fly as he rode past. Using his legs and balance, Trillion directed Kewatin to pivot.

Returning, he shot another arrow into the man's chest, but he stood.

The tanner, with two arrows embedded in his chest, swung his axe back and forth, each arc slicing men and steeds. Man and beast struggled to dodge the swings.

Trillion flung the bow aside, drew his sword with his right hand. Leaning forward, he grasped the saddle's pommel with his left. Gathering himself, he balanced on the saddle and let Kewatin's momentum propel him into the air.

He prayed that he could land behind the tanner, but instead, he found himself close to the man's right side. Crouching, he drew out a dagger with his left hand, pointed toward his back. Anger fueled his strength, for the brute had already killed and gravely wounded many. Trillion sank the dagger into the man's leg as he slipped past.

Circling, the tanner pulled it out and flung it aside. "There is no place for Airdle in Worstein." He swung.

Trillion's sword blocked the axe. He focused on the man's eyes and where he placed his feet. He pulled forth another blade, but it was short. Timing the next swing of the axe, Trillion thrust forward and pierced the tanner's lower chest and lung. Crouching as he pulled the sword back, he rotated to swipe the man with his blade.

The size of the axe and the length of its handle provided the opening he needed. The tanner focused on Trillion's short blade, extended his arm to sever Trillion's. With cat-like speed, Trillion rotated his torso to bring his sword down upon the tanner's arm. It fell, still clutching the axe.

Trillion pulled the axe free, broke off the head, and proceeded to force the tanner to the ground with the pole. As if filled with a demon's strength, the tanner kicked and punched. But he grew weak, sweat beaded on his brow, and Trillion managed to sweep his legs out from under him, flipping the man on his back.

Trillion retrieved his dagger lying on the grass and knelt

upon the man's chest, laying the blade upon his neck. "Yield!"

"Never!" He spat and cursed. "I'll never surrender to the unclaimed spawn of a brothel."

Trillion felt an old anger rise. *Lord, help, save us both.* "Be gone, demon of the night. I am no longer yours. Tanner, you do not have to serve the wicked ones. Yield to God." Preparing to hear more foul words, he tilted his head.

"I yield. You've won. Let me serve . . ."

When Trillion withdrew the blade upon the tanner's neck, he pulled out the arm trapped underneath him and plunged a short blade into Trillion's side.

A pulse shot through Trillion. Ignoring it, he sliced the man's throat with his dagger. If only he could have saved him. *All have free will to choose. That was his choice.* He was under no condemnation, for Christ had truly set Trillion free.

Trillion sat back on his heels, moving carefully. With each shift, he felt the blade slice deeper into his back. He reached around to gingerly pull it free. He pulled out a binding cloth from under his vest and bound the wound.

Standing, he surveyed the battlefield. Fewer lay unmoving than he had feared. The rabble had dissipated. He watched a number of rangers pursue on horseback. Trillion went to one who had lost a forearm. Blood dripped from the upper arm.

Trillion called out to a nearby ranger. "Lend your binding cloth. He needs our help."

The horseman handed his cloth to the prince.

Trillion bound the arm.

"What about you, Prince Trillion?"

"I must see if the rest can be helped." He tried to rise but found himself stumbling.

Ranger Zander rode toward them and dismounted quickly. Another ranger joined him.

Trillion felt his vision narrowing, the world darkened.

He tried to focus on two running toward him, but he had no strength. Falling to one knee, his sight blurred.

Zander reached the prince first and kept him from falling to the ground. The ranger, large of frame, lifted Trillion and walked to the healer station set up behind the orphanage.

Prince Joshua saw them coming and ran to them. "Prince Trillion! Does he live?"

"Yes." Zander continued walking. "We must take him to our ranger with a healer's pack. I will send a ranger to fetch you when we know of his condition." Joshua's steps slowed and stopped altogether. Forcing his hand not to shake, he headed back inside to talk to Bierl and the magistrate. The law was his domain.

The rangers dispersed the crowds. Karith and his men led the children down for first sup. Volunteers, along with Shelton's family, had already begun to prepare the meal. A father of four, Karith directed the order of the dining room, making the orphans feel at ease. The kitchen and dining hall buzzed with activity.

A ranger brought the news of Prince Trillion's wounding. Karith followed him to the side conference room where Bierl and Joshua walked with a magistrate. He tapped on the door frame. "Prince Joshua, does Prince Trillion live? Where is he?"

The prince approached the marshal and nodded. "They took him to Weirstone."

"So he will recover?" The marshal's face fell with the prince's grim look. "Of course, we will know in time. I request leave to guard them—"

Lord Bierl drew near. "Marshal Karith, in a short time we will have this well in hand to travel as a troop to Weirstone. But we have need of your care for the children. Soon we will have enough staff, along with Shelton's family, that we can journey back in good conscience."

The head marshal bowed stiffly and headed back to the dining hall.

The wagon, surrounded by rangers, tilted with the ruts.

"Slow down," called the ranger holding the wounded prince steady. He relaxed a little, feeling a faint pulse in the warrior's neck. Trillion's brave charge had saved many.

Trillion saw a verdant plain bordered by the most beautiful flowers he had ever seen. Figures approached, wearing robes of white with golden sashes. The instant he desired to know who they were, he knew their names. His ama, Queen Lillian, King Aaron, and many others walked to him with broad smiles, lit with God's love. Ama held out her arm. He heard in his mind, "I will come for you soon, at Eliziel."

The Lord appeared. Trillion knelt, and they talked mind to mind.

"Is this my time?"

A gentle hand rested on his shoulder. Pure love flowed. "Your son will be king. He will be the peacemaker. You must teach him all you know, and you have other tasks to do for Me. Not now but soon we will come for you. When it is time, go to Eliziel."

He almost reached for the hand as if to cling to the Lord. Yet they would sorrow so, Lisze and Wilm, if he stayed. Hard though it was, he yielded. "Your will be done, Lord."

Darkness descended and pain shot up his back. His body bounced, hitting hard boards. Trillion's eyes flew open. He struggled to steady his breathing. Trying to talk brought up phlegm with coughing.

The ranger rolled him gently to help him clear his lungs. "Rest easy, Prince Trillion. We'll be at Weirstone soon."

"What happened? Did we win?"

"Most certainly." He shared what news he could.

Trillion remembered the vision. Had he been given a glimpse of heaven? *Oh Lord, give wisdom for the days ahead.*

They arrived at the capital of Worstein Holding in a short time.

Lisze, Wilm, Cesim, and many others greeted them at the steps to Weirstone. The dining hall had been converted into a healer's suite, and the Dunilian healer had been summoned.

The wound was not as deep as had been feared, and within three days Trillion was up and about. Lisze and Wilm were overjoyed and took some time together in the castle.

All waited for the rest of the troop to return. It would be soon, according to reports from the wounded who had returned.

A day later a fast courier brought news that Lord Bierl, Prince Joshua, with the rangers and marshals, would arrive later that day.

Trillion stood beside Lisze, Wilm, Cesim, and Katrina. Giselle spied them coming up the lane and ran with the news. "They're here!"

They rode into the courtyard. Prince Joshua could hardly believe his eyes. He dismounted, handed over the reins, and walked quickly to Trillion. "Brother, you look well!"

"Quite refreshed. They have an excellent healer here." He examined Joshua's dusty clothes and circles under his eyes. "I see you need some tending. A feast has been prepared, and we must hear the news. Will you have to remain here?"

Joshua hugged his brother. He greeted Lisze and Wilm. "Some fresh spring water, then coffee, if they have it?"

"You jest, fair prince." Lisze laughed. "Worstein has better coffee than Airdle, I'd say." She led the way. "All is ready, and Lady Katrina has ordered warm baths prepared. Wash first, eat, then we can talk."

They paused, hearing Lord Bierl order Ranger Zander and Marshal Karith to refit and be ready for the next engagement.

Bierl turned to Katrina, who wrapped him in a warm embrace. "And for us?"

His lady smiled and took his arm, escorting him to their home. "Of course, but wash first, then sup."

They ate in the lower dining hall. Katrina, Lisze, and Giselle helped the staff clean up as the men sat, drinking the last of their coffee or tea.

Lord Bierl leaned forward. "We need to confer. I'll try to keep it short, if you're not too tired?"

Joshua shook his head.

"May Prince Wilm join us?" Trillion patted his son's knee.

"Of course, in my library."

They followed Bierl up the stairs and down the hall.

"Wilm, tend the fire," Trillion said, waiting to see where he should sit.

Bierl pulled a few more chairs around the hearth. He surveyed their faces. "While we had victory at Invien Springs and with the mayor on our side, the matter of Severn plagues my mind."

"My Lord, I must say your Judge Halperin is exceptional and would be a good replacement for Severn." Joshua saw Bierl's nod.

"I will see it done." Bierl stared into the fire. He shifted and focused his eyes. "We were wise to not tell the time of our leaving, for I suspect Severn's men are here in Worstein Holding as well as entrenched at Tierney Fair. This is only the beginning." He paused, but none asked any questions. "Prince Joshua, you must help the king see why we took these actions against Prince David's associates. If he signs a decree to block our actions, we will cede from the realm and secure our borders." Bierl looked at the judge with a level gaze. "Plans are already in place for erecting a wall across the King's Highway north of Stolein and closing the gap in Tierney Ridge."

Joshua leaned forward. "Of course, I'll take copies of the

cases you showed me, along with the other evidence we collected at the orphanage."

Lord Bierl patted Trillion's knee. "We are so very thankful for your recovery. You can help Stoddard, the Imbus Ayisin, and the free plainsmen remain united with Airdle. I do not take any joy in fracturing the land of Lamoria, but I will if forced. In days to come, if all goes wrong and not right, Lamoria will consist only of Tholen, Airdle, and Dornan. I pray the Lord will open the king's eyes, and Prince David is transformed as Prince Trillion has been."

Prince Trillion remembered the Lord's words. This would be his next task, along with preparing his son. He glanced at Wilm sitting beside him. There had been a change in him, and he suspected it had happened at Wolf's Bane.

Wilm went to the fire to pull the logs together.

Coming to himself, he turned to Bierl. "I pray that I can help mediate. Prince Joshua and I have talked about me training to be a judge."

"I'll take that up with the king." Joshua folded his arms. "Hopefully he will approve."

Bierl smiled for the first time. "This is great news. I hate to ask this of you, but how soon can you ride? Should I send some rangers to add to Marshal Karith's few he brought with him?"

Prince Joshua nodded, his head spinning. He glanced at Trillion.

"That offer will be gratefully accepted. Can you send six rangers? They can respite at Stolein and make their way home from there. How soon will be of the Lord's choosing."

"Well spoken, Prince Trillion." Bierl sat back. "Prince Joshua, would you open in prayer? I will close."

While at first sup the next morning, Lord Bierl received couriers from various cities and towns.

"This is most unusual. I must read these now." Bierl headed for the nearest room.

Trillion glanced at Joshua. "Send for Marshal Karith?"

"Wait for the facts, Brother."

Lisze, Katrina, and the staff who had not yet left for work lingered, wondering about what had happened.

Bierl returned in a short time. "Judge Severn and Healer Trent have fled. Severn torched his seaside house where he had housed copies of his judgments. Courthouses with their archives in several towns had been set to fire, including Invien Springs and Tierney Fair." He shook his head. "This will complicate our investigation into suspicious court cases. I've already spoken to Halperin about petitioning the investigation you had mentioned, Prince Joshua." He sighed. "From what I've read, the people are incensed, as many houses and barns were also lost due to the fires."

Katrina shook her head. "This is terrible news."

Bierl nodded. "Your aid groups, my dear, will have to be called up again." He looked at Joshua. "And if he succeeds in crossing our border, is his warrant valid in the other councils?"

"No, but I'll take a copy of the warrant and your reports. The king can issue one for his arrest anywhere in Lamoria."

Trillion stood beside Bierl. "I should send for Marshal Karith. The marshals can help. What do you need?"

Bierl bowed his head. "Many thanks, Trillion and Joshua, for coming to help us. I must call an emergency council, muster our rangers and people to aid the burnt towns. See the king and secure the warrant."

"But if Severn is no longer still in Worstein—" Trillion furrowed his brow.

Joshua exchanged a grin with Bierl. "Brother, with a warrant from the king, he can be detained anywhere in Lamoria by any ranger, marshal, or sheriff."

"Of course." Trillion turned to Joshua. "Could you be ready today?"

"With this news, though, my rangers can escort you as far as Tierney Fair." Bierl waited for Prince Joshua's decision.

Trillion nodded. "We can arrange escort to Airdle at Stolein. I will confer with Karith." He paused. "Lisze, can you rouse Wilm and find Cesim?"

"We'll be ready within a turn." Lisze rose to leave.

Joshua sighed. "We should make haste for Airdle Castle. I leave the details to you, Trillion and Marshal Karith." He headed for his room.

Trillion embraced Bierl. "Prayers will be raised for Worstein."

"And I will pray for all of you at Airdle. Godspeed, Prince Trillion."

Chapter 21

Prince Trillion and Prince Joshua Meet with the King

Later that day, Prince Joshua, Trillion, Lisze, Wilm, Cesim, and Karith with his marshals rounded the bend to Stolein Way Station's courtyard. The posted guard announced their arrival. Karith's wife, Lady Dara, and his two older children, Rian and Loralie, came out to meet them.

Stable boys gathered their horses, and they stood on solid ground.

Lady Dara, with her heart-shaped face and long, flowing black hair, approached Trillion and Lisze. "It's good to see you again, Prince Trillion. Happy you have recovered." She turned to the tall woman beside him. "And this must be Lady Lisze. I'm Lady Dara. So glad to you could visit our way station."

Lisze curtsied slightly. "I've heard much about you. Nice to finally meet. And this is my son, Wilm."

"As we did not know you would be coming, I've sup to prepare." Dara waved to a tall boy. "Here is my eldest, Rian. He can help you find rooms." She added, "And have the stable boy fill the tubs with bathwater."

"May I help with the meal, Lady Dara?"

"You are our guests today. Settle in, for you all look in need of respite." Dara went to greet Prince Joshua who was trying to work out the kinks and sore ankles from the long ride.

Trillion glanced around for Karith. Seeing him enter the

middle barn, he said to Lisze, "Have our bags brought up and see Wilm, Cesim, and Joshua are well situated."

With a brief wave, he headed to the barn. Past the door, he called, "Marshal Karith, may I see you?" When the head marshal came his way, he said, "Sorry to intrude, but may we have four marshals to escort us to Airdle tomorrow? If we ride hard we should make it in one day."

Karith took him aside and rested his hand on Trillion's shoulder. "We might be hardened for days of riding, but Prince Joshua is not. Wilm could probably manage, but he's still young. Lisze and Cesim need rest."

"What if we rode to Seagull Bay and continued on to Airdle when Joshua is ready?"

"Wiser plan, my prince." Karith looked at Trillion's straight shoulders and his direct gaze that showed little hint of fatigue. "You've made a remarkable recovery. May it continue, but take sup with your family." He stepped back. "I'll have your escort ready by morning."

In the middle of the third day, Princes Joshua and Trillion and the group arrived at Airdle Castle.

Prince Joshua headed to his suite not far from his offices.

Trillion turned to Lisze. "See our bags are taken up to our suites on the second floor. Settle in. Sup in our room tonight?" With her nod, he continued, "Is Cesim well?"

Lisze shrugged her shoulders. "Wilm and I can handle everything. I'll send Cesim to the healers." She lifted a brow. "And you?"

"I have to meet with Head Marshal Vaughn."

"It's settled? What you really want?"

"Where God is leading me." Trillion stepped close and reached for her hand. "I had a chance to rescue the orphans, but God is calling me to aid Prince Joshua in ridding the rest of Lamoria of those seeking to destroy our land. For that, I must become a lawreader."

Lisze reached for his hand. "My prayers go with you."

"Pray my men will be given a fit commander." He headed to the marshal's office. Years before he would have dreaded becoming a lawreader, but now he felt instead a small measure of joy. "Yes, Lord, I will see Your will done."

Trillion gave himself a day with his family before he went to find Joshua. It felt strange that his brother hadn't visited or sent news of their meeting with the king.

He entered Joshua's office and saw him surrounded by piles of parchments, with bound books of cases on a side table. "The work waited for your return. There were none to handle these cases?"

"These are the ones my judges have forwarded to me. The rest were approved and bound." Joshua eyed the bound cases. "However, with what I've learned at Worstein, there are a few more I want to examine. Did you have a question?"

"When will we meet the king?"

Joshua sighed. "The king recently returned from touring Dornan Council."

"With Prince David?" Trillion asked. His heart skipped a beat with his brother's nod.

"His clerk tells me he has matters to attend to but will see us as soon as he can." Joshua sat back and folded his arms. "I must trust the Lord's timing. I have rewritten my request to investigate suspicious judgments in every council."

Trillion leaned forward, suspecting he knew where Severn was hiding. "Has the king reversed Worstein's actions?"

"No, in fact it's as if nothing of consequence happened."

Trillion thought a moment and tried to lighten the mood. "We'll find out soon enough, Brother. I resigned from the marshal service." He tried not to wince at Joshua's broad smile.

"Good to hear. I've the request ready for you to train as a lawreader. May you someday replace me."

He froze, remembering his time in the wagon returning to Weirstone. "I know this is where I need to be."

Joshua glanced at the document before him. "I pray he meets with us soon as I am anxious to go home."

"I'll pray for that." Trillion left to rest while he had the chance.

That afternoon in his office, Joshua reviewed the request for authority to investigate suspicious cases throughout Lamoria. It could be a private decree. Copies would not have to be made and announced throughout the land.

A royal clerk knocked on his door. "Your audience with the king is granted. You may see him now."

Joshua again felt the hand of the Lord directing events. "Prince Trillion will be attending as well." Praying for wisdom and grace, he walked to Trillion's suite, with the clerk trailing behind. In a short while they headed to the king's offices by the Hall of Judgment.

The clerk announced their arrival.

They stepped past the clerk to stand behind the chair in front of the desk. "King Wallace, thank you for agreeing to see us."

The king looked up with lifted brow. "Prince Trillion, you wish to confer with us?"

Joshua cleared his throat. "As the prince played an integral part in the events at Worstein, I felt it was time to include him in these meetings."

"You may sit." The king leaned over his large, finely polished desk.

Prince Trillion brought a chair and sat next to his brother.

Prince Joshua opened his folder and pulled out the copies from Worstein. He stepped through what had happened, the state of the orphanage, and the corrupt cases approved by Severn. When the king said little, he slid across the king's desk the request to issue a warrant for Judge Severn and the petition to investigate decisions throughout the land. "My lord, we would not want such judgments to have been rendered anywhere in Lamoria."

The king stared at the documents. "I will need to read these." He raised his eyes. "Anything else?"

With that, the petition for Trillion to train as judge was placed before him.

Wallace slapped his hand on the request and stared out the window. Without turning his head, he said, "Prince Trillion, you may leave. I have some items to discuss with Prince Joshua."

The door closed. Silence hovered. Joshua waited for the king to speak.

"I've heard disturbing reports from Worstein."

Joshua tried to ascertain the king's state of mind. "What reports? How were they disturbing?"

"Some well-respected leaders of Worstein have fled the council. I heard reports that Trillion convinced you and Lord Bierl that they committed crimes."

"I'm glad I had a chance to view the situation firsthand." He tried not to yield to impatience. Hadn't he made the case clear? "Lord Bierl brought these matters to my attention, not Prince Trillion. I was skeptical at first, and so I spoke with Judge Severn directly. It was a shock to hear that he supported the oppression of orphans. I've shown you the cases proving the corruption of Judge Severn and his judges." Trying to find something good to say, he added, "I am pleased to report that the Council of Worstein will pursue these matters. They elected Judge Halperin as the new Supreme Judge of Worstein."

The king did not answer. He tapped his fingers together.

"The crown lies heavy. I am caught between many. One judgment helps one but hurts another."

"Which is why we have always sought wisdom from God, as King Solomon did. And may I say, Father, you have always kept close to the Lord and His law. It is for this reason, I come before you. I fear what has happened in Worstein's courts could also be happening here. Many judges and law-readers know how to keep the letter of the law while violating its spirit. Have you heard what had happened to Lisze's father's land grant?"

The king nodded but did not speak. His shoulders slumped. Joshua perceived a weariness in his eyes. He allowed his father to think through what he had heard.

They both startled with a page's rap on the door.

"Enter," the king said.

The page brought the usual midafternoon tea and sweet bannock.

"Bring coffee for Prince Joshua."

Wallace sipped his tea and glanced at the decree waiting for his signature. "And this warrant is your remedy?" He shifted, lines of tiredness upon his brow.

Joshua drank the coffee while he listened to his father ramble about the burdens of sovereignty. "You are in my prayers, as always, Father. Take what time you need." Joshua stood. "Should I remain at the castle for questions?"

The king rose and stepped around the desk. "I have much to think about. You have been away from home a long time. Do you believe your brother is being truthful about his change of heart? Could he have deceived Lord Bierl?" Wallace looked intently at his son, the esteemed legal scholar.

"Why do you ask that, Father? Did you not send him to Wolf's Bane?"

"He refused to return with Marshal Rysen and created these problems with Lord Bierl."

"Since Trillion's conversion there has been a remarkable transformation. The man we knew he could be has emerged. He is reborn in Christ. Father, believe the evidence I've shown you."

"You consider him fit to be a judge one day?"

"Most certainly. And with his language skills, we would not have to rely on interpreters."

The king returned to his desk. "I will sign your request for Trillion to train as a judge. Fetch my clerk for a candle and sealing wax."

Joshua watched as the clerk stepped through the process of sealing a decree. The page to be sealed and signed by the king was placed in the center of the desk. The clerk held a short stick of colored wax over the candle, tipped for droplets to fall upon the lower left corner of the page. Then the king, making a fist, impressed the ring of his left finger upon the wax. Afterward, he used an ink-dipped quill to sign the document. The clerk snuffed out the candle and retired to his desk.

"I'll let Trillion know." Joshua left.

He headed directly to Trillion's rooms. Hearing a low "Come in," he stepped through the door. His brother sat by a table with the Leaves of God opened.

"So Prince David's at it again?" Trillion turned to his brother when he sat beside him.

"Yes. Father did approve your training. I reminded him of your fluency in Amhavran and Regnard." Joshua paced. "I showed him everything. I don't understand why he would listen to lies. Surely, he's seen the change in you."

"Until my former life is paraded before him. Remember, as the crown prince, David has much influence over the king."

"He learned well from his mother how to manipulate our father."

"Glad I'm not king. Must be hard with all the demands. Pulled in every direction." Trillion sighed. He attempted a smile. "Now, you need to go home to Lady Jessica and not come back for a while."

"But your training."

"Your chief judge and the clerks will be more than able to begin my schooling. It might be a while before I graduate to your tutelage." He rose and hugged his brother. "That we worked so well together thrills my heart. Enjoy your seaside estate and say hello to Lady Jessica for us."

"You're right. Time to go home."

Trillion watched him leave. Somehow hearing his suspicions had come true hadn't deepened his despair but brought a measure of determination. God had tasks for him to do, and no one, not even David, could stand in his way.

In moments, Trillion was dressed to ride and left to find his family. Cesim was not in his room, and he assumed everyone was at the stables.

Lisze and Wilm rode in the paddock. "Where is Cesim?"

Wilm headed to the fence near his father. "Cesim is at the healer's. A little cold, or something." He noticed Trillion's riding breeches and unadorned tunic. "Can we go for a ride?"

"Absolutely."

After the outing they rode to Airdle City to see Arlen and Patrice's new home on Second Street. They received a tour of the saddlery shop, and Patrice invited them to stay for last sup.

"You'll be busy," Lisze said to Patrice as they cleaned the kitchen.

"I've resigned as head cook. They already have the replacement picked out."

"I will miss you, but it's time." She glanced at her friend wearing a loosely fitted tunic under her apron. "Oh, have you news?" Lisze embraced her friend when she smiled broadly and placed her hand on her belly.

They rode home, and Trillion insisted the stable boys care for their steeds. "They'll be fine," he assured them. "It's getting late."

Wilm walked with them up the stairs and announced he would find Cesim.

"Report back, young man," Lisze said.

Trillion revived the fire, and Lisze sat in a nearby chair. "I didn't have a chance to ask how the meeting with the king went."

He pressed his lips together and gave her the news. "But God will make a way."

"He always does." Lisze looked at the hourglass. "Where is Wilm?"

At that moment, Wilm stepped in. "Come, Cesim is very sick! His chest sounds funny. The healer seems worried. They've given him the same bed you had, Aba."

They both rose. "We will see him right now."

They headed to the healer's suite and walked in. No one was in sight. "Ahh, he must be back in his room."

"No, he's behind the curtain." Wilm pulled it aside for them to step through. They heard hoarse coughing and quickened their steps.

"Cesim, we've come to check on you." They found him on a bed along the wall, nearest to the hall.

Trillion sat on the short chair next to the bed. He gazed in astonishment at the sudden change in Cesim. His eyes were sunken with dark rings around them, and his cheeks hollowed. When the old man coughed deeply, Trillion rose to help him clear his lungs. Heat radiated from his back, and the skin on his hands was paper thin, almost translucent. "We hadn't known you were so sick."

Wilm walked to the other side of the bed.

Cesim reached for Wilm's hand. His lips cracked when he tried to smile. "Good lad, you are here." He shifted and tried to wet his mouth. "The light burns my eyes. Someone's pounding a spike into my head."

Trillion found a cup of water on a table nearby and gently wet Cesim's lips.

"Who will watch over the lad?" Cesim flicked his eyes to Wilm. "But I will watch you from heaven. Go forth and conquer, never doubting."

"Master Cesim, we pray for your recovery." Wilm gently touched Cesim's shoulder.

"Our times are set by God. It's been a good life. Take care of your fine lady."

The healer walked around the curtain.

Trillion asked, "Are you heading home soon?"

Anselm glanced at the curtain. "Follow me into my room."

They entered the apothecary room.

The healer shut the door and looked at them with set lips. "Plan for his last days. His friends need to come and spend whatever time they can with him."

"We are his family now."

They paused, hearing Cesim's rasping coughs. "I've assigned a royal guard to fetch me if he worsens, but there is not much I can do for him."

Lisze glanced at Trillion. With his nod, she said, "Leave some teas out. I can prepare them. If he worsens, I'll send for you, but even healers need their rest."

Anselm pulled out a small square drawer and placed dried leaves of varying colors in a dish. "One cup if he grows short of breath. This will help his heart. I've set a pot to boil over the hearth. Adds moisture to the air. Don't let it run dry."

Trillion watched the healer leave. He shifted, uncertain of doing what had come to mind. Breathing in, he remembered he was a child of God and clean in Christ. "I'll tell the king. He should still be up. He will want to know. They had once been close." He glanced at Lisze and Wilm. "Can you sit with him?"

Trillion headed to the king's suites not far down the hall. He tapped and stepped in when he heard, "Come in."

The king sat in his chair. The Leaves of God lay open next to a tall candelabra.

"Trillion? What do you need?"

Trillion stood close to the door. "Father, Cesim is very

221

sick. The healer fears he might pass. He doesn't know how long he has left."

Wallace rose. "Then I will see him now. Is he awake?"

"Yes, and Wilm is with him." They walked side by side. Both paused when they stepped past the curtains. The still form on the bed seemed shriveled, barely holding onto life.

"Like when mother died," Trillion said, his voice low and sad.

"Taken too soon—so young and vibrant. Days still come when I miss her so." The king stepped forward.

"Wilm, let them have some time alone. Off to your bed."

The king sat on the chair and held Cesim's hand. "Hello, old friend. Did we think we would see these days?"

Cesim stirred, his matted hair clinging to the pillow. "Your Majesty."

"Easy, lie still. It is the way of things. I see the Lord has ordained days of rest."

"Did you hear? We have serious troubles." Cesim's voice, hoarse and weak, ended with a cough, followed by a groan.

"Perhaps that is why the Leaves of God urge us to fear not. I've heard Jesus is the first one we see when He comes for His own. He'll carry us on eagle's wings to His halls of Glory when our time here is done."

The king began to reminisce about their time together serving in the marshal squad.

The next day passed. Many came to sit with Cesim. Prayers were uttered at Sunday service.

Sunday night Trillion awoke with a start. He slipped on a pair of socks and walked to the healer's suite where Cesim lay. Sitting on the chair near the bed, he marveled that this man could call him friend and say that he had prayed for him.

Cesim stirred, opened his eyes, and looked past Trillion until he wrapped his warm hands around Cesim's.

"Prince Trillion, your faith has saved you. He will bring

us together. This time will pass . . ." His look grew distant again.

Trillion leaned forward, hearing the death gurgle in the old man's chest. About to rise and call for help, he felt the old man's grip turn to iron.

"Already done." Cesim paused to catch his breath. He waved away Trillion's attempts to bring up the water cup. "Our days are already written. My Lord . . ." Cesim's face brightened, his eyes looking upward in the dim candlelight. Then a breath exhaled, his chest flattened, and Trillion felt Cesim escape to God's kingdom.

"Goodbye, old friend, for you have been a friend to me, as I hope I have been to you." He crossed Cesim's hands over his chest, closed his eyes, told the guard posted for the night, and headed for bed.

They held the warrior's memorial at Airdle Chapel. Many came from miles around.

Trillion watched the king rise to give the eulogy. "Cesim has run his course, remaining true to the Lord and Lamoria. The plains will miss his walks; the troops will miss his wisdom in finding the right shoe and shaping it with great skill. We will miss his easy manner and pleasant company, his frequent quotes, and pithy sayings."

Ever a good speaker, the king paused for the light laughter that ran through the chapel. He then spoke of the early days when they rode together, facing the past threat from the Amhavran. He spoke of Cesim's daily walk with God.

After the service Trillion noticed the king heading his way. "Lisze and Wilm, go on ahead."

"My liege," he said as his father drew near. Formal titles were used in public.

The king stepped to the side and down a deserted short hall. "It happened so fast I hadn't thought of a guard for Wilm. Do you have someone you would like to recommend, Son?"

The breath caught in Trillion's throat. He had called

him son. Tears held back during the memorial flowed. He reached for his father's hand. "I will always love you, Aba. I forgive you."

Wallace looked at his son. "For what?"

Trillion dropped the hand and stepped back. "When Ama died, you sent me away."

"Merely to make sure they could keep an eye on you. Nothing changed between us."

"Of course . . ." Trillion set his lips to still any quivering. "Wilm is old enough and well known by the staff and the marshals. He no longer requires a guardian."

"He has grown over the summer. Remarkably so. As if he is now a youth, no longer a boy."

"Yes. Is there anything else?"

"No, you may go."

Trillion turned and walked quickly. His old anger tried to emerge. Stepping around the chapel, he wandered past flower gardens and found himself on the edge of the Airdle Cemetery. "I forgive him," he said. "Lord, bless him," he prayed.

Trillion's eyes roved the stones of the first two wives of King Wallace. He scanned the memorials again until he remembered. His mother had died at Eliziel, and his father had allowed her to be buried there. *You will be placed beside her.*

Raising his eyes, he beheld the blue sky with wispy clouds and the air held scents of flowers and late summer fruits. Cesim had said it—his days were fixed.

"With You, Lord, I will always have an Aba. May I fulfill my purpose in You." When he turned, the courtyards and Airdle City came into view. The task of restoring Lamoria far exceeded his difficulties and hurts. "May I do Your will, Lord, for our land."

Chapter 22

Winter in Airdle

Autumn fled the day Trillion began his lawreader training, and Wilm's classes resumed after a short break.

Winter meant cold rains, blustery winds, and muddy roads sometimes up to a horse's knees. Higher passes could be blocked with snow. Most settled in their holdings, towns, or encampments, living off the harvest and tending to indoor chores. Prince Joshua traveled weekly on good days, but even then, couriers brought summaries when necessary.

Trillion advanced quickly through the courses. If Joshua could not come to the castle, he rode to Seagull Bay for the day, sometimes with Lisze. Wilm's days were filled with school and his training in horsemanship and arms.

A month later, after taking sup in the dining hall and Wilm busy with homework in his room, Trillion and Lisze pushed their chairs in their room closer to the fire.

Trillion announced, "We will be having sup in our rooms tomorrow. I've invited a special guest."

"Who is it?" Lisze asked with wide eyes.

Trillion pressed his lips together. "Should I or shouldn't I tell?"

Lisze rose and set her hands on her hips. "No secrets, remember! Besides you know how terribly I handle them."

He smiled. "Oh yes, your unexpected birthday party." Trillion stood and embraced her, feeling her soft skin. "I have invited Master Horseth to dine."

"Horseth, the language teacher?"

"The very one." He lifted his head. "Wilm is ready for tutors to advance his learning of Amhavran and Regnard."

Lisze sighed, her gaze growing distant.

Trillion pulled her toward him again. "No worries. I've made all the arrangements. Sup will be here." He did add, "But I want this to be a secret for Wilm. No telling."

"No telling."

Horseth slicked back his curls, checked his vest, and adjusted his cap before changing his mind to hold it behind his back. He was Amhavran with blond hair and blue eyes. Squaring his shoulders, he approached the page standing at the doorway to Prince Trillion's suite.

"Master Horseth, as requested." When the page looked at him blankly, he said, "Go in and make the announcement."

Prince Trillion met him near the door of the large sitting room. "Master Horseth, you are most welcome."

"Prince Trillion, Lady Lisze, Prince Wilm." He bowed with a broad smile.

Wilm's face grew somber when his teacher looked at him. "Master Horseth, may I confess?"

"Yes, Prince Wilm."

"I apologize for not paying attention or giving heed to your lessons last year, but I wish to master the language and the ways of your people."

"Is that so? What brought about this change?" Horseth glanced at Trillion and Lisze.

Wilm shuffled his feet but gave no explanation.

Trillion said, "Wilm, I have asked Master Horseth to tutor you on the Amhavran, their ways, speech, and writings." Trillion reached for a package on a nearby table. "We can start with this." He unwrapped a large book.

Horseth smiled. "Queen Lillian's Amhavran Leaves of God?"

"Yes." Trillion passed it to his former language teacher.

Wilm stepped closer to his teacher, who let him see the pages. "What writing is this?"

Swallowing a laugh, Horseth said, "The Amhavran have

always dwelt in the mountains. We avoided the plains before your people arrived generations ago. We already had a written language, not like the one Daniel created for the Lamorians." He raised a brow. "Are you ready to learn not only how to say hello and enter a family's lodging in our cities, but to also master their written speech?"

"Yes." He glanced at his father. "This is for Master Horseth?"

"No, son, this is for you. The easiest way to learn to read Amhavran is by reading God's Word. If you become stuck, you can compare with ours."

"Along with many other lessons." Horseth glanced at Trillion. "When will you add the Regnard tongue?"

"I've arranged a tutor from town, but the Amhavran studies are primary."

"Good to learn languages in one's youth. Teaching your son will be an honor." Horseth leaned toward Wilm with brows pulled together. "Prince Wilm, in my class, you are the student, understand?"

"Yes, Master Horseth."

"Listen to Psalm 23." Trillion took the Bible and read the passage.

"Queen Lillian was gifted in languages. She could pick up a dialect in one turn and was the heart of the language program here. She has not been forgotten." Master Horseth reached for the book and read another passage. "Young prince, your first lesson will be learning to read the script."

A knock on the door was followed by pages bringing in their meal. During sup and after, Horseth began to talk about the ways of his people.

The days flew by. Ever mindful of his brief visit before the gates of heaven, Trillion worked to learn how to love a distant father. The king eventually signed Prince Joshua's decree to investigate claims. Examining decisions and investigating as quietly as possible, Trillion enjoyed working beside his brother. The corruption was not as obvious as in Worstein, but it lurked under the surface. Nothing had come of the warrant for Severn's arrest, and he remained in hiding. At the end of the workday, Trillion would pray with Joshua for the Lord to heal and save their land.

As the winter waned and days lengthened, Prince Trillion continued to pour his knowledge of the languages and the peoples into Wilm. Setting aside a rigid schedule, he would choose a tongue for the day, exasperating Lisze.

One day after last sup, Wilm corrected his mother. "No, Ama, say it like this."

"And now I have two speaking in tongues in my own chambers." Lisze laughed. "I was not gifted in languages."

"Son, say it with respect. Your mother spends her days helping any who have needs throughout the castle."

"What was it this time? Regnard? Makes my head spin." Lisze headed for the side table and held up three folded and sealed parchments. "Mail call for Prince Trillion and Wilm!"

Wilm asked, "Who wrote this time?"

"Open them up and tell us." Lisze handed one to Trillion and two to Wilm.

"Logan, as usual. Fillan does not write as often." Wilm scrunched his nose. "Maybe preparing for his first child, and fishing for himself?"

"Yes, Son." Trillion smiled with Lisze's knowing gaze. "It's what adult life looks like. Not a lot of time to spare."

"Esrilin won't be back to Airdle. Head Marshal Vaughn sent him on another mission but doesn't say what it is."

Lisze tilted her head. "Secrets. And Esrilin's letter to you, my love?"

He carefully released the seal and read the letter through. Setting it aside, he glanced at Lisze.

"What?" She leaned forward, wanting to know.

Trillion rose. "Wilm, you can read those by candlelight. Didn't you want to ride with your friends to Dornan Ridge? I think it's dry enough by now."

"Right! I can go?" Wilm was out the door in moments.

"Now Trillion, what's happening?" She accepted the letter and read it. "The Ayisin chiefs, the plainsmen, and Stoddard Council request your presence at the spring Eastern Gathering. That's wonderful. Hadn't you told me you wanted to help bring the peoples together?"

Trillion sat back down. It was time. "Remember when I was wounded by the tanner? You thought I would die. It felt like I had."

Lisze sat beside him and held his hand. "It's like I went up to heaven, but didn't cross over. Hard to explain." Trillion stroked her hand and told her what had happened. "My days are few. I don't know when, but we need to spend as much time together as we can." He pulled back, feeling the failure of the lack of progress in being the peacemaker the Lord had called him to be. "I can't even reconcile with my father. How can I bring the tribes together?"

"Trillion, you've pulled away from the king since Cesim's funeral."

"I forgave him, and he acted as if I had accused him of doing wrong."

"My love, you know how disconnected and single-minded Joshua can be." Seeing his nod, she said, "The king is the same. He's often not aware of others' feelings. Many assume it's because he sits on the throne, but I've seen Joshua act the same way."

"I know I must love him as he is. So it's not my fault." He stood. "Prince David's cohorts will be with him." Picking up the letter, he met her gaze. "But Esrilin and Thielen will both be there. I can ask for their help if need be. The Lord must have told him to warn me." Trillion set it aside. "Nothing will come of it unless the king chooses to send me. And I will take Wilm with me."

Lisze stood. She at first wanted to protest, forbid it, but as she met his gaze, she knew this was also of the Lord.

"Fear not," he said, giving her a full embrace.

"Fear not, for there's always something we can fear." She turned her head to plant a kiss on his cheek. "And I will pray that you do well, Prince Trillion, every day you draw breath. May you heal rifts and bring people together at the Eastern Gathering at Whistler's Ridge."

Chapter 23

The Eastern Spring Gathering at Whistler's Ridge

Trillion passed the tests to become a recording judge able to certify court decisions. Wilm, able to carry on a conversation in both Amhavran and Regnard, attended the higher-level language classes at the Airdle Day School.

One chilly morning, Trillion received a summons to go to his father's office. Seeing the room empty, he sat down and waited.

The page had said the king talked with Prince David and Ricard in the Judgment Hall. Recalling Esrilin's letter, he wondered if the Ayisin's request would be honored.

He rose when his father entered.

The king sat in his chair. "Trillion, as you know the Eastern Spring Gathering at Whistler's Ridge will occur after Easter this year—a little over a month away. Prince Joshua had considered going, but cases in Tholen will keep him here. Also, the Ayisin and plainsmen have requested that you gather with them."

"Prince Wilm would like to go."

The king smiled for the first time. "He can accompany you as clerk and help the marshals."

"Will we journey there with you?" Perhaps this way he could regain rapport with his father.

"I will leave early to travel with Prince David through Dornan."

Trillion kept a neutral face. "May we ride with Marshal Thielen and his squad?"

"Of course, I expected it." The king sat forward and tilted his head.

He recognized the sign of dismissal and rose. "Have a good day, Father." He knew better than to repeat that he loved him.

Back in their rooms after sup he shared the news.

Lisze nodded. "What I suspected."

Wilm's grin went from ear to ear. Trillion resisted the urge to tousle his hair.

The king's approval for the trip launched days of planning. Wilm could talk of nothing else. Trillion admired his wife for helping acquire items and seeing that they had enough clothes for their growing son, even though he knew she had apprehensions about the trip.

Their prayers grew more focused each night. Lisze joined with him in praying for peace and for success in Trillion's tasks.

The week before they would leave, after returning from dining with the king and the guests he had invited, Trillion laid out the maps on their table. "Thielen said we'll take the Roanin Trail, north of Dornan Hills, straight to the gathering."

"Naturally, at a stiff pace. Wilm, you've never been to the city of Whistler's Ridge." Lisze touched his shoulder. "We skirted the edges of its commons on our way to the springs. The fair and gathering fields are southeast, a settled area of rolling farms and fenced-in herds."

Trillion told Wilm, "We will be occupied with the gathering of the chiefs. The ancient phrase for council meetings." He laughed when Wilm scrunched his face.

"We studied about that already. I'm the only one in class who can go!"

Wilm followed his father's finger as he traced their journey along the Roanin Trail heading northeast. The hills of

Invien ran north and south with their higher peaks near the Amhavran border. Rounded, heavily forested mounds spanned Whistler's Ridge's northern expanse. He bent forward to see the details of the city and its common lands, as well as the marketplace and fairgrounds. A drawing identified the gathering place where they would meet with Marshal Esrilin and his squad.

The day arrived.

Trillion watched Wilm headed toward Marshal Thielen, who stood beside their horses, packed and ready to leave. Wilm was formally dressed, wearing an embroidered cloak over his jerkin bearing the Airdle shield.

The notable squad leader turned to Wilm and strictly charged him, "You will be responsible to see the horses are well cared for and dry wood obtained."

Wilm nodded and could hardly keep his feet still with his excitement.

They had no mishaps along the way. Trillion prayed for wisdom and an even temper, for he felt inner warnings from the Spirit.

As they crested the last rise, Trillion brought his steed equal to Thielen's. Whistler's Ridge gleamed in an early afternoon's sun. Spring flowers flanked the road as it narrowed before dropping to a settled plain. Dornan Council stretched out before them, dotted with towns and clumps of houses bounded by fields ready for planting and lush green grass divided into pastures.

Wilm asked, "Is this what all of Dornan looks like?"

"The southern portion but not to the east and the northern plains." Trillion looked eastward. "It's been a long time since I've traveled these roads."

"I would like to see the other councils. I've never been that far north."

Beyond the city of Whistler's Ridge, tall streamers and banners outlined rows of market stalls. Farther ahead, Wilm spied long buildings near corrals surrounded by raised benches, with a tall pole beside a large stone firepit. He gazed upon the place of gathering, spoken of in their history books, recalling the tales his teachers told of alliances, intrigue, and deception. Wilm had imagined it looking grander and more foreboding than just glistening stones by a pole with the Airdle crest and Dornan flag.

Marshal Thielen led the squad to the main tents and gestured for another marshal to gather the horses.

"Wilm, go with them to secure the horses. Marshal Bid will walk you back to our tent." Trillion smiled, remembering when his mother, Queen Lillian, had sent him off with the commission to assist at a gathering. Wilm's chest seemed as broad and full as his had been those many years ago.

Wilm took the reins for their three, as well as four others. Bid gathered the squad's mounts while another young marshal led the pack horses to their tents. The tents were in a row, bearing the banner of each house waving in the breeze. He assumed the House of Airdle would be along the first row, near the tents of meeting. Rows of distant tents displayed Ayisin banners. Wilm recognized the banners of the clans from Roanin, Tholen, Stolein, and Dornan. A series of small enclosures with lean-tos were close to a set of stables.

Wilm increased his pace when he recognized Esrilin standing by the small paddocks.

"Greetings, Marshal Bid, you have two corrals for your mounts. Divide them up as necessary." Esrilin looked at Wilm. "And we have a tall stable boy in our midst. Wilm, what of the royal mounts? Stabled or put to pasture?"

Wilm stood beside Esrilin and realized that he came to

the marshal's shoulders. He smiled broadly. "It's great to see you. Thank you for your letters."

Esrilin smiled and stepped back to look at Wilm. "You've grown. I can't call you little one anymore. Stable boy, answer the question."

Wilm answered, "Marshal Esrilin, may they be pastured to graze? Have a good spot?"

"Here, at Whistler's Ridge? Young prince, do you insult the grass found in this valley?"

He laughed and walked beside the marshal.

"And Prince Trillion? Is he well? I hear he has quite recovered." Esrilin led him to the opening in the fence.

"For the most part. He can school his own steed." Once the horses were in the paddocks, Wilm turned to hug Esrilin. "I've missed you so."

"And I, you, but from your letters, I know that you are learning many valuable lessons at Airdle. I pray you have time together with your father. Our destinies are fixed by God, and woe to any who would stand in His way. The marshal service is my call from the Lord." Esrilin glanced at the youth growing into a man. "Are you glad you will squire at Worstein? I've heard good things about Lord Bierl."

"I am, but it will be a long time away from home."

"You have a few more years yet." Esrilin glanced about at the comings and goings of many. "Now, Prince Wilm, to your duties. Many are praying this gathering will help our people come together."

"As are we, Marshal Esrilin." Wilm, with one last check that the gate had been secured, headed for the main row of tents.

A waiting marshal led him to the third tent with flowing banners. Two ornate seats set on rugs woven with the Airdle crest occupied the back of the enclosure. The king sat on the right and Prince David on the left. His father hovered by the king's left side. No Ayisin or Sanderfield were in sight. He recognized many from Airdle and Dornan, as they sometimes visited Airdle to see the king. Prince David led the session, recognizing the delegations, giving them a short while to speak. When most had assembled, he announced the schedule for the gathering.

As the bell for last sup sounded, Prince David rose from his chair and turned to the king. Together, they walked to the dining hall. Prince David's aides formed a phalanx around them. Prince Trillion moved to stand beside his son toward the back as the large group followed the king.

Leading men, mostly from Airdle and Dornan, greeted the king and his firstborn warmly, accompanying them to the feast. Lord Nordrum, along with the mayors from the largest cities, had spoken of the prosperity of their councils. It had been too long since the king had toured Lamoria. The settled towns snuggling up close to common lands had at first alarmed him, but their glowing reports set him at ease.

"Where are Prince Trillion and Prince Wilm?" The king had assumed they were following at a distance and would join them in the dining hall.

"They've been requested to meet with another group." Prince David followed Marshal Rysen to a large tent set off by itself.

David smiled when the king, upon entering the tent, gazed at its transformation into an ornate banquet hall. Soon, the right to rule would be his. Until then, his father, who often couldn't see past empty flattery, needed to come to another opinion on some critical matters.

The advancement of Lamoria depended upon it.

King Wallace walked with his son to the head table. He lifted his brow at the large round tables filling the area. They approached a long, ornately decorated table with two kingly chairs occupying the center.

An aide pulled out a chair and helped the king sit facing the assembled dignitaries from Airdle and Dornan. Gold-trimmed dishes and fine silver graced their place settings.

Wallace asked, "Prince David, where are the other councils?"

"My lord, as we are a diverse country, we each have our own concerns. These are the leaders of the settled lands."

Wallace reached for a chalice, but his son set another one before him. Unsettled, he had hoped at least representatives of all the councils could dine together.

"We've prepared a special banquet." David winked at Severn and the leaders from Worstein who had fled their council. Healer Trent smiled at the crown prince.

The king took a sip, feeling the wine settle his nerves. He glanced at the men at his table.

Prince David rose and lifted his chalice. "All hail High King Wallace and the land of Lamoria."

The men replied, "Hail High King Wallace . . ."

The king shifted uncomfortably in his chair with the title.

Prince David spoke before any could state the pledge of Lamoria. "And the House of Airdle, thanks to the hospitality of Lord Nordrum and former Mayor Dunne of Whistler's Ridge, present this feast in recognition of our fine land, Lamoria." With a hand clap, pages entered with laden platters and bowls for the tables. Waiters served each plate and refilled the cups.

King Wallace cringed at the ostentatious display. Yet the wine was exceptional. The roasted lamb and beef filled the tent with tantalizing aromas.

Prince David sat. "King Wallace, I'd like you to hear from Judge Severn, as well as the mayors and businessmen from Worstein. They are as troubled as we are by Lord Bierl's opposition to their visionary leadership. They desire that the Council of Worstein work closely with the House of Airdle. We must be able to rely on Worstein Council to stand against any attacks from the Amhavran, lest they overrun our lands."

"Now it's the Amhavran invading?" The king felt an inner warning rise.

"My lord, you need to hear what these men have to say concerning the charges laid against them by Prince Trillion."

"But didn't Lord Bierl and the Council of Worstein arrive at these decisions because of the advice of Prince Joshua?"

"Have you examined the evidence for yourself?"

"I relied upon Prince Joshua's wisdom and experience."

Prince David leveled his voice. Every eye at the table focused upon them. Now was the time to lay the seeds of his rule, beginning with setting matters right in Worstein. "Prince Trillion has only recently passed the tests of law-reader and judge. He lacks experience." He looked sharply at Severn and continued, "Prince Joshua can be swayed. It's happened before."

The king's mind was too muddled to assemble a fitting rebuttal.

"Trillion, as we well know, has been graced with charm and flattering speech. He's put on the robes of faith and led you down a twisted path." David swept his arm to the side. "Our nation has grown. Our towns spread out. New inventions and designs provide for our people's needs, and we require workers for our trade halls as well as our fields." He increased the intensity of his voice and leaned closer to the king. "My brother is of the people who cling to the old ways as if they were written by God Himself. A great injustice has been done, investments lost, progress forestalled, due to prejudice and lack of vision."

"I've not seen such duplicity in Prince Trillion these past months."

"My lord, if you may permit me to speak." Healer Trent glanced at David. "He's not changed his ways. Despite his protestations, he's not made things right with those he cheated. He lay with a woman. I saw it myself when he was at Roanin."

Others added their own stories, defending their actions.

Ashes formed in the king's chest. "What of the reports of forced servitude, substandard housing, and wretched food?"

"The tales of a few aggrieved workers. You know how people can exaggerate an inconvenience into a wrong done. Have you confirmed the accusations, Your Majesty?" Prince David asked. "Have you completed your own investigation or did you rely on Prince Joshua, who has been swayed by Prince Trillion? Who knows what they paid Trillion to levy these ridiculous charges on forward-thinking leaders of the council only seeking to improve and better the towns."

The king shook his head. "No, Prince Joshua brought proofs with his report."

"What can be done now?" Prince David asked. The group around him bowed their heads in the king's direction.

"File your appeals. I will study the documents myself and command Prince Joshua to open an investigation to discover the facts." He raised his hand, hearing the groans. "Prince Joshua has served well and never supported flawed judgments. I will confirm his findings, but I do not have time to oversee the investigation. Prince Joshua is more than capable as Supreme Judge of Lamoria. We will see justice brought forth. If you have endured your losses since then, you can wait for a proper examination to discover the truth." King Wallace looked at each one, pleased to see them nod and lower their eyes.

The marshals' dining tent filled with horsemen, plainsmen, and elders.

The meal was lavish and delicious, made more so by their long day. The roasted lamb was tender and well-seasoned. Root vegetables, some creamed and buttered, followed by pudding cakes occupied their attention. As the meal wound down, Prince Trillion rose. He glanced toward his son. "Ready?"

"Father, do we return to the meeting tent?"

"A different one. Follow me." Wilm worked to keep up with his father, who stepped through the crowds to tents past the paddocks. Wilm recognized some of the Ayisin from Tierney and Worstein.

Trillion slipped into the back of a tent, and Wilm followed. He found himself standing on the outer edge of a large circle of leaders sitting cross-legged on thick rugs. They made room for their prince. Wilm found a place to kneel near the tent canvas and listened as they welcomed his father.

Aiden, former chief of the Imbus Ayisin, rose and began to pray. He acknowledged Trillion and Wilm. The prince approached the Ayisin elder for the traditional greeting.

Trillion surveyed the group, mostly of the outer provinces, but also small holding lords and tradesmen from the two largest regions. "Thank you, Chief Aiden, for whether we have much or little, dwell in town or the plains, travel following the stars or well-laid paths, we are all one before our mighty God." He raised his hand and pointed one finger into the air.

All said, "Lamoria is one. Our God is one. Our law is one."

"Today we have come to listen, to hear your grievances, and to seek solutions that will lessen tensions between our peoples."

Most began with complaints of Prince David's marshals not helping with the attacks upon their lands. Many blamed bandits, but some accused greedy plainsmen and townsmen. Suggestions were offered, and the discussion flowed. Trillion moderated, finding solutions to some issues.

Wilm noticed Marshal Thielen's second approach Esrilin. A young page entered to leave saddle bags and bedrolls near the head marshal. The pile looked like their luggage, but the throng was too thick for Wilm to make his way across until the meeting broke up. When the meeting ended, he headed toward Esrilin.

"Marshal Esrilin, what are these?"

"Your bags. You will be camping in my tent."

Prince Trillion approached, noting Wilm's broad smile, and listened to the marshal's explanation.

Thielen stepped into the meeting tent. "We've been dismissed to patrol the perimeter."

"Who is guarding King Wallace?"

"Prince David's squad under Marshal Dunne."

Trillion sucked in his breath. "You must find a way to insert two trusted marshals into the king's guards. Some of the most suspicious attacks were perpetrated when that squad was in the field. That said, I welcome retiring with you, Marshal Esrilin."

The marshals helped them with their luggage, and they left for Esrilin's large tent. Two of his men cleared an area in a side wing. "We can erect a curtain for privacy, Prince Trillion."

"Nonsense," Trillion said with a smile. "Like camping, right, Wilm? This will be a welcome respite for us." He glanced at Wilm. "Set up our bedrolls. I need to make a quick report to the king. He has probably also retired to his tent."

Trillion noted his brother Ricard's mare was still tied at the railing near Prince David's tent. Slipping past, he looked about for the king's tent as more had been erected since their arrival that afternoon.

"Prince Trillion," said a page bearing Prince David's insignia. "The prince told me to fetch you."

"Of course, where is the king's tent?"

"Prince David will tell you everything. Follow me."

Trillion paused, wishing he hadn't come as the page turned toward the dining tent. Raucous laughter and the scent of liquors made his jaw tighten. Feeling the Holy Spirit's warning, he prayed as he followed the page.

"So you found my wandering little brother," Prince David said with thickened, almost slurred speech. The men crowded around him burst into laughter.

Trillion waited at the entrance, not far from David's table, keeping his face neutral.

"Come to tattle on someone to the king?"

He knew better than to state the king had requested a report of his meeting with the Ayisin and plainsmen.

"Now a mute, or is that a deaf-mute?" Cupping his hand to his ear, David leaned forward and furrowed his brow as if unable to hear.

Laughter erupted again.

"Listen, Trillion of the Ayisin, Brother!" David's spittle reached the man sitting next to him. "Very soon, things will change for the better, and you will be able to take your place with your people. So nice you can perform Prince Joshua's service to the more distant parts, but some injustices cry out for reversal." He swirled the last of the dregs in his cup and drank it down. A waiting page refilled it. "Nothing to say?" Prince David raised his brows.

Trillion fled before his brother could follow with a servant's dismissal. Riotous laughter flowed from the tent. He had been not merely shut out, but publicly humiliated. He should be used to this, having grown up with it. Trillion paused his steps, forcing himself not to glance back at the tent. His law studies were in vain. Once the king passed and the crown sat on his brother's head, he had better live far away from Airdle.

Trillion found his way to Esrilin's tent. Low voices and friendly laughter filtered out. He stepped in and allowed his eyes to adjust. The group felt familiar and friendly.

"Father!" Wilm said, coming up to his side. "You're . . . what happened?"

"Nothing we need to discuss." Trillion rested his hand on his son's shoulder, which was now nearly equal to his. "I'm glad the marshals invited us to rest here. It's too noisy there."

Esrilin laid out a pad on the circle lit by a lamp in the center. "That was quick. You must have given the short version."

"They moved the king's tent, or I couldn't find it." He relayed the sparsest of details.

Esrilin said, "The Ayisin and Keyayisin encamped among the trees are eager to meet with you."

Trillion held back a sigh and felt a familiar tiredness begin to descend. "It's been too long since I've been on the eastern plains."

"Father passed the tests to become a chief judge like uncle," Wilm said. His voice faded away with Trillion's sharp look.

"We heard and were glad to know you will assist him. All the councils need his oversight."

"Agreed, but I will probably not be overseeing any of the judgments in Airdle or Dornan." When Esrilin met his gaze with a knowing look, his gloom deepened. His brother's display was more than just a drunken night's jesting in front of guests. "Tell me of the Weaver's Plain canyons, eastern grasslands, and shores."

Esrilin, quiet as always, allowed his men to speak.

As the night wound down and Wilm had slipped into his bedroll, Esrilin said to Trillion, "Tomorrow, I will take you to the outer camps. The less said at Prince David's meetings, the better."

The next morning Wilm woke to the smell of breakfast cooking over an open fire. His nose twitched and his stomach growled with perpetual hunger. Seeing his father still asleep, he slipped out of his bedroll, pulled on his boots, grabbed his jacket, and headed out.

Esrilin and several marshals sat on benches around a glowing fire, cooking link sausages on sticks.

"Our prince has emerged." One gestured to a coffeepot perched on warm stones. "Drink coffee now?"

"I've been drinking that for a while." Wilm retrieved his cup and poured the thick brew, along with some grounds. "Um, with pulp."

A marshal led him to a side table loaded with plates, utensils, cooked eggs, and pastries.

"No wood-fired bannock?"

"This is civilized camping."

"Without the snared rabbit either." Wilm filled his plate. He sat near Esrilin. "When do the meetings start?"

"Not for a while. They drank late and will sleep it off. There will be a midday feast, followed by competitions at the parade grounds. Many will make deals and settle disputes during that time. A courier brought a message. Prince Trillion's time to see the king will be in the afternoon after the events. He can sit most of the day with the Ayisin."

Esrilin stood. "Wilm, when you're done, let's see who sits by their fires."

They sauntered along the row of tents, fire circles found at every third one. Large stones, peeled logs, and benches surrounded smoldering firepits. Esrilin stopped to talk with early risers, and many greeted the marshal by name.

By the fourth firepit, Eriason, who had seen Wilm at Public Judgment, patted the stones beside him and invited them to sit. With a quiet call, a boy close to Wilm's age brought a steaming cup of strong tea sweetened with cream and sugar, along with bannock slathered with lard and salt. Wilm ate half of it before he remembered to thank them. He tried not to blush at their soft laughter.

"Are you hungry young one growing into a man? Like my Lukas." Eriason gestured for his grandson to join them.

Trillion approached and sat down. "Esrilin, your marshals told me where you went." He greeted by name the ones he knew.

Eriason asked, "Will we have a chance to talk with the king?" He set down his tea. "Perhaps he could come to us—not go to the big tent."

"That would be a wise request. Prince David has plans for the king's time, but I will try to find a way to ask him." Trillion accepted a cup of tea. "Good wood and good fire make the best tea."

They sat without speaking for a time, drinking in the presence of the others.

Eriason said, "We were nomadic ages ago. We built huts along the lakes and rivers for fishing, houses near fields during the growing season, and lived in tents to gather berries for making pemmican with lard and smoked meats. Some clans roamed the plains for the herds—horses and cattle. Life had its rhythm, but today many leave their houses only for short trips. The blessings of this land and trade with the townsmen have filled our homes." He leaned forward. "Some now want to divide the common lands, put up fences, build more roads. Where are the herds to go? Must we pen our horses and keep cattle in muddy feedlots?"

Others sitting around the firepit added their concerns.

Trillion asked, "Is this a problem at Imbus? I thought all made use of the open plains."

"North of Tholen Falls, that is truth, but south of there, even to the passes, some of Dornan talk of dividing the land into parcels for sale. They would build towns, estates with houses and barns. They'd fence the Weaver's Plain. Our forests and fields in Imbus lack room for large herds. Some have already been pushed out and are clearing northern forests for grazing."

"They want to fence Weaver's Plain, the richest grasslands of the realm?" Trillion looked at their grim faces.

"The common lands are vital for horsemen to release their herds and cull the free-range horses. There were no problems between the townsmen, plainsmen, and our people. The few who did not respect herd markings were pursued by all and handed over to the marshals for judgment. You know this." All nodded with Eriason's words.

"That is not what Prince David has been saying." Naseran, a tall plainsman, joined the conversation and tales flowed of missing herds, as well as fences and buildings constructed in common lands.

"Prince Trillion, we need to ask the king if he agrees with Dornan's plans."

Naseran folded his arms. "Prince David's friends, the holding lords and town-spawned rich, grow fat off our labors. Strangers run through our lands unchecked and unchallenged."

Prince Trillion rose. "The king has heard some of this but not of the settling of the common lands. He will have to take up this matter with Dornan Council." So, this was the motive behind many of the attacks in the east. David's boldness sent a chill down his back. For he would not be condoning these actions if he did not feel he had the support of the southern councils.

Chapter 24

The King's Heart Is Turned

Too soon, and yet not soon enough, a courier came to bring Trillion to the king. Thankfully, the meeting tent with the throne chairs was quiet as the king enjoyed afternoon tea.

"Ahh, Trillion, come sit."

Trillion perched on the edge of the other large chair.

"The Word says in order to make a pure judgment, one must hear both sides of a matter." King Wallace set down the teacup beside a plate of fine pastries. He turned his head to look at his youngest son. "You have just completed your studies. Perhaps we had you sit for the qualifying exams too soon. I hear injustices have occurred in Worstein. Surprised Prince Joshua went along. Did he consider all sides?" The king took another sip of tea. "I have sent couriers to Prince Joshua. He will investigate the actions taken at Invien Springs. It seems you have been deceived by those seeking to undo the progress of the region."

Trillion's heart dropped, and he could not find his voice.

The king looked at his son. "I know you are easily swayed, but the truth will be made manifest, as the Word attests. Prince David recommends you practice your law-reading skills with the Ayisin from now on. After all, they are your people." He cleared his throat. His brows drew down. "The reports I've heard . . . I didn't think you would return to your former ways."

Trillion stood, his face a mask. His head spun and his hands felt clammy. Would the king always believe these lies about him? Hadn't the months of living in the castle proved his transformation? Wetting his lips, he tried to take courage. "The people humbly request you meet them at their fire circle."

King Wallace shifted, adjusted his jerkin, and reached for a pastry. "They can come later today for Public Judgment—same as on a full moon hearing at Airdle Castle. If this was urgent, why did they wait for the Eastern Gathering and not come to Airdle?"

"Your Majesty, you should see them in private to hear what they have to say. This settling of the Weaver's Plain—"

The king slapped his hand upon his knee. "Does everyone stand against progress? The people of Dornan need the space and will only encroach nearby tracts. I have been assured the vast plains will not be diminished by a few extra towns and holdings."

He tried one last time. "My King, as you said—"

"I've heard enough. Let them come in the next few turns and level their accusations for all to hear. Perhaps they will not be as brave when those with whom they disagree are standing nearby." The king waved his hand in dismissal.

"As you wish, my liege." Trillion left. He found Esrilin and led him into the marshal's tent. His shoulders slumped as he repeated the king's words.

"So, Prince David and the men pushing for fencing the plains will be there? It's not surprising." Esrilin reached to console the prince. "I will let the Ayisin know and encourage them to go. The king must hear this from them."

"I fear Prince David has already swayed his mind."

"Didn't Prince Joshua show the king proof of the crimes of both the supreme judge and his associates?"

"Prince David can be very persuasive."

Esrilin raised his brow. "As long as you were a prince uninterested in helping lead the realm like Prince Ricard, you were no threat."

"He cannot tolerate that I have joined with Prince

Joshua." Trillion turned to go. What of the path the Lord had set before him? Where was the victory?

"Prince Trillion, long has our esteemed judge sat by passively, overseeing court decisions in the castle. You have been the first one to encourage him to step up for all of Lamoria. That is a mighty act indeed." Esrilin rested his hand on Trillion's shoulder. "I have a message for you. The chiefs and elders of Imbus and Stoddard have invited you and Prince Wilm to tour their region after the fair. Also, the Keyayisin welcome you to kindle a fire in their lodge. The changes in you have been noticed."

"So, this is what it's like to suffer for doing good and not evil. Easier to read about in First Peter than to live it." Yet, the Lord's joy was still his. *Lead me yet, Lord.*

"Let us follow our great God, despite what men may say of us. Prince Wilm is currently schooling the horses with the younger marshals. He's having quite the fun with practice wooden swords. I'm sure he'd enjoy your company at the exercise yards." Esrilin stepped back. "I'll convey the king's invitation for the Ayisin and plainsmen to come to the meeting tent."

"Thank you. I'll be along as soon as I get out of this formal attire."

Trillion found his son with the marshals and watched them charge, trying to unseat each other. On foot, while the horses ran about them, they clashed with wooden swords. When a stable boy brought Kewatin, he joined the fray.

Marshal Thielen led the Ayisin and plainsmen to the meeting tent. Prince David put them in the back of the line and refused to let them present their concerns as a group. Lawreaders, mayors, and councilmen stood by to refute each claim until the hour passed, and three marshals attempted to herd the rest out. Eriason, of the Ayisin, and Naseran, a plainsman, pushed their way to the front to address the king.

Prince David blocked their passage. "Can't you see? The king has tired. The hour is up, and we need the tent cleared for the banquet!"

The king stood and proclaimed, "The time has passed. Come to Public Judgment at Airdle where we will have more time to hear your concerns."

The men bowed and withdrew.

Prince David gestured for Marshal Thielen to approach. "You have been reassigned. You will assume command of Marshal Esrilin's squad, and he will lead the Stoddard Contingent."

Thielen bowed. "Has Marshal Esrilin been informed of this change?"

King Wallace waited for the marshal to complete his bow. "His new orders will be waiting for him at Stoddard Way Station. Tell him I send him there to clean up a squad that has lost its way. After all, if they were doing their job, how would these incursions have happened? The invaders must have passed through the northern territories of Stoddard."

"I will convey your wishes, Your Majesty, as well as your faith in his leadership." Thielen turned, his face a set mask.

The large marshal dining tent became a council meeting of sorts. The disgruntled plainsmen had assembled at Esrilin's invitation to sup. Marshal Thielen's news hadn't encouraged anyone. Trillion avoided making any assurances.

Having heard that the king would return to Airdle Castle through Dornan with Prince David, Trillion accepted the northern tribes' offer. He penned a letter to the king requesting permission to tour the northern councils and wished him a safe journey home. He added a personal letter to Lisze.

Trillion noticed Wilm's intense look mixed with concern. "Your ama knows you will enjoy seeing other parts of our land and meeting the ones who had helped her. You'll also meet my mother's people."

"I want to go, but won't she be lonely? Couldn't she join us?"

"The king depends on her service. We'll not linger long." He lifted his brows. "Marshal Esrilin will go with us to the Stoddard Way Station by our northern border."

Trillion had offered to stay as long as the Ayisin and plainsmen leaders wished, but after the cold reception with the king, they were ready to leave for home. Having secured the location of the king's tent, he visited with Esrilin.

They waited until the page had readied the tent for the king to retire. In the shadows, Trillion slipped alone into the tent and waited, hidden behind a screen. He heard the king enter and bid the page goodnight. Assured they were alone, he stepped into the light. "Father."

King Wallace turned, his hand shaking slightly.

Trillion moved to his side to stabilize him. The liquor was strong on his father's breath. "Let me help you."

King Wallace wrenched his arm free. "I can manage." He sat and stared at his son. "My wayward son, unstable as water."

Trillion's rehearsed speech faded away. Prince David had turned his father against him. "I will pray you have a safe journey home."

"Prince David needs to be with me now. Did I tell you he and Prince Ricard will be moving back into the castle? Your quarters by the garden will be renovated. As I recall, you enjoyed staying there earlier. It's time for him to take the mantle, to learn while I'm still around to guide him. He will be your king someday. I pray you will support him."

"If we may be permitted. The Imbus and Stoddard leaders have invited Prince Wilm and myself to tour their lands. Also, the Keyayisin have extended invitations as well. If you are agreeing?"

"That sounds like a good plan. You will be weeks on that trip, more than enough time to move you out of your quarters." The king looked at his son for the first time. "I pray you will remember what we taught you as a boy. What you do reflects upon the House of Airdle."

Trillion stood to full height and met the king's gaze. "As a Christian, Father, there is now no condemnation for me. Since that day I have ever strived to follow God and live righteously. We will be most grateful for the new suites. I thank you for your agreeing to our trip. We will leave on the morrow."

The old king nodded but did not rise. He sighed tiredly.

Recalling the love for others the Lord commanded, Trillion stepped toward his father. "I love you, Father. I will ever hold you in my prayers. May you rest in Christ your Savior." He placed his letters on a small side table. "I will fetch your chamberlain." Trillion left the tent.

Esrilin waited outside. "It's done. We leave at first light."

By the time they returned to Esrilin's tent, Wilm was fast asleep.

"Prince Trillion, the Imbus Ayisin and plainsmen have called for a prayer meeting. You are welcome to join us. If Wilm weren't so tired, I know he'd want to go," Esrilin said.

"You may call me Trillion, and I will call you by your given name. You have shown yourself to be a friend and are always welcome at my fire circle. I'll grab my bag."

"Thank you, Trillion. And I value your efforts to heal our land. Your faith is evident. The meeting has already begun. I'll lead the way." They walked together, united in one Lord, unified in the Spirit.

"Their fellowship is led by a plurality of elders with few earning their living through preaching. While their elders are scholars of God's Word, they also have professions. You will enjoy their breaking of bread service." Esrilin consulted his note. "The theme is Jesus Christ our Deliverer, though you may share whatever God has placed on your heart."

"I am ready."

A large plainsman's tent, crowded with men sitting in concentric circles, was filled with songs of praise. Trillion paused before the opened flap, feeling unworthy.

"Prince Trillion, we are glad you have come." Pagiel, with broad hands, gestured for him to enter and sit at the head of the innermost circle.

Room was made, and the two latecomers found their places. Trillion pulled his bag forward and drew out a thick, hand-bound book. He listened as one spoke of the Lord's gracious mercy and His complete salvation.

"Jesus saves to the uttermost." The man talked of his transformation decades ago as if it had happened yesterday. Others followed with various scriptures portraying regeneration and new life in Christ.

Trillion felt the cares for the people from David's corruption and his father's coldness fall away as he worshiped in the Spirit with other believers. Prayers for his brother David and his father arose. *Oh Lord, show them Your love.*

After the last song, Pagiel stood with an open Leaves of God. "The Lord has impressed upon me that despite what is done to me, I must not let anyone push me to sin. We are not to answer evil for evil, but instead good for evil." He read from Romans chapter twelve. "God calls us to extend love to our enemies, even if they are of Lamoria. Give that cup of water, plate of food, and pray for them. Personal retribution and retaliation are not an option for followers of Jesus Christ. We must stand against evil as we are commissioned, according to our laws. As we saw in the book of Acts, at the appropriate time, the apostle Paul demanded his rights as a citizen. But we are not to take vengeance."

Trillion followed the passages cited in the Amhavran text. Even though the elder had moved on to other passages,

Trillion found himself transfixed by Romans 12:14. "Bless those who persecute you; bless and do not curse them."

The Amhavran had many words for blessing: the blessing of a worker to his master, a lord to his servant, or to the merchant in the marketplace. The word chosen in Amhavran for that verse was not any of those, but that of a husband to his wife, a parent to a child, or the blessing one would extend to a close intimate friend.

Prince David had always been his enemy. Since his conversion, he kept the peace by avoiding his half-brother. Today he had to pray for the Lord to bless David as if they were and had always been close friends.

The room fell still. Trillion looked up. All eyes rested on him. He stood with the Amhavran book in his hands. "When brothers make themselves our enemies, we are torn, pierced, struck down. Those we had trusted who should be our friends are transformed into bitter enemies. Hate, anger, rage come easily and naturally in our flesh. But did not our Lord die for them as well? Did not His blood shed on the cross cover their sins? And if they would turn, if they would surrender to God and confess their sins committed against us, would not the God of heaven forgive them? So, in hopes, even if they do not, or we never see it, we must as God commands pray for the Lord to bless them." He turned to the verse and read the Romans passage in the Amhavran tongue. "For those who speak this language, did you notice? It is the blessing of a beloved friend or a father for his son. Pray for me that I may utter such a prayer for my own brother, Prince David." Trillion felt the Lord's joy burst forth.

One requested a song. Trillion went to sit, but Naseran came to his side. "Thank you for sharing that. We need to hear your answers about Wolf's Bane and Worstein."

"Of course." When the last note sounded, he described what had transpired in Worstein, as well as the decision of the king to reexamine the actions taken by Prince Joshua and

Lord Bierl. "We will continue to seek to find these invaders. If you see strange intruders report it to the marshals. Prince Joshua is helping with the investigation. Your complaints have been recorded by the king's clerk and will be entered into the records of the realm. It has been good to sit with you at this gathering."

Trillion looked to a far corner of the tent. Was his time coming to go to Eliziel? He spread his arms, looking at each one. "I welcome the invitation of the Imbus and Stoddard to see once again their forests, plains, and towns. Prince Wilm and I will be heading north with you tomorrow." A blessing from the Lord flowed from his lips.

Many came to greet him. Naseran took him aside, and they discussed the king's tour with Prince David.

"I assume you have no influence on Lord Nordrum," said Naseran.

"None. It would be fair to say that in the past I allowed him to influence me. He supports these changes for the Weaver's Plain?"

"Yes, along with Burgher Dalson and the mayors of the largest towns, including Whistler's Ridge."

"Do they not know where their beef comes from?"

"Oh, they think they can be raised in feedlots, the same way they like to house their chickens in coops." Naseran laughed.

Trillion laughed with him. "May the Lord guide you."

"Is Lord Bierl aware of Prince David's plan?"

"His rangers are in readiness to withstand any attempts to bring back the deposed judges and officials. Those efforts would be met with force and a declaration of independence from Airdle," Trillion said.

"Alas, we have no holding lord willing to take such a stand here. Lord Nordrum is a merchant at heart. I think he dreams of towns and roads throughout all of Dornan. It took

255

the Word of God Daniel brought to unite us. It seems we have walked away from our only hope."

"You speak truly. If Prince David had come to faith, we would not be having these problems."

"Oh, Prince, even the faithful can be swayed. Why else would the apostle Peter warn us to beware of lions seeking to destroy us?"

"Also truth. Our prayers go with you."

"And mine with you. May you find your place."

"Here as well as in the Lord's heavenly kingdom." Trillion had no idea why he said that. But he knew his days were numbered. How many remained? He must go to Eliziel and pass the torch to his son.

Chapter 25

The Tour of Imbus and Stoddard

Wilm recognized some landmarks once they cleared the outskirts of Whistler's Ridge. He never realized he had passed so close to the city. Years ago, he and Ama had taken a trip across the Weaver's Plain to visit fishing villages, and he had played in the warm ocean.

Now, he rode beside his father and Esrilin. Many questions ran through his head, but he held his peace as both men said little. Marshal Thielen had assumed command of Esrilin's squad and traveled with them until they reached the path heading to the eastern side of the Weaver's Plain.

The Imbus River surged down from the southernmost parts of the Invien Cliffs, along Tholen Ridge, and dropped to Tholen Falls. Crossing the plains, it filled its banks and lapped the floorboards of a wooden bridge. The stone supports seemed secure, but some boards were cracked with holes. Wilm directed his attention to his steed.

They took the western path that skirted the barren, rolling expanse of the Imbus Wastelands on their right. The first waypoint consisted of a few sagging lean-tos. With Prince Trillion's nod, Wilm set snares and helped others gather wood for their fires. The changes to the squads and his father's obvious gloom dampened his eagerness to visit the Imbus, Stoddard, and Keyayisin.

He was afraid to ask why the light had left his father's eyes.

The next day they reached the edge of the forests that dotted the narrow valleys between the Imbus Wastelands and Tholen Ridge. Wilm had read that the hills reached higher as one traveled north. He had never been past this point and stared at the groves of white trunks, the undergrowth not yet sprung up from the winter's chill. In the distance, what could have been mistaken for clouds appeared to be mountaintops still white with snow.

The Imbus Ayisin made a scrumptious meal for last sup, and Wilm wolfed his down. Even their bannocks were as good as his mother's. He listened and spoke little. As several began to turn to their bedrolls, Wilm asked his father to go for a walk. Trillion and Wilm followed the moonlight illuminating the white trunks of a stand of trees on the forest's edge.

He walked closely by his father's side. "I love you, Aba. Can you share your heart?"

Trillion looked toward his son, so innocent. He slipped his arm around Wilm's shoulders and sighed. "How I long to do so." The moon's light lingered along the path through leafy branches. "Wilm, because of my past sins, some are slow to accept that my transformation is real. I hope you never have to experience being doubted, scrutinized. The king has believed the lies about me that Prince David and his friends told him. Don't ever let this create problems with your grandfather. But know this, ever his eldest son has swayed him. My father's compassion sometimes leads him to allow the wicked to prosper."

"Is that what happened when you went to find the king?"
"Yes."

"Will I be able to visit him at his fire?"

"I hope so. But Wilm, you will always have my love. And you know the love of Jesus. His Holy Spirit dwells within you. We must pray for your grandfather to hear God and not follow men."

Trillion stopped to face his son. "Very soon we'll leave the castle. Already they are preparing our quarters for Prince David's return." He described the changes. "We'll visit Prince Joshua and Lady Jessica. Probably move to Worstein."

The trail turned and the path opened before them. The moon, shrouded with translucent clouds, cast its light through a gap in the trees. The clouds parted. The air brightened as the moon's rays shone a stairway to heaven. They stood transfixed.

Trillion stumbled, and Wilm reached out to steady his father. He glanced between the earth and the heavens. The moon's silvery light sparkled as if shining through a mist. "Father, what do you see?"

"My future is not dim, but black. The Lord has already charted our days."

A warning from the Spirit rose up. "Why must we go to Eliziel?"

Trillion faced his son. "God showed me that I will be buried by my ama, Queen Lillian."

"At Eliziel." Wilm shuddered and embraced his father as if he could keep him and never lose him. He wanted to protest, yet he feared that would increase his father's pain. "God's will." Wilm said after a while.

"Amen and amen." Both turned toward the camp.

"Ready?" His father moved with him. Wilm felt a shudder dance up his father's back and heard a deep cough.

"I love you." Soon it would be a year since he had first met his father. Wilm slipped his arm around him.

When the clearing came into view, Trillion halted his steps. "They say you were born at Imbus."

"I was? So that's what they meant, the Ayisin who saw me at my first Public Judgment."

"Esrilin, Cesim, and his men sheltered your mother with the Imbus Ayisin." Trillion patted his son's hand. "When we go to the Imbus, we will try to find the ones who helped her during your birth. I wish to thank them for sheltering you and your mother during that time."

"Aba, does my mother know about this trip?"

"I sent a letter. I very much wish she could join us."

"She's missing us. Will she be upset we have to leave the castle?"

"I see the bond between them, your mother and the king. But I know her heart still longs for the plains and her horses."

"I think the king will find a way to have her stay."

They found their bedrolls. Wilm tried to sleep, but his father coughed again.

The following morning, Wilm cleaned three rabbits and roasted them. A few woke late and stumbled out of their bedrolls. The Ayisin tending to the bannocks in two pans shook his head and laughed. Wilm reached for the coffeepot, enjoying the rich aromas wafting in the breeze. Water for tea boiled furiously in a fire-blackened pot. He watched the Ayisin eat, pack, and be ready for the trail in a short time.

They did not linger long in each village or town. The forest Ayisin were more settled than he had expected, with log homes similar to those of the townsmen. Wilm watched how his father moved easily among them. Their greetings were friendly in their quiet way, and many spoke of Queen Lillian, Trillion's mother. They stayed longest at Aiden's town. Its roads flowed with the land, connecting to homesteads with horses, cattle, gardens, and racks for drying stretched furs.

The next day, Esrilin followed narrow paths to a small grouping of four houses. "I'll check and make certain this is the place where you were born. I've only been here a few times."

Esrilin dismounted and knocked on a door. After Esrilin stated the reason for their visit, several women came out to meet them. A few of the older women had been midwives who sheltered Lisze.

They welcomed the travelers. Wilm tried not to squirm when a few pinched his cheeks, exclaiming how tall he was. His father thanked them for their care of Lisze and his son.

"You are blessed, young man," one said to Wilm. Their quiet smiles radiated joy, and gracious spirits endued their simple stew and pies with heavenly flavors.

Within three days, they found the Stoddard Way Station at the northernmost part of the council at a large crossroad leading to the Amhavran Mountains. Gray walls of stone rising to the sky marched north. Tall trees with dark trunks squeezed grazing lands into narrow strips. They would be leaving Esrilin behind when they headed south to the trail west to Worstein through Havransen Pass.

The way station, with one main house, a long barn, and a few outbuildings, looked old and worn. The roof of the main station house had been patched. The fences were in disrepair, and the barn looked as if it would fall down with the next storm. A number of scraggly horses looked up from their small paddocks.

Wilm hitched the horses to the post while Esrilin and Trillion entered the foyer to the main house. Wilm joined them. Sometime later, a young marshal escorted them to a clean, bright, airy open room with counter, tables, and chairs.

"Son, meet my friend, Marshal Targon." Trillion spread his arm, and Wilm walked up to a middle-aged man with thick black hair cut short, a slight mustache, and a firm grip.

"So, you have a son. Fourteen, fifteen?"

"I'm thirteen now."

"Sit, help yourself to coffee." Targon pointed to a coffee-pot suspended not far from a smoldering fire in the hearth.

Wilm took mugs from a nearby stand, filled them, and brought them to the marshals. He noticed the dark circles beneath his father's eyes, and his flushed cheeks.

"Coffee, Father?" When his father barely nodded, he asked a young marshal hovering nearby where the pump was.

He returned with fresh water in time to hear Esrilin relay the news that he would head the squad at Stoddard.

"Have your new orders arrived, Targon?" Esrilin asked.

"Here?" The man snorted. "We're lucky if we're paid or receive supplies."

"Where would you like to go? I could put in a good word for you. Where is the rest of your squad?"

"More than half are local. They live with their families and come in for their shifts at the station or head out straight for patrols. This is the northernmost way station in Stoddard. Now that the Sanderfield have ceded from the realm, in reality, if not on parchment, it seems Airdle considers we have little need of marshals here. We have difficult terrain to cover."

Esrilin shifted in the chair, looking at maps of Stoddard Council on the wall. "Had you been able to engage the intruders?"

"We've come close. I think they know we're looking for them as they are careful to vary their routes. This is a vast forest. A small group can easily slip undetected along deer or elk trails. Harder to hide on the open plains. But we haven't seen any sign for a while." Targon rubbed his chin. "Whoever they are, they're skilled, slipping past as if they were wraiths, but they leave the same signs as other men—smoldering fires, bones stripped clean, footprints."

Esrilin considered the man of Stoddard who would likely resign if forced to leave his council. "Would you consider being my second? Together, we could restore this station, see it properly funded and staffed. Which way station manages your supplies?"

"Whistler's Ridge."

"Has it always been this bad?" Trillion asked. "I remember this being a valued station because it borders the Amhavran eastern territories. After all, Stoddard bore the brunt of the Amhavran Wars in my father's day."

"Since Prince David assumed command of the marshals, we've been mostly on our own. Many spend half their time trapping, guiding, or working for the landholders. One went back to blacksmithing. Some days we can barely afford his services to have our own horses shod. At least there's always deer or elk we can harvest."

Trillion looked at Esrilin. "Clefisch Pass would be no better as a resupply point, but Marshal Karith, the Stolein Way Station keeper and head marshal, could advocate for you. He's close to Prince Joshua, who would be able to remind the king of your valued service."

"We're a little different, but we follow marshal standards."

"Good to hear. This posting requires men knowledgeable of the terrain," Esrilin said.

"And its people. We're a hardy lot, and it takes diplomacy to deal with local matters."

"Targon, we can make a list of the back pay, supplies, and needed repairs," Trillion put in. He glanced toward Wilm. "I could use a clerk."

"Sure," Wilm said.

"We're pretty self-sufficient. Most supplies could be obtained locally if we had the coin. We have a small breeding herd we use to secure feed and other staples. Bartered three young horses for last winter's hay and oats."

"Culling your herd for supplies should never occur at a king's way station." Esrilin frowned.

"Welcome to Stoddard, head marshal," Targon said.

"Marshal Esrilin will find a way to make things work, and with his contacts, he'll be able to secure proper support from Airdle." Wilm stopped, realizing he had spoken out of turn.

"Well, young prince, I appreciate your commendation. I know of your Marshal Esrilin and the tales of his exploits." He exchanged glances with Esrilin. "I accept the offer to be your second. Good to share the burden of this outpost." He emptied his mug. "I have a few arrangements to make now, summoning the cook and debriefing the findings of the day squads, but after, I can give you a tour."

Esrilin rose. "May I shadow you?"

Targon nodded.

"Bring the pay records. Wilm and I can work on the requisition report," Trillion said to the Stoddard marshal.

"Come into my office." Targon moved to the last door behind the counter and let Trillion enter first. Once they were seated, Targon looked hard at Trillion. "How long have you been sick?"

Wilm glanced between them.

Trillion touched his shoulder. "Easy, Son, we've known each other since I was a boy. Came with the king and queen on their tours. He let me serve here during my earlier years."

"Came from the Eastern Gathering?" Targon asked.

Seeing Trillion's assent, the marshal said, "Prince David knows you're a threat. Heard great things about you from the Worstein rangers. We share watch of Havransen Pass with their rangers."

Trillion's shoulders shook with a deep cough.

When Wilm touched his father's hand, it felt warm.

"We'll probably be going to Worstein. Smoothed that over." He described Prince David's plans for the Weaver's Plain.

"He'll not last long as king. If you could hold on, do well at Worstein, perhaps you could right the path of the House of Airdle."

Trillion slid his eyes away. "Need a little rest, that's all." He glanced at his son and added, "And those teas your mother packed for me."

"Shall I?" Wilm worked to keep from trembling, for he could not forget their walk in the light of a silver moon. *Take not my father, Lord.* He pushed down a rising dread to give heed to his father's answer.

"Later tonight will be soon enough. But now we have an injustice to correct, and you will be my clerk. Ready?"

"Absolutely."

Targon brought out meticulously kept records. "You'll have to make copies as I won't part with the originals."

It took a few days for them to complete the report and for Esrilin to settle in with the new squad. Trillion had rested and was feeling better, but his deep cough lingered.

"Are you sure you can make the trip, Trillion?" Esrilin glanced at Wilm, seeing lined furrows in his forehead.

"The trip will take less time if you head for the Havransen Pass." Targon pointed to the northernmost east-west pass to Worstein that offered a direct route to the Keyayisin council lands.

"There are steep rises, and Havransen is the highest of the passes through the Invien Cliffs. Trillion, rest here. We can call for a healer."

Trillion traced the route with his finger. "I must go to Eliziel, and this is the only way. The southern Imbus route will take too long. Besides, Wilm's been wanting to see the Northern Mountains." He noticed his son's enthusiasm to ride the pass. "Once we reach the summit, it's all downhill from there. With summer upon us, each day grows warmer." Trillion sucked in his breath for the next round of coughs. He brought a handkerchief to his mouth, then tucked it away.

Esrilin caught Targon's eye. "Prince Trillion, Sunday is in two days. Take your rest. By the first day of the week, we can have a healer come."

Wilm sat still as stone. His father's slumped shoulders, sunken eyes ringed with dark tints, and deepening coughs whispered that death's presence drew near.

Trillion looked at each in turn. "We will not delay. Son, we'll take our ease at Eliziel. Their healers are renowned." The main city of the Keyayisin spanned the Invien River lined by groves of silver birch, walnut, and peach trees. "Wilm, you've never seen the land of your grandmother, Queen Lillian."

"Or heard the songs of their choir with the strains of lute and harp," Esrilin said. "I will be with you in spirit, if not in the flesh. We have much to do to rebuild this station."

Targon took Esrilin aside, leaving Trillion to describe their journey to his eager son. "We can't make him stay, but ascending the eastern slope will be hard."

"Their steeds will bear the burden," Esrilin said.

"It's the thin air that concerns me. Have you seen the bloody cloths he left behind in his room? Even more reason for me to go with them. I would be amiss to send them without an escort. I'll take Marshal Nahshon with me as I want to meet Marshal Karith."

"A good idea. You can confer discreetly with Prince Joshua at Stolein. He is committed to bringing back unity and justice to Lamoria. I'll be more at ease knowing you'll be with them. Something is driving Prince Trillion to make this journey now."

"I wouldn't think of blocking his path."

Wilm rose early. After first sup, he helped Marshal Nahshon pack and prepare the horses. Hearing Aba's coughs when he entered the headquarters in search of his favorite pick to clean the hooves, he remembered he had forgotten to brew the tea.

He stepped through the dining room to the kitchen. "Has anyone seen my father?"

The cook shook his head. "Will he want eggs and meats for first sup?"

"I'll ask him." Wilm walked quickly to his room and drew out the tea leaves. He tapped on his father's door. "Aba, are you ready?"

Hearing hoarse coughs, Wilm pushed the door open. His father sat on the edge of the bed and stared at him with bloodshot eyes. "Aba! Can you ride?"

Trillion leaned on a small table by the bed to push himself upright. "We must leave today."

"I'll bring your tea. What can you eat for first sup?"

"Bannock with an egg. Not very hungry."

Midmorning was almost upon them when they were ready to leave.

After a final check, Wilm went to Esrilin and extended his hand, but the marshal embraced him in a hug.

"Go with God, Wilm."

"Be safe." There was so much to say, yet words could not express his love for Esrilin. "I will pray for you." He returned to the horses waiting at the hitching post.

The four mounted their horses and headed for the first pass. They would probably be forced to camp on the eastern slope at Amran's Spring, a pretty valley sheltered from the winds.

Their supplies were tucked in saddlebags and bedrolls. Wilm patted a small pouch secured beneath his jerkin that held the few medicinal leaves he had left.

Targon led, and Trillion rode behind him. Wilm kept his mount close by his father's. Nahshon held the rear.

The wide path headed due west through trees and undergrowth. Wilm drank in the musty scent of an aged forest. As the trail narrowed and pines overtook the hardwoods, the air lightened with hints of fragrant purple phlox with a sharp, aromatic odor that brought his senses alive. Every so often, the path opened on a rise and Wilm looked back to see the land sloping toward the Sanderfield with the seas far in the distance.

At the next rise, distant white peaks, visible in the north, took his breath away. Wilm kept his eye on the summits of the Amhavran as the trail rounded a bend and headed into forest again. The trees shrank and twisted, as if clinging to the sides of the mountain exacted a hard toll. He turned his attention to his father when he heard deep, hoarse coughing and watched his shoulders shake.

Holding in wordless prayers, Trillion barely noticed that Kewatin had slowed. Targon had stopped by a small lean-to near a flowing stream.

"Do we have time to stop?" Trillion brought Kewatin to a halt.

"The horses need the rest, and this is a good place for them to get a drink. We'll spend the night at Amran's Spring."

Nahshon led two of the horses to an open area by the lean-to. Wilm followed with their steeds. He glanced back to see his father sit on a bench, but knew he had to see the horses watered before he could take care of his aba.

After they were tied near a grassy area, Wilm hovered by his father. Targon said, "We will take our sup at Amran's Spring. It's sheltered with good water. We can enjoy a meal there with a campfire."

"A good plan." Trillion turned for the next round of coughs and headed for the trees.

The sun passed overhead and began to dip, sometimes drilling into Wilm's eyes when the trail switched back up the slope. They rounded the north side to see the length of the Invien Cliffs marching up to the peaks of the Amhavran. The towering mountains dominated the horizon. The trail turned, and short trees surrounded them as they dipped into the valley of Amran's Spring. Hummingbirds hovered around spring lilies that separated short grasslands from groves of trees. Wilm saw a small cabin with a lean-to on its near side, and a large firepit with sitting stones.

Nahshon tended to the horses. Wilm, carrying their bedrolls and saddlebags, followed Marshal Targon into the cabin. He spied a fire kit along with pots and pans. "Marshal Targon, may I boil water for tea here?"

"Use the outside fire. Add enough to the pot for coffee. We'll heat meat and beans for sup. But we need a fire kindled in the cabin. Do you know how to start a fire?"

Wilm held back his laugh. "Of course! Do you stop here often?"

"Long ago I tended the fires for your grandfather's squad as we prepared to fight. Marshal Rothsum was as comfortable in the mountains as in the plains or the sea."

"I would be interested in hearing your stories, Marshal Targon."

Wilm checked on Aba sitting by the outside fire already kindled by Nahshon. "You build a good fire."

"We'll need more wood. Fetch logs from the pile beside the cabin."

Wilm ran to bring firewood stacked by the side of the cabin. He noticed his father shivered as the air chilled with the setting sun. Wilm helped him move into the cabin. Fetching a heavy jacket and lap robe for his father, he headed outside to make the tea. Wilm entered the cabin, handed the mug to his father, and perched on a nearby seat. Nahshon brought sup on plates into the cabin.

"Well, Prince Wilm, are you ready for the tales of the Amhavran War that were fought at this very spot?" Targon leaned toward the eager youth.

"Did you say you were with Marshal Rothsum? Was Master Cesim also there?" Wilm asked.

"Cesim was a marshal then. He had taken a small group to scout the Amhavran position. They discovered the Airdle troops had been surrounded. A large number of invaders were heading for this pass, and we were Lamoria's last defense. They intended to burn the towns and plains of Stoddard. We sent a scout with the news to the rest of the marshals. We feverishly contrived traps, laid siegeworks, and stockpiled arrows. After all, we had the high ground."

"But that would be at the summit."

"Ah, the enemy knew these peaks. They wished to trap us unawares by taking a side pass south under rock ledges and sneak through this valley. Marshal Rothsum devised a scheme to let them think their plan had worked.

"Along the forest's edge, we waited in gullies and depressions. We sprung the trap, encircling them. Hand to hand we fought with all our might, for a man will more zealously defend his territory above a stranger's. This was our homeland. There is no other Lamoria in all the world. The moon lit the grassy plateau, and we fought on, throwing them off the mountain."

Wilm looked wide-eyed at the marshal's face glowing in the fire's light.

Targon turned to Wilm. "War is never glorious or pretty. The stench of broken bodies with their rotting flesh clung to this place for too long, but it was necessary to protect our people."

"What I recall of my history lessons, that was the turning of the tide and the granting of the term, King Wallace's Mighty Three. One was your grandfather, Wilm, and another walked by your side," Trillion added.

"And we've lived in the shadow of that peace for two generations? Is that right?" Wilm shivered, trying not to picture Targon's words too clearly. "What if that happens again?"

Targon shrugged his shoulders. "Lord Durtswin, an Amhavran clan leader, instigated the invasion. After the slaughter of Havransen's Pass, their name for it, the other clan leaders, tired of the bloodshed, surrendered Durtswin's head to the king."

Wilm gasped. "War is to be avoided above all else?"

"Making war rarely ends as cleanly as we imagine."

Trillion brought out his Leaves of God and read aloud. "'So we do not lose heart, for our inner self is being renewed day by day, though our body is wasting away. We do not look to the things that are seen but to the things that are unseen.'" He laid the book upon his lap to clear his lungs with deep coughs. "Second Corinthians, chapter 4, verses 16 and part of 18. I must find a privy." A shudder ran down his back. They would go to Eliziel. Should he tell Wilm?

Trillion stood. He had to find a place far enough away from the cabin to relieve himself and try to cough up what felt like wads of phlegm from his lungs.

Stumbling, holding his side, he tilted his head. Perhaps his eyes had adjusted, for it seemed as if lights lit the path to a distant rock. Curious, Trillion stepped around it to the edge of a cliff. The dark sky showcased myriads of stars.

He could no longer hold back the coughs that rose up from the depths of his chest. Wads of mucus, flecked with blood and small clods. Dizzy, almost fainting, Trillion leaned against a boulder.

Echoing in his mind, he heard *I will come for you at Eliziel.* Once again, an unearthly light showed the way to the cabin. Not quite clear of the pines, Wilm stood. It was not right to hide this from him. He lifted his arm. His son walked toward him and leaned into his embrace. "If only we had more time here, but we will be together for all eternity."

Wilm swallowed, nodded, and shoved down protestations. They hugged for a while. He wished they did not have to part.

He will rule one day. The Holy Spirit's whisper thrilled Trillion's heart and brought sorrow at the same time. For if the only son of the youngest prince would take the crown, war would have indeed returned.

Back to the cabin, Trillion walked over with as much

strength he could muster. He sat on the stool. "Much better."

Targon said. "Good to hear. We will escort you to Eliziel before turning south for Stolein. The coastal highway is broad and flat, Prince Trillion."

"Much appreciated."

The riders rounded the summit at noon and headed on the downward trail. Wilm noticed Aba's breathing had settled, and he sat higher in the saddle.

They headed north to a bridge and crossed the Invien River. They drew near to the Eastern Ranger Station. A ranger ran to meet them.

"Greetings, welcome to Worstein." He paused and stared at the four. "Prince Trillion, you have returned! And Marshal Targon, please take rest at our station. We'll send a courier for Lord Bierl."

"I am on my way to Eliziel."

Targon came alongside the prince. "We welcome the respite. Shall we?" When the ranger turned to leave, he looked at Trillion. "They knew you were coming?"

"Probably hadn't expected us to come this way though." Trillion shrugged. "Lord Bierl has more important issues than worrying about us. It would be good for Stoddard to have open commerce with Worstein when the crown sits on another's head."

Wilm's head spun with the undercurrents of alliances seething beneath the surface.

Stable boys attended to their horses. His aba seemed to have recovered. Perhaps they would survive these days whole and intact.

A young ranger led them to a set of small rooms. Wilm carried their bags, but his father didn't follow. He dropped their gear by the bed and scurried back to the main hall.

"Targon, halt here. You can make the ride to Stolein in one day if you head out early tomorrow." Trillion stepped closer to the marshal, but Wilm could still make out his father's words. "In the days to come, when David is king, it will be good for Stoddard to have a close alliance with Worstein. Inquire how they have built up their rangers."

"Pushing out the marshals? We're not there yet."

"May it never be, but the future is uncertain."

After the sun had set, the long tables of the meeting room were joined together and covered from end to end with roasted lamb, pork, elk, bowls of rice, steamed corn, mashed squash, and raisin pies. Not only Lord Bierl, but the leading mayors of Worstein and Chief Zuar of the Keyayisin, with their attendants, filled the near side of the length. Rangers sat on either side of Trillion, Wilm, Targon, and Nahshon. Feeling the tension in the room, Wilm knew these men had not assembled to discuss their herds or the spring plantings.

The men of Worstein finished the meal and turned to slices of pie graced by ice cream flavored with peaches. As if with one thought, no words having been uttered, young rangers collected the plates and cleared the table. Stillness hovered, only broken by the crackling fire in the hearth.

Lord Bierl opened with questions. Prince Trillion answered each one forthrightly, not avoiding any issues.

Lord Bierl said, "You see here the ruling council of Worstein. You must convey to the king that we will not reverse the decisions that were made in this council to restore justice."

Trillion glanced at each one and said, "The reports and findings have been recorded and filed in Airdle's Judgment Hall of Records. Prince Joshua has talked with the king about the corrupt decisions and shown him proof."

The holding lord glanced at the other leaders and back to the prince. "Know this, if the Airdle marshals seek to move against us, we will meet them. Make sure Prince David is aware."

"I will encourage Prince Joshua to remind them both." Trillion brought up the situation at Stoddard.

Bierl leveled his gaze at Targon. "Our passes and entryways must be guarded. If Airdle will not see to these defenses, Stoddard must step up when the marshal service fails, as we have done here."

Targon said, "I understand, but we're not yet at that point. The incursions have ceased, and with Marshal Karith's help we will have the means to properly patrol our area."

The council probed for the rest of the news from the Eastern Gathering. Trillion did not hide the problems at Weaver's Plain.

Wilm, although tired, pushed himself to stay awake. Never before had he feared for their future. As the men began to take their leave, he noticed Lord Bierl gesture for Trillion to go with him. Wilm followed.

Trillion turned and said, "Wilm, go with Nahshon to check on the horses; see their hooves are cleaned and locate our tack. I will talk a short while with Lord Bierl and meet you in our room." He rejoined the Worstein lord.

"Walk with me, Prince Trillion." Bierl heard the prince's rough breathing. "Are you sick again?"

"Need a little rest," Trillion said.

"Prince Trillion, we fear the rise of David to the throne. He can do much damage. Can Prince Joshua help him bring in justice for all the peoples?"

Trillion breathed in the sweet night air. "My older brother has great wisdom, as you have seen, but does he have the steel to bring it about? Would he defy his brother? Prince David has no faith. I had no faith until a short while ago."

"And apart from your miraculous conversion, Worstein would have already withdrawn from Lamoria. And it seems now as if Stoddard and Imbus might be forced to do the same." He reached for the prince's shoulder. "Unless there is one with the gift of leadership who sees the path of one Lamoria for all her peoples."

Trillion turned to the holding lord and wished, with all his heart, he could agree, promise, pledge that if under King David the country burst asunder, he would lead the resistance to restore the land. But last night, the Lord's reminder at Amran's Spring could not be forgotten.

"What have you seen, Prince Trillion?" Bierl stepped back and tilted his head. "The best kings of old, the kings of renown, had not only sight to see the days but sight beyond."

"I've seen that my days are numbered, and I must go home to Eliziel. As mountain flowers burst into bloom during times of rain and sun to quickly fade, our lives are like a whisper." Trillion met Bierl's eyes. "The Lord will raise up the one He chooses in His time. By His power Lamoria was birthed." He looked up to the mountains. "The Lord is not done with Lamoria, but He will purge her. The prophecy of the king from the four branches of our people will come to pass. In time—the Lord's timing—the right will come again." He blinked away tears. "The path will not be easy. Help my son after I'm gone. Remind him that even in times of distress, God works still. That He has not turned His back on our people."

"Would it be too soon for Prince Wilm to squire next year? He seems mature for his age."

"Yes, he's still young. Was it too soon for him to have gone to the gathering?"

"Nay, I think this will help him survive. Already, we see not a boy, but a young prince."

Chapter 26

Trillion Goes Home to Eliziel

Trillion woke with a start. A great force lay on his chest, and his breath caught in his throat. Wilm, still asleep, snored softly.

He tried to roll to his side but an explosion of pain seized him. By force of will, he moved to the edge of the bed, swung his legs down, and stumbled to the door. He thrust it open wide enough to slip down the hall to the main room and out the front door, where the cool of the night still clung to the land. The sun barely peeked over the cliffs.

Shallow breaths and strength of mind could no longer hold in the coughs. They came in long, ragged groupings that brought a red liquid up the back of his throat. He pulled out a cloth to wipe his mouth. The blood was mostly bright, with shadows of dark clumps. He fought for life, for breath, for he must go home to Eliziel.

Eventually, he cleared his lungs enough to head back into the station for coffee or warm water to soothe his throat. No coffeepots or kettle hung in the fireplace. Trillion stepped forward to warm his hands, thankful for the heat as a chill from the depths of his being had risen up.

He turned to the other hall and found the cook working in the kitchen at the end of building.

Trillion asked the cook. "Coffee?"

The man grunted and gestured to a hearth on the far end large enough to heat water and make soups for squads. Fresh cream in a cooled pitcher added flavor to the hot coffee. He waved away the offer of sugar, for that often set the back of his throat on edge. "Are we the only ones up?"

The cook grunted and looked at him. "Last ones. Out on patrol already. The young prince up?"

"No. Did the marshals head out?" Trillion regretted having slept so long.

"The rangers will escort you to Eliziel when you're ready. Heard you cleared the pass yesterday."

"On horseback along a good trail—not quite the same as summiting."

The cook looked out the window toward the ridge.

"Climb the cliffs? Summit the peaks to the north?" Trillion asked.

"I did. Trader, woodsman, tracker, but now I cook. Do what needs doing."

They turned at the sound of steps on the floorboards.

"Coffee that good, Aba?" Wilm took a mug from a shelf, and poured a cup. He looked at his father. "Hungry for breakfast?"

"Not quite, but you go ahead."

The cook listed the choices, and Wilm requested a full breakfast. The cook smiled. "My kind of ranger; eat well, work well, as my granny used to say."

They were on their way, flanked by two rangers, within a few turns. The ride to the center of the Keyayisin, along the northern banks of the Invien River, could be traveled in a few turns at a canter. Thankfully, the rangers made no complaints about traveling at a walk, past freshly tilled fields, fences of wood or stone, outlined by tall, narrow trees. Birds sang, and early summer flowers were in full bloom. Tall oaks, chestnuts, and walnuts here and there leaned over the carefully graded, broad road.

The land leveled out onto a broad plain with what

looked like dark forests ahead. To Wilm, it resembled the woods along Wolf's Bane northeast side. "Is that the Keyayisin homeland?"

"Yes, it's been a long time since I've been back. My parents used to travel there in the later years before my mother's death. It took some time for her father to accept her marriage to the king." Trillion recalled those days when he journeyed with them. Warm days where all seemed right with the world.

The land slowly rose. Herds gathered in the distance. Fencing enclosed large grazing areas. Graceful homes were guarded by tall trees. Breezes from the sea wafted past them carrying a slight hint of salty air. The shadows cast by the leafy canopy turned the tree trunks deep browns and grays. The road headed north to a broad hill capped by a village of whitewashed buildings trimmed with vibrant colors.

"Eliziel, the city of the Keyayisin, one of the oldest settlements. Some say the people camped here long ago when they first came," said Trillion.

The rangers turned up a wide road to a building with tall glass windows overlooking the sea. Trillion stopped his horse to gaze at the rocky shore and the top ridge of Black Pearl Island far in the distance. Long, wooden planks burnished a golden brown with engravings along the borders led to a carved door. A man stepped out. His black hair was still long, thick, and heavy despite his lined face and sharp eyes.

"Remember my uncle, Chief Zuar of the Keyayisin? You saw him at the ranger station." Trillion added, "Be courteous." He cleared his throat with some coughs, squared his shoulders, and worked at not looking directly at his uncle, for that would be considered rude.

"Prince Trillion, Prince Wilm, welcome to the fire circle of Eliziel, where all who are of the people come." He gestured for the young men waiting by the hitching post.

Wilm dismounted and handed the reins to the one closest to him. He went to his father's side, ready to help.

Trillion cleared his lungs again. Wordlessly, they turned to Chief Zuar and mounted the steps.

The large great room had a sunken floor with a firepit in the center, surrounded by polished granite of marbled orange, gray, and dark stone. A flue drew up the smoke from a cedar fire, filling the room with a rich incense. Padded couches rimmed one side. Teapots and mugs were in place on two small tables on either side of the couches.

"You may sit on the couch or the pad," Zuar said. He extended his arm, and the prince drew him into an embrace.

"Uncle, thank you for receiving us. Please send a courier to Airdle Castle for my wife, Lady Lisze, to come with all haste." He slipped a note into the chief's hand. Trillion stepped back, struggling to draw breath without yielding to another coughing fit. The room swam, and his vision darkened.

Wilm moved to his father's side and caught him before he fell. Zuar helped place the prince on a nearby couch.

Zuar gestured to two attendants standing nearby. "Send for the healer." He glanced at Wilm. "Let's make him comfortable. How long has he been sick like this?"

Wilm glanced at the older man. "Since an accident a year ago. Last month we had hoped he had fully healed, but since the Eastern Gathering, he's not been doing well."

Trillion began to cough. Gurgles sounded. Red liquid poured out of his mouth. Wilm grabbed the nearest bowl, dumped out the fruit and held it, rolling his father forward. A stream of blood, frothy and with dark streaks, filled the bowl. Feeling helpless, Wilm begged the Lord to heal his father, prolong his life.

Zuar placed a hand on the boy. "Prince Wilm, the healers are here."

Wilm slid to the side but refused to release his aba's hand. Numbly, he watched them work to clear his lungs. The gray around his eyes, the pinched look, and his sallow cheeks pierced his heart. Their eyes met.

He watched his father sit up and moved his mouth as if to speak, but another coughing fit began. When Trillion swayed, the healers laid him back. His father drew breath once again. Wilm beseeched the Lord for his aba's life.

"Prince Wilm, we have sent a courier for your mother. We will take your father to the waiting chamber, an open, airy place where the people go when they are ready to pass on," Chief Zuar said.

The day became a blur. Four strong men placed his father on a litter and headed for a broad staircase leading to an open veranda with screens pulled open. The surge of the tide could be heard, and Wilm stepped onto the veranda to see a rocky coast a little south of Wolf's Bane.

Blinking away a few tears, he squared his shoulders and sat on the seat by the bed. His father, propped up, looked to the sky. "Aba, would you like to see the waves?"

Trillion clung to his son's hand. Wilm reached over with his free hand and felt his father's heart racing. Laying an ear on his chest as he had watched his ama do, he heard rumblings of air trying to move through blocked passages. Wilm sat up and noticed pain wash across his father's face.

A healer drew near and tapped his shoulder. "Prince Wilm, we can push the couch onto the veranda in a little while. We have a few more treatments."

Wilm moved aside.

The turns lengthened. After their treatments and a time of rest, Wilm helped his father sit up to see the ocean in the distance.

As the sun slipped below the horizon and warm lights from posted lanterns danced on waving branches in gentle sea breezes, Trillion said with a weak voice, "Push me back in and close the screens."

Wilm, glad they were alone without the healers and attendants hovering nearby, slid the couch back into the room and brought the screens across. He poured a small cup of tea and held it for his father to drink.

Trillion smiled, sipped, and sat back.

"Are you hungry?" Wilm cast about for the cookies and fruit left on his plate.

"No, Son." Trillion furrowed his brow. "Don't blame God for this. Thank Him for having given us some time together." He patted his son's hand, unlined and unscarred.

Wilm strove within. He would not plead for his life to be long, but he could not hold back. "Aba! Why now?"

Gathering strength, Trillion looked at his son. "If He takes me home, it is because my work is done." Coughing erupted again that he could not hold back.

Wilm held up a bowl to catch the stream pouring from his father's lungs. He heard the healers return before he saw them out of the corner of his eye. Stepping aside, he noticed Chief Zuar gesturing for him to come over.

"Let them provide the evening's treatment. It won't be long." He studied the young prince, tall for his age. "Couriers have been sent to King Wallace and Lady Lisze."

"Prince Joshua must come. I did not see everything at the gathering. There are things my father must tell him. Things the king needs to know."

"Prince Wilm, couriers also have been sent to Prince Joshua. Try to rest in this side room."

"I can't leave him alone."

"They will wake you when he's ready. He will not be left alone."

With heavy eyelids, Wilm walked with this man who was his great-uncle. He paused at the entrance to a small room with closed shutters and a soft down bed. "Chief Zuar, why have we not visited you before this?"

"I regrettably allowed disagreements to keep us apart."

Zuar sighed. "At one time, I had told your father never to return. Since the news of his change, I have been too slow to mend that mistake. Prince Wilm, I had not believed faith would find him or that belief could transform him. Forgive me, but today I can extend the compassion I failed previously to show him." He nudged his chin in the direction of the bed. "Take some rest. You will need it for the vigil ahead."

Despite himself, Wilm slept. Coming to a start, hearing a rough snore, he jerked awake and sat up. Crickets sang in the distance, creating a subtle cadence that blended with the sound of waves carried in on a slight breeze. Sheer curtains moved in the dim light of a small lantern outside his open door. All was silent. Wilm slipped out of bed and walked to the large room. A figure sat by his father's side. She turned toward him when he stepped close.

"Is he?" he whispered.

"Resting peacefully," the woman said, rising to let him sit by Trillion's bed. Without a word, she left the room.

Wilm bent close. The gurgling breath, though indicating his father still lived, sent a chill down his back. He reached for the hand closest to him and felt its warmth. He feared that touching his father's forehead would awaken him from what seemed to be a deep sleep. Whatever the healers had done seemed to have worked.

Praying, pleading, he sat by his father's side.

Later, Wilm awoke, realizing he had knelt by the low bed and fallen asleep over his father's side. Lifting his head, he saw his father staring up into a far corner of the room with a peaceful smile on his face that almost glowed.

"Son, I am happy you slept." His smile broadened.

"Father!" Wilm clung to his hand. The look in his father's

eyes troubled him more than the coughing had. "Why are the good so weak and the wicked so strong? If God allowed Lamoria to become the people of Airdle, why would He curse us?"

Trillion blinked as he shifted his focus back to this earth. "Nay, but a cleansing purge." He reached up to touch his son's arm. "Troubles we bring upon ourselves." He felt his strength slipping away. "Is your mother here?"

Wilm shook his head. "No, but it hasn't even been a day. The courier left last night. He probably reached Airdle with the sunrise."

"Not even a day." Trillion coughed only enough to clear his lungs. The draughts had dulled the pain, but the mass in his chest could still be felt. Trillion gripped his son's hand.

"I won't leave you, Father." He smoothed out the pillow and the bed. When Trillion slid to the side and invited him in, he rested beside him. Wrapped in an embrace, they slept again.

At noon of the next day, Prince Joshua came up the stairs and entered the room. The look on his brother's face proved the truth of the message he had received.

Wilm rose and let him take the low chair by Trillion's bed. He hovered to the side.

"Is Lisze with you?" Trillion asked.

"She's not here?" Joshua looked to Wilm for confirmation.

Wilm asked, "Did you get our message at the castle?"

"No, at Stolein. I was with Karith and Targon. They said I needed to hear the full story from you. Prince David is back at the castle." He patted his brother's hand. "We'll send another courier."

Trillion stared fixedly at Joshua. He grasped Joshua's

hand and relayed between breaths what Prince David had said at the gathering, the treatment of the plainsmen and Ayisin, and the state of Stoddard Way Station. "Can the king oversee Stolein? Roanin and Whistler's Ridge are already lost, but Stoddard needs help."

"I will take this up with our father." Joshua looked about, noticing Wilm sitting on a nearby chair. "Are there any you'd like to call?"

"Lisze and my father if he so desires." Trillion's eyelids fluttered.

"I will send an urgent message with a courier to Airdle and Marshal Karith."

Trillion squeezed his brother's hand. "Lisze?" he said, his eyes going out of focus.

"Coming soon, Brother. Rest and save your strength." Joshua rose. "I'll see the dispatches sent."

Wilm took his place by his father's side. The turns passed. Healers came and went. The day lengthened.

When the setting sun hovered over the horizon, Wilm heard quick, booted steps.

His mother stepped in, still in her riding leathers. She hugged Wilm and slipped into the seat by Trillion. Joshua ushered out Wilm and the healers.

"What did Ama say? Can Grandfather arrive in time?" Wilm watched his uncle turn to meet his gaze. The sorrow in Joshua's eyes confirmed his suspicions. "He's not coming."

"The last courier was instructed to give the dispatch directly to the king."

"That would be possible if the messenger could find a way past Prince David's guards. They kept Father from seeing the king. Even the holding lords, plainsmen, and elders couldn't gain an audience with their king. Has Prince David taken over the land?"

Joshua met Wilm's piercing gaze. "Not yet. I will find a way to show the king the truth. Tell him of Stoddard's neglect, of our unguarded border, of the necessity of Lord Bierl's actions in Worstein."

"We must pray he'll believe you."

Turns later, Lisze emerged and found Wilm and Joshua sitting in the main hall, staring dully at the fire in the circle.

"Wilm, he's calling for you." She held Joshua's hand. "Thanks for sending the courier from Stolein." She slumped, exhausted, on the couch and accepted a cup of coffee.

She had nothing else to say. What Trillion had told her in hoarse, gasping breaths she had confirmed when she put an ear to his chest. She believed the healers' assessment that Trillion had a growing mass in his left lung that had burst and was filling his chest. They had put in a tube to relieve the pressure, but that had only given him a few extra days. It had probably been there since the accident when his horse fell on him. "At least we had a year with him. How is Wilm taking it?"

Joshua said, "Hard. I think he finally understands that it will be soon."

"I doubt he'll live to the morrow. And the king? Any word?" When Joshua's distant gaze confirmed her suspicions, she spoke deliberately. "You must tell me everything he said to you about this trip. What happened? Hadn't the king requested he join the gathering?"

Prince Joshua relayed what Trillion had said.

"We've been removed from our suites. I will request a land grant from Lord Bierl. I think we can find a place in Worstein."

"Talk to Chief Zuar; he is Trillion's uncle."

"Who disowned him. I'm amazed he was allowed to die here since they wouldn't give him even a cup of water while he lived."

"Lisze, Trillion hadn't tried to reconcile, but his transformation has been noted. They extended an invitation before he left the gathering. God drove him here. Even if reconciliation is on a deathbed, it is still peace in God's sight."

"Amen." Lisze bent her head.

"And Lisze, I've pledged to protect you and Wilm. You will not be abandoned. If you have to, you can stay with us until you find a home. Jessica looks forward to spending time with you."

"Many thanks." They looked up when Wilm appeared, tears running down his face.

"Come quickly," he said.

They followed him up, hearing the death gurgle with Trillion's every breath. His arm had been raised, but he turned his head to hug Lisze. "My love, you were always my one and only. There were no others. Praise God for His grace in giving me time with you and Wilm." He reached for his son's hand.

"I go to my God and your God, joining my mother and many others." He glanced at them with loving eyes. "Life is short. Live it well. Good God." The hand dropped, the eyes fixed, and the chest emptied of breath.

Lisze leaned over him. Wilm rested his arm on his mother's shoulders, feeling them tremble and shake with her grief. Despite his prayers, God had taken his father. He lifted a dry face to his uncle who stood, narrow and stooped, tired and worn.

The healer marked the time and left the chamber without a word. Chief Zuar sent dispatches throughout the land of the Watcher's Memorial for Prince Trillion of the House of Airdle.

Chapter 27

Prince Trillion's
Watcher's Memorial

The Keyayisin Watcher's Memorial shared with the people the last words spoken to those who watched as a loved one passed to eternity. The Keyayisin Meeting Hall overflowed with concentric rings of pads curving around a raised firepit with carved leaves of metal directing the cedar smoke up in a circular motion. For Prince Trillion, his wife, his son, and one brother sat on the dais. Not even Chief Zuar joined them for only these three had come to sit with the youngest prince as the Lord of Glory called him home.

Prince Joshua shared the last words his brother had uttered. Lady Lisze, overcome with grief, her son by her side, tried but could not speak. Wilm hugged her and brought her to sit by Prince Joshua. Then Wilm turned and looked at the crowd filling the hall.

"Thank you for coming and honoring my father's life, for he wanted you to know that God is good, merciful, forgiving. He saves to the uttermost, as my father's life attests. Even though we only had a short time together, he poured himself into me. He spoke of God and His love, of His goodness, and of the hope we have that God loves the people of Lamoria and will never abandon them."

As he began to share Trillion's last words, he felt a commotion on the left side but did not glance that way. Transfixed by his father's vision, he remembered to pray and recalled his father's words over the last weeks.

"The four tribes—Airdle, Dornan, Ayisin, and Sanderfield—all came together as one people united not because we were the same, but unique because of a God of infinite possibilities. In Him, we can be one. Apart from Him, we will only divide and return to the darkness. God has not, and will never, forget Lamoria. As each of us walk with the one true God, He will lead us home. This God who delivered my father from sin into His light, who transformed him, can do the same for us if we stumble not, doubt not, and keep our faith."

Tears came with his final words, and he left the dais for Chief Zuar to lead the last song before the procession to carry Trillion's wrapped body to a grave.

As the three followed Trillion's form on a pallet, a figure came alongside them. Wilm turned, his brows drawn down. "Grandfather. You came?"

King Wallace embraced Wilm and Lisze. "How can I ask you to forgive me for not coming sooner? I hadn't known he was on his deathbed."

"We sent messages," Wilm said.

"I was told he would recover."

Chief Zuar, with three elders, led the procession to the White Groves. On a hill overlooking the sea, monuments of the people surrounded aspen trunks. They walked to the tree where Queen Lillian had been buried. Trillion would be placed beside her.

Chief Zuar approached the king. "This was his request. If you wish, we can erect a stone with his name, and he can be buried in the Stone Cemetery near Airdle."

"No, that they are here will remind us to keep a close bond and never let anything come between us, for that would be a great tragedy." The king shivered. "We must pray that our fractures can be stopped and the gaps healed. It begins here with the Keyayisin, one with Airdle and the Worstein. Let it spread throughout the land. That is the message from the Lord my son brings. Let it be the beginning of the turn."

Chief Zuar gave the reading from the Leaves of God and spoke of the hope Christ brings. Beginning with Lisze, Wilm, and Joshua, they laid a fresh bud on the bundle. Others walked by with their flowers. Wilm watched four men lower the bundle into the ground. Joshua threw in a handful of dirt. As Wilm followed, his chest nearly burst within him. He let the dirt, soddened by his tears, fall with settled ticks upon the rolls of canvas.

His father was gone.

Taken too soon.

Lisze's hands shook, and her lips trembled. She leaned against her son, who accepted the wad of dirt from her hand and let it fall. Rasping breaths led to renting cries that split the air. Wilm and Joshua helped her to a stone bench facing a crowned tree with branches that spread over the graves ringing its trunk.

King Wallace followed and sat near Lisze. They listened to the tones of the final verses—dust to dust, ashes to ashes.

" 'But only by the sweat of your brow will you eat your food until you return to the ground—because from it you were taken, for you are made from dust and to dust you will return.' Thus says the Lord, Genesis 3, verse 19," Chief Zuar said.

"Thus says the Lord," the people replied, and they, one by one, stopped to say a word, touch a shoulder, whisper their prayers.

Lisze's tears continued. Wilm stood to her left, stabilizing her with his arm. King Wallace patted her knee. Joshua stepped aside, feeling helpless, not knowing what to do.

Lisze turned to the king. "Your Majesty . . ." She wiped her face and set her jaw. "We will remove our items forthwith and leave the castle."

"Why would you leave, Daughter?"

"Prince David said his wife, Lady Esmerelda, would take my place." Her voice broke.

"This is nonsense. Lady Esmerelda has no more intention of managing the castle than a flitting hummingbird. It was at her insistence that they raise their family near Roanin, her family's holdings. No, my dear, Prince David has spoken out of turn. And to think that Prince Ricard would take up residence in the remodeled east wing suite? I don't think he would welcome that idea." The king lifted his brow. "Lisze, I've grown accustomed to having you around and miss you when you're gone. Would you be willing to be the lady of Airdle Castle? You've already taken up many of those responsibilities. When you are ready to return, your rooms will be waiting for both of you." He glanced at his grandson standing beside them. "The passing of my son Trillion does not mean you also must go. For that would only increase my sorrow past the point I could bear." Wallace's words died away on the breeze without an answer. "Why would you doubt your place by my side?"

"You broke his heart," Wilm said.

Lisze lowered her brow at her son. "Wilm! My liege, apologies for the prince who speaks out of turn."

"It's true! I saw it. Father told me what you said to him." Wilm stepped back, shocked by his rising anger. He squeezed his eyes to hold back tears. "But Grandfather, on his last day, as he waited for you to come, he said he wanted me to tell you that he forgave you. That he was right in God's eyes, and you would be friends again in the Lord's kingdom." His voice shook. Turning aside, he bit his lip and willed himself to shove down the pain. Did he even want to go back to the castle?

"Forgive me, all of you. No, I can't make excuses—not for this. I believed what had been told me, even though I knew how God had transformed my son. I should have left with the first courier you sent." The king wiped away lingering tears.

Wilm felt his back stiffen, but he could not ignore God's command. He touched lightly the king's shoulder. "I forgive you, Grandfather. He wanted me to remind you that he always loved you. I'm glad I've had a chance to know you. I love you, Grandfather."

King Wallace rose and embraced him. "Thank you, Wilm."

Releasing him, he said aloud, "The firstborn son is to be king. God made David firstborn." The king turned to them. "Pray, fervently pray, that what the Lord did for Trillion, He will do for David. He rebels against God, and because of this, he will not be a good king. But I will make things right." With a determined look toward Joshua, he continued, "I will support your efforts to return justice to all our peoples. Let the Council of Worstein know that I will not interfere in the steps they have taken to foster justice. David's leadership of the marshals will be restricted to the Airdle Squad. We must recall Marshals Thielen and Esrilin to survey all the way stations and squads to ensure they are serving and protecting the people."

"Grandfather, you must also stop the settling of the Weaver's Plain," Wilm said.

Wallace nodded. "We do have jurisdiction over the common lands. We must bring back the commission to oversee development of these areas, beginning with the Weaver's Plain. Joshua, have your aides prepare a report of the history of such administration and how it was managed."

"They say they need the room," Wilm said.

"So it shall be discovered if they are greedy or truly pressed for land."

"They seek to use areas easier to build on." Lisze stood and reached for his hand. "This is a good beginning, and I would be honored to stand with you."

King Wallace embraced Lisze and Wilm. His shoulders shook with his tears. "We all prayed to have more time."

"Let us rejoice in the time the Lord did provide," Joshua said.

The king fulfilled his promises and peace returned to Lamoria. Under Joshua, Thielen, and Esrilin's direction, landholders and plainsmen, townsmen and holding lords felt a measure of justice return to the land. The Weaver's Plain and other common lands were preserved, and Targon resumed command of a revitalized Stoddard Way Station. Good relations continued with Worstein, and ambassadors were sent to Sanderfield to open up commerce with the other councils.

Prince Trillion's Letter to Prince Wilm, His Only Son

Prince Wilm and Lady Lisze returned to Airdle with the king. He prayed for the Lord to abundantly bless his grandfather, who shouldered the burdens of a nation.

A few days after their return, his ama asked him to take last sup with her in the prince's suite.

He rapped on the door and entered. His ama sat still, gazing into the distance, holding a letter in her hand.

"Son, please come." She wiped away a tear and held out the folded parchment. "The Lord told your father many things he hadn't shared with us. There are no accidents with God. That you are of the founding four, raised on the plains with the marshals and later made a grandson of the king, was no mistake."

Hearing the page call with last sup, Lisze began to rise.

"I'll get it, Ama." He set the letter on the table.

They ate, feeling the presence of the other. After the meal, Wilm reached for her hand, praying for both of them to heal.

"Ama, I am glad for our year together with Aba."

He left with the letter, entering his room across the hall. Wilm set the letter on a side table but could not bring himself to open it. Finally, exasperated at himself, he broke the seal.

Dear Son,

Our time was too short, yet we know God has His reasons.

The Lord showed me that your birth had been planned long ago. God gave me the task to be a peacemaker, and I was able to help. But you will be the peacemaker of the prophecy.

Do not worry. The Lord will not bring this to pass until you are ready. There will be hard days ahead, but never forget, to you will be given the right to bear the crown of the king of Lamoria.

Forget not what we taught you, cleave yourself to God, for He will be your strength. He will be your guide. He will overshadow you.

Every moment with you was a treasure from the Lord.

With all my love, Your Father, Prince Trillion

www.ingramcontent.com/pod-product-compliance
Lightning Source LLC
Chambersburg PA
CBHW052001020726
47501CB00004B/957